James Barnet

The Martyrs and Heroes of Illinois in the Great Rebellion

Biographical sketches

James Barnet

The Martyrs and Heroes of Illinois in the Great Rebellion
Biographical sketches

ISBN/EAN: 9783337213480

Printed in Europe, USA, Canada, Australia, Japan

Cover: Foto ©Raphael Reischuk / pixelio.de

More available books at **www.hansebooks.com**

THE

MARTYRS AND HEROES

OF

ILLINOIS

IN THE GREAT REBELLION.

BIOGRAPHICAL SKETCHES.

Edited by James Barnet

Dulce et decorum est pro patria mori.

ILLUSTRATED WITH PORTRAITS.

CHICAGO:

FROM THE PRESS OF J. BARNET, BOOK AND JOB PRINTER,

No. 124 Lake Street.

1865.

THIS
VOLUME
IS DEDICATED
TO THE LOYAL AND THE
BRAVE.

BY THE EDITOR.

In the following pages we can only give a few notices of that mighty host of brave men from Illinois whose blood has watered the battle courses of the late Rebellion in our land, and whose lives have been laid down as a holy sacrifice on the altar of their country.

If, in the fulness of grief, relatives or friends have embellished the obituaries with seeming superfluity or endearment, we would not seek to rob them of such garniture; for it is fitting that the loved ones of their bosom should be fully decked out in the robes of moral heroism when "sleeping the sleep that knows no waking." What nobleness—what bravery—what pangs and sufferings endured for our sakes—none can truly tell. They have triumphed, and Providence smiles upon the victors.

Our task may not yet be finished, if the friends or relatives of those who are unnoticed will gather up the records of their patriotic dead and transmit them to the undersigned.

JAMES BARNET.

" Being Dead, yet Speaketh."

" With us their names shall live
 Through long succeeding years,
Embalmed with all our hearts can give,
 Our praises and our tears."

" Rest on your battle-fields, ye brave,
 Let the pines murmur o'er your grave,
 Your dirge be in the moaning wave—
  We call you back no more!

O, there was mourning when ye fell,
In your own vales a deep-tone knell,
An agony—a wild farewell,
  That haunts us evermore.

Rest with your still and solemn fame!
The hills keep record of your name,
And never can a touch of shame
  Darken the buried brow."

" Their memory is heard upon the mountain,
Their memory sparkles in the fountain;
The smallest rill, the mightiest river,
Rolls, mingling with their fame forever."

CONTENTS.

The names with asterisks (*) indicate portraits accompanying sketches.

ABRAHAM LINCOLN.

PRESIDENT LINCOLN.

" HONOR AND SHAME FROM NO CONDITION RISE;
ACT WELL YOUR PART—THERE ALL THE HONOR LIES."

ABRAHAM LINCOLN having been called from amongst us to occupy the exalted position which he filled so worthily, and with whose sledge-hammer of duty and principle, toil and honesty, the Rebellion received its heaviest blows until it collapsed, ILLINOIS claims him as a martyr and a hero—one who suffered for his heroism, and who fell in the hour of victory.

The sixteenth President of the United States was the son of Thomas and Nancy Lincoln, and was born in Hardin (now Larue) county, Kentucky, on the 12th of February, 1809. When he reached his seventh year, he was sent to a school kept by Caleb Hazel, who lived in the neighborhood of his father's log cabin, and whose exercises consisted of the two fundamental branches—reading and writing. Owing to the family moving to another State, Abraham had to relinquish his practiced studies for a life of hard work on his father's farm, a year covering the entire schooling he received. The journey from Kentucky to Spencer county, Indiana, he has been heard to declare, constituted one of his hardest trials of pioneer experience.

Hardy toil, blended with sport in the woods with his rifle, simple but healthy fare, and repose in a loft, beneath the roof of the hut, formed the daily routine of outward physical being of our hero, and such an existence as imparted vigor and strength to his system.

In the autumn of 1818, he had to mourn the loss of his mother, an excellent woman, who had religiously trained him in the ways of pleasantness, and moulded her son's impressible nature in the paths of honesty and wisdom, which gave him the grand characteristic title in later years of "Honest

Old Abe"—a cognomen that princes might envy, and a like title that every virtuous youth should strive to acquire. He never afterwards mentioned her name but with the deepest reverence —a suggestive fact as to his close adherence to the sacred but often-neglected injunction that children should honor their parents.

A year after this bereavement, his father married Mrs. Sally Johnston, a widow having three children by her first marriage, who proved a good and kind mother to her step-son.

Aside from his outdoor labor, our subject took pride in his early studies, and his diligence soon won him the regards of his instructors. He was quick to learn, considering his condition, and was gifted with a retentive memory. Books were eagerly sought after, and the getting of them his chief anxiety. His father aided him greatly, however, in obtaining those he asked for when desirable, and endeavored always to procure them for the use of his son.

In this way (says Mr. Raymond) he became acquainted with Bunyan's Pilgrim's Progress, Æsop's Fables, a Life of Henry Clay, and Weems' Life of Washington. The "hatchet" story of Washington made a strong impression upon Abraham, which is illustrated in the following tale:

Mr. Crawford had lent him a copy of Ramsey's Life of Washington. During a severe storm, Abraham improved his leisure by reading this book. One night he laid it down carefully, as he thought, and the next morning he found it soaked through with water. The wind had changed, the rain had beaten in through a crack in the logs, and the book was ruined. How could he face the owner under such circumstances? He had no money to offer as a return, but he took the book, went directly to Mr. Crawford, showed him the irreparable injury, and frankly and honestly offered to work for him until he should be satisfied. Mr. Crawford accepted the offer, and gave Abraham the book for his own, in return for three days' steady labor in "pulling fodder." His manliness and straightforwardness won the esteem of the Crawfords, and, indeed, of all the neighborhood.

After leaving school, and until he was eighteen years of age, he was constantly engaged in the avocations of a backwoodsman — cutting down trees and splitting rails — and in the evenings occupying his time reading such works as he could borrow in the neighborhood. A year later he was hired at ten dollars a month to go to New Orleans with a flatboat loaded with stores, which he accomplished to the satisfaction of his employer, by disposing of the goods to advantage.

In March, 1830, his father determined to remove with his family to Illinois—still westward—being induced to this step from the glowing accounts which were circulated of the fertile soil of the Prairie State. Traveling with wagons drawn by oxen, Abraham got one in charge, and in two weeks reached Decatur, Macon county, where the family settled on a tract of ten acres, on the north side of the Sangamon River, and about ten miles west of their halting place.

Here a log cabin was built, and the erection of a fence sufficient to enclose the lot was the next improvement—a work that young Lincoln assisted in performing. Thus, in all the various employments in which he was engaged, Abraham was active, earnest and laborious—dignifying labor with an effort he never was ashamed of, but glad to think that he was useful to himself and to his kind. The following year the aspirations of manhood took hold upon him, and he resolved to seek his fortune among strangers. His parents and friends, on witnessing his departure, were sad, and loth that he should go; but this step, to him as to others the most momentous, had not been taken without due deliberation, and he went westward to Menard county, where he was employed on a farm near Petersburg; then at Sangamon lent a hand in building a flatboat, taking another trip to New Orleans; afterwards becoming a clerk of a store at New Salem.

In 1832, the Black Hawk Indian War breaking out, he joined a volunteer company, and was chosen Captain. In war as in peace, he was prompt and efficient in the discharge of duty, his patriotism scorning danger and defying fatigue. This initiation of military life no doubt served him well when he became by virtue of his office Commander-in-Chief of the armies of the United States, and which has been proved by the orders issued and plans laid by him for the capture and destruction of "Stonewall" Jackson's army while it was threatening Washington in 1862.

On returning from the campaign, he was nominated and ran for the Legislature, but failed in securing a seat, although he received in his own precinct 277 out of 284 votes. This was the only occasion he was ever beaten before the people. He next opened store, with a stock of goods on credit, which, proving unprofitable, he sold out. At this time, he received the appointment as Postmaster of New Salem.

Still eager for information, he had gained a knowledge of grammar, and was attaining an insight into the profession of the law, when he became acquainted with John Calhoun, afterwards President of the Lecompton (Kansas) Constitutional Convention, who proposed to aid him in his studies. At the same time he practiced surveying, in which he was successfully engaged for over a year.

In 1834, he was elected to the Legislature, by the highest vote ever cast for any candidate, and was re-elected in 1836, 1838, and 1840. During these terms he first became intimate with Stephen A. Douglas, but little dreamt of the antagonistic position they afterwards assumed towards each other before the country. Both were the architects of their own fortunes, and both achieved an eminence of political glory that has now become historical.

In 1836, he obtained a license to practice law, and in April, 1837, removed to Springfield, and went into partnership with John T. Stuart. He rose rapidly to distinction in his profession, and was especially eminent as an advocate. An incident in his early practice is thus related:

At a camp meeting in Menard county, a fight occurred, which resulted in the death of one of the participators. A son of Mr. Armstrong, of Petersburg, who gave Lincoln employment when he went out into the world to work for himself, was charged and arrested for the crime. A true bill was found against him, and he was placed in jail to await examination. As soon as Mr. Lincoln became aware of the case, he wrote a kind letter to Mrs. Armstrong, stating his anxiety that her son should have a fair trial, and offering, in return for her interest in him while under adverse prospects some years before, his services gratuitously. Investigation assured the attorney that his client was the victim of a conspiracy, and he determined to effect a postponement until the excitement subsided. The day of trial, however, at last arrived, and the accuser positively testified that he saw the prisoner thrusting a knife into the heart of the murdered man. All the circumstances he remembered perfectly; the deed was committed about half-past nine o'clock at night, and the moon was shining brightly. Mr. Lincoln carefully reviewed the testimony, and then conclusively proved that the moon did not rise until an hour or more AFTER the murder was committed! Other discrepancies were shown, and, in half an hour after the jury retired, they returned with a verdict of "not guilty."

The young man and his mother had been awaiting the final result with agonizing suspense. No sooner had the words dropped from the foreman's lips, than the mother swooned in the arms of her son. He raised her and pressed her to his heart with words of glad reassurance. "Where is Mr. Lincoln?" he exclaimed, and then ran across the room and grasped his deliverer by the hand, with a heart too full for utterance.

Mr. Lincoln returned the warm pressure, and then cast his eyes towards the west, where the golden orb of day was still lingering. Half turning around, he said to the prisoner, tenderly, "It is not yet sundown, and you are free."

Few could restrain their emotion, as they observed Abraham Lincoln obeying the divine injunction of comforting the widowed and fatherless.

On the 4th of November, 1842, he was married to Miss Mary Todd, daughter of the Hon. Robert S. Todd, a lady of accomplished manners and refined social tastes.

In 1844, he was Presidential Elector in favor of Henry Clay, and canvassed the States of Illinois and Indiana in his behalf, addressing large audiences with marked success.

In 1846, he was elected a Representative in Congress from the Central District of Illinois. In Congress he voted for the reception of anti-slavery memorials and petitions, for motions of Mr. Giddings for committees to inquire into the constitutionality of slavery in the District of Columbia, and the expediency of abolishing the slave trade in the District, and other such propositions. He voted for the Wilmot proviso every time it was presented; and he stated, in his contest with Judge Douglas, that he had voted for it, "in one way and another, about forty times." In January, 1849, he offered to the House a scheme for abolishing slavery in the District, by compensating the slaveholders from the treasury of the United States, provided a majority of the people of the District should vote to accept the proposal. He opposed the annexation of Texas, but voted for the loan bill to enable the Government to defray the expenses of the Mexican war.

Mr. Lincoln was a member of the Whig National Convention of 1848, and urged the nomination of General Taylor. In 1849 he was a candidate for the United States Senate, but the Legislature being Democratic, elected General Shields.

After the expiration of his Congressional term, Mr. Lincoln applied himself to his profession with successful diligence, adding both to his fame and fortune, until the repeal of the Missouri Compromise called him again into the political arena. He

entered with energy into the work which was to decide the
choice of a Senator in place of General Shields, and it was
mainly owing to his exertions that the success of Judge
Trumbull, the Republican, and his election to the Senate,
was attributed.   At the Republican National Convention in
1856, which nominated Gen. Fremont for the Presidency, the
Illinois delegation unanimously urged Mr. Lincoln's name for
the Vice-Presidency.

On the 2d of June, 1858, the Republican State Convention
nominated Mr. Lincoln as their candidate for the United States
Senate, his opponent being Judge Douglas—two well matched
champions of opposing political views.   Douglas' superior skill as
a debater, however, was more than met by Lincoln's plainness
and logic ; the strategy of the one being counteracted by the
tactics of the other.   The contest that followed was one of considerable fervor, which led many of the people to form opinions
and choose party who had not thought so deeply upon matters of
government before. The election day at length arrived, when the
popular vote stood: for the Republican candidate, 126,084; for
the Douglas Democrats, 121,940 ; for the Lecompton candidates,
5,091.   But the vote for Senator being cast by the Legislature,
Mr. Douglas was chosen, his supporters having a majority of
eight on joint ballot.   During this campaign, Mr. Lincoln paid
a glowing tribute to the Declaration of Independence, from
which we copy the closing extract:

You may do anything with me you choose, if you will but heed these sacred
principles. You may not only defeat me for the Senate, but you may take
and *put me to death*. While pretending no indifference to earthly honors, I
do claim to be actuated in this contest by something higher than an anxiety
for office. I charge you to drop every paltry and insignificant thought for any
man's success. It is nothing; I am nothing; Judge Douglas is nothing.
*But do not destroy that immortal emblem of humanity—the Declaration of
American Independence.*

The promptings of his unselfish nature found a response, and
he was pronounced to be a leader of men. People became anxious to hear and see the one who uttered such lofty sentiments.
Like seed dropped into good ground, his words took root, and
sprung up in a fruitful harvest of supporters to the great prin-

ciples of liberty and humanity—truths that overcame the destructive policies of doubt and corruption.

To gratify public curiosity, a writer thus gave a pen-portrait of Mr. Lincoln:

He stands six feet and four inches high in his stockings. His frame is not muscular, but gaunt and wiry; his arms are long, but not unreasonably so for a person of his height; his lower limbs are not disproportioned to his body. In walking, his gait, though firm, is never brisk. He steps slowly and deliberately, almost always with his head inclined forward, and his hands clasped behind his back. In matters of dress he is by no means precise. Always clean, he is never fashionable; he is careless, but not slovenly. In manner he is remarkably cordial, and, at the same time, simple. His politeness is always sincere, but never elaborate and oppressive. A warm shake of the hand, and a warmer smile of recognition, are his methods of greeting his friends. At rest, his features though those of a man of mark, are not such as belong to a handsome man; but when his fine dark gray eyes are lighted up by any emotion, and his features begin their play, he would be chosen from among a crowd as one who had in him not only the kindly sentiments which women love, but the heavier metal of which full-grown men and presidents are made. His hair is black, and though thin is wiry. His head sits well on his shoulders, but beyond that it defies description. It nearer resembles that of Clay than that of Webster; but it is unlike either. It is very large, and, phrenologically, well proportioned, betokening power in all its developments. A slightly Roman nose, a wide-cut mouth, and a dark complexion, with the appearance of having been weather-beaten, complete the description.

In his personal habits, Mr. Lincoln is as simple as a child. He loves a good dinner, and eats with the appetite which goes with a great brain; but his food is plain and nutritious. He never drinks intoxicating liquors of any sort, not even a glass of wine. He is not addicted to tobacco in any of its shapes. He never was accused of a licentious act in all his life. He never uses profane language.

A friend says that once, when in a towering rage, in consequence of the efforts of certain parties to perpetrate a fraud on the State, he was heard to say: "They sha'n't do it, d—n 'em!" but beyond an expression of that kind, his bitterest feelings never carry him. He never gambles; we doubt if he ever indulges in any games of chance. He is particularly cautious about incurring pecuniary obligations for any purpose whatever, and in debt, he is never content until the score is discharged. We presume he owes no man a dollar. He never speculates. The rage for the sudden acquisition of wealth never took hold of him. His gains from his profession have been moderate, but sufficient for his purposes. While others have dreamed of gold, he has been in pursuit of knowledge. In all his dealings he has the reputation of being generous but exact, and, above all, religiously honest. He would be a bold man who would say that Abraham Lincoln ever wronged any one out of a cent, or ever spent a dollar that he had not honestly earned. His struggles in early life have made him careful of money; but his generosity with his own is proverbial. He is a regular attendant upon religious worship, and though not a communicant, is a pew-holder and liberal supporter of the Presbyterian Church in Springfield, to which Mrs. Lincoln belongs. He is a scrupulous teller of the truth—too exact in his notions to suit the atmosphere of Washington, as it now is.   *   *   At home, he lives like a gentleman of modest means and simple tastes. A good-sized house of wood, simply but tastefully furnished, surrounded by trees and flowers, is his own, and there he lives, at peace with himself, the idol of his family, and for his honesty, ability and patriotism, the admiration of his countrymen.

On the 18th of May, 1860, the Republican National Convention, which assembled at Chicago, nominated Mr. Lincoln for President of the United States, and that nomination was ratified by the people at the ensuing election in November. The electoral vote was subsequently proclaimed by Congress to be as follows:

For Abraham Lincoln of Illinois,..180
  " John C. Breckenridge of Kentucky,...... 72
  " John Bell of Tennessee,... 39
  " Stephen A. Douglas of Illinois,.. 12

On hearing of his nomination while at the *Journal* office in Springfield, he received the news in silence, remarking before he left the room—"There is a little woman down at our house would like to hear this; I'll go down and tell her." No doubt he wished to commune with himself and advise with his safe counsellor as to the acceptance or rejection of his appointment to the highest gift of the nation.

The load he had to bear was heavy—human strength was weak; but he chose to endure, and with his firm purposes to do right, constitutionally, before all the people, he left his hallowed home for the city of Washington, on the 11th of February, 1861, when he delivered a farewell address to his fellow-citizens in the following words:

My Friends: No one not in my position can appreciate the sadness I feel at this parting. To this people I owe all that I am. Here I have lived more than a quarter of a century. Here my children were born, and here one of them lies buried. I know not how soon I shall see you again. A duty devolves upon me which is perhaps greater than that which has devolved upon any other man since the days of Washington. He never would have succeeded except for the aid of Divine Providence, upon which he at all times relied. I feel that I cannot succeed without the same Divine aid which sustained him, and in the same Almighty Being I place my reliance for support; and I hope you, my friends, will all pray that I receive that Divine assistance, without which I cannot succeed, but with which success is certain. Again, I bid you all an affectionate FAREWELL.

His course towards the White House was a continued ovation incidental of politics and the conflict that had yet but feebly been perceived, until he arrived at Harrisburg, the capital of Pennsylvania, when it was found expedient to change his route to thwart the devilish designs of treason. The South desired his election that they might the more closely hug their belief in secession; but, at the same time, fanaticism essayed to prevent him reaching Washington. They could not live at peace, for they had begun to prepare for war. Power in high places had been wrested out of their hands, which they would not submit to. Their cherished institution was insecure; they madly would retain it—spread it widely—and even fight for it! The last resolve came first, which proved to be the beginning of the end.

On the 4th of March, 1861, Abraham Lincoln was inaugurated as the Sixteenth President of the United States, with imposing ceremonies. In front of the capitol he delivered his address, from which we give a short extract:

The chief magistrate derives all his authority from the people, and they have conferred none upon him to fix the terms for the separation of States. The people themselves, also, can do this if they choose, but the Executive, as such, can have nothing to do with it. His duty is to administer the present government as it came to his hands, and to transmit it, unimpaired by him, to his successor. Why should there not be a patient confidence in the ultimate justice of the people? Is there any better or equal hope in the world? In our present differences, is either party without faith of being in the right? If the Almighty Ruler of nations, with his eternal truth and justice, be on your side of the North, or on yours of the South, that truth and that justice will surely prevail by the judgment of this great tribunal, the American people.

The eyes of the whole civilized world were bent on Abraham Lincoln, the man of the people. Some were beaming with delight, that now they had found one honest man in power—one who would try to do right for right's sake, despite jeer or taunt. Some were lighted up with scorn and contempt, as their system of oppression was in fancied danger, for they hated the people. Some were gleaming with avarice at the thought that now the nation's extremity was their opportunity.

They all had their reward.

One, the infamy and disgrace of fine and imprisonment; one, the inward satisfaction at the triumph of justice; and the other, in exile, despair and death.

The speeches and State papers of President Lincoln so exhibit a plainness and a faculty of "putting things," that they became subjects of criticism and arrested the attention of even the literary circles of refined Europe. Rev. J. P. Gulliver, in a communication to the N. Y. *Independent*, relates the substance of an interview he had with the Chief Magistrate bearing upon and illustrating this mental phenomenon, which we insert:

"I want very much to know, Mr. Lincoln, how you got this unusual power of 'putting things.' It must have been a matter of education. No man has it by nature alone. What has your education been?"

"Well, as to education, the newspapers are correct—I never went to school more than twelve months in my life. But, as you say, this must be a product of culture in *some* form. I have been putting the question you ask me to myself while you have been talking. I can say this, that among my earliest recollections I remember how, when a mere child, I used to get irritated when anybody talked to me in a way I could not understand. I don't think I ever got angry at anything else in my life. But that always disturbed my temper, and has ever since. I can remember going to my little bedroom, after hearing the neighbors talk, of an evening, with my father, and spending no small part of the night, walking up and down, and trying to make out what was the exact meaning of some of their, to me, dark sayings. I could not sleep, though I often tried to, when I got on such a hunt after an idea, until I had caught it; and when I thought I had got it, I was not satisfied until I had repeated it over and over, until I had put it in language plain enough, as I thought, for any boy I knew to comprehend. This was a kind of passion with me, and it has since stuck by me, for I am never easy now, when I am handling a thought, till I have bounded it north and bounded it south, and bounded it east and bounded it west. Perhaps that accounts for the characteristic you observe in my speeches, though I never put the two things together before."

"Mr. Lincoln, I thank you for this. It is the most splendid educational fact I ever happened upon. This is *genius*, with all its impulsive, inspiring, dominating power over the mind of its possessor, developed by education into *talent*, with its uniformity, its permanence, and its disciplined strength, always ready, always available, never capricious—the highest possession of the human intellect. But let me ask, did you not have a law education? How did you prepare for your profession?"

"Oh, yes. I 'read law,' as the phrase is; that is, I became a lawyer's clerk in Springfield, and copied tedious documents, and picked up what I could of law in the intervals of other work. But your question reminds me of a bit of education I had, which I am bound in honesty to mention. In the course of my law-reading I constantly came upon the word *demonstrate*. I thought, at first, that I understood its meaning, but soon became satisfied that I did not. I said to myself, 'what do I do when I *demonstrate* more than when I *reason* or *prove?* How does *demonstration* differ from any other proof?' I consulted Webster's Dictionary. That told of 'certain proof,' 'proof beyond the possibility of doubt;' but I could form no idea what sort of proof that was. I thought a great many things were proved beyond a possibility of doubt, without recourse to any such extraordinary process of reasoning as I understood 'demonstration' to be. I consulted all the dictionaries and books of reference I could find, but with no better results. You might as well have defined *blue* to a blind man. At last I said, 'Lincoln, you can never make a lawyer if you do not understand what *demonstrate* means,' and I left my situation in Springfield, went home to my father's house, and stayed there till I could give any propositions in the six books of Euclid at sight. I then found out what 'demonstrate' means, and went back to my law studies."

"I could not refrain from saying, in my admiration of such a development of character and genius combined, 'Mr. Lincoln, your success is no longer a marvel. It is the legitimate result of adequate causes. You deserve it all, and a great deal more. If you will permit me, I would like to use this fact publicly. It will be most valuable in inciting our young men to that patient classical and mathematical culture which most minds absolutely require. No man can talk well unless he is able, first of all, to define to himself what he is talking about. Euclid, well studied, would free the world of half its calamities, by banishing half the nonsense which now deludes and curses it. I have often thought that Euclid would be one of the best books to put on the catalogue of the Tract Society, if they could only get people to read it. It would be a means of grace.'"

"I think so," said he, laughing; "I vote for Euclid."

Fairly ensconced in the nation's watch-tower, he now commenced his vigilant guard—a task harder than it had been his lot to share while in the backwoods of the West—which was relieved by the smile of affection and the innocent prattle of his youngest child in the rare intervals of pressing duty.

The boom of Sumter's guns sounded the alarm of war, and heralded the fact that conciliation or negotiation was a failure. Manhood and principle were almost forgot by politicians in vain endeavors at peace-making; but Abraham Lincoln kept perseveringly on in his line of duty—to uphold the starry banner and preserve the Union. The people supported him in all that he did, notwithstanding malice in the North and rebellion in the South. As a measure to weaken the enemy, he promulgated his first "Emancipation Proclamation," which proved to be fraught with happiness to the bondman, and made famous as a benefactor of mankind the name of Abraham Lincoln:

> For Abraham's the man to work out this plan
> By one * bold proclamation,
> And clear the way for a far brighter day
> To shine on our civilization.

Which was as follows:

I, ABRAHAM LINCOLN, President of the United States of America, and Commander-in-Chief of the Army and Navy thereof, do hereby proclaim and declare that hereafter, as heretofore, the war will be prosecuted for the object of practically restoring the constitutional relation between the United States and each of the States, and the people thereof, in which States that relation is or may be suspended or disturbed.

That it is my purpose, upon the next meeting of Congress, to again recommend the adoption of a practical measure tendering pecuniary aid to the free acceptance or rejection of all Slave States so-called, the people whereof may not then be in rebellion against the United States, and which States may then have voluntarily adopted, or thereafter voluntarily adopt, immediate or gradual abolishment of slavery within their respective limits; and that the effort to colonize persons of African descent, with their consent, upon this continent or elsewhere, with the previously obtained consent of the governments existing there, will be continued.

That on the first day of January, in the year of our Lord one thousand eight hundred and sixty-three, all persons held as slaves within any State, or designated part of a State, the people whereof shall then be in rebellion against the United States, shall be then, thenceforward, and forever free; and the Executive Government of the United States, including the military and naval authority thereof, will recognize and maintain the freedom of such persons, and will do no act or acts to repress such persons, or any of them, in any efforts they may make for their actual freedom.

That the Executive will, on the first day of January aforesaid, by proclamation, designate the States and parts of States, if any, in which the people thereof respectively shall then be in rebellion against the United States; and the fact that any State, or the people thereof, shall on that day be in good faith represented in the Congress of the United States, by members chosen thereto at elections wherein a majority of the qualified voters of such State shall have participated, shall, in the absence of strong countervailing testimony, be deemed conclusive evidence that such State, and the people thereof, are not then in rebellion against the United States.

---

* There were two proclamations in fact, but one was the virtual instrument which placed the name of Lincoln high on the scroll of fame, and blessed his memory through coming time.

That attention is hereby called to an act of Congress entitled " An Act to make an additional Article of War," approved March 13th, 1862, and which act is in the words and figures following:

Be it enacted by the Senate and House of Representatives of the United States of America in Congress assembled, That hereafter the following shall be promulgated as an additional article of war for the government of the army of the United States, and shall be obeyed and observed as such:

ARTICLE.—All officers or persons in the military or naval service of the United States are prohibited from employing any of the forces under their respective commands for the purpose of returning fugitives from service or labor who may have escaped from any persons to whom such service or labor is claimed to be due; and any officer who shall be found guilty by a court-martial of violating this article shall be dismissed from the service.

SEC. 2. *And be it further enacted,* That this act shall take effect from and after its passage.

Also, to the ninth and tenth sections of an act entitled "An Act to Suppress Insurrection, to punish Treason and Rebellion, to seize and Confiscate Property of Rebels, and for other Purposes," approved July 16, 1862, and which sections are in the words and figures following:

SEC. 9. *And be it further enacted,* That all slaves of persons who shall hereafter be engaged in rebellion against the Government of the United States, or who shall in any way give aid or comfort thereto, escaping from such persons and taking refuge within the lines of the army; and all slaves captured from such persons, or deserted by them and coming under the control of the Government of the United States; and all slaves of such persons found *on* [or] being within any place occupied by rebel forces, and afterwards occupied by the forces of the United States, shall be deemed captives of war, and shall be forever free of their servitude, and not again held as slaves.

SEC. 10. *And be it further enacted,* That no slave escaping into any State, Territory, or the District of Columbia, from any other State, shall be delivered up, or in any way impeded or hindered of his liberty, except for crime, or some offence against the laws, unless the persons claiming said fugitive shall first make oath that the person to whom the labor or service of such fugitive is alleged to be due is his lawful owner, and has not borne arms against the United States in the present rebellion, nor in any way given aid and comfort thereto; and no person engaged in the military or naval service of the United States shall, under any pretence whatever, assume to decide on the validity of the claim of any person to the service or labor of any other person, or surrender up any such person to the claimant, on pain of being dismissed from the service.

And I do hereby enjoin upon and order all persons engaged in the military and naval service of the United States to observe, obey, and enforce, within their respective spheres of service, the act and sections above recited.

And the Executive will in due time recommend that all citizens of the United States who shall have remained loyal thereto throughout the rebellion, shall (upon the restoration of the constitutional relation between the United

States and their respective States and people, if that relation shall have been suspended or disturbed) be compensated for all losses by acts of the United States, including the loss of slaves.

In witness whereof, I have hereunto set my hand and caused the seal of the United States to be affixed.

      Done at the city of Washington, this twenty-second day of September,
[L. S.]   in the year of our Lord one thousand eight hundred and sixty-two, and of the Independence of the United States the eighty-seventh.

By the President: ABRAHAM LINCOLN.
   WILLIAM H. SEWARD, Secretary of State.

As indicated in the foregoing document, he issued his second official Emancipation notice on the 1st of January, 1863, relating the States and parts of States that were then in rebellion, and declaring the slaves therein to be *forever* FREE, which edict he concluded in the following words:

And upon this, sincerely believed to be an act of justice, warranted by the Constitution, upon military necessity, I invoke the considerate judgment of mankind and the gracious favor of Almighty God.

The people came to the conclusion that these proclamations were destined to bring slavery to a timely end where rebellion was raging; and to overcome the anomaly of that evil existing with freedom in other parts of the country, a resolution was adopted in Congress to submit to the action of the several States an amendment to the Constitution of the United States, prohibiting the existence of slavery within the States and Territories of the Union forever. Illinois, by her promptitude, placed herself in the van of this needful movement.

Steadily did President Lincoln steer the ship of state, although his enemies were not few. His four years of servitude were about drawing to a close, when the Republican Convention met at Baltimore on the 7th of June, 1864, and renominated him for President. His aspiring opponent, Gen. George B. McClellan, was nominated by the Democratic party at their convention in Chicago; but their platform and candidate both showing signs of retrogression, they deservedly failed to win.

On the 8th November, 1864, the entire vote polled stood thus:

Abraham Lincoln, ...2,223,035
Gen. McClellan, ...1,811,754

The confidence of the people again strengthened the heart and purposes of President Lincoln in his administration of the Government. The platform of principles set forth by the nominating Convention received his hearty approval, being, next to the Constitution, his guiding star of office.

On the 14th of April, 1861, the flag on Fort Sumter was lowered to rebellion, and carried off by the brave few who had made a resolute but an unavailing defence. On the 14th April, 1865, the same flag, so long hid away, was flung to the breeze by the assembled throng on Sumter's battered walls:

> "'Tis the Star-spangled Banner, O! long may it wave
> O'er the land of the free and the home of the brave."

This was a day of rejoicing. Richmond had been taken. The mainstay of the rebels, Lee's army, had been defeated, broken, and were now prisoners. Their last hope was gone, and joy was in the North at the near prospect of returning peace.

Great preparations were making throughout the land for a celebration of triumph on the 17th April; but this *feu de joie* Mr. Lincoln was not ordained to witness. During the day, he was invited to visit Ford's Theatre in the evening, and it was also announced that Lieut. Gen. Grant would be present. About ten o'clock, while the play of " Our American Cousin" was progressing, a stranger, who proved to be J. W. Booth, an actor of some note, entered the box occupied by the Presidential party, and leveling a pistol close behind the head of Mr. Lincoln, fired, the ball lodging deep in the brain of the President. The assassin jumped upon the stage, shouting *"Sic Semper Tyrannis!"* the motto upon the escutcheon of the State of Virginia, and fled.

Human help to save the President was vain. He lingered on unconsciously until twenty-two minutes past seven next morning, when death relieved him of his suffering, and changed the gladness of the American people into a wail of sorrow.

> "'Tis the wink of an eye, 'tis the draught of a breath;
> From the blossom of health to the paleness of death,
> From the gilded saloon to the bier and the shroud—
> Oh why should the spirit of mortal be proud?"

"Treason," in its expiring throes, "had done its worst;" and as the Cain-like hand which smote our chief fell palsied in death, his life, other than as a warning, was declared to have been "useless."

The President's remains—accompanied by those of a darling son, who had been earlier called—moved to their resting place by the same route he had partly taken when appointed to occupy the chair of State, and were everywhere met with the symbols of grief and respect;

"And now, the Martyr is moving in triumphal march mightier than when alive. The nation rises up at his coming. Cities and States are his pall-bearers, and cannon beat the hours with solemn procession."

On the 4th of May, in a little knoll in Oak Ridge Cemetery, near Springfield, not far from his former home in the flesh, Illinois received back her son to her bosom.

> Hereafter his dearbought fame shall be
> The unfettered praises of the free.

CAPTAIN THOMPSON.

MARTYRS AND HEROES OF ILLINOIS.

CAPTAIN THOMPSON.

(OF THE REGULAR ARMY.)

CAPT. JOHN A. THOMPSON, of the 18th U. S. Infantry, killed in battle at "Hoover's Gap," Tenn., was born at Northampton, Mass., October 22, A. D. 1824, and was the son of Amherst Thompson of Chicago, whose father was a soldier of the Revolutionary War, was in numerous battles, and for more than thirty years drew a pension from the government. Col. Joseph Thompson, the father of Amherst, held a commission under Washington, in the Revolution.

John A. Thompson entered Amherst College, Mass., in September, 1842, where he remained until the commencement of his junior year, taking the first prize for declamation. In the fall of 1844, pecuniary considerations induced young Thompson to leave college, in which he supported himself partially by teaching, and with only a few dollars in his pocket, which was increased somewhat by the liberality of his uncle, John Thompson, Esq., a prominent banker of Wall Street, New York, he launched out upon the great ocean of life. He traveled to Virginia, where his genial disposition and interesting manners soon brought him employment as a teacher. Remaining in Virginia about a year, he emigrated to Missouri, where he was engaged in teaching some two years, when he returned to Amherst, Mass., and commenced reading law with the Hon. Edward Dickinson, of that place. Under the instruction of Mr. Dickinson, young Thompson advanced rapidly in his professional studies, and while a student, tried cases with much ability. After finishing his legal studies, he removed to Niles, Michigan, was admitted to the bar of that State, and at once

1

entered upon his profession. The "rough and tumble" of western practice at that time was well calculated to bring out the abilities of Mr. Thompson, and he soon became a popular lawyer of that region. He was for a time prosecuting attorney for the county of Berrien, Michigan.

In the summer of 1852, Mr. Thompson removed to Chicago, Illinois, where, for some eight years, he was engaged in the active practice of the law in connection with his brother.

While in Chicago, he engaged to a considerable extent in politics, and was a popular political orator and debater. Being a noble, whole-souled, liberal man, with hosts of friends, Mr. Thompson was, in the spring of 1855, by a large majority, elected City Attorney of the city of Chicago, and performed the responsible duties of that office, then embracing all the legal duties relating to city matters, to the satisfaction of all classes. In the ensuing year, at the request of the Common Council, in connection with his brother, Geo. W. Thompson, Esq., a well known member of the Chicago bar, he compiled and codified the ordinances and laws of Chicago, producing, out of a confused and tangled mass of city legislation, the present "*Municipal Laws of Chicago,*" a work which has justly received the praises of the public.

As a lawyer, Mr. Thompson was of the first-class for a man of his age—rarely excelled in forensic debate, an eloquent and polished speaker, often powerful in his efforts, and always honorable and high minded. Few men have been more popular in Chicago than he.

In 1859, Mr. Thompson was induced by his friends to settle in south-west Missouri, and removed his family to Granby, Newton county, Missouri, and was preparing to develop the lead mines of that region, when the threatening clouds of the Great Rebellion began to gather. Again and again did he with powerful eloquence appeal in vain to his fellow-countrymen to forbear to lay their hands upon the pillars of the Republic. Standing as he then did upon the bounds of civilization and beyond the line where loyalty ended and treason began, manfully and with heroic stubbornness did Mr. Thompson attempt to breast back the rising tide of rebellion in that section, until actual danger to his family compelled him to leave his new home with all its promises and hopes.

We extract from a report of a speech from the *Neosho Herald*, made by Mr. Thompson before he left:

"Who would strike the American Republic from the list of nations? Our country was not designed for destruction. The Temple of Liberty was not erected to be laid in ruins. Yon lofty tower dedicated to him 'first in war, first in peace, and first in the hearts of his countrymen,' was not intended for the ivy to creep upon its crumbling walls and broken columns. The Union of these States was not cemented with Revolutionary blood, to be dissolved. It cannot be without civil war, rapine, treason, annihilation;—it cannot be without marring the memories of the distinguished *dead* and overturning their monumental stones:—it cannot be without impeaching the patriotism of the eloquent Clay, or denying the logic of the irresistible Webster;—it cannot be without disputing the justice of our fathers' struggle for independence and blotting from memory the name of WASHINGTON, and with it his counsels of wisdom and affection. '*The Union, the Union—let it be preserved!*'"

He returned to Chicago in the spring of 1861, resolved to give the rest of his life to his country. He immediately applied himself to the study of military tactics, assisted in organizing the first Illinois regiments, and returned to Missouri, assisted Gen. Lyon in removing arms from St. Louis to Illinois for safety, and subsequently entered the government service as an assistant in the department of Gen. Fremont, who appointed him on his staff with the rank of Captain, for meritorious services. Being well acquainted with the country, and knowing many of the leading men of that State, Capt. Thompson was a valuable aid to Gen. Fremont, who committed to him important trusts and duties. When Gen. Fremont was relieved of his command, and his staff officers dispersed, Capt. Thompson once more returned to Chicago, and was preparing to organize a regiment of volunteers, when he was notified of his appointment by President Lincoln, to a Captaincy in the Regular Army, which was highly complimentary to him, as an appointment from civil life to that rank in the old army was an unusual thing.

His commission issued February 21, 1862, taking rank from October 26, 1861, and was credited to Missouri, through the efforts, principally, of the Hon. John S. Phelps, member of Congress from that State, a social and political friend of Capt.

Thompson. He always spoke of the kindness of Mr. Phelps with much gratitude.

He was assigned to the 18th United States Infantry, whose headquarters were at Columbus, Ohio, where he immediately reported for duty. This regiment not being full, Col. Carrington ordered him to return to Chicago and recruit a company of regulars, and he at once entered upon the work. At that time it was difficult to obtain men to enter the regular army, nearly all preferring the volunteer service, yet Capt. Thompson, by his energy and perseverance, speedily recruited one of the very best and most effective companies of troops that Illinois has sent to the war, which he drilled to a high standard of discipline. *"Captain Thompson's Regulars"* were the pride of Chicago while they were there. He was ordered back to Columbus with his company, and placed in command of "Camp Thomas," a camp of instruction for the 16th and 18th U. S. Infantry. The 18th Regiment (the largest ever in the American army) was composed of twenty-four hundred men—three battalions of eight companies each. The first battalion was soon ordered to the field, leaving Captain Thompson in command of the second battalion. At the time of one of the threatened advances of Gen. Bragg on Cincinnati, he was ordered with his battalion to that place to defend it, when he was placed in command of the "City Guards," composed of his battalion of regulars and some volunteer companies. Afterwards, he was ordered to the field in Kentucky, and placed in command of the batteries opposite Cincinnati. For a time he was in command of "Burbank Barracks," in Cincinnati. The alarm in that city having subsided, on the 13th Feb., 1863, by especial request of Gen. Rosecrans, Capt. Thompson, with his battalion, was ordered to the field in Tennessee, with the Army of the Cumberland, and took his post in the "Regular Brigade" of that army.

On the 23d of June, 1863, Captain Thompson, in a letter to his wife, writes: *"To-morrow we advance upon Bragg's army. If it should happen that I fall, remember and be happy in the thought that all this is for my country, my wife and child."*

Brave words of a true hearted man! and ere the sacred missive had reached his wife, the lifeblood of the noble martyr was poured out on the altar of that country which he loved so well!

The line of march of the Regular Brigade was on the Manchester road, leading through "Hoover's Gap," a strong position occupied by Johnson's, Bates' and Clayton's brigades of rebel infantry, the hills being well supported by batteries, all in position to resist the advance of Gen. Rosecrans. On the morning of the 26th June, Gen. Reynolds' division had surprised the enemy at this gap, but by desperate fighting the enemy had regained their ground, when the Regular Brigade was ordered into a charge upon these positions.

The correspondent of the N. Y. *Herald*, speaking of this charge, says: "The Regular Brigade in the centre and holding the advance, had a more beautiful field than either Walker on the right or Humbright on the left, and the charge which it made across the valley was the feature of the advance—the men moved in most beautiful order, the line never wavering or becoming broken until the fence behind which the enemy rested was reached. Here a brisk engagement ensued—the rebels were driven back in great disorder, throwing away their blankets and canteens. Our principal loss fell upon the 18th Infantry."

The second battalion of the 18th Infantry, commanded and led by Capt. Thompson, had the extreme advance of this charge, towards the close of which it became necessary to make an oblique movement, and while issuing the order "*right oblique march*," Capt. Thompson received a large minie ball, which passed through his bridle hand and thence into his body near the navel, lodging near the spine. He fell from his horse, and while Gen. Rousseau and staff, and Gen. Brannon and staff, had gathered around and were condoling with him, a rebel shell exploded in their midst, scattering the party. He was removed back to the hospital in Nashville, where he died of his wounds the ensuing Tuesday, June 30, 1863, surrounded by sympathising friends, a few hours before his wife reached him ! The last words of the gallant hero were: "*I now leave all with God.*"

His body was brought to Chicago by his wife and brother, and buried with full military and masonic honors in "Graceland," by the side of three of his children. He was a prominent member of several masonic bodies, being a Sir Knight in Apollo Commandery of Chicago, and a member of Lafayette Chapter of R. A. M., in said city.

In 1851, Mr. Thompson married Miss Elizabeth W. Lusk, of Newark, N. Y., a very estimable lady, who, with a young daughter, now survive him.

Capt. Thompson was an ardent patriot from the first, giving all his powers to his country. On the 22d day of April, 1861, when the news was received of the fire on Sumter, and Chicago was arming a force to fortify Cairo, he became highly excited and hastily arranged matters to start for Missouri the next morning. He gave a couple of horse pistols, which he brought from Missouri, to the Cairo expedition, and anticipating danger, made a hasty *will* of what little property he had, and started for Missouri with his revolver in his pocket, to battle for the old flag. He concludes this hasty *will* with the following patriotic bequest: "I give and bequeath my horse pistols to my country, hoping that by their aid the same may endure forever—and my revolver to the first soldier of the old republic who sends the first secessionist, in arms against his country, *to his long home.*"

From this time Mr. Thompson was in the service of his country until his death. His mind, temperament and business experience was well calculated to make him an excellent officer. He at once won the respect of the old army officers, and soon became an excellent military man. He was kept in commands above his rank, which corresponded in the volunteer service to the duties of colonel. In the field he always commanded his battalion, composed of eight full companies of troops, but the slow rule of promotion in the regular army kept him with the rank of "Captain Commanding." On his death, prominent officers of the Regular Brigade wrote, "that the 18th Infantry had lost one of its most valuable and gallant officers."

Gen. Rousseau writes: "I was just behind Capt. Thompson when he fell. He was a brave and efficient officer and an honor to the service, and fell gallantly fighting for his country."

Judge Swayne, of the United States Supreme Court, who became acquainted with Capt. Thompson, in Ohio, in a letter to his friends, says of him: "He was a gallant soldier, a gentleman of great worth and high character—an ardent patriot. His love of country and desire to serve her carried him into the military service. I had predicted for him, in my own mind, a brilliant career. I have met with no more striking or interesting man in the army."

Thus, in the full vigor of his manhood—his country still trembling in the balance—the laurel wreath of her deliverance almost within his grasp—amid the fury and carnage of the battle field—bearing aloft his tried sword and shouting *onward* to his brave battalion—the clarion notes of victory sounding in his ears—the swift, fatal missile of treason pierced him to the heart, and the noble John A. Thompson fell, to battle for his country no more!

Behold the grandeur of this spectacle!

In 1860, the Rev. Amherst L. Thompson, a younger brother of the subject of this sketch, fresh from the sacred groves of Andover, under the benevolent auspices of the American Board of Foreign Missions, and under *orders* from On High which he read in the Great Book, buckled on the armor of a *Christian* soldier and went forth to fight the battles of his Lord and Master in heathen lands. Leaving friends and kindred and comforts and home, he traveled over oceans, seas and continents, and at last unfurled the blessed banner of the Cross amid the benighted races of Central Asia. For a brief period, with Spartan heroism, did he battle the errors of a wicked populace, contending with the demons of darkness, superstition and crime, and *died* on the field of his labor—a noble Christian martyr, in the noontide of his heroic deeds!

A few months later, the brother, the subject of this sketch, beholding the mighty pillars of his loved country crumbling one by one beneath the rolling tide of a gigantic and wicked rebellion, likewise buckled on the armor of a *Patriot* soldier, and went forth from Chicago to fight for the honor and integrity of his native land. He eagerly grasped the glorious old banner of the Stars and proudly bore it onward into the midst of the fury and carnage of the battle field—and *fell*, a heroic, patriot soldier, dying for his country!

Ye Winds, which wafted the pilgrims to this land of promise! catch upon your broad wings and onward bear a record of this story! Let the selfish, the sordid and the base, read it—let him who would strike at the vitals of his country, read it—let posterity see what a Christian can do for his God—what a Patriot can do for his country!

Brave, noble, illustrious brothers! the splendor of these achievements shall ever radiate amid the folds of those sacred banners under which you fell—emblems which, by the blessing of God, shall symbol forth to distant ages a world redeemed and a nation saved!

And when, in the "good time coming," the fragments of this wicked generation shall be gathered into history, good men, philanthropists and Christians—

> "Will, by their pilgrim-circled hearth,
>   Talk of thy doom without a sigh;
> For thou art Freedom's now and Fame's—
> *Two* of the few, the immortal names
>   That were not born to die."

CAPTAIN DENISON.

Capt. CHARLES EDWARD DENISON was born at Woodstock, Vt., on the 30th of May, 1827. At the age of fourteen, he entered Norwich University, a military college, under the charge of Gen. T. B. Ransom, (father of Gen. T. E. G. Ransom, of the Army of the Mississippi,) who fell at the head of his command at the storming of Chapultapec in Mexico. Young Denison graduated in 1845. After leaving college, he was employed on the Passumpsic River Railroad, Vermont, as civil engineer. In 1852, he was on the Cincinnati and Marietta Railroad in a similar capacity. In 1853, he removed to Peoria, Ill., and was employed there as civil engineer on the Peoria and Oquawka, the eastern extension, and other roads. In 1856, he took an active part in raising a military company in Peoria, called the "National Blues," and was elected their first captain.

At the first call of the President for 75,000 volunteers, he, in a few days, raised a company of three-months men; was elected their captain, and reported in Springfield, and formed Co. E of the 8th Regiment Illinois Volunteers—Col. Oglesby. This regiment went direct to Cairo. Soon after, some influential friends, then in Washington, obtained for him the appointment of a captaincy in the Regular Army—a promotion quite unexpected to himself, but a well merited compliment to so brave and noble-hearted a soldier. He was assigned to the 18th U. S. Infantry, and to the command of Co. B. He immediately reported for duty at Columbus, Ohio, where this regiment was then forming. He remained there during the summer of 1861, filling up and drilling his company. In the fall, the first battalion of his regiment was ordered to the field in Kentucky, and joined Thomas' division of Buell's army.

Capt. Denison was with the "Regular Brigade" of that army in their many long and tedious marches through Kentucky and Tennessee: now skirmishing with the enemy, now guarding

railroads; again marching with all the celerity possible, to take
part in some important conflict, as at the battle of Mill Springs,
Ky., and the second day's battle of Shiloh. He was at the siege
of Corinth, the battle of Perryville, Ky., and the conflict at Stone
River, where, on the forenoon of 31st Dec., 1862, in that severe
engagement, in a cedar thicket, while leading his company, he
was wounded in the knee with a round shot. He refused to be
carried to the rear, but lay where he was wounded, and continued to encourage his men until they were forced back and
the ground on which he fell was occupied by the enemy. He
remained there until the ground was retaken in the afternoon
by our forces, when he was carried to the field hospital and
had his limb amputated. He lingered on until the 15th of
January, 1863, when death claimed the valiant officer as its
own. He was highly esteemed by his brother officers as a true
man and a noble soldier.

Capt. Denison, by education and natural endowments, was
well fitted for the place which he held. He had long desired
a position in the army, and had he been fired with the ambition
for distinction that many possess, he might have held a higher
rank, but in his singleness of purpose, he aimed only to serve
his country, and he did it well.

Capt. Denison was married twice, and leaves a wife and three
children to mourn his loss—a daughter by his first wife and two
sons by the last.

His remains were conveyed to Peoria, and buried in Spring-
dale Cemetery.

MAJOR APLINGTON.

ZENAS APLINGTON was born in Broome county, New York, on the 24th of December, 1815. His father, James Aplington, was a Baptist clergyman. We have nothing to record of his early life, but may presume it to have been a period of struggles like those of most American young men of humble parentage, as the education he received was limited, his opportunities probably being but few in number.

About the year 1837, Mr. Aplington emigrated to Buffalo Grove (by the Indians called *Nanusha*), Ogle county, Illinois, where he fixed his permanent residence. His early occupations there were successively those of a farmer, a blacksmith and carpenter (conjointly), and a merchant. As a builder, he erected the Lee county jail at Dixon, and a number of other substantial buildings in his own neighborhood. As illustrating the versatility of his talents, it may be said that though an excellent mechanic, both as carpenter and blacksmith, he never served an apprenticeship at either occupation. While a farmer, he resided upon and cultivated a farm, which subsequently became the site of the now thriving town of Polo.

On the 27th of April, 1842, he was married to Caroline, daughter of William and Jane Nichols—a most estimable lady, by whom he had six children, all of whom are now living.

In 1855, he contracted with the Illinois Central Railroad Company for the building of the section of their road passing through the town of Polo, which dates its prosperity from the completion of that road. Mr. Aplington, owning the land, at once laid it out in town lots, and by liberal terms and generous enterprise secured the rapid settlement and building up of the town. The rapid increase in the value of his landed property made him a wealthy man. Subsequently, during the crisis of 1857, he met with heavy pecuniary losses, and became again reduced to comparative poverty. So that he was first poor, then rich, then poor again.

In 1858, Mr. Aplington was chosen State Senator for the district, comprising the counties of Ogle, Carroll, Winnebago and Boone. He served but one session in this capacity (his term being uncompleted at the time of his death); but brief as was this service, he achieved an enviable reputation as a legislator. His native shrewdness, genuine talent, imperturbable good nature, unflinching integrity and untiring energy gave him at once a large influence in our legislative councils. His votes were ever on the side of the right, and in the Capitol, as at home, the poor and the oppressed always found in him a friend and an able and eloquent advocate. It is noteworthy, that among his warmest *personal* friends were senators and others, who most strenuously opposed him in partisan contests.

When the rebellion broke out, in 1861, Mr. Aplington lent his whole energies to the cause of the country, and performed efficient service in raising volunteers. In August, of that year, he organized a company of cavalry, of which he was chosen Captain. When the company arrived at Springfield, they joined the 7th Illinois Cavalry, Col. Kellogg, of which regiment Capt. Aplington was elected Major. In this capacity he for some time commanded the post of Bird's Point, and was with Gen. Pope at the taking of New Madrid and Island No. 10, where he performed important service.

On the 8th of May, 1862, Major Aplington was with our advanced forces near Corinth, Miss., in command of a battalion of his regiment. Here he was ordered, by Acting Brig. Gen. Paine, to charge upon the rebel infantry in a dense wood. He remonstrated against doing this, alleging that his men would be cut to pieces without accomplishing any good. Upon the repetition of the order, he mounted his horse, and turned to his men, saying, "Boys! you hear the General's command. We must obey orders. Follow me." He then dashed gallantly forward upon three or four regiments of rebel infantry, himself several paces forward of his men. One rebel, who essayed to "pick off" the brave commander, was stricken down by a blow from his stalwart arm. A second was more successful, and a rebel bullet entered Major Aplington's head, just below the eye. Dropping his sabre, he crossed his arms upon his breast, a calm smile settling upon his features, and fell from his horse—dead. A contest then ensued for the possession of the body, which his men succeeded in bearing from the field.

The remains of Major Aplington were taken to his home in Polo for burial, where the closing of all business, and the universal attendance of all classes at the funeral obsequies, testified the estimation in which he was held in the community in which he had lived.

In person, Major Aplington was tall and powerfully built, and his early occupations added largely to his muscular powers. He was possessed of great native talent, and though his early education was limited, by diligent study and careful reading he made himself thoroughly acquainted with the history, resources and needs of our country and the principles upon which our Government is founded. The village debating clubs always found him an active member; and we find him on the stump and in the forum an able advocate and a prompt debater, and a cool, clear-headed legislator. He was frank, open, and even somewhat eccentric in his manners; but we have yet to know the person who ever received from him a harsh or unkind word. The gentleness and kindness of his nature were shown in all his intercourse with his fellows. Unswerving in his integrity, kind and generous to the poor and needy, liberal and even profuse in his public services, he was universally esteemed, and wielded a large influence in his own community and wherever he was known. Amid all the "ups and downs" of fortune through which he passed, his generous heart and his conduct to his fellow-men knew no change. As a Christian patriot, he gave his life for the salvation of his country, that he might leave to *his* children the precious birthright of freedom which *he* had inherited. Brave as a lion, gentle as a woman, true as steel, all men loved him, and all men bewail his loss.

LIEUTENANT PRICE.

WILLIAM DELANO PRICE, the second son of William H. Price and Sarah A. Delano, was born March 1st, 1843, at Chillicothe, Ross county, Ohio.

In the autumn of 1849, his parents removed to LaSalle county, Illinois. His early youth was devoted to the occupations of a prairie farm, and was marked by a quiet, genial cheerfulness and gentleness, which made him a favorite in the family and amongst his few acquaintances.

He very early manifested an untiring industry in the intellectual occupations of his home, and a quiet and dauntless courage that disregarded danger when duty called him to confront it. At fifteen years of age, he called to his assistance a still younger companion, and the two with difficulty and at great personal hazard, saved two other and older companions from drowning.

As his character was gradually unfolded, the manifestations of uncommon intellectual promise became so decided, that his parents acceded to his wish, and he entered upon a preparatory course of study in September, 1859, at Lake Forest, in the academy connected with Lind University.

At this school he spent two years, to what purpose is explained by the following extract from a letter of the Rev. W. C. Dickinson, Professor of Languages, of the Academy: "Your son, in point of intellectual endowments, gave great promise. His scholarship was always high; few here, if any, have ever surpassed him. He had a true love for learning. The motives that prompted him as a scholar, were such as could not have failed, I think, to lead him to honorable distinction in any profession he might have chosen. He had *qualities* of mind, also, of rare excellence. His literary taste and judgment were uncommonly mature and fine. His delicate sensibilities, as they manifested themselves in his compositions, I greatly admired. One does not often find a fancy so exuberant and yet so correct, in one of his age. Of his fidelity to all duties as a member of this school, I can only speak in praise. He was always in his place, always ready, and with a cheerful interest in his work. His genial disposition made him a favorite with all. Cherishing no jealousies or enmities himself, he was the object of none from others. All loved to claim him for a friend, and imitate his excellences. In moral character, he was pure and manly. For a period of many weeks, he was deeply interested in religion. He did not feel ready to make a public profession, but I cannot feel otherwise than that the impressions he received here, remained in permanent effect upon his character."

Upon the close of the summer term of 1861, "thoroughly prepared to enter any of the eastern colleges," he came home. In the spring of that year, a class attended to military drill for a short time, under the late Col. Ellsworth, and afterwards under one of his pupils. This constituted a meagre experience, but it illustrated for William elementary military principles, and afforded a foundation for intelligent industry to build upon.

Repeated attempts to get a cadet's warrant, at West Point, having failed, he determined to enter the service of his country as a soldier. With the patient industry which marked all his efforts, he immediately set at work to improve his knowledge of drill; and when, in the ensuing October, he entered the 53d Regiment of Illinois Volunteers, then being organized at Ottawa, it is believed that he was fully the equal in thorough and accurate knowledge of drill, and in the faculty of applying it in the instruction of others, of the best informed officers of that regiment.

The ability to bring recruits being avowedly the only recognized qualifications for holding a commission in the regiment, he entered Company A as a private, and upon the organization of it was appointed Orderly Sergeant. The duties of this position he discharged without intermission for a single day, until the 5th day of September, 1862. At this time he was ordered by the Commandant of the regiment to assume the duties of Second Lieutenant. How he discharged the somewhat trying and invidious duties of orderly sergeant, may be safely left to the testimony of the members of Company A, and to the superior officers of the regiment.

His kindly temper and suavity of manner were, in him, the allies not of weakness, but of power. His instance is a signal proof of the character of the cruel fallacy a thousand times iterated and reiterated, that an officer who discharges his duty well, must of necessity provoke the ill-will of his men.

He was formed for a leader of men, and endowed with the power of exerting the strongest of all influences upon them. Were they in camp, on the march, or in the hospital, he shunned no labor that could promote their comfort or improvement. Incapable of doing intentional injustice himself, nothing so excited his indignation as injustice to soldiers by others. They understood him, confided in him, and loved him.

Neither in his diary or in his correspondence with his relatives, is there any complaint or notice of wrong or injury sustained by himself. A single gleam of his consciousness that he was more than commonly trusted by official superiors, emanates from only one entry in a fragmentary diary he kept during a part of his year of service: "Sept. 3d, 1862. We are on picket on the Hernando road, three miles south-east of Memphis. The sun is just setting and the boys are variously occupied; some are reading, some playing cards, others cooking, and some are just starting out after sweet potatoes and tomatoes. I am, as usual, in the most advanced squad, out of reach of the officer of the day, and of every one else who might consider it necessary to keep a strict watch upon us. Every wagon which passes out is searched, and any newspapers or suspicious articles are taken."

The next entry in the diary is under date of Sept. 6: "We are on the march again; some say, for Bolivar. Yesterday I was detailed to act as 2d Lieutenant until further orders."

Various incidents and reflections are entered from the 8th to the 14th, of which the last was written in camp, at Bolivar, and is concluded with the remark: "I was quite sick upon the march, and came very near having to be carried. But I persevered in tramping on without help, and finally walked out of it at the rate of 18 miles a day. One poor fellow was taken sick just after starting, was placed in an ambulance, and died there before the end of the journey."

Following this, are notices of various incidents of camp life, and on the 3d of October, 1862, occurs the last in the diary: "I have neglected writing for some time. However, very little has passed of any significance. I have been sick for some little time, although I've been on duty until the past two days; a dose of calomel has salivated me and put me in an uncomfortable position. Regular battalion drills are held every afternoon, and if persevered in, will be productive of much good."

Thus, whilst he was borne down by illness, the last line traced by his hand in the scanty record of a year of hardships and dangers, stands an indelible witness that the idea of duty was always present with him.

He exerted his influence habitually with the men of the company, to prevent their doing wanton injury to the unfriendly inhabitants of the country which was the theatre of operations, denouncing such as both wrong and hurtful to themselves.

On the 3d of October, Lieut. Price wrote and posted a letter to his parents, and one to his former school and room mate. He also learned that the 53d had orders to march early the ensuing morning. His superior officers and his comrades urged him, on account of his enfeebled condition, to remain in hospital, at Bolivar. He would not be persuaded to remain.

The division (4th of the army of Gen. Grant) marched on the morning of the 4th, towards Corinth, and at about four o'clock P. M., after a weary and hurried march of some twenty miles, came in contact with the enemy five or six miles west of the Hatchie River. Slight skirmishing ensued, and the division bivouacked. Lieut. Price was on picket the last half of the night, or through the early morning hours of the 5th of October. At daylight, he was evidently so ill, that he was again urged to stay with the wagon train. His refusal was now more decided than before, for the division was in immediate contact with the enemy, and a battle inevitable. The division moved, the second brigade in front. The enemy retired rapidly, with but one effort to take up a position west of the river, from which he was instantly driven across the Hatchie. He then placed his guns in position on the bluff east of the river, and formed his line on the river bottom, sharply followed by the second brigade.

Here the first brigade, under Gen. Lauman, was ordered up. He accompanied the 53d Illinois across the bridge under a shower of shell, grape and canister. The regiment was ordered to the extreme right, to a position between the road and river; here, for a third of a mile, but a few rods apart. Whilst executing this movement, a regiment of the second brigade, which had preceded it, came running back and broke through the line of the 53d, throwing it also into confusion. At this point, the Captain of Company A became separated from his command. Some ten or fifteen minutes time were spent, under a galling fire, in restoring order and reforming the line. The 53d moved forward to its position, steadily and in good order, Company A being led and commanded by Lieut. Price. On arriving at the desired position, near a slight elevation on the river bottom, which afforded an imperfect shelter against the shower of missiles hurled by the enemy against the feeble line, the 53d immediately commenced firing. As Company A assumed its place in the line, its youthful commander said to the men: "There they are, boys—give it to them!"

Acting Orderly Sergeant S. B. Baldwin, of Company A, (who was recommended for promotion, for bravery and good conduct in the battle,) writes, on the 9th, to a brother of Lieut. Price: "We were ordered to lie down and commence firing. We were so exposed to the enemy's fire, that had we raised half way up, ours would have been the fate of many others. I, for one, kept low, and I kept telling the other boys to do the same. But William was sitting up a little behind the boys, telling them to keep low, and cheering them up, when he fell. I saw him at the moment the bullet struck him, taking effect in his right side and coming out under his left arm. He fell, and died without a struggle."

The following is an extract from a communication, dated on the battle-field, the day after the battle, and addressed to one of the Chicago papers: "In closing, allow me room for a tribute of respect to one of our gallant dead, Willy Price, lately advanced to a lieutenancy in Company A, who, for nearly a year, as Orderly Sergeant, has been the pride and favorite of his company. His promotion was hailed by the whole regiment with joy. Courage and kindness, firmness and gentleness, sound judgment, and a high sense of honor, combined in him to make a soldier and a gentleman. No brighter offering was ever laid upon the altar of liberty and patriotism."

D. F. Hitt, late Colonel of the 53d Regiment, says:

"In relation to Lieut. Wm. D. Price, who fell at the memorable battle of the Big Hatchie, while nobly and bravely commanding Company A, I beg leave to say, that he was one of the best and most promising young men that it has ever been my privilege to become acquainted with. I never knew or heard of his drinking anything stronger than tea or coffee. I never heard of his playing at any kind of game. Books, tactics and his military duties, seemed to be his all-absorbing delight. Always in his place, and always ready to do, and do it willingly, too, whatever was ordered by his superior officers. He was kind, but strict and prompt with his men, and very attentive to all their wants and necessities, as well as to seeing that each one did his duty actively and correctly. He was one of the most apt scholars in military studies that it has been my luck to meet with, either in the army or military school, and he seemed by nature well calculated for camp life. I noticed, particularly during the five or six months' campaigning prior to his death, that he stood the hardships of heavy marching, and severe night and day, and often double, duty, much better than a great many men of a great deal more experience. He was neither clamorous nor restive, but naturally quiet and determined. Always candid, he meant what he said. He was fearless and brave, and was esteemed and admired both by the officers and men, especially the officers of our regiment, and his loss deeply mourned by all."

No superior officer impugned his fidelity or efficiency, and the privates of the company gave affecting testimony to the goodwill they bore him. One of them writes, four days after the battle, in which he fell: "His loss is mourned by every man in our company; kind to all, he showed the man in all his actions." Another manly and brave soldier, who followed his lead in battle, who was near him, and saw him killed, said quietly and feelingly to a friend: "If there was ever an angel on earth, Willy was one."

It is due to his memory to state, that from the vices and indulgences which sully so many otherwise estimable and brave soldiers, and the prevalence of which in the army is the cause of uncounted calamities, he was wholly exempt. So conscientious was he in this respect, that he persistently declined all share in the amusement of card playing, the almost universal resort for relief of the monotony of camp life, assigning as his reason, that if he became fond of it, the consequent indulgence would interfere with his duties. His recourse for occupation in leisure moments, which were few for him, was a professional book. He was continually extending his knowledge of the theory as well as the practice of the art of war.

On the morning of the 6th of October, he, together with the other dead of the regiment, clothed as when he fell, was tenderly buried by his comrades—his blanket constituting for him the only envelop at their command. His name and rank were traced on a board at his head. One week thereafter, loving hands raised the body, placed it in a metallic case, and returned with it to Bolivar the same night.

On the 14th October, Company A, and members of other companies, of the 53d Regiment, attended at the railroad depot. Gen. Lauman, Commandant of the Post, also came and assumed the office of directing the transfer of the body to the car. He had before said to the friends who had it in charge : " He was a gallant officer, a very gallant officer ; he died in the performance of his duty."

An escort of young men received and took charge of the body, at Ottawa, on the morning of the 17th, at three o'clock. And on the 18th, crowned with the victor's wreath, and enveloped in the folds of the flag in defence of which he died, he was borne from the Episcopal Church, again by friendly hands, to a grave in the cemetery amongst his kindred.

Thus perished, before he had completed his twentieth year, a soldier, who promised to become an ornament and support to his country. Like Fillan, the young son of Fingal, on his first battle-field, he has fallen without his fame.

> " His leaf has perished in the green,
>   And while we breathe beneath the sun,
>   The world, which credits what is done,
>   Is cold to all that might have been."

COLONEL SCOTT.

COLONEL SCOTT.

"He died too early," is the fitting thought of those who know the young Colonel of the Zouaves.

JOSEPH R. SCOTT was born in Brantford, C. W., in 1838, of Scotch parentage, from whom he inherited the valorous spirit and untiring energy of that never-conquered race. He came to the United States when he was twelve years of age, and not long thereafter engaged in what he had fixed as his pursuit in life—mercantile business. In 1856, he commenced the formation of the National Guard Cadets, in Chicago, afterwards famous throughout the country as the United States Zouaves. In the early progress of the organization, the lamented Ellsworth came to Chicago, and Scott, finding in him a kindred spirit, pressed him to accept the Captaincy, while he acted as Lieutenant. Thus it was that these two, lacking what in certain circles is considered the one thing without which all others fail —a military education—laid the foundation of a fame that will remain when the schools shall perish from memory. Not that military education has not its uses, but that it has its abuses, and that many are so endowed by nature as to lay down rules for education, and transcend the routine of meaner minds. Military genius, when coupled with energy and valor, is more than the equal of military skill, science or education, call it by what name you will. This is what they possessed in an eminent degree; and when the record of valor is made up, side by side with the noblest of the land will appear the names of Scott and Ellsworth !

A few days after the firing upon Sumter, Scott was elected Colonel of a three-months regiment, composed largely of the Zouaves and the Chicago Highland Guard. He was one of the youngest colonels in the service, being only about twenty-two; but superiority in skill and capacity were conceded him by his seniors, and his regiment was held to be the best drilled in the department. This regiment, at the end of "the three months' service," was reorganized "for three years or the war;" and at this juncture, Scott's characteristic generosity again shone out: though the choice of his regiment for colonel, he voluntarily

gave way to John B. Turchin, a veteran warrior, and became
second in command. What a scathing comment on those who
seek preferment through subterfuge and knavery. Scott's first
and last thought was his country and the 19th. Under this
leadership, his regiment took the field. Their name was a
household terror to rebels—they fell like an avenging Nemesis.
More than once they were denounced by the enemies of the
Government for having inaugurated in their department the
rule not to starve where there was enough and to spare in the
hands of armed rebels, and hoary villains and cowardly assas-
sins, with rebel instincts, were mean enough to charge them as
robbers and murderers; but to those who knew the glorious
19th and Jo. Scott, such wicked charges had no foothold of
belief. The 19th went on, and left some of its brave boys in
Missouri, Kentucky, Tennessee and Alabama—not to be forgotten, but to draw the hearts of a nation saved to the scenes
of its suffering and the birth of its immortality: thus

"The workmen die, but the work goes bravely on."

In August, 1862, Turchin having been promoted to a briga-
diership, Scott again became the Colonel of the 19th, in which
position (though at times acting as commander of a brigade) he
continued to the time of his death. The battle of Stone River,
so fearful in its character and so grand in its results, wove a
garland of immortality for Scott. He had been holding the
impetuous valor of his men in check during the slowly passing
hours of the bloody strife—their deep murmurs were heard as
they gave vent to their disappointment in not being permitted
to share the glory of the field—when, in an agony of despairing
hope, the voice of the General in command was heard ringing
all over the field, "Who'll save the left?" Before the echo
had died out, the exultant voice of Scott was heard in reply—
"the 19th Illinois!" and in an instant, leaping from his horse,
waving his sword overhead, he dashed onward, shouting "forward, 19th!" "double quick!" "charge bayonets!" The
brave fellows, with their wild, quick, Zouave cry, rushed to the
rescue, and the enemy fled in wild dismay—as clouds fly before
the hurricane. The left was saved, but the 19th lost what it
loved next to its country's weal—Scott fell, mortally wounded,

at the head of his column. He was removed to his home in Chicago shortly afterward, was carefully nursed by his devoted wife and anxious-hoping friends, and had all the help that surgical science and skilful treatment could afford, but all of no avail. He died from the effects of his wound on the 8th of July, 1863.

> " He has fought his last battle;
> He sleeps his last sleep;
> No sound can wake him to glory again :"

Yet how fondly we linger at his tomb and almost refuse to believe him dead. His noble, manly form—his flashing eye and joyous laugh come back upon us with such counterfeit of life, that we fail to realize that he is dead.

In looking back, we see in him no ordinary man, but one possessing a *something* which made him different from his fellows—possessing a divine appointment to work more mightily the machinery of the age and to give new impulses to life. Such as he are not, as many say, the creatures of circumstances—they are not the mere uprising of the moment : they are the workmen of such scenes as the American people have been passing through—

> " Time's rushing loom they are seated before,
> To weave the divinity's life-breathing robe,"—

circumstances bring them out to view, and afford a field for their energy and God-given vocation.

While as a soldier we might linger over his memory, there are other traits in which he is equally dear to our hearts. He was a good son of a loving mother, a fond husband of an affectionate wife, and the father of a beautiful child, and to them the loss is irreparable. Every thought that goes back to his character and glorious death, opens up the wounds of their hearts afresh. They see not so much the faithful soldier—the country's pride—as the loving heart. They almost forget the eye that kindled in wrath as it waked to the presence of the country's foe, in the eye that dwelt in fondness upon the domestic hearth. Thus the lightning that gilds the cloud, and adds terror to the angry storm, reveals to the weary traveler the abode of hospitality. His character, like the cloud of old, was darkness to his enemies, but a pillar of light to his friends, and he is but one of many the country weeps for in this her day of regeneration.

As deeds of valor inspire with fervor the poetic imagery of the muse, and in order that the glory of the 19th Illinois, with their brave leader and companions in arms who fell at Murfreesboro, should be perpetuated, the following "Battle Scene" has been written by R. Tompkins, and set to soul-stirring strains by Geo. F. Root:

"WHO'LL SAVE THE LEFT?"

Thro' two long days the battle raged
  In front of Murfreesboro,
And cannon balls tore up the earth,
  As plows turn up the furrow ;
Brave soldiers, by the hundred, fell,
  In fierce assault and sally,
While bursting shell hiss'd, scream'd and fell,
  Like demons in the valley.

The Northman and the Southron met,
  In bold, defiant manner—
Now vict'ry perched on Union flag,
  And now on rebel banner ;
But, see! upon the Union's left,
  Bear down, in countless numbers,
With shouts that seem to wake the hills
  From their eternal slumbers.

The rebel hosts, whose iron rain
  Beats down our weaker forces,
And covers all the battle plain
  With torn and mangled corses ;
Still onward press the rebel hordes
  More boldly, fiercer, faster,
But Negley's practiced eye discerns
  The swift and dread disaster.

"Who'll save the left?" his voice rang out,
  Above the roar of battle,
"The Nineteenth!" shouted Colonel Scott,
  Amid the muskets rattle ;
"The Nineteenth be it—make the charge!"
  Quick as the word was given,
The Nineteenth fell upon the foe,
  As lightning falls from heaven.

Over the stream they went, into the fight,
Cutting their way on the left and the right,
Unheeding the storm of the shot and the shell,
Unheeding the fate of their comrades, who fell :
Onward they sped, like the fierce lightning's flash—
Onward they sped, with a tornado's crash—
Onward they sped, like the bolts of the thunder,
Resistlessly crushing the rebel hosts under,
'Till, wild in their terror, they scatter'd and fled,
Leaving heaps upon heaps, of their dying and dead ;
And the shout that went up with the set of the sun,
Told the charge was triumphant, the great battle won.

MAJOR CLARK.

MAJOR CLARK.

Major ALPHEUS CLARK was born in Seneca county, Ohio, on the 30th of April, 1823. In 1837, he removed from there to Lyndon, Whiteside county, Illinois, and in 1850, left for California. He returned to Lyndon after an absence of three years, well satisfied with his trip. He was married the following winter, and remained in that place a loved and highly esteemed citizen, *strictly* temperate and religious, and of very strong anti-slavery principles, he being one of the old abolitionists at a time when that party was very unpopular. Great firmness of character was the chief feature of his mind, that displayed itself more forcibly in actions than in words. As Captain of the Home Guards of Lyndon, he heard the trumpet sound of war, and love of patriotism led him on the path of duty.

In August, 1861, he, in connection with Capt. Clendenin, raised a company in Whiteside county for Farnsworth's 8th Illinois Cavalry. When the regimental election for officers took place at St. Charles, Capt. Clendenin being elected Major, Lieut. Clark was unanimously chosen Captain of Company C. Just before the battle of Beverly Ford, his recommendation for the appointment of Major of his regiment was forwarded to the Governor of Illinois, which was confirmed, and his commission issued, to take rank from the 24th of May, 1863. It was sent to the regiment, but did not reach him until after his death, which occurred on the 5th of July, 1863.

Capt. Clark's company was one of the four companies which were doing picket duty on the right of the army, and bore the brunt of the attack of Stonewall Jackson's advance on the 26th of June, 1862, from 8 A. M. to 3 P. M., being then compelled to fall back before the superior force of the enemy.

He was with the army of the Potomac in its advance on Manassas; followed its successes and reverses through the peninsular campaign; was at Williamsburg, in the seven days' fight in the front of Richmond, in the retreat to the James River; was with it in Maryland, engaging the enemy at Poolsville, Barnestown, Middletown and Boonsboro, and with the advance into Virginia, fighting Stuart's Cavalry at Philamont, Union, Upperville and Barbour's Cross Roads, and had a part in the memorable battles of Fredericksburg and Chancellorsville.

In the battle of Beverly Ford, one of the most desperate cavalry conflicts of the war, it devolved upon Capt. Clark, as senior captain, to command the gallant 8th, all the field officers being sick or on detached service. With a coolness that has made him proverbial, he led his men into the fight, and when by reason of a rash charge against heavy odds, the 8th New York Cavalry were driven back in a confusion which threatened to bring panic and disaster to the whole army, Capt. Clark intrepidly checked the disorder of our own men and broke the advancing columns of the enemy. It was at this moment that a rebel Major, leading a squadron of cavalry, rode within thirty paces of the Captain, and halting, presented his revolver and fired. The fire was returned by Capt. Clark, and it has been told by an eye-witness, that nothing could exceed the perfect coolness and *nonchalance* with which the two foemen continued to exchange their leaden compliments. A shot from the Major, however, took effect in Capt. Clark's left hand, disabling him from managing his horse, and he was forced to give over the command to Capt. Forsyth.

Captain Clark's wound gave him but little uneasiness. He was sent to the Seminary Hospital in Georgetown, D. C., to await the slow process of healing, and was, on application, granted leave of absence to visit his home. On examination, however, it was found necessary to perform an operation on his hand, to remove the bones which proved to be broken.

A little circumstance may here be mentioned to show the spirit of the man: Major Beveridge, of the same regiment, who was sick in the same room, left it in the morning, and gave as his reason for doing so, that he disliked to see the operation performed. "I could stand it," said the Major, "if he *would only complain*, but to see him endure the torture without a groan, as he will be sure to do, is more than I wish to look at."

The operation was apparently successful, and the wound seemed in a fair way of healing. He was, however, afflicted with chills for a few days, but no apprehension felt for his

safety, until it soon became evident that the blood had been
insidiously absorbing the matter from the wound, and that his
system was badly poisoned. Everything that science or skill
could suggest was done for him, but the death-rattle in his
throat too plainly told that he was past all medical remedy.
He received the announcement with the same calm demeanor
that he would receive an order in camp. He expressed a sub-
missive obedience to the will of God, and a christian readiness
to die. He spoke feelingly of his home and family, and gave
orders respecting his effects and the disposition to be made of
his body. His last rational words were of his beloved wife and
children. Later in the day he became delirious, and, with a
face wreathed with smiles, he was, in imagination, again in the
saddle at the head of his squadron. He continued to talk
almost to the moment of his death: now placing his men on
picket; now forming in line of battle; now meeting a charge
of the enemy; now ordering an advance; urging his men forward; cautioning against surprise; ordering an arrest of those
who faltered in their duty, or encouraging those who were
battling gallantly. Like the exiled Corsican on St. Helena, he
died a true soldier; but, unlike him, he was moved by patriotism,
not ambition. His last words were—"We'll march them up
by fours."

Kind words soothed his dying moments, as quietly, calmly,
and with scarcely a struggle, he breathed his last breath out;
fond hands smoothed his pillow; fair fingers plucked beautiful
flowers to rest on his pulseless breast, and stout hearts heaved
heavily as his spirit took its flight. He was beloved by all who
knew him; commended as one of the coolest and bravest men
in his regiment, and without an enemy in the army.

Major Clark's remains were taken from the Seminary Hospital, Georgetown, to his beloved home in Illinois, where,

"After life's fitful fever, he sleeps well."

JOHN HARRIS KINZIE,

MASTER ON THE GUNBOAT, "MOUND CITY."

JOHN HARRIS KINZIE was born on the 20th October, 1838. His father was John H. Kinzie, the oldest living citizen of Chicago, having been brought to this frontier post in the year 1803. His mother was Juliette A., daughter of Arthur W. Magill, late of Middletown, Conn. From his earliest childhood, John evinced a passion for machinery and things pertaining to the application of mechanical principles. Before he was six years old he would lie upon the floor with his paper and pencil, copying from a book which had been given him, the engraving of a steam engine, placing the A, B, C, etc., to mark the different parts; after which he would seize upon some one to listen to him while he explained which was the piston, which a valve, with the mode of their operation, until he fancied he had made the whole quite plain.

To develope and improve this taste, his parents, after a few years passed at Jubilee School, (Peoria co.,) placed him under the care of Rev. Roswell Park, D.D., of Racine College, and afterwards sent him to the Polytechnic Institute at Troy. He had, subsequently, the advantage of instruction from Professors Peck and Trowbridge, at Ann Arbor, Mich. He acquired a more familiar knowledge of the practical application of mechanical science, while with H. Berdan, Esq., making the tour of the chief commercial cities, with a view of establishing the famed Mechanical Bakeries, and in the employ of the Illinois Central and Rock Island Railroads.

The energy and enthusiasm with which he threw his whole soul into each pursuit, attracted the notice and engaged the interest of even the gray-haired observer, while the amount of scientific and philosophical knowledge he had acquired, often prompted the remark, "I must see that boy, and talk with him again."

His marriage with Miss Elvina Janes of Racine, took place on the 21st April, 1861—three days after the first Proclamation

JOHN HARRIS KINZIE.

of the President calling for volunteers. His brother, and most of his young friends had enlisted. John's mind was in a state of doubt and perplexity—"I feel as if I must go," he said, "and yet, as if I *ought* to wait a while."

In the month of June following, his father was appointed Paymaster in the Army, and John accompanied him as his clerk for a few succeeding months, visiting Washington, St. Louis, Cairo, and other posts. Notwithstanding, however, the aptitude for business which he displayed, and the facility with which he acquired the necessary routine, he found the employment irksome—nothing but mechanical or engineering pursuits would satisfy a natural bent, rendered still more determined by cultivation.

He quitted his clerkship for a service on one of the government transports at Cairo, and it was while here that he attracted the notice of Admiral (then Commodore) Foote, who conferred upon him the appointment of Master in the Navy. He received his commission on the 4th January, and having, two years previously, passed his examination for the Navy, reported for duty on board the gunboat Cincinnati.

The "Mound City" was still in the course of construction, and before she was entirely completed, John was transferred to her, to assist in superintending her preparation for service. On the 23d February, he was able to announce in a letter to his parents, "The Cincinnati, with Flag-Officer Foote on board, has weighed anchor, and signalled us to follow. We're bound for Dixie." Some accident to the machinery, however, obliged them to return from the Cumberland River, which had been their first destination. Their next goal was Memphis. The progress of the fleet from Cairo to Memphis is matter of history. John's reports to those he loved best, were always of the most gay and cheerful character. He knew that after the fearful accident to the Essex in Tennessee River, the hearts of those who loved him were never at ease on his account, and he strove to convince them that there was no danger for him, even while, as it afterwards appeared, fully appreciating the defects in the construction of the Mound City, and living under the shadow of her coming doom.

From "Above Island No. 10," on the 29th March, he writes: "The rebels have fired at our boats for fourteen days and thirteen nights, from five different batteries, in all thirty guns, and have never hit us yet. Pretty poor shooting at 1¾ miles!" And again: "We have not fired a gun for nearly three days, and everything looks very quiet. The rebels finding that rifled 42-8 inch and 13 inch shell had an injurious effect on the human system, coolly moved their camps out of the way, built casemates to their mud forts, sunk their floating batteries to the water's edge, and during the night they build up what the mortars tear down by daylight." The Federal forces entered "No. 10, that once stronghold of secesh," on the 11th April. A demonstration was made by the enemy on the 9th May. It was described in few words: "The rebels came up this morning, but the Cincinnati, Cairo and Mound City drove them back again."

The first serious engagement of the Mound City was at Plum Point Bend, on the 10th May. Describing this, John writes: "We had a pretty lively time last Saturday. We fought ankle deep in water." (The Mound City, it will be recollected, was run into by the rebel ram Van Dorn and sunk.) "The Sponger at one of my guns was shot, and I jumped into the port and rammed the shell home—when that gun was fired, it crippled the ram. I had my hands full, I can tell you."

The Mound City was, providentially, got into shallow water, so that, although the officers and crew prepared "to leave their good ship," and possibly even life itself, they escaped for the present.

For his conduct in this affair, John was openly complimented by his superior officers. The testimony of one is: "In the service he was the bravest of the brave. I can bear witness to his coolness in action, his gallantry, and his efficiency. We have had many opportunities of seeing him placed in trying circumstances, in which he acquitted himself bravely and honorably."

The boat was brought up to Cairo for repairs, and when in order, proceeded, without further adventures of importance, to Memphis.

To the loving friends at home, all danger to their brave boy seemed now over. Memphis had been looked upon as the haven at which perils and hardships should cease. They were, therefore, not prepared to hear of a new tour of duty—an expedition to raise the blockade by rebel gunboats of the Arkansas and White Rivers. The boats assigned to this service were the Mound City, as flag-ship, Capt. Kilty, the St. Louis, Lexington, and the tug Spitfire.

They reached the " Arkansas Cut-off,"* on the White River, on the morning of the 14th June, where the tug, being sent sixteen miles up the river to reconnoitre, made prize of the magnificent steamer Clara Dolson. The fleet was accompanied by the transports New National, White Cloud, and Jacob Musselman, bearing the 46th Indiana regiment, Col. G. N. Fitch, whose object was to capture the transports which the rebels had run up White River.

The fleet cautiously and carefully ascended the stream, information having been received that the enemy had a battery or series of batteries about 80 or 90 miles above the mouth. These batteries, which were situated on a bluff in the bend of the river, were reached on the morning of the 17th June. Of the engagement which there took place, the particulars are probably unknown to few throughout our land.

The Mound City had the lead, and the St. Louis kept up a spirited firing, being unhit by the enemy's balls. At length the Mound City moved on, past the lower battery, supposing that, as it had slackened its fire, all existing danger was over. Both boats ceased their firing, fearing that the balls might hit, instead of the enemy, our own brave Indiana troops who had landed below, to attack the batteries. While thus lying, with her stern a little to the southern shore, awaiting anxiously the result of Col. Fitch's movement, the Mound City was struck by a plunging shot from the upper battery. It passed through the iron-lined casement, struck and exploded the steam-drum of the engine, instantly filling the boat with the scalding vapor.

John was standing upon the drum at the moment. "How he got into the water," said a survivor, "I never could conceive, but the first thing I knew after I reached it, he was swimming

---

* It is called the *White River Cut-off*, on the Arkansas River, and *Arkansas Cut-off*, on the White River.

near me. I observed that the rebels were drawn up upon the
bank, and were firing at us as we were in the water. I called
to him to make for the lee of the boat as I was doing, but I
think he was trying to get off his belt and sword, which hindered
him in swimming, and he made for the small boats instead. I
saw several throw up their hands and go down as the shot
struck them in the water."

The boats of the Conestoga and Lexington put off to the rescue of the victims. Shots were fired at them, but the brave souls
on board counted not their lives dear, so they might save their
suffering comrades. As John was lifted from the water, three
bullets struck him, taking effect in each arm, and in the hips;
another passed through the handkerchief which an officer, his
friend, was dipping into the water in order to bathe his face.
Every kind attention was lavished upon him, for, to use the
words of the sailor quoted above, "Everybody loved him and
wanted to do something for him."

Col. Fitch's bayonet charge upon the batteries had been successful, and the men who but a short time before had revelled in
their wanton barbarity, were now prisoners, or wounded, or gone
to their long account. This news was told to John as he lay in
his agony. "Have we taken the fort?" he asked. On receiving
an answer in the affirmative, "then," said he, "I am content to
die." The friends who had so tenderly ministered to him,
saw him placed with others on board the Jacob Musselman,
under Capt. Huntoon, to be conveyed to Memphis, and thence,
if he survived, to Cairo, where he hoped his young wife would
meet him, in compliance with a letter he had dictated to her. A
few lines from the pen of a loving friend will complete the sad
picture:

"There is something touchingly beautiful in the record of his
death, as made by one who was with him at the time, which
gives assurance that his last moments were those of peace.
Says this writer: 'At first it was thought he would recover, but
he failed rapidly towards morning, and at four o'clock, on the
morning of the 18th, just as the sun was kissing the tree-tops
on the banks of the great river, his spirit passed away.'"

GENERAL FARNSWORTH.

Brigadier General ELON J. FARNSWORTH was born in Green Oak, Livingston county, Michigan, on the 30th of July, 1837. In 1854, his father, James P. Farnsworth, removed from Michigan to Rockton, Winnebago co., Illinois, where he still resides —a farmer. His only brother died in Michigan before their removal to Illinois, and shortly after their removal his mother also died. In 1855, his father sent him to the university at Ann Arbor, Michigan, where he remained until the winter of 1857–8, when he joined the army of Gen. Johnston (then on its way to Utah, to suppress the Mormon difficulties in that territory) as an assistant in the Quartermaster's Department. He remained with the army in that distant frontier and in traveling over the Western territories, until the breaking out of the Rebellion in 1861. Love of adventure, buffalo hunting, etc., frequently led him to make long journeys on horseback through the mountains and over the plains of the "Far West," and it was there doubtless that he gained such a mastery of the horse as subsequently gave him the reputation of being "the best rider in the army."

News of the Rebellion reached him in the summer of 1861, and he immediately hastened home to join the 8th Illinois Cavalry, which his uncle, Gen. John F. Farnsworth, was then organizing. He was made Battalion Quartermaster, but soon thereafter, by an election, he was promoted to the Captaincy of Co. K of that celebrated regiment. During all the battles of the Army of the Potomac, he never missed a fight or skirmish in which his troop were engaged, and which are said to be forty-one in all.

He was brave and daring to a fault, and so kind and considerate to his men, that he early became their pride and boast. Whenever a scout or reconnoisance was to be made, Captain Farnsworth was almost invariably placed at its head, and so

3

intrepid was he in his attacks, and so watchful in his movements, that his name became a terror to every bushwhacker along the lines.

For his skill and daring on one occasion, the following complimentary order was issued:

HEADQUARTERS 1ST CAV. DIV.,
March 31, 1863.

General Orders, No. 15:

I. The General commanding takes this occasion to thank Capt. Farnsworth of the 8th Ill. Cavalry, for the gallant and efficient manner he has performed the scouting duty intrusted to his charge. The score of prisoners taken from the enemy is largely in his favor, and the skill and adroitness displayed in the capture are worthy of high commendation.

II. This order to be published at the head of each regiment in this division.

By order,   BRIG. GEN. PLEASANTON.
A. J. COHEN,
To Capt. E. J. Farnsworth, 8th Ill. Cav.   Capt. and A. A. G.

The compliment was well merited, and to his genius and bravery much of the celebrity of the regiment is due.

In May, 1863, Gen. Pleasanton placed him upon his staff as Aid, and so well pleased was he with the man, that he nominated him to the office of Brigadier General, and the news of the appointment reached him while on duty in the field. Our cavalry was then at Frederick City, Maryland, moving towards Pennsylvania in pursuit of the rebels. Gen. F. was at once assigned to the command of the 1st brigade of the 3d division of cavalry—consisting of the 1st Vermont, 1st Virginia, 5th New York and 18th Pennsylvania Cavalry—with a battery of artillery. With his brigade Gen. Farnsworth moved rapidly forward. On the 30th of June he had a severe fight with the rebel cavalry under Stuart, routing and defeating that celebrated officer.

On the 3d of July, Gen. F. was ordered by Gen. Kilpatrick, who commanded the 3d division of cavalry, to charge the right flank of the rebel army. The rebels (infantry) were posted behind a *stone wall*, and a little in rear of the wall was still another fence. They also had their artillery posted in such manner that they could pour a deadly fire of grape and canister upon the flanks of an advancing column. Gen. F. reconnoitered the ground in person, and reported to Gen. Kilpatrick that a charge at that point would be madness, and would only result in the loss of his men. General K., however, ordered the charge to be made. The gallant young hero replied: "Very well, I'll not send my men where I do not go with them." The correspondent of the New York *Times*, who was with the cavalry, gives the following account of this terrible charge, one of the bravest, most gallant, but most disastrous, of any during the war:

"The 1st Vermont, Col. Preston; 1st Virginia, Maj. Copehart; and the 18th Pennsylvania Cavalry, Col. Brinton,—were in position to charge. The 1st Vermont, 1st Virginia, and a squadron of the 18th Pennsylvania, led by Gen. Farnsworth, dashed forward at the word until the stone wall was reached. A few men pulled the rail fence away from the top of the wall. Gen. Farnsworth leaped his horse over, and was followed by the 1st Vermont—the enemy breaking before them, and taking a position behind the second fence. The few rods between the two fences, where our men crossed, was a fearfully dangerous place, the little force receiving the concentrated fire of three lines from front and both flanks. The witnesses of the movement stood in breath-less silence, their blood running cold, as the chargers gained the second fence. Man after man was seen to fall, Gen. Farnsworth among the rest. · He is killed!' gasped many a one, looking at that fatal spot. But no—that tall form and slouched hat are his—he lives—and all breathe again. His horse had been killed. A soldier gives him his horse. The General again mounts, and dashes on. The enemy here make a more formidable stand, but are driven away, and the whole force go dashing, reeling over the fence in a whirlpool of shot and shell, such as is seldom ever witnessed even by soldiers. The constant roar of musketry and artillery on the main field gave the scene a peculiar grandeur. It was fearfully grand. The second fence crossed, and new fires were opened upon this brave band. To retreat at that point was certain death, and the only chance of safety was to advance, and advance they did for between one and two miles, to the rear of the rebel army, in sight of the coveted train, but at what a cost! Dispersing, the men returned under a galling fire as best they could. A few did not get back to their command for hours—many never came. The list of missing gradually lessened, and hope led us to look anxiously for the return of Gen. Farnsworth; and when, with morning's dawn, no tidings from him were heard, then hope said he was wounded—a prisoner—he has been left seriously, perhaps dangerously, wounded at some house by the roadside. Vain hope! Messengers were sent in every direction to search for the missing spirit. It did not seem possible that he could be dead, and yet so it was. He fell just after crossing the second fence, his body pierced with five wounds. There some of the Vermont boys found him two days after, (the rebels having fallen back.) The brave, noble and generous Farnsworth has gone to his last rest, and the sod which covers his grave has been wet by the tears of those who loved and honored him while living. His name will ever be held in remembrance by every member of the 3d division."

Gen. Farnsworth was possessed of rare beauty both of person and of soul. No man who knew him failed to admire his great social attractions, nor will they soon forget his tall, athletic frame, dark flashing eye and finely moulded features. There fell no braver soldier on that field of carnage.

The following letters are from that excellent and gallant officer, Major Gen. Pleasanton, who commanded the cavalry corps, to the uncle of the subject of this sketch, and Captain Drummond, of Gen. P.'s staff, who superintended his burial, and announced his fate to his friends:

HEADQRS. CAV. CORPS, ARMY OF THE POTOMAC,
July 6th, 1863.

Gen. J. F. FARNSWORTH:

Dear General: I deeply regret to announce to you the death of Brig. Gen. Farnsworth, late Captain 8th Illinois Cavalry. He was killed while leading a charge of his brigade against the enemy's infantry in the recent battle of Gettysburg. His death was glorious. He made the first grand charge against the enemy's infantry—broke them—when found, his body was pierced with five bullets, nearly a mile in rear of the enemy's line.

He has been buried in the *cemetery* at Gettysburg, and the grave is properly marked. The enemy stripped the body to the *undershirt*—an unheard of piece of vandalism, as the General was in his proper dress.

Accept my warmest sympathy. You know my estimate of our late friend and companion in arms. We have, however, a consolation in his brilliant deeds in the grandest battle of the war.   Very truly yours,

A. PLEASANTON.

Gen. J. F. FARNSWORTH:

Gen.: You have already heard of the death of your nephew, Gen. E. J. F., killed in the action on the 3d. I was with him not five minutes before he fell, gallantly charging the enemy's infantry at the head of two of his regiments. His body was brought in last night, and at 3 A. M. of the day, I buried him with one of his captains, each in a good, rough box, in the Gettysburg Cemetery. He was shot through the pelvis, and had two balls through the left leg, one of which shattered his ankle.

Farnsworth's loss is mourned by all. He had just got his star, and fell in a gallant endeavor to prove to his new men his right to wear it. While by the light of a single lantern I dug his grave, instinctively the lines of Sir John Moore's burial at Corunna came in my mind.

" We buried him darkly at dead of night,
The sods with our bayonets turning,
By the moonbeam's misty struggling light,
And our lanterns dimly burning.

" Slowly and sadly we laid him down,
From the field of his fame fresh and gory ;
We carved not a line, we raised not a stone,
But we left him alone in his glory."

T. DRUMMOND,
Capt. and Prov. Marshal Cavalry Corps.

In July, Gen. J. F. Farnsworth visited Gettysburg, disinterred the remains of his nephew, and after embalming, removed them to Illinois, where now sleeps the heroic brave. He rests, to be remembered with the honored dead who have fallen in defence of their country, and a nation mourns the inestimable loss.

LIEUTENANT COLONEL SMITH.

Col. MELANCTHON SMITH was born in Rochester, N. Y., on the 25th of March, 1828. His father was a military man, and served his country as captain at the battle of Queenstown, in the last war with Britain, where he received much commendation for his skill and bravery. He dying while his son was a child of only a few summers, young Smith was brought up in the family of his uncle, Melancthon Starr, in New York city, where he remained until he was about twenty years of age. He then became connected with a mercantile house, and traded extensively in the Southern and Western States. In 1854, he settled in Rockford, and commenced business as a merchant. Finding in this employment insufficient scope for his active and nobly-ambitious spirit, he abandoned, after a few years, the pursuit of trade, and devoted himself to the study of law, for the science of which he possessed an ardent love and a fine mental adaptation. He studied in the office of Judge Anson S. Miller, of Rockford. Being admitted to the bar in 1859, he engaged with ardor and ability in the practice of his profession, till the political campaign of 1860, with the momentous issues then at stake, called him away from professional to public and patriotic efforts for the redemption of the country. He threw his whole soul into this campaign, speaking earnestly and eloquently on the great questions of the day, in the counties of Winnebago, Boone and Jo Davies.

The winter of 1860 he spent in Washington. The following spring he received the appointment as Post Master of Rockford, in consideration of the valuable services he had rendered. Upon the call for 75,000 men, he made an effort to arrange his business, so that he might raise a company, but was unsuccessful: he, however, spent time and money freely in assisting the late Col. Nevins, of the 11th Regiment, to raise and equip his company. When the next call came, it found him ready and anxious to do his part. He obtained permission from the P. O.

Department to leave his office, and by his efforts raised, in a few weeks, a company of 100, which included some of the most sterling and wealthy men of the county, and joined the 45th, or "Lead Mine Regiment," at Galena. He was soon elected Major, and drilled the entire regiment — *alone* — for a year. The efficiency of the 45th has proved how well the task was accomplished.

It was a remarkable circumstance, that some years before, when there was no speck or thought of war in this country, he had, from his own military instinct, joined the company drilled by the lamented Col. Ellsworth; and the knowledge and skill in military tactics learned under that distinguished master, availed him much afterwards, and contributed not a little to his usefulness and distinction in the field.

Col. Smith was present at the battles of Fort Henry, Donelson and Shiloh, and at the siege of Corinth, Gen. Logan gave him command of the advance skirmishers for four days. He was the *only Major* that Gens. McClernand and Logan mentioned in their official reports, none below the rank of Colonel being usually reported. They call him a "brave and efficient officer—worthy of any position assigned to him."

Soon after the occupation by our army of Western Tennessee, he was appointed Provost Marshal of Jackson, in that State, and remained there for several months, discharging the duties of his trust with fidelity and vigor. Afterwards, he was transferred to a larger and more important post, and appointed Provost Marshal of the district of Memphis. Of the fidelity and success with which for three months he discharged the laborious and trying duties of this office, no better testimonial can be given than the fact, that when, in accordance with his own expressed desire, he had been removed to his regiment at Vicksburg, a delegation of the merchants of Memphis waited on Gen. Grant with a petition that he be recalled to that important post, which request was immediately complied with.

Though fully aware that an effort was being made for his return, and that his recall was more than probable, such was his desire to rejoin his regiment and participate in the impending battles, that he did not wait to know the result, but started

immediately on his first order for Vicksburg; and though he
learned soon after his arrival, that Gen. Grant ordered his recall, he sought and obtained permission to remain until after
the fall of Vicksburg, coveting the danger and glory of the
battle-field more than the immunities of civil office and the
comforts of domestic life, which, in the intervals of toil, he
could there enjoy.

On the afternoon of Thursday, June 25th, a corps in Gen.
Logan's division was ordered to storm Fort Hill, in the rear
of Vicksburg. The assault was successful, but attended with a
fearful sacrifice of life. Foremost in the fray was the gallant
45th Illinois, and foremost of these was Lieut. Col. Smith, who
had command in the absence of the superior officer. At the
very beginning of the engagement, while in the act of cheering
on his men, he fell wounded in the head by three balls, one of
which entered and lodged in the brain. He immediately felt
in himself that his wound was mortal, and expressed his consciousness of the fact with the words, " I die as a true soldier,
and as I would wish to die."

He lingered in a state of half-consciousness for nearly three
days, repeatedly expressing his satisfaction with his fate, and
his entire willingness to die for his country. He expired on
Sunday morning, June 28th, in the 36th year of his age. His
remains were brought to Rockford, and on the occasion of his
funeral an eloquent discourse was delivered by the Rev. H. M.
Goodwin, from the text—2 Timothy, iv. 7—" I have fought a
good fight."

Col. Smith possessed in an eminent degree all the qualities
of a good soldier: courage, enthusiasm, self-devotion and fearlessness of danger, supported by a firmness and fortitude and
self-reliance that made him equal to every duty which a soldier
is called upon to perform. Combined with these was a rare
gallantry of spirit, and a noble generosity that won for him the
respect and love of all who had enough in common with him to
know him. One of the most marked traits of his character—
which no one could be with him an hour without feeling—was
his high and almost chivalrous sense of honor, showing itself by
a quick sensibility to, and a supreme scorn of, whatever is mean

and unworthy. This sprang not from a selfish fear of reproach, without regard to principle, but from the deep probity and moral rectitude of his character. He was honorable in all his transactions, not out of regard to some factitious code of honor, but because he was true to his own personal convictions. The sincerity of these convictions made him earnest in expressing and uncompromising in asserting and maintaining them, which exposed him often to misjudgment and unpopularity with those who did not appreciate their ground and honesty.

Before deciding to enter the army, he made the question a subject of devout and earnest prayer, and the decision when made was a religious consecration to the service of his country, expecting never to return, but to die on the field of battle.

He was not without faults, but they were defects and imperfections rather than vices, and of the worst of them it could be said, they "leaned to virtue's side." The life and death of this valiant soldier affords a beautiful lesson to young men, which is summed up in the words of the poet:

> "Be just and fear not.
> Let all the ends thou aimest at be thy country's,
> Thy God's and truth's; then, if thou fallest,
> Thou fall'st a blessed martyr."

LIEUTENANT COLONEL WRIGHT.

Lieut. Col. JOSEPH C. WRIGHT was born in Rome, Oneida county, N. Y., on the 7th of January, 1821. He graduated at Captain Partridge's Military School, in Norwich, Vt., and afterward studied law, and was admitted to the bar at Oswego, at the early age of twenty years. About the year 1853, he abandoned the profession of law, and became engaged in the grain business, residing mostly in Chicago, although he frequently visited and maintained business relations with Oswego.

As a lawyer, he was successful in an eminent degree, his natural and acquired attainments having fitted him specially for an advocate, and as such, he was engaged in some of the most important cases in the State of New York.

As a merchant, Col. Wright's character is worthy of emulation. Engaged in a business which is in its very nature extra-hazardous, it was not strange, nor to his discredit, that in the crash of 1857 he found his name on $40,000 worth of paper, not his own, but for which he was responsible! To his honor, however, be it recorded, that every single dollar of this was paid, and that, too, out of his earnings since the date named. In all his operations he was bold and persevering; and if they were not always successful, pecuniarily, they were invariably carried through without the loss of honor or integrity. He was honest to a fault, for if a doubt existed on which side the beam turned, it was a rule with him to decide against himself. There are few men in the produce trade who have handled as much grain in the same period, and the number is still less who have had fewer litigations. He never forgot that while he was a merchant he was still a man, and that he also professed to be a Christian. Even when, in the dark commercial days of 1857, he saw his fortune melt away like snow, he manfully gave up, to pay his debts, every dollar he could control, and that, too, at a time when creditors were generally eager to compromise on the first offer, and it was the custom among many to adopt the French motto—*Sauve qui peut*—"Save himself who can."

Col. Wright proved himself to be a true soldier. As a member of the Board of Trade, he eloquently urged the formation of those regiments which now bear its name, and was offered the Colonelcy of the first that was raised—the 72d. Being a civilian, however, he modestly declined the honor, and when offered the Lieutenant-Colonelcy, at once showed his sincerity by accepting it, even at a great pecuniary loss to himself and family. In the camp he carried with him that high gentlemanly bearing, kind disposition, and Christian practice, which had been his custom everywhere; and while no officer was more sincerely loved and respected—nay, almost idolized—by his men, there are few who ever deserved it more. To those above him in station, and to those below, he was the same at all times and all places; and no private can say that he was ever received less courteously, and his wants attended to less promptly, than if he had been a staff officer. During the long period from his enlistment till the investment of Vicksburg, the regiment did not meet the enemy in battle; but on the 22d of May, when Gen. Grant ordered the assault on the enemy's works, owing to the indisposition of Col. Starring, he had to assume the entire command of the regiment, which he did in a manner which reflects everlasting honor on his head. Not satisfied with the usual position of an officer, like the lamented Lyon, sword in hand, he led his men clear up to the rifle-pits, where he received, from rebel hands, his death wound. This, however, did not break his spirit. When visited by the correspondent of the Chicago *Tribune* in his tent, immediately after his arm had been amputated, he cheerfully said: "Never mind, 'Bod,' I have one arm left with which I can guide my horse; the carrying of a sword is only for effect anyhow;" and even later, after he had arrived in Chicago, he talked with the writer of this on the probable future scenes and events in this sanguinary struggle of freedom against slavery. He had nothing to say about grain, of prices current, or of markets. His whole conversation was of our country and its sacred cause—his aspirations how much he could accomplish for its good. In reply to a suggestion in reference to his condition, he said: "If God spares my life, and I regain my health and my country needs me, I will as cheerfully give this right arm to the cause as I have already given my left." This patriotic yearning was denied him, and after sickness and suffering, he died a true soldier.

As a citizen, Col. Wright was justly admired. Carrying with him everywhere his Christian character, he won hosts of friends among all parties. In the social circle, few had such conversational powers, which he used in a manner free from all taint and corruption. But he was pre-eminently a lover of his family hearth, and to those who knew him thoroughly, the genuineness of his patriotism is better appreciated by the fact of the sacrifice it was to absent himself from his own fireside. Gifted with an eloquence which we can say was scarcely equalled west of the lakes, he was, for many years, the leading speaker of the Chicago Board of Trade on all public occasions; but never more will the rooms of 'Change resound with the tones of his silvery voice—never more will his oratory adorn the commercial chambers of the emporium of the West.

The Board of Trade, on learning of the death of Col. Wright, appointed a committee to draft resolutions of regret and to confer with the family in making arrangements for his funeral. On the 7th of July, a procession, marshalled by Col. Tucker, marched to the house of T. B. Carter, and accompanied the remains from there to the Second Presbyterian Church, when, after service, they were conveyed to the Michigan Central Railroad Depot, to be taken to Oswego. On arrival there, a somewhat similar order of arrangements was carried out. During the services, however, a beautiful incident occurred which will be long remembered. A dove—fit emblem of the "peace which passeth understanding"—flitted into the church, and alighting on the organ, seemed to shake down from its wings benediction on the scene, sitting fearlessly amid the wailing minors of the music, as if it were a messenger sent to fly up to heaven's chancery with the record of the hero's life, well spent, and freely given to God and his country. His body was interred in Riverside Cemetery amid the rattling crash of musketry, to await the last roll call before the Great Commander.

LIEUTENANT BEALS.

Lieut. JEDEDIAH BEALS, son of Alvord and Charlotte Beals, was born in Geauga county, Ohio, in June, 1836. His father, in the spring of 1863, became totally blind, and unable to see a single object. He gave two sons to the service when the Rebellion broke out—one, the subject of this sketch; the other, discharged on a surgeon's certificate for disability, after serving nine months. The mother of Lieut. Beals (now deceased) was a sister of the late Thomas Beard, Esq., who founded the city of Beardstown, Cass county, Illinois.

In 1842, Lieut. Beals emigrated with his father, mother, brother and several sisters, to Cass county. His father was a farmer, and his son, the Lieutenant, followed this occupation until the year 1857, with the exception of the time he was engaged at school. He received a good English education, the last of which he procured at the High School at Beardstown, under the superintendence of Prof. J. Barwick. In 1857, he became engaged in the engineer corps on the Rock Island and Alton Railroad. In 1860, he took a contract on the same road in Greene co., and finished it the same year. In March, 1861, he went to Cedar Rapids, Iowa, expecting to engage in the railroad business in that vicinity; but immediately upon the breaking out of the Rebellion, he returned home and sought a place in the army. He went to Springfield, and joined the 32d Regiment Illinois Volunteers. Before the regiment left for the seat of war, he was furloughed, with permission to recruit: and by the last of December, 1861, he had enlisted, in the vicinity of Beardstown, 24 men, whom he took to Carrollton, Greene co., and with Capt. H. W. Manning formed Company E, of which he was appointed 1st Lieutenant. Co. E was attached to the 61st Regt. Ill. Vols., Col. Jacob Fry, which was mustered into the service, March 7th, 1861, at Benton Barracks, Mo., and immediately proceeded to the theatre of war in Kentucky. The first time the regiment was under fire, however, was in that field of carnage at Shiloh.

At the battle of Shiloh he was much exposed, but escaped in that terrible conflict without a scar, although the exposure and fatigue brought on sickness a few days afterwards, in consequence of which he remained an invalid for a short time in camp. His anxiety, however, for active duty induced him to return to his post before he had sufficiently recovered, and that imprudence brought on a typhoid fever, to which he succumbed. He was sent to the Hospital at Evansville, Ind., where he died on the 11th of May, 1862.

Lieut. Beals was an amiable and unassuming young man, courteous to all, obedient to his superior officers, and kind to the men under him : full of patriotic zeal, he gave his affections to his country when danger first hovered around her. On entering the service, he was asked by a friend whether he had counted the cost and danger. "Yes," said he, "if I had a thousand lives, they should all be hazarded in defence of my country."

That Lieut. Beals was a good soldier, is known from the testimony of his superior officer, Capt. W. H. Manning, in a letter to the writer of this, who says :

"Whilst writing on this subject, I would wish to state, that I consider his loss as one that cannot soon be supplied. As a companion, he was always cheerful, and disposed to look on the bright side of everything—as an officer, he was prompt and efficient in every duty—on the battle-field, he was brave almost to recklessness, and on the dreadful day of Shiloh, he won the admiration of every officer and man in the regiment. Ever since he left, especially since I heard of his death, I have felt as one bereft indeed. May he rest in peace, and may a sympathizing Saviour comfort his sorrowing and afflicted friends."

P. Beals, brother of the youthful Lieutenant, went to Evansville and brought his body home for burial. His funeral took place on a pleasant Sabbath afternoon, when a large concourse of friends and citizens convened in the Congregational Church at Beardstown, to manifest their love and respect for the deceased. An eloquent sermon was preached by the Rev. Mr. Twining. The brave, the noble, the kind and affectionate young Lieutenant was then laid in his grave by the side of his kinsmen, there to sleep and wake not until the morning of the resurrection.

LIEUTENANT MEACHAM.

Lieut. HENRY GOODRICH MEACHAM, son of Dr. Silas and Rebecca Meacham, was born in the town of Maine, Cook co., Illinois, on the 18th of January, 1841. Bereft of his father at an early age, under the judicious guidance of his mother, he developed such rare mental and moral qualities as ripened subsequently into a noble manhood. In his fifteenth year, he left home for Evanston, Illinois, to prepare for a collegiate course, where, after studying two years, he was admitted to the Northwestern University in September, 1858, and graduated in the class of 1862.

In the year 1861, at the breaking out of the Rebellion, when many of his companions and classmates had responded to their country's call, he felt that he must go. His mind was much exercised upon the subject, but after mature deliberation and advice of friends, he thought it best to complete his course of study. His strong patriotism, however, did not permit him long to enjoy the comforts of home and the society of friends, to which he was ever most strongly attached. A few weeks only, after receiving his diploma, came the President's second call for volunteers, and, renouncing all his long-cherished plans of scientific and professional study, young Meacham, unprompted by any one, and purely from a sense of duty, enlisted as a private in the 88th Regiment Illinois Volunteers, on the 25th of July, 1862. A few months afterwards, he was promoted to a Lieutenancy. In this, as in all other positions, he was ever faithful, commanding the respect and esteem of his brother soldiers and superior officers.

After sharing in hardships, toilsome marches, and dangers of battle at Perrysville and Stone River, and the subsequent duties of camp life, his constitution, not naturally robust, gave way, when he was for a time off duty. During his convalescence, his regiment was ordered out on a forced march to meet the enemy. Still feeble and utterly unfit for duty, he insisted on joining his

company, that there might be no lack of service on his part
when there was work to do for his country. After a march of
some hours, he sank to the ground from utter exhaustion, and
was borne back to the hospital at Murfreesboro, Tenn., where,
after an illness of one month, he died on the 1st of April, 1863.

> " He, the young and brave, who cherished
>   Noble longings for the strife,
> By the wayside fell and perished,
>   Weary with the march of life."

His brother, R. W. Meacham, who was with him during the
last days of his sickness, immediately brought his remains to his
home in Brickton, Ill., where his funeral and interment took
place, April 9th, on which occasion a discourse was delivered
by the Rev. Dr. Bannister, under whose instructions young
Meacham came during his senior year in college.

His character possessed many traits which would mark him
as a model young man. His residence in the University was
characterized by an unvarying course of exemplary, good conduct. In his appropriate work he was diligent, critical and
thorough—prompt in meeting every requirement, and performing his allotted labor, not esteeming it drudgery, as many do,
but from the high motives which dignify the nobler class of
minds. Possessing rare natural endowments, both mental and
moral, he had gained such chasteness and breadth of culture as
few at his age attain unto. He exhibited a Christian deportment for years, and united himself to the Congregational Church
at Elk Grove on the eve of his departure for the field. His
sincerity of purpose, the transparency of his character and
motives, his manly bearing, his kind and genial spirit, his pure-
mindedness, and his patient and painstaking devotion to his
work, cause his memory to linger with us in fragrance and
beauty.

MAJOR MEDILL.

MAJOR MEDILL.

Major WILLIAM H. MEDILL, of the 8th Illinois Cavalry, mortally wounded in pursuing the rebels after the battle of Gettysburg, was born in Massillon, Ohio, on the 5th of November, 1835. In the spring of 1838, the family removed to a farm in Pike township, Stark county, Ohio, where he remained on his father's farm until he was fifteen years old, when, in 1850, he went to Coshocton, Ohio, and commenced learning the printing business in the office of the Coshocton *Republican*. In April, 1852, he removed to Cleveland, Ohio, where he took a situation as a compositor on his brother Joseph's paper, the *Forest City*—afterwards called the *Leader*. At the end of six months, he took the foremanship of the *Leader*, which situation he held until the fall of 1855, when he removed to Chicago, where he joined his brother James in publishing the *Prairie Farmer*. In the fall of 1858, he disposed of his interest in the *Prairie Farmer*, and went to Canton, Ohio, where he established the *Stark County Republican*. He worked hard and faithfully to get his new paper on a paying footing; but his means were limited; the receipts at first were small, and the cash outlay considerable; the promises made to him at the outset, by politicians, were not fulfilled, and after six months' effort, not realizing the success he anticipated, he sold the paper and returned to Chicago. During the short period he owned the *Republican*, it was a pungent and attractive sheet, handsomely printed, and filled with interesting matter. In politics, like its proprietor, it was radical Republican.

On his return to Chicago he obtained a situation as a compositor on the *Daily Tribune*, of which his brother Joseph was part owner and editor, and worked at the case from the spring of 1859 until the breaking out of the Slaveholders' Great Rebellion in the spring of 1861. During this period he spent his leisure hours in storing his mind with useful information. He

4

read history, reviewed his elementary studies, and when the war broke out, was spending his evenings in the Commercial College of Bryant & Stratton, and in the lyceum of the "Young Men's Literary Union," of which he was a zealous and popular member. During his boyhood years his education had been neglected, and now when he was arrived at manhood, he perceived the imperative necessity of making up for lost time and preparing himself for future usefulness. He desired to be an editor of a successful daily paper, and with this object in view, was industriously fitting himself for the responsibilities of that calling when the news was flashed to Chicago on the night of the 14th of April, 1861, that the rebels of South Carolina had fired on the United States' fort, Sumter, and had bombarded its heroic handful of defenders into surrender. He declared, on the instant of the arrival of the sad intelligence, that he would volunteer on the first call for men to help revenge the insult to the National flag and to crush the parricides that had lifted their daggers against the life of the Great Republic. He had watched and studied the gathering storm of rebellion for months, and had come deliberately to the conclusion that there was but one way to deal with the insurgents, and that was to grapple them and crush them by military power. He contended that there was no other possible cure for the disease, save sabre, grape and bayonets.

The news of the capture of Fort Sumter was published in Chicago on the 15th of April. A meeting of young men of the Literary Union was called to assemble at Bryant & Stratton's Commercial Rooms on the evening of the 17th. Several brief speeches were made; one of them by Major Medill, in which he set forth the cause of the Rebellion and its cure, and pledged himself to join the first military company that might be raised, as a private soldier, in obedience to the promptings of patriotic duty. A muster roll was presented, when sixty young men— himself included—put down their names. On the next day he joined the Barker Dragoons, and soon after found himself doing picket and other duty at Camp Defiance, Cairo, where the company remained for six weeks. On the 1st of June, Gen. McClellan, then recently appointed to command, visited Cairo

to inspect the troops and fortifications. He was so much pleased
with Barker's Chicago Dragoons, that he immediately adopted
them as his body guards, and ordered them to join him at
Clarksburg, Va., which they did the week after. For the next
two months, the Chicago Dragoons were actively engaged in
contests with the rebels. First there was a brisk skirmish at
Philippi; next a fight at Buckhannon; then came a hard fight
at Rich Mountain, July 8th. On the 11th was the battle near
Beverly, in which the rebels were routed, losing 200 killed and
wounded, and leaving 300 prisoners, several pieces of artillery
and all their baggage in the hands of the Federal troops. In
this battle the Chicago Dragoons dismounted and fought as
sharpshooters, doing considerable execution with their revolving
carbines. Private Medill distinguished himself for dash and
daring. When the order to charge was given, he was among
the foremost of his company to open the attack on the enemy.
The fighting was done Indian fashion — every trooper took
shelter behind a tree or log, and dodged forward from one to
the other. In this encounter Private Medill became engaged
with a Georgian lieutenant. Each was behind a small tree
about sixty yards apart. The rebel fired first, but missed his
aim. Medill raised his carbine and fired, but hit the sapling
behind which the rebel stood partly concealed; he then sprang
forward, calling on the rebel to surrender or he would let daylight through him. The officer threw down his gun and
handed his sword to his captor, who marched him to the rear,
feeling proud of the achievement. The sword he brought home
as a trophy, and it is now in possession of his brother Joseph.
After the battle of Beverly, the Chicago Dragoons joined the
pursuit, and helped to give the finishing blow to the enemy at
Carrick's Ford, where the rebel Gen. Garnett was killed and
1200 prisoners taken. The remnants of the enemy's force fled
over the Greenbriar Mountains, vigorously pursued for considerable distance by our troops. The last seen of them they were
double-quicking it towards Staunton. In a letter, dated Beverly,
July 16th, he complains that the army had ceased its pursuit.

We are 12,500 strong, (he writes,) with five batteries of flying artillery.
The rebs. are utterly demoralized. McClellan ought to pursue them to Staun-

ton, and then make a forced march on Richmond, which we could easily capture and hold by the aid of the fleet. It would take us but a week. The
country is full of provisions, and most of the way, the road is good and easy
to travel. Now is the time to strike vigorously at the secessionists. If I
commanded this army, the pursuit would certainly be made. I like our General, but I think he is too cautious ; he lacks boldness and enterprise.

Though but a private soldier and little skilled in military
tactics, he exhibited foresight and daring—essential qualities
for an officer, and with the history of the campaigns in Eastern
Virginia before the reader, few will deny but that his suggestions were feasible.

On the 10th of August, the Chicago Dragoons, having served
a month over their time, returned home and were mustered out
of service. After a fortnight's rest and recreation, he resolved
to re-enter the service of his country for three years or during
the war; not that he liked military life, but from the promptings
of patriotic duty. On the 24th of August, 1861, he applied to
Gen. Farnsworth for permission to recruit a company for the
afterwards famous 8th Illinois Cavalry, which, on the 26th, was
granted, on condition that the company be raised in two weeks.
The State at the time was covered with recruiting officers, and
competition for men was sharp ; but taking hold with his accustomed vigor, before the fortnight had elapsed, he had his company filled and sworn into the service for three years. He was
unanimously elected Captain, and when the field officers came
to be selected, a majorship was easily within his reach, but he
declined it on the ground that he would rather be in direct
command of the men who had joined his company out of friendship to himself, than to hold a higher and easier command where
he would be in a measure separated from them. This feeling
of mutual friendship continued until the day of his death, and
when the news was made known in the company that their old
captain was no more, there were few of those bronzed warriors
that did not weep bitter tears of regret, or make new vows of
vengeance on the rebels who had deprived them of their beloved
companion in arms. This feeling of strong attachment grew out
of no licence he gave them, for he was a strict disciplinarian,
and insisted upon a full compliance with military rules and

orders. But he won their confidence and love by watching over their personal comfort, showing them kindness when sick, preserving their health, defending them against aggressions, and in the hour of battle setting an example of coolness and bravery, but never recklessly rushing them into danger and destruction. By these means he always had the largest, best drilled and most efficient company in the regiment. In acknowledgment of their confidence and esteem, his company presented him on New Year's, 1862, with a handsome sword and a brace of Colt's revolvers.

Refusing to be major at the outset, Gen. Farnsworth made him ranking captain, and it happened that for several months of the summer and fall of 1861 he was in command of the regiment, when he performed the duties of colonel to the satisfaction of his superiors, and established his ability to command.

In October, 1861, "Farnsworth's Big Abolition Regiment," as the 8th Illinois Cavalry was called by the Potomac army, marched passed the White House, 1164 strong, in review by the President. It was composed of unconditional Unionists, who equally hated slavery and rebellion; a better or harder fighting regiment has not gone to the war, nor has any performed more service or inflicted greater damage on the enemy.

The fall of 1861 was spent near Washington, drilling, and the winter in Alexandria, as part of the garrison, where the regiment was constantly in a quarrel with the military governor, Gen. Montgomery, a rebel sympathizer, who took sides with the secesh inhabitants, removed the American flag from houses owned by rebels, and drove off editors of outspoken Union newspapers, and spent his leisure hours in denouncing the Abolitionists as being the cause of the war. With such a man the 8th Illinois could not harmonize. Montgomery succeeded in getting the regiment removed from their comfortable quarters and sent to camp on a low, wet piece of ground some distance beyond Alexandria, where 240 men were soon down with fever from the effect of exposure to rain, snow and knee-deep mud. Thirty-five brave boys died, and Captain Medill, in his letters home, bitterly laments the loss of four of his company—victims of the proslavery malice of Montgomery.

The spring campaign opened early in March, by the sudden and unexpected evacuation of the feared and famous Manassas. An extract from a letter written by the Major, April 19, 1862, may prove interesting:

*   *   Well, we have actually taken Manassas without firing a shot. Astonishing is it not? For nine months it has stood as a menace and as a stumbling block in the pathway of the army. It was looked upon by many as an earthquake standing ready to swallow up all who might venture too near its yawning mouth. We have been assured by spies, by deserters, by Richmond and New York newspapers, that the country all about Manassas was naturally as impregnable as Gibraltar—that it had been converted into one tremendous fortification; the hill-sides being honey-combed with rifle-pits and covered with masked batteries. On March 10th, we started for the famous stronghold. I will not relate the feelings and talk of the soldiers, except that each considered himself a martyr about to be sacrificed for the sake of his country.

The first day's march brought our regiment within eight miles of the world-renowned stronghold: to-morrow, the great battle would begin! The evening was spent cracking jokes. One said, our march reminded him of the fable in Æsop, of the tracks that all led into the sick lion's den—none leading out, and that he expected no tracks of this army would ever lead towards Alexandria. Next morning "boots and saddles" sounded, and forward we started, spread out like a fan as skirmishers, every minute expecting to run against a masked battery, or be blown up by a hidden torpedo or mine. At nine, a halt was ordered. My Lieut., Hynes, who is acting Provost Marshal on Gen. Sumner's staff, galloped up to our regiment and cried out, Manassas was evacuated two days ago, and the rebel army has skedaddled across the Rappahannock! Incredulity was on every man's face, but the messenger declared it was true, and that Gen. McClellan was then occupying Beauregard's headquarters; that the rebels had run off in a panic, that their works of defence were all shams, that Gen. Sumner said that they had not numbered 60,000 men. That we all felt sheepish you may well imagine. Here was an army of almost a quarter of a million held at bay by this handful. For the first time, we began to lose confidence in our commander. All that Lieut. Hynes told us proved true. When we came upon the rebel lines, there was nothing to be seen but an open country, dotted over with little, trifling earthworks. The ditches and breastworks were poor apologies. I leaped my horse over all the obstructions met, with ease.

On the top of a point of ground, where we first came upon the plains of Manassas, was an earthwork, on which the rebels had planted a number of wooden guns. By the way, I observe that some of the New York and Philadelphia papers deny that any wooden cannon were mounted in any of the forts, but I know better. There were a dozen or more in this one fort, as nearly every officer of my regiment can testify, for we handled them.

All the stories you have read about the wonderful strength of Manassas are *bosh*. I have seen several battle-fields, but never beheld a piece of country in Virginia so favorable for a fair, stand-up, give-and-take fight. The strongest protection the rebels had was the natural banks of Bull Run, a small stream a few yards in width. We could have flanked them on either wing, and crushed them like an egg-shell. Manassas will go down in history as the biggest humbug on record. Any time during the past four months it might have been taken, if our leaders had been as willing to show the way as the soldiers were of following.

We have given this long extract from Major Medill's private correspondence, because it relates to one of the most important events of the war, described by a close and honest observer.

The 8th Illinois and other cavalry were ordered to pursue the retreating rebels to the Rappahannock. The Illinois troopers had the advance, and Major Medill (then senior captain) commanded the leading squadron. At Bealton's Station he came upon a battalion of rebel cavalry, drawn up on a hill-side to receive him. The Major promptly brought his front into line, and ordered his squadron to charge. Away they dashed on a gallop, and when within 100 yards, delivered a well directed fire from their carbines. The rebels broke and fled, and then commenced an exciting horse race for several miles. The rebels scattered, and the Major ordered his men to disperse as skirmishers, after them. The pursuit was continued to the Rappahannock, where most of the rebels escaped across a bridge, which they burned as soon as over. The rebel loss was two killed, twenty wounded, and twelve taken prisoners. After this gallant little affair, the Illinois cavalry returned to Alexandria and embarked for Fortress Monroe. Nothing of interest transpired after debarking until the battle of Williamsburg, May 5. From the dense forests that enveloped the battle-field, the cavalry could take no part in the action. After the rebels were defeated, however, the 8th Illinois vigorously pursued the foe in his retreat—the Major's squadron leading. About a thousand prisoners were captured, mainly by the Illinois cavalry. The army of Gen. McClellan moved slowly forward towards Richmond. On the 18th of May, Major Medill was sent out with his battalion on a reconnoisance towards the Chickahominy Creek. He got within 12 miles of Richmond, and had a sharp skirmish with some rebel infantry and cavalry. He captured a

few prisoners and a negro returning to his home from Richmond, who had newspapers of that morning and letters written
but a few hours before in Richmond: they described a great
panic existing in the rebel capital; the enemy expected that
McClellan would march immediately on the city; their army
was demoralized; the defenses were defective; the terrified
officials were removing the public archives, and no doubt was
expressed or entertained but the Federal army could march in
and take the place. This information was promptly placed in
the hands of Gen. McClellan; but the golden moment was not
improved. The battle of Fair Oaks was fought and won, but
not followed up. The right wing of the army, under Gen.
Porter, took position at Gaines Mill, and went to fortifying; the
Illinois cavalry was pushed forward to Mechanicsville, and performed picket duty along the Chickahominy, as far north as
Hanover Court House. On two or three occasions the Major
pushed his reconnoisances within sight of Richmond. He complains very bitterly in a letter, dated June 17th, of the gross
negligence of the regular cavalry under Col. P. St.-G. Cook,
for allowing his brother-in-law, Gen. J. E. B. Stewart, to pass
through his pickets and lines to the rear of the army, capturing,
destroying and burning as he went, and escaping unmolested.
Cook exhibited no vigilance or energy, but was never court-
martialed, because he was an aristocrat and a regular. He did
not start in pursuit for several hours, then took a wrong road,
and marched slowly. He says if his regiment had been put in
pursuit of Stewart, they would have given a lively chase, and
that he never would have had twelve hours' time to build bridges
across the Chickahominy on which to escape. In a letter, dated
June 25th, he says:

Before this reaches you, the long gathering storm-cloud will break. We
have wasted a month here in inaction. Our army is doing two things: ditch
digging and dying; the sickness and mortality this hot weather in those marshes
are terrible. While our army is wasting away, the enemy is rapidly growing
stronger by means of a sweeping conscription. We are 40,000 fewer for duty
than we were a month ago, and the rebels are 50,000 stronger than they were a
few weeks since. I have just heard that Stonewall Jackson, with 30,000 men,
has arrived from the Shenandoah Valley, and taken position on our right, near
Hanover Court House. If this be so, a battle may take place at any hour.

I am disgusted at the way this fine army is employed. One part is ditch digging, and another stands guard over the plantations and property of slaveholders, whose sons are in Lee's army, fighting us. Our generals will never put down this Slaveholders' Rebellion by pursuing a proslavery policy. The chief support of the rebellion is derived from the labor of four millions of slaves, who supply the Commissary and Quartermaster's Departments of the enemy, and support the families of the rebel soldiers besides. We must knock away this great pillar of their edifice, else we shall never succeed in putting down the revolt. I am not sanguine of the result of the impending battle; our boys will make a stubborn fight, but McClellan has waited too long. He has neglected his opportunity. Mark my words.

The next day, sure enough, the first of the bloody scenes of seven days' battle began at Mechanicsville; the day after, Gaines Mill was fought and lost, after a long and terrible contest, in consequence of the neglect of the General-in-Chief to reinforce the right wing of his army, which was obliged, for twelve hours, to resist the whole rebel army. The 8th Cavalry, in this battle, did all that was in their power in rallying and returning stragglers to the front, charging on the enemy's flanks, and finally helping to cover the retreat. The Major distinguished himself for coolness and bravery in this as well as in the subsequent operations, until the army found itself at Harrison's Landing, July 2d, 1862.

From that time until September, when the 8th Illinois Cavalry found itself engaged with the enemy in Maryland, there is little personal history to relate. He was much depressed in spirits at the result of the seven days' battles, and fearful of foreign recognition of Confederate independence. He continues, in his letters, to deplore the proslavery spirit and influences that prevailed at the headquarters of the army.

When the army withdrew from the Peninsula, the Major's regiment formed the extreme rearguard—and himself had command of the rearmost squadrons. Not a few slaves found asylum in that regiment as it fell back to Yorktown, and hosts of them owe their deliverance to the Major and his radical troopers, who never let slip a chance to relieve the rebel F. F. V.'s of this very "peculiar" kind of property.

Owing to the sickness of the senior officers, the Major was the ranking officer, and took command of the regiment on its

arrival at Yorktown, and continued in command during all of
the subsequent campaign, in which he greatly distinguished
himself, frequently receiving the thanks of Gen. Pleasanton,
the chief of cavalry.

The 8th Illinois Cavalry reached Alexandria, Sept. 4, 1862,
but they had scarcely landed before they were ordered to
Washington, and thence marched direct to Rockville, Md.
Lee's army had crossed the Potomac after defeating Pope's
troops, and occupied Frederick City. The old army of Mc-
Clellan's was hastily reorganized and united with the bulk of
Pope's and Burnside's corps and other troops, and marched at
once to prevent Lee from seizing Baltimore. The Major's
regiment led the vanguard of this movement, and on the 9th of
September became engaged with J. E. B. Stewart's rebel cavalry
at Damascus and Tenallytown, beating them in each encounter.
Next day a sharp fight took place at New Market, in which the
rebel cavalry were severely handled. Soon after, the gallant
affair at Boonsboro occurred. The place was held by two regiments of Stewart's cavalry. The Major made a hasty reconnoisance, and concluded he could win. He formed his men,
and placing himself at their head, ordered a charge. Away
they dashed on a full gallop right into the place, where a hard
hand to hand conflict ensued; revolver, sword and pistol were
freely used on both sides, but the impetuosity and pluck of the
Illinois troopers carried the day, and the discomfited rebels
beat a hasty retreat, leaving nearly 200 killed, wounded and
prisoners in the hands of the victors, besides all their baggage.
The 8th Illinois lost less than forty men in the engagement.
In following up the flying foe, a hard fight took place a few
miles beyond Boonsboro, at Middleton, in which infantry and
artillery were brought up by both sides. The enemy was defeated, and retreated to South Mountain, where a very desperate
contest ensued, ending in the defeat of the rebels, in which the
Major's regiment took a conspicuous part. The rebels fell back
behind Antietam Creek. This was Sept. 15th. On the 17th
took place the hard fought battle of Antietam, resulting in the
defeat of the rebels. The 8th Illinois, under Major Medill, and
the brigade under Gen. Farnsworth, were employed to support

an artillery attack on the centre of the rebel position, in order
to relieve Gen. Burnside from a cross-fire that was consuming
his men. Those relieving batteries were pushed far forward,
and completely silenced the troublesome guns of the enemy.
The Major often afterwards said, that if Gen. McClellan had
sent forward half of his reserves, under Porter, that lay idle
all day, the rebel right wing could easily have been crushed, as
it might have been assailed in front and flank at the same
moment. McClellan was duly notified of the important heights
gained by the artillery and cavalry, but he neglected to improve
the tempting opportunity. After the rebels retreated, the Major's regiment, as usual, was in the advance of the pursuit, and
picked up a large number of prisoners.

On the 2d of October, the 8th Illinois had an encounter with
the rebels, in which the Major exhibited superior strategic as
well as fighting qualities. His brigade made a reconnoisance
to Martinsburg, Va., into which they dashed and captured a
lot of rebels, rescued some Union prisoners, and got a quantity
of plunder. There was a large rebel cavalry force under Gen.
Fitzhugh Lee, not far off, that entered the place just as the
Federal cavalry was leaving it. Gen. Pleasanton placed the
8th Illinois and a battery of flying artillery, both under Major
Medill, as the rearguard, which the enemy "pitched into" at
once. After a running fight for some distance, the Major left
one gun with his rear squadron, and sent the other five pieces
forward to a high spot of ground, and had them masked and
trained to sweep the road. Meanwhile the rearguard and its
gun took up successive positions and skirmished vigorously.
The rebels, seeing but one gun, pressed hard after, and tried to
capture it by a charge. When they came rushing on headlong
to within a couple of hundred yards of the masked battery, the
Major gave the signal for his men to clear the road, which was
instantly done. Whereupon the whole battery opened with
grape, canister and shell right into their column. The result
was, that scores of men and horses were piled together on the
road in a common destruction. While they were in confusion,
the Major ordered his men to ride into the fields along the roadside and pour a volley into their flanks—the Major heading the

charge himself and emptying the contents of his revolver into the broken and flying enemy. The rebel loss was 150 men, including prisoners. The 8th Illinois lost but 16 men. The remainder of the march back to Sharpsburg was unmolested. Gen. Pleasanton highly complimented the Major on the complete success of this piece of strategy, and for the able manner in which he handled the rearguard. It was about this time he was promoted to Major—having previously been senior Captain of his regiment.

It was soon after the occurrence last related, that Gen. J. E. B. Stewart made the famous raid—measuring the circumference of the Potomac army. Several bodies of Federal cavalry were started in pursuit of the contumacious rebels, among others the famous 8th Illinois Cavalry, commanded by the subject of our sketch. The greatest difficulty was to find Stewart's track. The Major was started on the wrong road, and after traveling some twenty-five miles, finally got on the right scent; but the rebels had a long start of him. Away went his troopers and the 3d Indiana Cavalry and their battery of artillery, on the gallop. Night came on, but the pursuit was kept up regardless of the darkness. Over hills and mountains, down into deep valleys, and across creeks and ravines, rode the gallant 8th Illinois and Indiana boys. A cold rain poured down, adding to the gloom and difficulty. The Major seized and pressed native guides to pilot the way. With these, and the light of two tin lanterns, he vigorously pushed ahead. When day broke, he learned that the enemy was at least fifteen miles in advance, and pushing south in the direction of Washington. For twenty-five hours his men had been in the saddle, and neither they nor their horses had eaten a bite. Many of the latter had broken down, and other horses were seized to take their places. A halt for rest and refreshment was ordered of a couple of hours; then "boots and saddles" was sounded, and off went the cavalcade again. The troopers pushed forward as fast as it was possible to urge on their poor jaded brutes. Finally the regiment reached the Monocacy where it empties into the Potomac, just as the rearguard of Stewart's troopers were fording the river and making their escape into Virginia. A few shells were thrown after them, but the game had escaped; and what made it the more provoking, within four miles was a strong force of infantry and cavalry that knew of their coming, and could easily have stopped their crossing. The mortification of the Major and his comrades may be imagined, but can hardly be described. In this extraordinary pursuit the 8th Illinois Cavalry rode a distance of 88 miles in thirty-two hours, including all stops and delays. It is needless to say that both men and horse suffered severely.

A few days after this event, the Major obtained a brief furlough to visit his friends in Chicago. He had not been off duty a day for almost fifteen months. On his arrival he was warmly welcomed by his friends and acquaintances. The Mercantile Literary Union, of which he was an active and popular member at the time he joined the army, gave him a generous banquet at the Briggs House, and congratulated him on his promotion, and his prospects of higher military preferment for worthy and gallant conduct. After enjoying the society of friends and relatives for a few days, he hurried back and joined his regiment.

When the army of the Potomac crossed the river and marched to Fredericksburg, the 8th Illinois Cavalry was in the advance, skirmishing all the way there. A month afterwards, the great battle of Fredericksburg was fought and lost. The Major's regiment was an idle spectator of the terrible conflict, and could take no part in the fray. The regiment spent the winter doing picket and scouting duty in the peninsula between the Potomac and Rappahannock rivers, where they made themselves a terror to the smugglers and rebel conscript agents. When the 1st of January came, the President's proclamation of freedom to the slaves of rebels went into effect. The Major celebrated that day by taking a battalion of his cavalry, visiting all the plantations for many miles around, and liberating and bringing into camp nearly one thousand "contrabands." The rest of the regiment were not idle, but scouted about the country on similar business. Before nightfall, King George county, where slavery had reigned for 200 years, was free soil!

The Major entered into no service with more alacrity and hearty zest than in giving freedom to the loyal bondsmen of rebels. He did it from motives of humanity for the poor slave, and for the purpose of weakening the enemy. He contended that from the labor of the slaves the rebels derived their chief strength, and that military policy, to say nothing of humanity, required that they should be deprived of that great support.

Early in the month of May, the 8th Cavalry was divided into three battalions—one under Major Medill, and another under Major Beveridge, and the third under Major Clendenin, and sent down the peninsula between the Potomac and Rappahannock on a scout to break up smuggling, capture guerillas, and drive out the rebel conscript agents. They were gone ten days, during which time they seized an incredible quantity of smugglers' goods, burnt 100 boats of every size, from a schooner down to a dug-out, made a hundred prisoners of guerillas, captured a number of the "conscriptors," and swept Westmoreland, Richmond, Lancaster and Northumberland of able-bodied, adult slaves. When the regiment returned, it brought back a singular train, consisting of scores of wagon loads of contraband goods, droves of cattle, horses and mules, a hundred cut-throat looking prisoners, and over 1500 shouting, singing and praying negroes—some mounted on mules, others on their masters' wagons, and part on foot. As the cavalcade filed through the lines of the army, it was greeted on all sides with loud laughter and louder cheers, at the "grand haul" the Illinois troopers had made from the secesh. Hundreds of the contrabands became soldiers in the Union army, and are proving their right to be free by loyal devotion to the stars and stripes.

The battle of Chancellorsville was fought May 2–3. An important part of Gen. Hooker's plan embraced a great cavalry raid on the rear of the rebel army to destroy their trains, railways and bridges, burn up their army stores, and then sweep down to Richmond and capture it if found to be slightly defended. The plan was well laid, but badly executed. The cavalry was divided into two divisions of 4000 men each, and two batteries of flying artillery to each: one was commanded by Gen. Stoneman, with whom went the 12th Illinois, under Col. Davis; the other division was commanded by Gen. Averill, with whom went the 8th Illinois, under Col. Gamble. The plan was, for the two divisions to cross the Rappahannock some distance apart, and form a junction at Gordonsville, and thence sweep forward towards Richmond on their grand raid. Meanwhile Gen. Hooker would strike Lee's forces with the main body of his army. Stoneman crossed the Rappahannock, and pushed boldly for Gordonsville. Averill also crossed, and marched timidly forward until he reached a ford on the Rapidan, which was disputed by a couple of rebel regiments with two guns, and there he remained a day and a half, afraid to force his passage across, and then marched back, having accomplished nothing. He remained idle all of the third day within three miles of the left flank of Stonewall Jackson's corps while it was whipping and driving Howard's 11th corps. There that splendid cavalry force lay supine, listening to the roar of the great battle going on within three miles, when, if it had pitched into the rebel flank, there is no doubt but that it would have changed the fate of the day, and converted a bad defeat into a great victory, for such an attack would have been wholly unexpected by the rebels.

Stoneman ascribed the partial failure of his expedition to Averill's bad conduct, and Hooker deprived him of his command. Instead of being dismissed the service, he was sent to Western Virginia and given another command! In speaking of the disgraceful and supine part he and his brave regiment were made to play in the battle of Chancellorsville and the raid on Richmond, the Major always expressed regret and mortification.

Shortly after this time he had a severe attack of bilious fever, aggravated by diarrhœa; but a sound constitution and temperate habits, and his great anxiety to rejoin his regiment, carried him safely through. Lee's army had commenced its famous march on Pennsylvania, and Hooker's cavalry were constantly engaged with the rebel cavalry and picket forces, for the purpose of discovering the enemy's intentions. A hard cavalry fight took place, June 9, near Warrenton Junction, in which Captain Smith and Major Clark were mortally, and Major Forsyth severely, wounded—all officers of the 8th Illinois. When Major Medill heard of the fight, he got up, sick as he was, ordered his horse, and started to join his regiment. The excitement and anxiety to take part in the actions caused his system to throw off the fever, and enabled him to do duty in a few days. He writes, June 10:

My sickness has not troubled me half so much as to be left behind my regiment when there is warrior's work to be done. I cannot submit to this fever, and shall mount my horse and join my regiment if it takes two men to hold me on.

Shortly after, he joined the regiment and took part in the desperate cavalry contest at Aldie and Upperville, in which he greatly distinguished himself. On that occasion, the cavalry division of Gen. Buford encountered the rebel cavalry under Gen. Stewart. Col. Gamble's brigade, of which the 8th Illinois was the advance, charged on the rebel force drawn up in front of the Aldie Gap of the Blue Ridge. The 3d Indiana acted as skirmishers, and the 12th Illinois as supports. Early in the fight, Lieut. Col. Clendenin, who commanded the 8th Illinois, had his horse slightly wounded, and retired from the field. Maj. Medill, being next in rank, then took command, and, until the battle was won, behaved with a bravery, a skill and a gallantry that won the admiration of all who witnessed his conduct. In charge after charge he led his men on the rebel ranks, routing and scattering them. His regiment defeated, successively, two Virginia and one North Carolina cavalry regiments. His favorite weapon, in making a charge, was the revolver. He would dash his men right up to the rebel squadrons, who, in the melee, would unhorse scores of them with their sure and deadly six-shooters. He considered a sabre no match for two revolvers in a close encounter either with cavalry or infantry. In this engagement the 8th Illinois lost but 40 men—most of them being wounded by sabre cuts, while they put *hors du combat* over 250 of the enemy, besides capturing 100 prisoners. In the course of the fight, Major Medill captured the commander of the 11th Virginia Cavalry, with which his regiment was engaged at the moment. The incident is thus related by an eye-witness:

While the Major was rallying his men, after one of our charges, I saw, at a short distance over the field, a rebel horseman, with drawn sword, chasing our Sergeant Major, who had got mixed up with the rebels. Major Medill, who happened to be near, put spurs to his big bay horse, and in a few bounds was close to the "reb.," who raised his sword aloft and shouted "surrender!" The

Major brought his revolver to an aim, and was in the act of pulling the trigger, when the fellow dropped his sword and cried out, "Don't shoot, I surrender." He saved his life by just a second, as more than one bullet would have lodged in his body the next instant. The prisoner proved to be the Colonel of the 11th Virginia Cavalry, and big enough in a fist fight to have whipped two of our Major; but on the field of battle, size confers but little advantage.

Immediately after this cavalry battle, Gen. Hooker discovered that the rebel army was marching along the opposite side of the Blue Ridge, making for Maryland. He at once put his army on a forced march to head them off. The cavalry brigade, under Col. Gamble, consisting of the 8th and 12th Illinois, 3d Indiana, 8th New York, and a battery, led the advance, and reached Gettysburg on the 30th of June, and immediately charged on two rebel regiments occupying the place and drove them back. Next day, July 1, Buford's division of cavalry (including Gamble's brigade) lay in camp. July 2d, the bloody and terrific battle of Gettysburg began. The rebels advanced early in the morning to the attack. Gen. Reynolds' force—the 1st and 11th corps—did not arrive on the ground until 9 A. M. For the three preceding hours, Buford's cavalry managed to hold the enemy in check by successive and rapid charges on their flanks, compelling them to halt and change line several times, and actually captured quite a number of prisoners, and inflicted on the rebels ten times the damage received. In these brilliant charges, the 8th Illinois was conspicuous for its audacity and success. Major Beveridge led the right—being the ranking officer, and Major Medill the left of the regiment.

After the infantry came up, the 8th Illinois and its brigade were ordered to the left of the line, to prevent a flank movement on the part of the enemy. From that time until the battle ended, the brigade gave the rebel infantry great annoyance, materially retarding his advance, by making frequent, bold dashes at them. In this way, the 8th Illinois saved a whole brigade of infantry and a battery from being captured, by compelling one of the rebel surrounding lines to halt to repel the daring charge of the Illinois troopers, which enabled our infantry brigade and their battery to escape.

After the great battle was over, and the beaten enemy com-

5

menced their retreat, the two Illinois cavalry regiments began shooting and slashing the rebel rearguard, capturing trains and taking prisoners, until Lee's army stood at bay at Williamsport and Falling Waters. In this pursuit those regiments captured over 2000 prisoners and 809 rebel army wagons, fighting with the enemy's rearguard almost at every mile of the distance.

During this pursuit, the gallant Major pressed on the retreating columns with all his vigor and energy, and looked forward with radiant hope to the moment when the further retreat of the rebels would be stopped by the swollen waters of the Potomac. He felt sanguine that Meade's victorious army would attack without delay the broken and demoralized graybacks, now notoriously short of ammunition and provisions. He believed the campaign was about ending with the total destruction of the invading host, and that the rebellion was on the eve of receiving its death-wound. Full of this belief, he urged on his comrades to strike boldly at the fleeing foe, and give them no rest until they laid down their arms.

On the afternoon of July 6th, the Major's regiment reached the vicinity of the Potomac at Williamsport, and there discovered the rebels engaged in building a bridge over the river to facilitate their escape. The regiment and brigade charged at once on the enemy's pickets and drove them back, capturing a large train of wagons, which were set on fire. Forty or fifty prisoners were also taken. The enemy were found to be in considerable force both of cavalry and infantry; but it was deemed highly important to seize the bridge. A brigade of regulars took position on the right, and the cavalry on the left of the road. Gen. Buford ordered half the 8th Illinois to dismount and go forward as skirmishers. At the time the order was given, Major Medill was attending to some duty at a little distance. On his return, he learned that half of his regiment had gone forward under Capt. Hynes. He at once remarked to Major Beveridge that "a field officer should command the battalion. If you have no objections, I will go." Assent being given, he borrowed a carbine, mounted his horse, and spurred after his men. As soon as he reached them, he stepped in front of the centre and shouted, "Come on, boys;" and away the line swept

through a field on a quick step. At the opposite side of the
field, behind a barn and some fences, were stationed a large
force of rebel infantry, who opened a heavy fire on the advancing skirmish line. When the field had been more than half
crossed, seeing a group of rebels in plain view but a short distance ahead, the Major called on his men near him to give the
fellows a volley, and raising his own carbine, took aim. At
that instant, a minie ball struck him nearly in the middle of his
body, making a frightful hole one and a half inches long by an
inch wide, and of unknown depth. The ball passed through
the lower edge of the breastbone, and slanting downwards, went
through his lung and lodged somewhere near his backbone. He
was soon borne from the field to the woods in the rear, and
thence on stretchers a few miles to a church, where his wound
was examined by the surgeon of the regiment and pronounced
mortal. He was next day conveyed to the army hospital at
Frederick City, suffering greatly from the motion of the vehicle.
Meanwhile, the battle went on until nightfall, neither party
gaining much ground, when our men fell back.

Capt. Waite, in a letter to his father, thus writes respecting
the Major's fall:

Major Medill went to the front and took charge of the three squadrons of
dismounted men fighting as skirmishers. They moved forward at a quick step,
and with a "hip," "hip," in the very best of spirits. In a few minutes the sad
news came back to us that our noble Major was mortally wounded, and soon
after several soldiers came slowly along, bearing in their arms the gallant officer.
A ball had entered his breast, and we believed him past recovery. I cannot
describe the sadness and gloom which this misfortune cast over the entire
regiment and brigade. Officers and men all felt that we had met with a severe
loss. The Major had been with us through many a hard fight. His conduct
at the late desperate cavalry battle near Aldie, had particularly won for him
the confidence and esteem of all the officers and men present. The gallantry,
bravery and coolness displayed by the Major on that occasion were very highly
spoken of by all. His genial, kind-hearted and generous nature had made him
a favorite with the officers of the regiment; while his integrity of character and
strict discipline as an officer, had won our confidence and respect. There is
not a man in the regiment but mourns his fall.

As soon as he reached the hospital, his friends in Chicago
were notified by telegraph of his wound. His eldest brother—

editor of the *Tribune*, hastened to his side, and remained with him till death came. For the third and fourth days after receiving the wound he seemed a little better; the pain had subsided, and he began to feel some hope of ultimate recovery. He conversed freely on all topics; made his will with composure, giving a number of keepsakes to his friends, but bequeathing to his mother the most of his property. On the sixth day, pain and inflammation increasing, he abandoned hope of recovery; but from then until the hour of his death, he exhibited wonderful calmness and fortitude. The same fearless heroism, that had carried him triumphantly through many a fearful contest with his country's foes, stood by him when brought to face the king of terrors, unaided by the excitements of the battlefield and the support of robust health.

His fine physical constitution succumbed but slowly to the destroyer, and enabled him to survive ten days with a wound that would have proved fatal to most men in twenty-four hours. His mind at times was flighty, chiefly from the effects of the opiates administered. Still, he retained his consciousness until within fifteen minutes of his last breath. He expired, without pain or struggle, at 10 o'clock, July 16, 1863, surrounded by a large number of his beloved companions in arms, who wept over their dying comrade as bitter tears as if he had been their nearest of kin.

While the Major lay in the hospital at Frederick, he would constantly inquire whether Meade had yet ordered an attack on Lee's beaten troops. His mind was in a state of feverish anxiety for the assault to begin, lest the enemy would escape across the river. Lee's army, he said, was wholly in our power, and it only required a little daring and enterprise on the part of Meade to capture or kill every rebel composing it. Oh! for Joe Hooker, he would say; if he commanded now, not a rebel would escape.

At last, the bad news was brought to him that the rebels had escaped without a blow being struck at them. He was in agony at the information. "I wish I had not heard it," he exclaimed. "I am going to die without knowing that my country is saved and the slaveholders' accursed rebellion crushed. The capture of Lee's army would have ended the war in sixty days; now it may drag on for years. It was cowardice or weakness that let the rebels escape." He was greatly consoled, however, by the news that reached him of the capture of Vicksburg and Port Hudson, and the reported fall of Charleston. "Ah!" said he, "blood will tell; it takes the *Western* boys to handle the rebels."

He deplored the hostility to the prosecution of the war evinced by "Northern Copperheads," as he called them, and declared that "there was more danger from a divided North than from both the rebellion and foreign intervention. Let the people of the Free States be united and stand together, and in the end they will triumph over all opposition, and reclaim every seceded State to the Union."

In giving directions concerning his body and funeral, he said that he desired his remains embalmed, and dressed in the full uniform he wore when he fell on the battle-field; that he desired the Rev. Robert Collyer to preach his funeral sermon, because he had declared that the soldier who died to save Liberty and Union, would himself be saved at the judgment-seat of Heaven. He also desired that he should be buried by the Chicago military, and that his remains should repose in Graceland Cemetery, because it was under the control of Thos. B. Bryan, Esq., a true-hearted Union man, and a zealous and devoted friend of the soldier.

His requests were all strictly carried out. His pall-bearers were eight officers of his own rank. His remains were escorted from the depot, on their arrival at Chicago, to the residence of Joseph Medill, Esq., by the Chicago Zouaves, where the last sad rites to the noble hero were performed: they were escorted to the cemetery by a battalion of the 65th Infantry, under Col. McChesney, and the members of the Chicago Typographical Union, of which he had been a respected associate. At the cemetery, six volleys were fired by the escort, and the remains were deposited in the receiving vault.

Our narrative is ended. We have hastily traced the career of one of the martyr heroes that Illinois has given for the salvation of the Union, and in the long roll, no nobler, braver, or truer patriot has sealed his devotion to his country by his heart's blood.   He was an ardent, thorough devotee of Liberty; his whole soul was in the holy cause of Union.   Every energy of his nature was bent to the accomplishment of the success of the great cause.   He was as fearless as his own sword, and as cool in the battle as on parade; he set an example of gallantry, honor and integrity that won for him the esteem and confidence of all his companions, without incurring the envy or jealousy of any.   We but reiterate the unanimous voice of his beloved regiment, the brave, old 8th Illinois Cavalry, in ascribing to him great executive ability as an officer wherever he had an opportunity to exhibit it, and in making the sad prediction that, had he lived, he would have won his way to high station and reputation in the army.   He fell in the morn of life, full of promise—a courteous gentleman, a whole-souled patriot, and a brave soldier.

LIEUTENANT COLONEL LOOMIS.

LIEUTENANT COLONEL LOOMIS.

Lieut. Col. REUBEN LOOMIS was born in the year 1826, at Mount Washington, Massachusetts, of a very respectable family, of which he was the only son. His father, David Loomis, migrated with his family to Ohio while Reuben was quite young, and where he grew to manhood, thoroughly trained to habits of industry on his father's farm.

In the spring of 1853, he was married to Miss Mary E. Hess, a very estimable and worthy lady, who still survives him.

In the year of 1856, he removed with his family to Du Quoin, Perry county, Illinois, and located on a farm in the vicinity of that flourishing town, where he resided until September, 1861, being universally esteemed as a good citizen and a strictly honest man.

At the commencement of the rebellion he took strong ground in favor of sustaining the Government, and putting down disloyalty. He was fearless and outspoken in defense of his country's rights, and took no pains to conceal from Southern sympathizers, with whom he came in contact, his utter detestation of their conduct.

As the rebellion increased in magnitude, and the call for "more men" became urgent, his convictions of duty induced him, at considerable sacrifice, to leave his farm and remove his family to town, and engage in recruiting a company of cavalry, which he soon accomplished, and which, when organized, unanimously elected him their captain.

On the 30th day of September, 1861, Capt. Loomis started with his company for Camp Butler, Illinois, where they arrived on the 5th of October, and on the 9th were mustered into the United States service by Col. Pitcher, and attached to the 6th Illinois Cavalry Volunteers, and was lettered as Company I.

Capt. Loomis soon afterwards returned to Du Quoin, and obtained additional recruits sufficient to fill his company, with whom he returned to Camp Butler on the 8th November.

On the 19th of the same month, the regiment, under command of Col. Thos. H. Cavanaugh, was ordered to Shawneetown, Ill., leaving Camp Butler on the 20th, arriving at Du Quoin on the 21st, encamping there until the 25th, arriving at Shawneetown on the 27th, where they were encamped until Feb. 20th, 1862, when the 1st and 2d battalions left for Paducah, and the 3d battalion for Smithland, Kentucky.

While at the latter place, Capt. Loomis, with his company, made several excursions through the surrounding country with marked success, gaining the credit and respect of his superior officers.

On the 27th of March, the 3d battalion joined the regiment at Paducah, and while there Company I, under the leadership of its brave captain, made several trips into Tennessee of unusual daring, considering the very inferior arms and equipments with which the men were at that time provided.

In the month of April, Col. Cavanaugh having resigned, Major B. H. Grierson was promoted to the Coloneley, and through the recommendation of his superior officers, Captain Loomis was appointed Major, and received his commission as such from Gov. Yates, to rank from April 25th.

On the 8th of June the regiment moved to Columbus, Ky., and on the 19th, to Memphis, Tenn., remaining at Memphis and vicinity until 26th November, making frequent incursions to Tennessee and Mississippi, with invariable success.

On the march to Tallahatchie and northern Mississippi, the "Sixth" had the advance of Gen. Sherman's corps, and protected the rear of Gen. Grant's army on its return from that expedition.

During the winter of 1862–3, the regiment was encamped at Lagrange, Tenn., though kept almost constantly in motion.

In the month of December, the Lieut. Colonel having resigned, Major Loomis was promoted to fill the vacancy, and Col. Grierson being assigned to the command of a brigade, Lieut. Colonel Loomis took command of the regiment in January, 1863, in which command he remained to the day of his death.

On the 29th of March the regiment had a very severe fight near Belmont, which elicited the following complimentary order:

Headqrs. 1st Div. 16th Army Corps, }
Lagrange, Tenn., April 2, 1863. }

General Orders—No. 46.

By direction of Major Gen. S. A. Hurlbut, Commanding 16th Army Corps.

The General commanding the 1st Division returns thanks to the cavalry, which, under the command of Lieut. Col. Loomis, of the 6th Illinois Cavalry, so gallantly repulsed an attack made upon them at midnight by a rebel force, outnumbering them threefold, near Belmont, Tenn., on the 29th of March, 1863. By such determined fighting true glory is won, and we cannot think of our brave men, springing from their slumbers, aroused by a murderous volley, and rushing upon the foe and routing him, without a thrill of pride. Well does our country merit such glorious service, and may all our troops largely render it whenever opportunity may be afforded.

It is hereby ordered that a copy of this order be addressed to each commissioned and non-commissioned officer and private who participated in the affair referred to, as evidence of his bravery and good conduct.

(By Command.)   Brig. Gen. Wm. Sooy Smith,
                         Commanding 1st Division.

Hoffman Atkinson, A. A. G.

On the 17th of April, the regiment, under command of Col. Loomis, started with Col. Grierson's brigade on the expedition known as the famous "Grierson Raid," through Mississippi, arriving at Baton Rouge, La., May 2d, 1863.

They were engaged in several fights in that vicinity, and participated in the siege of Port Hudson, in which the skill and bravery of Col. Loomis was fully tested and found most worthy. After the fall of Port Hudson he returned with the regiment to Memphis, remaining there until the middle of August, when they were ordered to Germantown.

Col. Loomis was in command of the regiment in the fight at Ingraham Mills, on the 12th of October, and at Wyatt, Miss., on the next day, in both of which the regiment bore a conspicuous part, and for which he was highly complimented by his commanding officer.

His untimely death, which occurred on Monday the 2d day of November, 1863, sent a thrill of horror through the entire regiment, and caused a feeling of regret and sadness in the breast of every officer and private in that department of our army.

His remains were escorted to Memphis with military honors, and every testimonial of respect was shown to his memory at that place.

Capt. L. B. Skinner, commander of his first and much-loved Company I, was appointed by Gen. S. A. Hurlbut to convey the lamented Colonel's remains to his heart-stricken widow, who is left with four helpless little ones to mourn his irreparable loss. His remains were interred with Masonic honors at Du Quoin, and followed to the grave by hundreds of the citizens of the town and vicinity.

Flags were displayed, draped in mourning, business houses were all closed, and the whole community mourned its honored dead.

At a meeting of the citizens of Du Quoin, resolutions were adopted expressive of their horror-stricken feelings at the manner of his death and detestation of the man who caused it, closing with the following:

That in the death of Lieut. Col. Loomis, the nation has lost one of her bravest soldiers and purest patriots, and this community one of its most honored citizens.

That we deeply sympathize with the bereaved family of the deceased, in this terrible calamity.

That the thanks of this community are tendered to Major General S. A. Hurlbut, Commander of the 16th Army Corps, for the appropriate tribute of respect paid to the deceased.

The Masonic fraternity at Du Quoin also passed a series of resolutions, expressive of their respect for and attachment to their deceased brother; as did also the military Masonic Lodge with which he was connected.

In regard to the manner of his death, the following correct account, as furnished by Major C. W. Whitsit, and published in the Memphis *Bulletin*, is herein copied:

HEADQRS. 6th ILLINOIS CAVALRY, }
GERMANTOWN, Nov. 7, 1863. }

EDITOR "BULLETIN:"

SIR,—I am much grieved to see that the unhappy wording of the notice of the shooting of Lieut. Col. Loomis, our late much loved Commanding Officer, by Major Herrod, which appeared in your paper of the 4th, the impression is made that it was the result of a personal quarrel while at supper. Such was not the case; and to correct the impression, which is doing injustice to the memory of the deceased outside of the regiment, where the circumstances are unknown, allow me to state the circumstances as they occurred:

At the time, the entire effective force of the 6th Illinois Cavalry was out under command of Lieut. Col. Loomis, assisting in the general operations against Gen. Chalmers' movements. Major Herrod being left in command of the ineffective force in camp, did some important official business over his signature, as "Major Commanding Regiment." Lieut. Col. Loomis, thinking it an injustice to him and his regiment, took occasion to reprimand Maj. Herrod for his unwarrantable assumption of power.

Some bitter words passed during the interview, which was in the forenoon of the day on which the murder was committed. At dark Maj. Herrod came to headquarters and enquired for Col. Loomis, who, he was told, was at supper, but would soon be in. He proceeded immediately to the Lucken House, near half a mile distant, where Col. Loomis boarded, and where Col. Hatch and several other officers were at supper. Meeting Col. Loomis in the hall he accosted him thus: "Col. Loomis, you said this morning thus and so, in the presence of Col. Hatch; take it back or I'll kill you." Col. Loomis replied in a mild tone: "Maj. Herrod, you have got a pistol in your hand, and I am unarmed. If you want to kill me, kill me." Maj. Herrod immediately fired; the first shot knocking him down, the second entering his breast, killing him instantly. He fired three more shots at the prostrate body, none of which took effect.

This is a statement of the case just as I believe the evidence in the case, taken at a proper time, will make it appear. By publishing it you will do justice to the deceased and a favor to his friends in the regiment, the men of which were almost universally attached to him, both as an officer and a gentleman.

CHAS. W. WHITSIT, Major,
Com. 6th Illinois Cavalry.

Maj. Herrod was immediately arrested by Col. Hatch, and conveyed to Memphis in irons, to await his trial.

Below is a copy of the resolutions passed by the officers of the regiment:

GERMANTOWN, Nov. 9th, 1863.

At a meeting of the officers of the 6th Illinois Cavalry Regiment, of which Major C. W. Whitsit was Chairman, and Lieut. J. H. Benham, Secretary, the following officers—Capt. Joseph Corker, Capt. F. Charlesworth, Capt. W. D. Glass, Lieut. Geo. A. Anderson, and Lieut. H. F. Patterson—were appointed a Committee to draft resolutions, which were unanimously adopted as follows:

WHEREAS we, the officers of the 6th Illinois Cavalry, feel it incumbent on us, as associates in arms with our late lamented Lieut. Colonel, R. Loomis, and treasuring toward him many happy remembrances, contracted through many trials and dangers on the field of battle in support of our country's flag, and in the quiet camp, to give his widowed wife and fatherless children an expression of the feelings of regard we entertain toward him while in our midst.

AND WHEREAS, it pleased Almighty God in his providence to suffer the life of our beloved Lieut. Colonel to be taken away. Therefore, be it

Resolved, That in him the country has lost a brave and sagacious leader, a true patriot and an ardent lover.

2. That we as a regiment and officers, have lost a gallant commander, long to be remembered by us.

3. He endeared himself to us by his kind and gentlemanly bearing, his attachment to the service, his irreproachable character, his unassuming modesty, and never flinching in the hour of danger to expose his life with his command whenever duty called, as we have witnessed on many a bloody contested field.

4. That we most sincerely mourn and lament his loss.

5. That we tender to his poor, sorrow-stricken wife and children our heartfelt sympathy with them in this their greatest trial.

6. That in their loss they have lost an affectionate husband, a kind and indulgent father ; his mother a dutiful son, and his sister a tender brother.

7. That we most devoutly commend them to Him who is a husband to the widow and a father to the fatherless.

(Signed)   C. W. Whitsit, President.

J. H. Benham, Secretary.

LIEUTENANT JAMES,

LIEUTENANT JAMES.

The subject of this memoir, Lieut. EDWARD ARTHUR JAMES, was born in Adams, Berkshire county, Massachusetts, on the 17th day of September, 1839.

His parents were natives of Glasgow, Scotland, who emigrated to the United States and settled in North Adams in 1833.

After a residence there of ten years, the family removed to Illinois, and the father of Lieut. James (who now fills the arduous and responsible position of Provost Marshal of the 1st District of Illinois) purchased a farm in the town of Barrington, Cook county, where he lived with his family a considerable time, and which farm he still owns.

Here, amidst the quiet and peaceful pursuits of a country life and the endearing surroundings of a happy home, the subject of this memoir spent his early days.

He was possessed of a mild and pleasant disposition, and was much loved, not only by the members of his family, but by all of his young associates, to whom his agreeable manners, his obliging disposition, the energy with which he entered into all their youthful sports, and the kindly feeling with which he sympathized with them in their misfortunes, greatly endeared him and secured for him a lasting place in their affections, which will never be obliterated.

He received a good common school education, improved by one term at a select school, and one at the Garden City Academy, and having adopted mercantile pursuits as a profession, he qualified himself by studying at Sloan's Commercial College, in the city of Chicago, of which institution he became a graduate.

In 1858 he went into the employment of his elder brother, William—now Major of the 72d Illinois Volunteers—as a clerk, and remained in that capacity until the sale of the business by his brother in 1860.

At the breaking out of the war in the spring of 1861, he was employed in the Quartermaster's Department in this State, under ex-Governor Wood, and discharged his portion of the arduous duties of that important position with the most exemplary fidelity, until the State organization of that department was suspended, by the General Government assuming the control of it in all the States.

In the winter of 1861-2, he joined Capt. W. H. Bolton, of Chicago, in raising the distinguished Battery which bears his name, and so energetically was the good work prosecuted that in February, 1862, the Company was mustered into the service of the United States as Co. L, 2d Regiment Illinois Light Artillery, when the subject of this memoir was elected junior 1st Lieutenant, and was duly commissioned as such.

About the middle of the following March, the company was ordered to the field, and left for Benton Barracks, St. Louis, where their horses and guns were supplied.

After being thus prepared for active service, the company departed for Pittsburg Landing, and arrived there shortly after the bloody and memorable battle of Shiloh, and having joined the noble army of the Union, it participated in the siege of Corinth until its evacuation by the rebel forces under Beauregard.

For some months the battery to which Lieutenant James was attached remained in that vicinity, taking part in most of the skirmishing which took place during the ensuing summer, but unengaged in any action of much importance till the bloody conflict at the Hatchie, in the following October, in which battle Company L bore a conspicuous part, and received most honorable mention for heroic conduct in the various official despatches of the Generals in command—in all of which the name of Lieut. James is mentioned with distinction.

It may not be out of place in this connection to furnish the following brief extracts from official documents relating to that engagement, which will show the estimate formed of Lieutenant James by his superior officers.

In General Veatch's report the following may be found:

As soon as this disposition was made, a section of Capt. Bolton's Battery, under the command of Lieut. James, was brought up and shelled the house and barn in a most effective manner, driving out the rebel picket, which fled to the woods on the left.

The guns by which this distinguished service was rendered were served by the lamented officer of whose career this is a brief and imperfect sketch.

In the same report the following notices of Co. L are also found :

The batteries during this time had got into position, Bolton near the road and Burnap on the right, and were doing most efficient service. The firing at first was splendid from the rebel batteries, but it gradually slackened, and it was evident they were being disabled by the telling shots from our side.

And again :

Bolton's and Mann's batteries had crossed the bridge, and kept up a vigorous fire on the enemy.

In the official report of Capt. Bolton, the following is found :

I was ordered by Gen. Veatch to forward one section to shell a house and barn in which the enemy were concealed, about 450 yards distant, on the left of the road leading to the river. This section I placed in command of Lieut. James, who fired six shells at the premises, all of which, upon examination afterwards, proved effective.

I was then ordered to take my battery across the bridge and occupy a position on the east bank, which was effected under severe fire from the enemy.

In carrying out these orders Bolton's Battery was the first to cross, Lieut. James' section being in the advance. The fire from the rebels was most severe, and the Lieutenant's horse was twice wounded before the position was won.

The following is from Major General Hurlbut's address to the artillerymen of the 4th Division, on the occasion of the presentation of a rebel flag to Capt. Bolton's Battery of Chicago Light Artillery, October 11, 1862 :

To this Battery (Chicago Light Artillery,) I present this flag, captured mainly by their exertions ; as at the field of Shiloh I found it necessary to have dismissed from the service one battery for its dastardly conduct, so now I have the pleasure of saying *that every officer and every soldier observed his duty.*

Capt. Bolton, I have the pleasure of presenting to you these colors, to be disposed of as your Battery may decide.

Remember, all of you, that you must at all times be ready whenever you are called upon, *to do the same good work that you did at the Hatchie.*

In a letter from Major C. C. Campbell, Chief of Artillery on Maj. Gen. Hurlbut's Staff, we extract the following :

I commanded all the artillery at the battle of the Hatchie. I saw this flag (that presented to Capt. Bolton's Battery,) unfurled and borne aloft amidst three columns of infantry advancing to take Spear's Battery. I being at the time within three hundred yards of the enemy, I read the inscription, " Clark County Farmers," and immediately after giving my orders, saw that flag stricken down by a shot fired by Lieut. E. A. James, of Bolton's Battery, who at the same time poured such an incessant charge of grape and canister on the advancing foe that they were driven from the field, leaving their colors behind them.

The Major, (after speaking of his own illness,) says :

Lieut. Ed. James, of Bolton's Battery, died in Chicago of the same disease. He staid with me the last night he was here, and left for Chicago the next day. He has fought his last battle. A braver boy never lived. He was under my eye all the time at the battle of the Hatchie, and was in fact my best officer.

For some time before the battle, Lieut. James had been suffering from that terrible disease of camp life, diarrhœa, and was at the time of the engagement so debilitated, and suffering so acutely, that his superior officers urged him to abstain from taking part in the coming conflict ; but his ardent spirit, his glowing patriotism, his determination to lead his section of the battery, (the men of which loved him to adoration, and would follow him devotedly wherever he chose to lead,) and his own unquenchable desire to earn for himself fame and honor as a soldier, caused him to disregard the advice which had been forced upon him. He went into the fight sick and exhausted, but, nevertheless, was in the saddle from early morn till the close of day, when the battle was won, and he earned the distinction which will ever encircle his name.

But the honor was dearly purchased—life was the price to pay. Within a few days the inroads of the disease became so terrible that he was completely prostrated, and having received leave of absence from Gen. Hurlbut, he with difficulty reached his home, where, on the 2d November following, surrounded by his sorrowing family, he breathed his last, and another young life, for the cause of freedom, was laid on the altar of his country.

In years to come, when the history of this great war shall be read as a thing of bygone days, the name of Edward A. James will be found high up in the niches of the temple of fame, enshrined in the hearts and watered by the tears of an appreciative, grateful, and, let us hope, a reunited and happy people.

CORPORAL DAVIS.

CORPORAL DAVIS.

Corp. REDECK WEED McKEE DAVIS was born on the 28th of June, 1836, in the city of Wheeling, Virginia, and when only one year old came with his parents to Peoria, Illinois. He was the youngest son of the late Samuel H. Davis, a veteran printer and editor, well known in New York, Virginia and Illinois.

McKee Davis was a precocious child, and acquired the elements of learning very rapidly, but was always quiet and gentle in his disposition, cool and deliberate in judgment and action—evidently domestic in his habits, he thought his home the most blessed place in the world.

He was, however, full of life, brilliancy of wit; active, generous, and brave almost to a fault. We will pass over the early part of his life, merely glancing at the time when he entered life's great arena, and with a printer's "stick and rule," to work as a "jour" in Peoria, Bloomington and Davenport.

Next we find him in possession of a small printing establishment in Onarga, Iroquois county, where for some time he published and edited a weekly journal known as the Onarga *Mercury.* Here, also, he was united in marriage with Miss Caroline E. Newell, daughter of T. A. Newell, one of the founders of that town; after which, not being sufficiently sustained, he removed to Peoria and again entered an office as a journeyman.

At the commencement of this unnatural war, his soul was fired with an ardent desire to go forward in defense of his country's flag, which had been so basely attacked at Sumter, but so well defended by the gallant Anderson and his noble band; but the ties of a wife and widowed mother deterred him.

At the third call of his country, in 1862, he could resist the impulses of duty to his country no longer, and on the 22d of July of that year he enlisted in the 77th Regiment of Illinois Volunteers, Co. E. This regiment has been truly a fighting

6

one. At Arkansas Post the 77th distinguished itself, and so in every battle in which it has taken a part.

In a letter to his wife, Corp. Davis says: "My parting with you was sad indeed, and prepared me for scenes of the same kind on leaving Peoria, the home of my childhood. Dear, beautiful city, shall I ever behold thee again? Tomb of my honored father, farewell! Memories of bygone days, visions of the blessed past will cheer me on my onward march, while love of country will nerve my arm to defend with my life if need be, her rights and her flag. In Cincinnati and elsewhere we have been received with cheers and kindly greeting; but in this little city (Covington, Ky.) 'on the old Kentucky shore,' but two houses were seen with the stars and stripes—we cheered them lustily."

Of the first skirmish he was in on their march from Covington to Richmond, Ky., he says: "You know, dear mother, I am not a coward, but as we neared Livingston we encountered a squad of the enemy—a pretty large squad, too. A skirmish ensued, and as the bullets whizzed about my head like a hail-storm of lead, I never was so completely 'scared' in my life, and the first time I fired, the gun 'kicked.' After that, however, I could load and fire as well as any of them, and faced the haughty foe with a firm and steady purpose to perform my duty bravely and faithfully. I am of the same metal as the foe, for I, too, am a Southerner, but, thank God, I am one who loves the old ship of state. In this skirmish I had a narrow escape; a bullet passed through my cap."

In marching through Kentucky they were in many severe skirmishes, made long, tedious marches, and at Richmond made some important captures.

After the battles at Vicksburg on the 28th, 29th and 30th of December, 1862, he wrote: "Our division (A. J. Smith's) suffered greatly, but my life has been thus far spared. We hoped our forces would be triumphant, but the enemy was too strongly fortified. At the third day's battle we beat a hasty retreat."

At Arkansas Post he was wounded; but before receiving the wound he had acted a most courageous part. In a letter, after this battle, he says : "The heart-rending sights I have witnessed since entering Fort Hindman, no pen can adequately describe. One poor fellow, a noble-looking rebel, too much so for a rebel, held in his hand the picture of a beautiful woman and her babe —no doubt his wife and child. He was dead, but in the agony of death, seemed to have pressed this fond memento to his breast.

"About noon on Sunday, January 11th, 1863, the battle of Arkansas Post commenced in earnest. Our regiment was held as a reserve, a mile from the scene of conflict. A comrade and myself (John McIntyre) were together: we spent the leisure time afforded us in talking of death, reading the Bible, and prayer. While thus engaged the order came to advance at double quick. We rushed forward and went into the hottest of the fight. We left-flanked and commenced the fire, crawling very cautiously, and rising now and then to see the faces in the front. I tell you it was a solemn time. The 28th Ohio had got out of ammunition and we had to go ahead. We rushed past them, and met a regiment running ; we cheered them on by a shout of 'God and our country,' and they took fresh courage, rallied, and faced the enemy. We had got to the end of the road and were driving the enemy gloriously, when I was wounded and taken off the field. Soon after, poor John McIntyre was killed, but I trust that in that hour of prayer a few hours previous, he was prepared for his great change."

He was in front of Vicksburg doing good service in digging the canal ; was afterwards at Milliken's Bend ; was in all the series of battles from Grand Gulf to the rear of Vicksburg, fighting bravely and also doing good work as opportunity offered in his heavenly Master's service.

On the 22d of May he received a mortal wound on the left thigh, while nobly defending the flag of his country. The limb was amputated, but he sank beneath the shock to his system, and on the 27th, at perfect peace with his Saviour, he passed away. His last words were, "My God, my wife and child, my country for which I die."

The following is an extract of a letter from the Chaplain of the 77th Regiment, addressed to the mother of Corp. Davis :

Near VICKSBURG, May 29th, 1863.

DEAR MADAM : I would fain be the messenger of good news to you, but God in wisdom has ordained otherwise.

We had hoped your son would be able to bear the shock to his system by amputation, but the ordeal was too severe. He lingered till the night before last, when he dropped away.   *   *   *   *   .   *   *   *   *

I would again bear testimony to his truly Christian character, and to his devotion to his country—his brave and soldierly bearing at all times.   *   *

We buried your son's body on a hill beside others who fell with him. It was my privilege to perform that last sad office for him, and to pray for you and our suffering country beside his open grave. May the Lord comfort and bless you, my friend.

WM. G. PEARCE, Chaplain,
77th Illinois Volunteers.

Mrs. M. B. DAVIS.

Solemn funeral services were held in the Congregational Church at Onarga, on the Sabbath after the sad notice of his death was received, when a most appropriate sermon was delivered by the Rev. Mr. Winters, from 2d Cor. iv., 17–18.

CAPTAIN WARD.

Capt. GUY CARLTON WARD, the eldest son of Alva and Priscilla H. Ward, was born at Scipio, Cayuga county, New York, March 21st, 1831.

In boyhood he was of a retiring disposition, but of studious habits—faithful, truthful and manly in all his actions. He seemed to pass from youth to manhood at a very early age, taking a position among men, and acting an earnest, firm and noble part in life. He was above all other things a dutiful child, promptly obeying his parents in all their commands. He was free from all low and debasing conduct, never being known to be guilty of any mean or belittling action, but conducted himself as if he thought that life was real and earnest. He looked the stern and solid realities of the world full in the face, and with a stout heart and strong will he determined to conquer in the great battle of life. He was always regarded as a diligent student, especially in history and biography. He was well read in the politics and current literature of the times. His early manhood was passed in Ohio, where he struggled hard with his parents—who were blessed with a numerous family—to obtain an honest livelihood and be known and honored amongst men. At the age of nineteen years he went to Cincinnati and learned the trade of a house mason. He served his time as an apprentice with Mr. John Earhart, with whom, at the expiration of his apprenticeship, he entered into business as a partner. He served as an apprentice and partner in business for five years. The firm failed through the operations of the principal. A noble and brave man's qualities shine in adversity as well as in prosperity. Capt. Ward's first attempt in business resulted in a bitter experience. He left Cincinnati and settled in Du Quoin, Perry county, Illinois.

While in Cincinnati, Capt. Ward had connected himself with the Freemasons, among whom he was always held in the highest esteem. He was Master of the Lodge in Du Quoin, and also held responsible positions in the Royal Arch Chapter established in that place. In the Grand Lodge his learning and talents as a bright and intelligent mason were brought into requisition by his appointment as a member of important committees. He ever in all the commanding positions which he occupied among the masonic fraternity, acquitted himself with satisfaction to his friends and honor to the institution. He was the chief man in starting and sustaining a Lodge of Masons in connection with the regiment to which he belonged. He was untiring in his labors and constant in his devotion to the principles of the order.

Capt. Ward settled in Du Quoin just as that thriving village was starting into existence. His deportment was so praiseworthy in all the relations of life that he at once won the confidence and esteem of the leading citizens of the place. He was for several successive years elected Town Trustee, and was also President of the Board. His habits of industry and his strictly moral character, ranked him among wise and good men as a young gentleman of high promise and commanding usefulness in the world. He had been taught the great truths of Revelation by his parents. These he firmly believed; his faith in them was never shaken. He united with the Presbyterian Church in Du Quoin, of which William S. Post, D.D., now Chaplain of the 81st Illinois Infantry, was at that time pastor. The warmest friendship and most intimate relationship always existed between Capt. Ward and his friend and pastor, the Rev. Dr. Post.

In the year 1857, Capt. Ward married Miss Lizzie Bell Robinson, only daughter of William and Nancy Robinson, of Clermont county, Ohio. Their first child, Anna Cora, died in the summer of 1859, at the age of eight months. Mrs. Ward died of that cruel and lingering disease, consumption, March 12, 1861, leaving Capt. Ward with one little son named Willie Post. Soon after this domestic affliction, the flag of his country was fired upon at Fort Sumter, which aroused all the lofty patriotism and sublime devotion to the stars and stripes which glowed in the brave and manly breast of Capt. Ward. He immediately went to work with all his energies—his whole soul being enlisted in the righteous cause—raising volunteers for the Union army, on

the first call of the President for 75,000 men. The company
was soon raised. C. H. Brookings, who fell bravely in the siege
of Vicksburg, in May, 1863, was chosen Captain, S. R. Wetmore
was elected 1st Lieutenant, and Guy C. Ward, 2d Lieutenant.
This was the first company raised for the service south of the
Ohio and Miss. R. R., which, after its organization, became Co.
G, 12th Illinois Infantry, Colonel (now General) John McArthur,
commanding. The company was named by the ladies the "Du
Quoin Braves." They left Perry county on the 28th of April,
and were mustered into the service on the 3d day of May, at
Springfield. During the three months of their enlistment, the
regiment was stationed most of the time at Cairo, Ill. When
the regiment was reorganized, and enlisted for three years or
during the war, Lieut. Ward was unanimously elected Captain.
He recruited his company in a short time, and rejoined his regiment with an intelligent and resolute band of men. The regiment was soon ordered to Paducah, Ky., where he remained till
it was deemed necessary to occupy Smithland, when his company was sent as part of the garrison of that post. He remained
there until arrangements were made for the attack on Fort
Henry, when he was ordered back to his regiment at Paducah.
The regiment left Paducah, Gen. Smith commanding the division, Colonel McArthur the brigade, and Lieut. Col. Chetlain
the regiment. The division landed three miles below Fort
Heiman, and moved to the assault at once. The enemy fled
and left the works in our possession. From here the regiment
marched to the attack on Fort Donelson. Through that eventful siege and battle Capt. Ward sustained his share in all the
fatigues and hardships attending the memorable contest. On
Saturday morning, Feb. 15th, when attacked by the enemy at
daylight by overwhelming numbers, "he led his men to the conflict with as much coolness," says Capt. Wetmore, whose sketch
of Capt. Ward we are quoting, "as he would have done had it
been a dress parade." His regiment was flanked three times and
forced back, but never lost their order or formation. Finally,
when out of ammunition, the regiment was ordered back, and
soon after the enemy retired without effecting the object of cutting his way out of the fort. Gen. McArthur spoke in the

highest terms of the coolness and courage of Capt. Ward. Five men were killed and twenty-one were wounded in his company.

After the occupation of Fort Donelson, the regiment was ordered to Clarksville, Tenn., and in a few days, still on to Nashville; thence back to Clarksville, where the regiment received their baggage, which had been left at Fort Heiman. The men had been seventeen days without tents, blankets, or a change of clothing.

Here the company lost the first man from sickness since the first organization of the regiment on the 26th day of April, 1861—a period of eleven months—which shows the care and attention they had received from their Captain during all that time of exposure, which included everything to which a soldier is subject. There were plenty of houses belonging to secessionists in Clarksville, but they were considered too good for Federal soldiers to use.

From here the regiment was sent by steamer to Pittsburg Landing, where it was engaged in the battle of Shiloh. Capt. Ward had not been able for duty for a long time; Lieut. J. F. Watkins, who commanded the company, was seriously wounded in the first day's fight at Shiloh. The 1st Lieut., J. McArthur, was on Gen. McArthur's Staff. No commissioned officer being on hand to command the company, Capt. Ward left his cot and led his men in the second day's engagement. The loss of the company was heavy in the battle. The men maintained in this hard-fought contest their well-earned reputation for firmness and bravery. When the regiment was ordered to Corinth in pursuit of the enemy, Capt. Ward started with his men, but he was ordered back to camp, where he remained very sick with diarrhœa for a long time, till he was sent to Cincinnati. As soon as he regained his health, he returned to his regiment at Corinth. He was engaged in the battle of Iuka, but from the position which was assigned the regiment it did not take an active part in the conflict. After the battle of Iuka, part of the regiment, under Capt. Ward's command, was ordered to Burnsville; the rest, commanded by Col. Chetlain, went to Corinth. On Friday the 3d day of October, the companies in charge of Capt. Ward were ordered from Burnsville to Corinth.

During the night, Capt. Ward, with his men, slept on their arms on the battle-field at that place, ready at the word of command to renew the engagement with their companions in arms in the morning. The 12th Regiment, then in command of Capt. Ward, was held with the rest of the brigade to which it belonged, as a body of reserve. One of our batteries was captured by the rebels, but before they had time to turn the guns on our men, the 12th Illinois Regiment, in conjunction with a regiment from Ohio, was ordered to charge upon the enemy and retake the battery. In leading his men to this gallant charge, waving his sword in his hand while rallying his "Braves," shouting in a clear, shrill voice, which was distinctly heard above the thunder of battle, "Onward, men, onward," Captain Ward fell, pierced through his head with a minie ball. He fell just at the moment victory was perching upon our banners—not only those of the 12th Regiment, but also of the whole Union army. No man fell in that bloody contest more conspicuous for heroic daring than Capt. Ward. With him perished in the same engagement several of his brave men.

In a general order issued by Gen. Rosecrans after the battle, the name of Capt. Guy C. Ward was mentioned with the highest meed of commendation and praise as one of the heroes and martyrs in the stern and awful conflict. His remains were brought home to Du Quoin by his father, where his funeral was attended by an immense concourse of mourning friends. He was buried with Masonic honors in the graveyard, where rest by his side his beloved wife and child. A beautiful monument has been erected to his memory with the appropriate lines—

> "How sleep the brave, who sink to rest
> With all their country's honors blest."

CAPTAIN TUCKER.

Capt. Lansing B. Tucker was born in the city of Rochester, State of New York, on the 28th of May, 1844. He was an unusually intelligent boy, and of an affectionate disposition.

He early manifested a talent for mechanical arts, and a taste for a soldier's life, which was encouraged by the military associations of his family, his father, Col. Joseph H. Tucker, having been connected with the volunteer service during the entire life of Capt. Tucker.

Among his earliest studies were works on military organization, tactics, science and discipline. For some years prior to the breaking out of the present war, he commanded a military company composed of students in the Chicago University, where he was also a student.

He was universally esteemed by his teachers and fellow students, always prompt and proficient in his studies, and exceedingly frank and manly in his intercourse with all.

At the commencement of the war, he earnestly entreated permission to volunteer into the service of his country, although but sixteen years of age, yet, from his manly appearance, he would have been regarded as some years older. His family did not encourage his entering the service at this time, on account of his youth and their desire to have him complete his studies. However, in the year 1862, upon the urgent call of the Government for fresh troops, his entreaties could not be longer resisted, and he, together with many of the students comprising the military company in the University, volunteered their services, and organized a company for the 69th Regt. Ill. Volunteers, of which he was immediately elected Captain.

Although the youngest officer in his regiment, Capt. Tucker was regarded as its best drill master, and was a universal favorite among both officers and men. His regiment was placed on duty at Camp Douglas, in charge of prisoners of war, where it was stationed when Capt. Tucker was taken sick of camp fever. For two weeks he lay uncomplainingly on a bed of sickness and suffering, and no murmur escaped his lips: once only, he expressed regret to a friend, who stood at his bedside, that he could not have passed away amid the "cloud and lightning" of the battle-field, fighting for his country's flag. Almost his last thoughts and words were of his country. At times, when in the delirium of fever, he expressed anxiety for the welfare of his men, and gave orders in regard to his company. He died on the 18th day of August, 1862.

The funeral obsequies occurred on Thursday. Aug. 20th. in the grove of the University grounds, at Cottage Grove, near Chicago. The military escort on that occasion consisted of the whole of the 69th Regiment, in command of Col. Hough. The music was supplied by the Light Guard Band, and was peculiarly touching and appropriate. Rev. Dr. J. C. Burroughs, President of the University, delivered the funeral discourse, after which an opportunity was afforded all present to look at the corpse of the deceased soldier. The coffin containing his mortal remains stood upon a platform erected for that purpose, in the centre of the group, and was enveloped in that time-honored emblem of a soldier's fidelity and love—the Stars and Stripes. At the head of the coffin, draped in black, hung the beautiful silk flag which the young ladies of the Dearborn Female Seminary, Chicago, presented to the University Cadets, of which the deceased was Captain, June 21st, immediately after its organization. Capt. Tucker received the flag, and replied to the address of the young ladies in the following words:

We give you our warmest thanks for this beautiful banner, and, as we receive it from your fair hands, its every shining star and glowing stripe becomes dear to our hearts. We do not know how soon our country may need our little band; but we are ready to respond to her call, and, under this flag, march to "victory or death." We shall never cast to the breeze its folds without thinking of the *fair ladies* who gave it to us, in their defence, and for our country's glory we shall fight valiantly, wreathing our banner with triumph, or finding in its folds a winding-sheet.

On June 7, 1861, at the solemn funeral of Judge Douglas, the University Cadets, under command of Capt. Tucker, were assigned the duties of a guard of honor to receive the procession, and mounted guard around the grave, their lines encompassing an area of about three acres.

The publication of the classes of the University—the *Index
Universitatis*—thus discourses:

Among those who have gone to the field of battle, are a large proportion of
the young men who have filled our colleges. We have been obliged to bid
farewell to many of our fellow students, who have felt it their duty to give up
the delightful pursuit of knowledge—to leave our classic halls, and go forth
to fight the battles of their country. Many of them have breasted the storm
of battle, and stood firm in the thickest of the fight, winning laurels for bravery
and daring. Some have been wounded, and others have fallen by disease.
Among the latter is the much-lamented Capt. Tucker, who, before he entered
the army, was Captain of our University Cadets, and had won the affection of
the entire company, as well as of his fellow students.

The following order, by Lieut. Col. Pickett, gives an estimate
of the esteem in which the young soldier was held:

HEADQRS. 69th REGT., CAMP DOUGLAS, Aug. 18, 1862.

Special Order, No. 28.—The Lieut. Colonel commanding has the painful
duty of announcing to the regiment the death of Captain Lansing B. Tucker,
at the residence of his father, Col. Joseph H. Tucker, this afternoon at half-
past one o'clock.

In making this mournful announcement the Lieut. Colonel commanding cannot permit the occasion to pass without paying a brief tribute to the memory
of our brother officer. But young in years, having but recently reached his
18th birthday, he was yet old enough to understand and practice the duties of
a soldier and a Christian gentleman. A strict disciplinarian, who required and
enforced implicit obedience, he yet bore in mind that his soldiers were MEN.
The decease of Capt. Tucker was no ordinary calamity at the present time,
when our country needs the help of all her sons.

With a well balanced and well disciplined mind, a brave, warm, true heart,
and a fixed and settled determination to make a military life his profession, it
is but the truth to say that had his life been spared, he must have risen to distinction as a defender of his country's flag. All his thoughts seem to have
been engrossed with his duties as a soldier, and even in his last moments, when
the kind physician endeavored to soothe his pains by the administration of a
cool draught, he said: "Wait, wait, till the fight is over! Forward!" In
his dying moments he did not forget Company C. But why extend this
eulogy? Many of you enjoyed his personal friendship, and all respected his
soldierly qualities. Though but two moons have waxed and waned since we
made his acquaintance, his true nobility of soul bound this regiment to him
with "hooks of steel." Truly can it be said of our boy-captain,

"None knew him but to love him,
None named him but to praise."

T. J. PICKETT,
E. M. BEARDSLEY, Adjt.   Lt. Col. Com'dg 69th Regt.

LIEUTENANT EAMES.

Lieut. CHARLES A. EAMES was born in Rushville, Schuyler county, Illinois, on the 18th of April, 1840. His parents, Cutler Eames and Abbie F. Eames, are still living, and reside in Beardstown, Cass County. They are natives of Boston, Massachusetts, and resided there until 1835, when they emigrated to the West, and settled in Rushville. In 1846, they removed to Beardstown. At that time their son, Charles, who was six years old, entered the juvenile department of the public school, where he continued in attendance until December, 1835. From the time he entered school until leaving it, after acquiring the highest branches of an English education, no pupil was more esteemed by his teachers, and none sooner mastered their lessons in the academic department. In mathematics he excelled, his mind being peculiarly adapted to the solution of difficult problems. His preceptor, the Rev. Professor J. Barwick, gave him the highest meed of praise as a scholar, and a young man of the most correct deportment. At school, and in his subsequent business, he evinced that logical quality of mind that fitted him for the exercise of strategy and command in the field.

In December, 1855, he became engaged as a clerk in the banking-house of J. C. Leonard & Co., in the city of Beardstown, and remained constantly in their employ, faithfully discharging his duties, until he entered the army. When the first company was organized in Cass county by Capt. Thomas Thompson, for the war, in the spring of 1861, Chas. A. Eames left his situation and a salary of seven hundred dollars per annum, for the position of a private soldier in Company A of the 14th Regiment. Some of his associates sought to dissuade him, but the noble youth was fully determined to give his services to his country. Whatever the dangers and privations might be, he was sure to reap the rich reward of an approving conscience.

After serving two or three months in the 14th, he was granted a furlough, with permission to recruit. After recruiting some time, he, with his men, were attached to Company G of the 32d Regiment Illinois Volunteers, of which he was elected 2d Lieut. Co. G was commanded by Capt. Jonathan Moore—the regiment by Col. John Logan.   This regiment held Fort Henry while General Grant's army besieged and captured Fort Donelson. While there, Lieut. Eames acted as Assistant Adjutant of the regiment.

The phenomena of mind is not always truly made by externals. Lieut. Eames was only known and appreciated by those who came in contact with him ; he was reserved in his manner, and generally taciturn with those whose age seemed to him to demand an acknowledgment of superiority.   Mr. Leonard, in whose employ he had been for seven years, had the most implicit confidence in his accuracy and integrity.   The connection of the two partook more of the character of a paternal relation than one based upon mere interest.   No heart was more sad than that of his old friend and patron when the young Lieutenant was consigned to his early tomb.

In the army, by reason of the close association necessitated by the discipline, he soon became endeared to all the members of the company, and especially to the officers of the regiment. In the organization of the 32d, it was, like nearly all other volunteer regiments, composed of undisciplined officers and men, and unskilled in the science of war.   An opportunity was, therefore, afforded to those whose minds were adapted to the science, to recommend themselves to the notice of their superiors.   Lieut. Eames, though unassuming in his manner, was vigilant and energetic in the performance of his duties, and hence displayed those qualities of mind that recommended him to the regard of his commanding officer.   It was stated by Col. Logan that he was the best disciplinarian in the regiment ; never did he see any one that learned the tactics with such facility, and, in the field, his mind seemed to comprehend combinations intuitively.

At the battle of Shiloh, Captain Moore, being advanced in years, was unable to lead the company to the field, and the 1st Lieutenant, whose fighting proclivities led him to the river, the command devolved upon Lieut. Eames.   On the 6th of April, the first day of the battle, Company G was ordered to the support of a battery, which the enemy endeavored to take. When the company took a position near it, the Lieut. ordered his men to lie down; and while they were partially protected from the murderous fire of the enemy, Eames stood up a little in the rear and calmly surveyed the field of carnage, until orders came to take another position. During this time the fire from the enemy on and about the battery was severe and incessant. Presently, orders came to the company to half-wheel and march to the left, and in executing this order they had to cross a fence. Just after crossing, Lieut. Eames was struck with a ball and fell dead, pierced through the heart. When the battle was over, on the evening of the next day, his comrades found him on the same spot where he died, and carried him from the ground.

Thus fell the noble youth, the affectionate son, the pride and joy of a mother's heart. It is said that "death loves a shining mark." The ball that pierced his heart could find no more shining mark on the bloody field of Shiloh. A life with high hopes, with the promise of distinction in the field, and honor and sweet enjoyment in the peaceful walks of life, was offered up on the altar of his country.

During his leisure hours, Lieut. Eames had applied himself to the study of German, and had mastered that language. While in the service he carried with him a German Testament, and after the battle of Shiloh, the book, with his name in it, was found on the field and brought to his mother.

His brother, Francis C. Eames, on hearing of his death, proceeded to Pittsburg Landing, procured the body and brought it home for interment.

The memory of his sweet and peaceful life may be effaced, but the blood of the martyr that enriches the soil of the Union shall not be forgotten by a grateful people.

PRIVATE AUSTIN.

ABRAHAM HARRISON AUSTIN, son of Freeman and Phœbe Austin, was born on the 16th of February, A. D. 1844, in the town of Porter, county of Niagara, state of New York, where the family remained until the autumn of 1850, when they removed to the town of Ophir, Lasalle county, Illinois, which has since been their residence.

Abraham was studious, energetic and determined, and endowed with quick and accurate perception, so that whatever subject his mind grappled with, it was as speedily mastered.

On the war breaking out, he wished to enlist, but his age prevented him. The solicitations of his friends held him back until the call of "six hundred thousand more," in August, 1862, when no further persuasion could influence him. His only reply to their entreaties was—"My country needs men; many must go, and I am one. Many of those who go will fall, and it may as well be me as some others. I would rather die than live to see my country destroyed by traitors. If that day ever dawns, I do not want to live to see it."

He enlisted under Capt. W. H. Collins, Co. D, 104th Illinois Infantry, commanded by Col. A. B. Moore, on the 14th August, 1862, and was with the regiment through all its weary marches, sleeping most of the time in his blanket on the ground without a tent, until the battle of Hartsville, Tenn., on the 7th December, 1862, when he fell to the ground, pierced through the head by a rebel bullet. He lingered in terrible pain for about twenty hours, and died in the hospital, and was buried in a soldier's grave in the village churchyard, among his brother soldiers who "fought and bravely fell" on that field of battle.

His Captain says of him: "He was one of the best, if not *the best* soldier in the company—perhaps in the regiment." And, officially, in his final papers, he remarks: "He was ever a brave and faithful soldier. *Never asked* to be relieved from duty. He fell fighting at Hartsville, Dec. 7th, 1862."

LIEUTENANT WOOD.

Lieut. WELLINGTON WOOD, son of Timothy and Rebecca Wood, was born in the beautiful manufacturing town of Moline, Rock Island county, Illinois, on the 3d day of September, 1839. His father was one of the earliest settlers, and one of the parties who laid out the town in lots for settlement. Lieut. Wood here grew up a high-spirited and gifted youth, and fond of the natural sports of this period of gladsome life. During the spring of 1857, he attended the school at Evanston, Ill., and for some time the High School of Moline. He had an excellent and retentive memory, and his natural powers were of a high order, which we find first exercised in reading the "Declaration of Independence," for a Fourth of July celebration on Rock Island, in the year 1859.

At the age of twenty-one years, he, with a school class-mate, (C. W. Skinner, 5th Wis. Regt.) wrote a play in six acts, which was considered of some merit, and performed it at the Moline High School Exhibition.

He had commenced the study of law, but when the war broke out, the names of Scott and Ellsworth inspired him with emotions of patriotic ardor, and on the first call he enlisted as a private in the 19th Regt. Ill. Vols., (the Chicago Zouaves) now so noted for their discipline and fighting qualities. While at Chicago he was a candidate for the 2d Lieutenancy, but failing to acquire that position, he was immediately appointed Orderly Sergeant, in which capacity he served during the march through Missouri. At Cairo, Ill., he was temporarily attached to the 27th Regt. Ill. Volunteers, as Drill Master, for a period of four months. He was commissioned as 2d Lieut. of Company H, December 1st, 1861.

He was a graceful rider, and it ever appeared that his great object, his particular forte, was to ride horses and command men. He was a splendid marksman with both pistol and rifle, and as a sportsman, for "shooting on the wing," seldom met his equal;

7

in fact he excelled in almost everything he attempted, which
made him a favorite with all who knew him.

He combined in his nature all those elements essential to respect and love. Possessed of an active mind, disciplined and
refined by education, he united with it a kind and gentle disposition, rendering him at once a friend whose friendship, based
upon truth and honor, would outlive the cold embrace of death.
Manfully did he discharge his duties as a soldier. The records
of this war can point to but few (if any) nobler examples of
heroic devotion to his country than that of Lieut. Wellington
Wood.

During his campaigns with the 19th, he did not neglect writing home to his parents. In a letter to his mother, he writes:

Be comforted, dear mother, with the reflection that your absent soldier
sons * cannot, *will* not forget a mother's teachings, even amid the rough associations that now surround them. Although they may seem careless and
indifferent, a mother's influence is with them still. And now I must close,
bidding you be happy in the thought that your boys, now that they are far
from home, appreciate and love you more than ever, and we earnestly hope
that we may be able, in some measure, to reward you for your goodness and
devotion towards us.

In another letter, the Lieutenant writes:

Have you heard anything of Pitts? If you have, let me know; and now,
my dear father and mother, *you have two sons* in the Union Army. I hope
you do not regret it. The various changes and vicissitudes of war have widely
separated us. We may be thrown together in the heat of battle. We may
both fall—or *one* may fall, and the other live. If this should prove true, let
he that lives rejoice in his brother's blood, shed in a glorious cause. And
now, my dear parents, I hope you may ever cherish an honorable and happy
remembrance of your soldier sons.

Expecting a battle within a few days, he says:

But we are prepared for the trial. Those who survive will avenge the blood
of those who fall. Should it be my fate, dear mother, to be numbered among
the latter in the coming struggle, only remember that yours is the sorrow
common to thousands of hearts which have been lacerated and torn by the
fall of dear ones in the bloody strife. Think of the words of Ellsworth.
Cherish the consolation that I am engaged in the performance of a sacred

---

* This has reference to himself and his younger brother, Pitts R. Wood, of the 2d Iowa
Infantry, who has been in nearly all of the hard fought battles except Stone River and
Lookout Mountain. He was one of the first over the walls of Donelson. His comrade in
battle was shot down on one side of him, and his Captain (Slaymaker) on the other, during
the last mentioned engagement.

duty. Our country is writhing and bleeding on the altar of madness and treason, and *my* arm shall *never* be withheld as long as strength remains to strike a blow.

In another letter :

Dear parents and friends, rest assured that I shall do my duty at all hazards and under all circumstances. In the words of the lofty Ellsworth, (whose picture is now before me,) cherish the consolation that I am engaged in the performance of a sacred duty, and wherever I am placed, if my name shall happen to be pronounced, it shall never be attended with disgrace—NEVER.

In another :

What a sad condition our country is in; and the gulf between the North and the South is widening. We can scarcely hope to see the two sections re-united in peace and harmony again for many years. The South is getting more and more embittered against the North every day. This rebellion, which our Government at first thought to suppress in so short a time, has assumed a magnitude which will take years to effectually wipe out. But the duty of every patriot and lover of liberty is as plain as it was in the days of the revolution. The liberty of our fathers must be sustained at any price. Let every institution and law incompatible with a free and enlightened government be sacrificed—yes, even slavery, the bone and sinew, the root and branch and soul of the rebellion—be scattered and swept from the land and forever obliterated, to give place to a freedom and a nation which shall exist through all time.

C. W. Skinner, writing to a friend (a teacher in the Moline High School,) thus speaks of the Lieutenant :

But alas! those pleasant times can never be recalled. The old members * of our rhetoric class can never be assembled on the *hill* as in days of yore. The most brilliant star has fallen. Not among the friends of home and the scenes of his childhood did he fall, but amid the roar of cannon and rattling of musketry, Will Wood received his call to leave all things earthly. The host of friends he leaves behind will take comfort in the thought that he died in a noble cause, fighting for the Stars and Stripes, that symbol of freedom which now floats proudly over his grave. Like a brave soldier he breathed his last, and while we mourn him as lost to us, let us who still remain in the ranks, fight with a sterner purpose.

From the tone of several of his letters, it would seem he had a presentiment that he would never return to gladden the family hearth. In writing to a friend, he says :

I am unable to say when I shall see you; the nearest I can come to it is *sometime*, I trust. But, perhaps, I *never* shall. If so, I hope to be remem-

* I was a member of that "rhetoric class," and remember Will's writing several beautiful compositions. We usually called him "Young Thunder," on account of his deep, rich voice, or "Our Standard Bearer," in consideration of his beautiful pieces.

bered as one who, with all his faults and imperfections, loved his friends, *and loved his country.* If my spirit might be permitted to linger about the abodes of earth, it could hear no prouder encomium or behold not a more glorious inscription on my tomb than—*He died for his country.*

Illustrative of the manner in which he conducted himself while with the 19th, the following incidents are related: One morning, his uncle (D. B. Sears, Q. M. of the 27th Ill.) and Gen. Palmer were talking together when the Lieut. passed by, and as he passed on, said, " Good morning, uncle," at the same time saluting the two officers in his usual graceful manner. When he was out of hearing, the General turned to Sears with: "Who was that young man?" Sears told him it was Lt. Wood. " Who is Lt. Wood; I noticed he called you uncle?" " Yes," said Sears, " he is a nephew of mine." " Well," said the General, " *that was the most perfect salute I have seen since I've been in the army.*" Amongst his comrades it was frequently said, that whatever Will Wood did was according to "Army Regulations." At an exhibition drill of the 19th, on the stage in Nashville, Tenn., Wood was highly applauded for his skill. In writing to his friends afterwards, he thus characteristically spoke of the circumstance :

"The papers puffed us, . . . and . . . The rebels cursed us."

At the battle of Stone River, the Lieutenant was at the head and a few feet in advance of his company, waving his sword above his head and cheering on his men, when the fatal ball, supposed to have been shot by a rebel sharpshooter, struck him just to the right of the clasp of his sword belt. The ball passed through the belt, but lodged in his body, the force of which knocked him down, and sent his sword several feet from him. After he fell, his first words were—" Give me my sword." His comrades placed him behind two cottonwood or sycamore trees, and went on to assist in taking the rebel battery, and, as they came back a few minutes afterwards, they found the Lieut. had recrossed the river ; but they never knew how he had got over. They secured an ambulance and conveyed him to the hospital ; and while lying there beside Col. Scott, the Surgeon came and examined the Colonel, saying, " *You're* all right ;" * then turning

* Appearances were then favorable for Col. Scott's recovery, and were so up to within a short time even of his death.

to the Lieut., said, "I wish I could say as much for *you*." This statement, to one so lately full of vigor, somewhat discomposed the Lieut., and he anxiously bent his eyes upon the Doctor, with the eager inquiry—"What! you don't think it's going to kill me, do you, Doctor?" "Much depends upon yourself," was the only reply that could then be given. His strength of constitution did not avail him, however, in this his last extremity, and he passed away on the following Sunday.

The annexed tribute to worth and bravery, which appeared in the Chicago *Tribune*, announced to his friends, the fate of the gallant Lieutenant:

HOSPITAL, NASHVILLE, Tenn., Jan. 30, 1863.

It hath pleased Almighty God to take from us Lieut. Wellington Wood, of Company H, 19th (Chicago Zouaves) Illinois Volunteers. The gallant Wood fell in battle at Stone River, while bravely leading his men in action, in defense of his country's cause. He was a youth in years, but a host within himself, and endeared to every member of our unconquered and gallant regiment. In him we have lost an officer of great merit, a perfect gentleman in deportment, and a thorough soldier. On picket duty and upon the battle-field he was always in the right place. He was not only an honor to his regiment but to the country he defended, and when his manly form was stricken down in battle his comrades in arms bore his corpse to a place of safety, and secured it for his friends at home—Moline, Illinois. Moline, you have lost a citizen, a soldier, and a gentleman. Young and comely, brave as the bravest, he was one of the many heroes of the 19th who fell in that battle ; but there are yet enough left, who will avenge the death of our brother soldier, Wellington Wood. The 19th, one and all, deeply sympathize with his friends at home in his death ; but they may rest assured that the army to which he belonged will long cherish the name of Lieut. Wellington Wood.

WM. P. WHITE,
Corporal, Co. G, 19th Illinois Volunteers.

Mr. R. K. Swan, of Moline, was dispatched for the body, and on returning with it, funeral services were held in the Congregational Church in Moline. Escort duty was performed by a company of soldiers from Post McClellan, under command of Capt. Robt. M. Littler. At the church, prayer was offered by the Rev. Mr. Milliken, the pastor. The sermon was preached by the Rev. Mr. Hitchcock, from Matt. ii. 15, and Luke ii. 35.

He was buried with military honors in Moline Cemetery, and on the monument which marks his resting place, is the wished-for inscription—

"HE DIED FOR HIS COUNTRY."

COLONEL ROBERTS.

Col. GEORGE W. ROBERTS, son of Pratt Roberts and Ann Wilson Roberts, was born in East Goshen township, Chester county, Pa., Oct. 2d, 1833. In May, 1844, he entered the celebrated school of A. Bolmar, at Westchester, Pa., where he remained four years. He completed his academic studies at the institution kept by Charles Bartlett, known as "College Hill," at Poughkeepsie, N. Y., and in May, 1854, entered the Sophomore class in Yale College, where he graduated with high honors in June, 1857. He received the degree of Master of Arts from his *Alma Mater* in July, 1860.

He studied law in the office of Joseph J. Lewis, Esq., in West Chester, Pa., and was admitted to the bar, Jan. 8th, 1858.

In 1859, he was the candidate of the Anti-Lecompton Democrats of Chester county, for the office of District Attorney, and although not elected, he received the full vote of the party.

He practised law in his native county until the spring of 1860, when he removed to Chicago, Illinois, and entered the office of E. S. Smith, Esq., a prominent member of the bar of that city, where he remained in the active practice of his profession until June, 1861.

A few days after the fatal error of the South in the bombardment of Fort Sumter, he resolved to do what he could to restore the authority of the Government, believing, as he said, that it was the duty of every man to do all in his power to put down the rebellion; that he had health and strength, and should lend his best exertions, and *life* if necessary, to the support of his country. He became a member of a company of citizens associated chiefly for instruction in military tactics, and drilled in the ranks for about two months. He then commenced recruiting for the 42d Regiment (1st Regiment Douglas Brigade) of Illinois Volunteers, to which object he devoted time and money. Immediately upon its organization he went into camp with it, and whatever of inconvenience or privation there was to be endured, he shared it in common with the humblest soldier under his command. He devoted himself to the study of military science, for which he had a decided taste and capacity, with a zeal and ardor which knew no relaxation, and rendered himself fully competent to discharge all the duties which any position he might be called to fill should demand of him.

On the 22d of July, 1861, he received a commission as Major of the 42d Illinois, and with this regiment soon thereafter left Chicago for the seat of war. On the 17th of September of the same year, he was elected Lieutenant Colonel, and on the 24th of December following, he was commissioned Colonel, in the place of Col. Webb, then recently deceased, which position he held at the time of his death.

Col. Roberts, with his regiment, took their place in the march with Gen. Fremont to Springfield, Mo. He distinguished himself at New Madrid; had command for a time at Fort Holt, near Cairo; was from thence ordered to Columbus, Kentucky, after its evacuation by the rebels; next proceeded to Island No. 10, where, in a daring and brilliant expedition, amidst the howling of the tempest and the gloom of night, he spiked the guns of a rebel battery, which had been successful in preventing the passage of our gunboats—an enterprise which men pronounced it madness to attempt. This was effected without the loss of a single man, although a minie ball sped within an inch of the Colonel's ear, as he stood up in the boat, after the feat was accomplished, calling to his marines to send her home.

He was thence ordered to Fort Pillow, from which place he accompanied Gen. Pope up the Tennessee River, and covered himself with distinguished honor at the battle of Farmington Roads, where, with his single regiment (the 42d Illinois) he held at bay for hours a rebel force five times greater than his own, and by his cool and determined valor, saved the day and prevented a defeat. At the siege of Corinth he was in command of a brigade, and rendered services which placed him in a position of most enviable prominence, and secured for him a name which few may hope to achieve. He was in the advance, and was the first man to enter Corinth. In a private letter to his father, dated May 15th, 1862, Col. Roberts says: "Brave old Palmer, who was last on the field, galloped down the line in an ecstasy of joy : ' gallant 42d,' he cried, as he swung his hat, ' I am proud to be your General ; I wish I was the father of every one of you.' I felt proud and happy to think that my men had won and received so distinguished a compliment."

He was thence ordered to Memphis, where he again distinguished himself by the efficacy of his movements against guerrilla bands, and in the surprise and capture of prominent and dangerous guerrilla chiefs. From thence, with his regiment, he was transferred to the army under command of Maj. Gen. Rosecrans, and at the battle of Murfreesboro', while in command of the 3d Brigade of Sheridan's Division, in the terrible onset made on the right wing of the Union army, on Wednesday the 31st of December, 1862, he fell with his face to the enemy, and met a death as glorious as his career had been noble and manly.

A writer in the N. Y. *Tribune*, describing the battles, and speaking of the casualties of the day, says : "Noble Roberts, Col. of the 42d Illinois, and commanding Sheridan's 3d Brigade, distinguished at New Madrid, Island No. 10, and the siege of Corinth, and conspicuous for his manly, personal beauty and chivalrous deportment, was struck down forever." He died as he would have wished to die. Amid the awful crash and shock of battle, the sky blackened with its smoke, and the earth shaking with its roar, gallantly holding his little band to face the fearful onset they were compelled to meet, that others might be saved— his strong arm raised, and his broad breast bared in defense of the country he loved so well—his soul took its flight.

And thus he died—so young, so noble, so brave. The poet has sadly but truly said :

> " The good die first,
> And they whose hearts are dry as summer's dust,
> Burn to the socket."

Had he lived a few days longer he would have received a commission as Brigadier General, the order for it having been issued. His remains were brought to his father's residence, Chester county, Pa., from whence, on the 19th day of January, 1863, they were conveyed to the Oaklands Cemetery.

Col. Roberts possessed a clear, discriminating and vigorous mind. In college he was noted for his mathematical talents ; and his early devotion to the science, founded on the most self-evident of truths, was clearly visible in his modes of thought, and gave character to his intellect. The knowledge which he acquired lay not in his head a crude, cumbersome map—his discriminating mind digested it and made it part of himself.

His mode of expressing himself was felicitous. He was endowed with the gift of language in no ordinary degree. His quick and ready intellect would call up from the rich and varied stores of his information whatever thought or fact the occasion demanded. His colloquial powers were remarkable, and he was a most genial and entertaining companion. He was a man of noble impulses, of high aspirations and lofty aims, and possessed a most kind and generous heart. Those courtesies which so smooth and beautify the otherwise strong and jarring intercourse of the legal profession, were *pre-eminently* his. A prominent trait in his character was to master whatever he undertook. No impediment, however great, could ever slacken his efforts or dishearten his ambition; whatever he did was done with the will and purpose and strength of a man. His physical strength was great, and he seemed to possess corresponding mental ability. He was always cool, and deliberate, and self-possessed, never disturbed nor disorganized, let the storm be ever so great around him.

The history of this war has not furnished the record of a man of more heroism and manly courage; and of that long list of military heroes who have died in their efforts for the liberties of mankind, there is not *one* whose memory will live longer, or whose fame will shine brighter than that of George W. Roberts.

On the announcement of his death, meetings of the members of the bar of Chester county, Pa., and of Chicago, Ill., of which he had been a member, were held, and appropriate resolutions adopted.

CAPTAIN SMITH.

Capt. JOHN G. SMITH was born in Whitehall, Washington co., New York, December 11, 1835, and when about six years old immigrated with his relations to DeKalb county, Illinois. This country being then new, his means of education were limited; but his naturally inquisitive mind thirsted for knowledge, and as he grew to maturer age, he took especial pains to acquire something more than a *common* education. He was a student for about two years at Mt. Morris Seminary, Ogle county, after which he was engaged about three years in teaching in Missouri. His disposition was kind, gentle and social. He had an agreeable word and pleasant look for every one. His friends were *many;* his enemies, if any he had, were *few.* At the breaking out of the rebellion he was still in Missouri, and narrowly escaped being drafted into the rebel army. Immediately on his return to his old home in Illinois, he volunteered into the service of his country, and was chosen 1st Lieutenant in Co. B, 8th Illinois Cavalry. He was mustered into the United States service Sept. 18, 1861, and, July 17, 1862, upon the resignation of Captain Whitney, he was promoted to the Captaincy, which position he held until his death.

In the cause of his country Capt. Smith was a most earnest and ardent worker. The true spirit of patriotism fired his bosom. His heart and soul were in the work, and his hand was ever ready to do what his heart and soul conceived.

As a companion in arms, he was sociable, affable and kind; modest and unassuming, yet true to himself and his country. He was universally esteemed by his brother officers and beloved by his men. As an officer, he was brave, daring and heroic. He never faltered in the presence of the enemy, and his delight always was to move upon the foe.

He went to the Potomac with the 8th Illinois Cavalry, and was never absent from his regiment. In the camp, on picket,

in its long and weary marches, and in its numerous and severe
skirmishes and battles, he shared with his regiment all its toils
and dangers, and performed his part in making for it an enviable history.

In March, 1862, he marched with his regiment to the Rappahannock, pressing the enemy as he fell back from Manassas.
In April of that year he sailed with the regiment down the
Potomac to the Peninsula; was in the battle of Williamsburg,
Mechanicsville and Gaines Mills, and shared in the perils of that
memorable campaign of the seven days' struggle around Richmond, and in that famous retreat to Yorktown. He arrived in
Alexandria on the last day of August, with the regiment, just in
time to enter upon the Maryland campaign, and here again he
confronted the enemy heroically at Poolesville, Queenstown,
Boonsboro' and Antietam. Recrossing the Potomac, he had
part in the fall campaign in Virginia, meeting the rebel hosts at
Philamont, Union, Upperville, Barbour's Cross Roads, Amis-
ville and Little Washington.

It was at Barbour's Cross Roads that companies A and B,
under the leadership of Captains Forsyth and Smith, charged
upon a rebel regiment and drove them from their guns; but being
unsupported, after a sharp and close contest with greatly superior
numbers, they were compelled to fall back with a loss of two
killed and five wounded.

Capt. Smith passed the winter of 1862–63 with his men, most
of the time on picket duty. The regiment was sixty days on
duty in King George county, guarding from the Rappahannock
to the Potomac.

Engaged in this perilous and arduous duty, and exposed to
the rains and storms of winter, ofttimes without shelter or tents,
Capt. Smith was never known to murmur or utter one word of
complaint. He endured all and suffered all like a true patriot
and hero, for his country.

He entered upon the summer campaign of 1863 with as bright
hopes as any of his comrades, but Providence saw things differ-
ently. In that most desperate and bloody cavalry fight of the
war, Beverly Ford, on the 9th of June, Capt. Smith, while holding the advancing enemy in check until our own scattered troops

would rally and form, was wounded by a minie ball in the left knee, breaking and splintering the bones. Still unflinching, clinging to his horse, he performed the assigned duty, checked the enemy, and led his squadron in good order from the contest.

From the field he was borne to the Seminary Hospital at Georgetown, D. C. Here the surgeon in charge decided *amputation* to be necessary. Even this operation failed in its antici-. pated effect, and on the night of June 16, 1863, the brave Capt. Smith died. He died for his country—he died as many brave soldiers have died—*like a hero*—with no loved ones near to calm his last moments, and to whisper to him of heaven. He had fondly hoped they might come; but a brother-in-law and sister did not arrive until after he had expired. His remains, embalmed and wreathed in flowers by strangers' fair hands, were forwarded to his friends at Sycamore, DeKalb county, Illinois, for interment. And near that beautiful town, on the prairies, calmly sleeps the noble warrior, lamented by his friends, and mourned by all who knew him. Of such are the armies of the republic composed, and by such suffering and anguish is our beloved country to be redeemed.

When taking his final leave of friends and home for active service in the field, Capt. Smith penned, *impromptu*, on a blank leaf in a book he then presented to a much-loved and favorite sister, the following beautiful lines, which not only show his goodness of heart, and something of the genius of the "rising man," but indicate clearly his motives for leaving the quiet of home for the field of deadly strife at the call of his country.

MUST GO.

The Ship of State rides on the sea,
　　Where foundering waves around her roll,
And there's a voice, which says to me.
　　Gird on thy strength and nerve thy soul
To serve thy country—thy duty first.
When she by traitors is accursed.

Hence upon the tented field,
　　Enthusiastically I go,
Determined not to leave or yield,
　　Whilst thou, my country, hast a foe ;
And if in strife my life shall cease.
In a soldier's grave I'll rest in peace.

I'll be remembered, sister dear,
　　Although my lot is far away :
Thy following prayers methinks I'll hear,
　　At morning's dawn and close of day.
High heaven rewards the good and true,
And blessings thence shall visit you.
To say good-by rings pleasure's knell,
But it must be said.—Adieu! Farewell!

　　　　　　　　　　　　　　J. G. SMITH.

Sycamore, October 13th, 1861.

LIEUTENANT CLARK.

Lieut. DANIEL NEWTON CLARK was born in Hartford, Vt., but at a very early age removed with his mother to Massachusetts. His early years were passed near the sea shore, where the wild waves chanted strange, sad music in his boyish ears, for beneath them his brave father lay buried.

Thirsting for knowledge, whilst yet a boy, he left his home with only his mother's blessing and the silent influences of her pious teachings to help him on his way. Fortune was chary of her gifts to him, yet, nothing disheartened, he struggled on until he had fitted himself for college, and entered Rochester University, New York, at the age of 24 years. Finding at length his means insufficient to go through a course of study, he left school, and with one "longing, lingering look" toward the old institution, and a deep-drawn sigh for what "might have been," he turned his steps to Illinois, where he spent his time alternately in teaching and agricultural pursuits.

Earnest and faithful in whatever his hands found to do, hopeful in adverse fortune, and possessed of sterling integrity of character, he won for himself many firm friends.

When the great war-cry sounded through the land, he paused and listened till his heart was moved to a high and noble purpose, and though with a strong presentiment that he would fall on the battle-field, his name stood enrolled among the first who offered themselves to their country, where his brave heart and strong right hand did nobly their duty till laid powerless by death.

He enlisted as a private in Co. B, 15th Illinois Volunteers, but had successfully won the position of 1st Lieutenant at the time of his death. The decimated ranks of the old 15th speak more loudly than tongue may utter or pen shadow forth, of their heroic deeds and sad, untimely deaths.

Donelson, Shiloh, Vicksburg and Jackson, bear each a proud

record of their bravery and devotion. Some lie there uncoffined; others have been borne back, as was the subject of this notice, to slumber near the places which so short a time before they had left in the flush of health and pride of manhood.

In a letter to a friend, after the battle of Shiloh, he says:

The first thing I saw, as the smoke of battle cleared a little on the enemy's side, was a large, new, secesh flag. Never shall I forget my feelings as the breeze unfolded it to our view. What! thought I, the *Stars* and *Stripes* give way for that Rebel flag? Never! and our hands and hearts were nerved with new strength to face the storm of leaden hail which seemed rained upon us.

Again, he says:

When I came off the ground, after seeing so many of our brave boys who had fought their last battle, I thought, what has been *their* fate may ere long be mine; yet I cannot say at that moment I felt intimidated, or to regret the step I had taken. No! though I cannot banish thoughts of friends and home, I am ready to meet the enemy. There is one happy thought—"It is not all of death to die." Though my body may fall on an enemy's soil, and even lie there unburied, thank God! death was never written of the soul.

Lieut. Clark died at Natchez, Miss., Sept. 23d, 1863, of fever, which terminated in congestive chills, after an illness of three days. Ever looking beyond this life to the *better* life to come, he was ready to go when he heard the call, "Come up higher."

LIEUTENANT ADAMS.

Lieut. ROBERT A. ADAMS, son of James H. and Eliza Adams, was born in the township of Green, Adams county, Ohio, on the 31st of March, 1841, from whence he emigrated to Whiteside county, Ill., in 1852. From that time he followed the pursuits of farming, and by his kindness and industry, soon won the esteem of most of his acquaintances.

When the rebellion broke out, he took a firm stand in favor of our glorious Union, and would have joined the army at the first call for volunteers, but his elder brother having left the family roof, and his younger brother having joined the 8th Ill. Cavalry, he considered it his duty to stay at home and take care of his parents. In 1862, however, when his country called for more men, he then felt it his privilege to give a helping hand to put down the wicked destroyers of peace and unity, and immediately went to work in assisting to raise a company of volunteers for the service. On the 9th of August, the company was organized at Albany, Whiteside county, and went into camp at Princeton, Bureau county, and from thence they went to Camp Douglas, Chicago, where they became Co. F of the 93d Regiment Illinois Volunteers. He was appointed 1st Sergeant of his company, and filled this position to the satisfaction of all his superior officers. He was never known to have omitted any duty, thereby gaining the regard and respect of his comrades.

In writing home to his friends, while at Camp Douglas, he portrays the kindly feeling of brothers in arms thus:

I am writing to-night without having tasted any food, as all the orderlies of the regiment took a vote of their companies on giving our suppers to a paroled Ohio regiment from Harper's Ferry, who, for three days, had nothing to eat excepting a few crackers. The vote was unanimous. I felt happy and slept more soundly after seeing those hungry soldiers eat our rations. This is the kind of material the 93d Regiment is made out of, who will never bring dishonor upon the grand Stars and Stripes. Trusting in a higher power than man, I shall endeavor to do my duty as a soldier. Fear not, dear parents, for me. If I fall, it will be for my country and that dear old flag. May it long wave.

In a letter to his sister, after speaking of home and friends, he says:

Alas! where will be the many voices which used to mingle with ours in days past and gone? Some will be sleeping their last sleep beneath a southern soil, while others will be marching onwards, trusting in God for victory to our arms. Friends need not grieve, but be comforted, for man never fell in a more glorious or more nobler cause.

Friends of the "Tornado Co." [the title of his company] can rest assured that they enlisted for the Union cause, and when called upon to go into action, will give a good account of themselves; and if any of them fall, all that they ask is to be remembered as among those who have done their duty as true patriots.

On the resignation of the 1st Lieutenancy of the company, Sergeant Adams was duly elected 2d Lieutenant on the 20th of March, 1863, at Memphis, Tenn. His regiment was ordered from thence to Lake Providence, under Gen. Grant. He was in the Yazoo Expedition, afterwards returning to Milliken's Bend, and from there to Grand Gulf, Raymond, Jackson, and Champion Hills.

On the 16th of May, Lieut. Adams received two wounds—a severe one in the left side, and another through the thigh and groin—which caused his death on the 29th, at the military hospital on Ball's Plantation, near Champion Hills, Miss. His father says:

His career was short, but his memory will remain in our hearts, and the cause for which we gave him will have our all, if need be, so that this accursed rebellion may be put down.

THE BROTHERS McCLINTOCK.

CAPTAIN McCLINTOCK.

Capt. HIRAM McCLINTOCK, eldest son of James and Phebeett McClintock, was born on the 18th of October, 1840, in Cook county, Illinois. His father being a farmer, Hiram was bred to the pursuits of a country life, until he attained the age of twenty, when he went to Pulaski, Ill., and taught school during the winter of 1860–1. In the spring he returned home, and at the call of the President for three months volunteers, he, with other associates, enlisted with Capt. Hugunin, on the 24th of April, 1861, whose command was mustered in as Company K of the 12th Illinois Infantry, Col. John McArthur commanding. The regiment immediately went to Springfield, as a rendezvous for drilling. About two weeks afterwards it moved to Casey-ville, where they spent four weeks in guarding the railroads. From this place they went to Cairo, where the regiment re-mained until mustered out of service. Hiram, not being well at this time, did not re-enlist, but returned home.

Soon after, a number of young men in Lyons formed a com-pany for military drill, and Hiram was chosen Captain. They continued their organization until the winter set in. He re-sumed his occupation of school teaching, and continued thereat till August. His patriotism at this time became too fervid for him to remain longer out of the service of his country, when men were so much needed to face a desperate enemy and save the government from the grasp of the despot, and he left school to commence the work of recruiting a company of infantry. L. Riley, a citizen, having got a muster roll, he and Hiram put their names to it, and went on together in getting up the com-pany, in which they succeeded. Hiram was elected 1st Lieut., and commissioned on the 5th of September, 1862. The com-pany took its place in the 127th Regiment Illinois Volunteers as Co. H. The regiment remained at Camp Douglas until the end of October, when it went to Memphis, Tenn. At this place they were joined with other troops and marched to the Tallahatchie, returning to Memphis. From the latter place they took transports to the Yazoo swamps, and fought the battle of Walnut Hills. This was the first engagement in which the Lieutenant took part, and from the testimony of both officers and men, no braver soldier was there. After that, the army moved to Arkansas Post, where the Federal arms were more successful.

About the middle of January, 1863, he went with the army to Young's Point and worked at the canal. In March, he went with what was termed the Black Bayou Expedition, returning to Young's Point.

At this time the captaincy of the company being vacant, Hiram was promoted and commissioned Captain, March 13th. After the expedition referred to, the 127th was engaged clearing a bayou of logs and brush, until the beginning of May, when Grant's army started for Grand Gulf and the rear of Vicksburg. He was at the battle of Champion Hills, where he conducted himself bravely. On the 19th of May, a general charge was made on the rebel fortifications. Capt. McClintock, with his men, had scarcely reached the defences, before which his Orderly and several others had been cut down, when he received two shots—one through the head, and the other in the breast—and fell dead instantly. Col. Eldridge, in communicating the sad intelligence to his parents, remarks :

My regiment is deprived of one of its bravest and most promising officers, the army of one it could ill afford to spare. He stood by me in the thickest storm of battle on that fearful day.

CORPORAL McCLINTOCK.

Corp. WILLIAM McCLINTOCK, the second son, was born on the 28th of March, 1842, in Cook county, Ill., and like his brother Hiram, followed the pursuits of farming. Feeling it to be his duty to answer to the call of his country, he left the plow and volunteered into Co. H of the 127th Regiment Illinois Volunteers, and was mustered in at Chicago on the 12th of August, 1862. Soon afterwards he was appointed Corporal. He remained with the regiment at Camp Douglas until the 1st of November, when they moved to Memphis and the Tallahatchie, returning to the former place; from thence, on transports, to the Yazoo swamps, and was engaged in the battle of Walnut Hills. At the close of that contest, he was taken sick with measles. which complaint was followed by typhoid fever. He was on the hospital boat at Arkansas Post, then taken to Young's Point in January, 1863, where he remained sick, and finally died with chronic diarrhœa on the 27th of February. His remains were disinterred and brought home by his father, and buried in the family ground at Lyonsville. His superior officers and associates in arms speak of him as a brave soldier, and ever ready to do his duty. He was of a quiet and cheerful disposition, and beloved by all of his acquaintances.

Brothers in life, brothers in battle, in death they were not long divided.

CAPTAIN WOODRUFF.

Capt. JOSEPH WOODRUFF was born in Syracuse, Onondaga county, N. Y., on the 7th of September, 1829, from which place he emigrated to Lasalle county, Illinois, in 1843.

He appears to have been patriotically inclined even in his more youthful days; for we find him answering to his country's call for troops for the Mexican war, enlisting in the ranks, and serving faithfully there until the close of that sanguinary contest.

Returning home, he settled in Marseilles, Lasalle county, where he was engaged in mercantile pursuits, until the breaking out of the present Rebellion. Fully convinced that his country demanded his manly assistance, he soon left the counting room for the camp. He recruited a company of men, and with them joined the 39th Illinois Regiment, (Yates Phalanx,) and was commissioned by his Excellency, Governor Yates, as Captain of Company K of that regiment, in September, 1861.

He participated in all the varied campaigns and excessive labors of that regiment until the day of his death, which occurred on the 23d of September, 1863, in Fort Gregg, Morris Island, S. C., and was occasioned by the bursting of a shell thrown from the enemy's batteries on Sullivan's Island.

Unassuming, yet courteous in his bearing, Captain Woodruff was highly esteemed by his civilian friends, who have joined with the survivors of his old company in erecting a fitting monument to his memory.

His body was embalmed and sent by the officers of his regiment to Marseilles, where he leaves a widow and two children.

Perhaps no better expression of the high respect cherished for him by his comrades in arms can be given than is found in the following order, published on the occasion of his death, and the resolutions adopted by the field and line officers:

HEADQUARTERS 39TH ILL. VOLS., }
MORRIS ISLAND, S. C., Sept. 25th, 1863. }

Special Order, No. 63.

With profound sorrow the Lieut. Col. Commanding announces to the regiment the decease of Capt. Joseph Woodruff, of Co. K, 39th Ill. Regiment, who died in regimental hospital, Morris Island, S. C., Sept. 23d, 1863, a few hours after he received a fatal wound from the enemy's gun.

Capt. Woodruff was among the many brave men who, after the first repulse of our inexperienced army at Bull Run, rushed forth with martial spirit to support the flag of our troubled country, and vindicate the majesty of her laws by rebels ignored. Leaving a lucrative business, a large circle of firm friends and a young and confiding family, he collected around his country's standard a company of patriots, and led them from his village home, Marseilles, Lasalle county, Ill., to Camp Mather in Chicago, where he linked his destinies with the 39th Ill. Regiment. The long and winding war-path over which he has gallantly led his company, the severe hardships and stern privations he has patiently endured, and the unaffected bravery and deep-seated patriotism he has ever evinced, form a part of our regimental history, and hence need not here be enumerated.

He entered upon the operations before Charleston with quiet yet commendable enthusiasm, and from the day his regiment broke ground for the first fort on Folly Island, to the evening the missile of death met him in Fort Gregg, he exhibited a determination of purpose, remarked by many and surpassed by none.

The ranking officer in the line, he was frequently called to command the regiment, and his official ability was such, that his fellow officers looked anxiously forward to the time when promotion should be granted him as a meritorious reward, but in this, they are only too sadly disappointed. On the evening of the 23d inst., just as he was transmitting his instructions to the officer who relieved him of his command in Fort Gregg, a shell from Fort Moultrie burst among his men, killing several, and so wounding him in the side, that he soon died. He was conscious to the last, and apparently resigned to his sad fate.

As an officer, Capt. Woodruff had an enviable reputation: ever ready for duty, he was never known to murmur, or question the propriety of an order, however laborious or dangerous the duty it demanded. Socially, he was a man admired by all who knew him, and in his friendship he was honest and sincere. He has fallen in the midday of his manhood, and in the very fort from which was fired the first rebel gun at Fort Sumter, the vibrations of which so thrilled with energy the great northern heart. He has fallen, but he fell in defence of a principle deeply enshrined in every loyal breast, and for the unity and perpetuity of a country that shall gladly honor her gallant dead.

Let the virtues of the deceased be emulated by his bereaved comrades who survive him, and by whom his memory will doubtless be perpetuated with a pleasing sadness.

As a token of respect to the fallen brave, it is hereby ordered that the usual badge of mourning be worn by the officers of this regiment for the period of thirty days.

By command of

O. L. MANN,
Lieut. Col. Commanding Regt.

S. S. BRUCKER, 1st Lieut. and A. Adjt.

At a meeting of the officers of the 39th Regt. Ill. Volunteers, called for the purpose of expressing the deep regret felt in the loss of a brother officer and friend, the following resolutions were approved and adopted:

WHEREAS, On the night of Sept. 23, 1863, Capt. Joseph Woodruff, of Co. K, 39th Regt. Ill. Volunteers, while on duty as officer in command at Fort Gregg, and when about to be relieved from the same, was wounded by a shell thrown from Fort Moultrie, which carried away a large portion of his right side, causing his death in a short time afterwards; therefore,

Resolved, That, while we recognize the hand of God in all things, we can but mourn the loss of our brother officer, and one of our country's noble defenders; and, while we so deeply regret the violent death which snatched from us one whose every act endeared him to all, whose loyalty, patriotism and bravery proclaimed him a true man and soldier, we cannot but feel that our loss is his gain, and that he has left a world of suffering and gone to join that band of noble patriots who have fallen before, and with him in their country's defence.

Resolved, That we tender our heartfelt sympathies to the family and friends in this their sad bereavement of a kind husband and generous companion, and trust that they may find consolation in the fact, that he fell while at his post and in the discharge of his duty, and that in dying he evinced, while sensible, that spirit of resignation which bespeaks the faith of a Christian.

O. L. MANN, Lieut. Col. Commanding,
CHAS. M. CLARK, Surgeon,
L. A. BAKER, Capt. Co. A,
C. J. WILDER, Lieut. Co. H,
} *Committee.*

LIEUTENANT BUCK.

Lieut. HENRY A. BUCK, only son of Allen and Amanda Buck, was born at Ypsilanti, Mich., on the 26th of June, 1837. From a child he was noted for his fearlessness and bravery, and a passionate love for truth and for the right was ever a distinguishing feature of his character. His behavior towards parents and sisters was that of a dutiful son and a kind, affectionate brother, as he grew up one of the truly noble, well educated and promising young men of Michigan.

In 1854, he entered the University of Michigan as a student, graduating in 1858. He then entered upon the study of law in the office of Messrs. Norris and Ninde, Ypsilanti; was admitted to the bar, and commenced the practice of his profession in the city of Grand Rapids with H. P. Yale. In June, 1861, he returned to the University, and received the degree of A. M. In November of the same year, while on business in Chicago, he enlisted as Orderly Sergeant in Company K, 51st Regiment Illinois Volunteers. This step he announces in a letter to his friends, where he says:

On very careful reflection, the conclusion is forced upon me, that honor and duty both call for a response to my suffering country's despairing cry to take up arms in her defence. Do not let this determination wound your feelings. I consider it a duty, and I know you will feel prouder of me when I return.

The regiment remained at Camp Douglas until the 14th of February, 1862, when it went to Cairo and occupied barracks at Camp McClernand, removing in a few days to Camp Cullom, Ky. From thence to Bird's Point, Mo., marching through Houghsville, Bertrand and Sykestown, encamping two miles from New Madrid. On the morning of the 13th of March they were drawn up in line of battle; an engagement was going on between the land batteries on one side and the rebel batteries and gunboats on the other. A battery was soon planted to bear upon their gunboats, and, after sharp skirmishing, succeeded in driving in the enemy's pickets. That night the rebels were compelled to leave New Madrid in great haste. On the 7th of April, they took transports, and landed in Kentucky at noon, marching off through the fields and woods; again crossing the line into Tennessee, following up about 2000 rebels, halting a mile from Tiptonville, an enemy's camp, and taking about 40 prisoners on the route.

After the evacuation of Island No. 10, on the 8th of April, when Gen. McKoon and 5000 rebels surrendered to Gen. Paine, Co. K was detailed to guard a boat load of prisoners to New Madrid. Soon after, they were ordered to Farmington, Miss., and participated in the engagement there. While here, the regiment was made the recipient of an elegant stand of colors, presented by citizens of Chicago.

On the 15th of June, Sergt. Buck was appointed by the Col. as Acting 1st Lieutenant, which position he filled until the battle of Stone River. During the summer months, they were occupied in guarding different points in Tennessee and Northern Alabama. On the 5th of September, they were ordered to Nashville: all the country south of it and east of Corinth was to be evacuated. After weary days of hard marching and some severe conflicts with the enemy, they reached the city on the 16th. At this time there had been no communication, either by telegraph, railroad, river, or otherwise, between Nashville and the North for several weeks. The regiment remained here until marching orders were issued to the different columns on the 26th of December. The entire army of Gen. Rosecrans was then in motion.

Soon after followed the memorable battle of Stone River. On the morning of the first day's fight, Lieutenant Buck was wounded in the left side by a minie ball—his diary then saving his life. Undaunted, he remained at his post until evening, when he was obliged to be carried from the field to the hospital. In two weeks after he reported for duty, and was placed in command of the company. Headquarters were established at Murfreesboro on Monday, the 5th of January, 1863. Taking up a position in front of the town, the exhausted army settled down into the quiet of camp life. On the 23d of June, Gen. Rosecrans issued orders for an advance in force against the

enemy.   To Gen. McCook's Corps (the 51st being attached)
the part of making the first advance was assigned.   Early on
the 24th they started out on the Shelbyville Pike, and on the
9th of July their brigade climbed the Cumberland Mountains
for five weary miles, then marched two miles on the sandy sum-
mit to the "University of the South," * and camped.   In this
beautiful spot they remained until August, then moved to
Bridgeport, Ala.

On the 6th of September, Lieut. Buck writes:

We are now in Lookout Valley, on the banks of Lookout Creek, at the
foot of Lookout Mountain.   Now "lookout," Bragg, for Rosy is after you.

This was the last letter received from him.   In a few days
the impending battle between Rosecrans and Bragg took place.
At Chickamauga, on the afternoon of the 19th of September,
Lieut. Buck fell while bravely leading his company to what
proved his own and nearly their whole destruction.   He was
killed instantly, being shot in the head, and fell without
uttering a word.

He died not only respected but beloved by both officers and
men.   Col. Raymond, when speaking of his death to a friend,
said—"I have lost my best officer."   His company, of which
only 8 out of 43 remained after the conflict, agree in saying a
purer man—a more brave and gallant officer, never lived.   His
letters, while with the regiment, all breathe a pure Christian
spirit, and express the noblest conceptions of life and duty.
He was a member of the Presbyterian Church of his native
place, and never sullied his profession amid the temptations of
military life, being careful to honor the cause of religion by a
faithful attendance upon its public service whenever an opportunity occurred.   No consideration could induce him to resign
his commission.   In answer to urgent wishes to return home,
he says:

I have sworn to serve my country honestly and faithfully, and as long as
God spares my life, I must and will fulfil my obligations.

He gave to his country continued service for nearly two years, being off duty not more than three or four weeks in that time, and never taking a furlough to visit friends. "A soldier (he writes at one time) has no business away from his command, if there is an enemy to meet." All his strength and energies were given for his country's salvation, and he fell a martyr to liberty. Although his remains lie in the soil of Georgia, the name of Lieut. Buck shall live in the holiest remembrances of his friends and appear with lustre on the heroic escutcheon of the Prairie State.

THE SAMSON FAMILY.

ANDREW F., aged 23, EDWIN S., aged 21, and HAMILTON SAMSON, aged 19 years, enlisted in Company H. 77th Regiment Illinois Volunteers, in August, 1862. They participated in the skirmishing or battle under Gen. Sherman, the following winter, at Vicksburg. Edwin was at the battle of Arkansas Post, and Andrew was at the siege and fall of the Mississippi stronghold —Vicksburg.

Hamilton died of disease at Young's Point, Feb. 4, 1863; Edwin at Milliken's Bend, March 25, 1863, and Andrew at Vicksburg, after its capture.

Their father, Rev. H. Sampson, of Minonk, Woodford co., thus closes the very brief record of his sons: "They were all the children we had, and we gave them to the Lord and our country."

MAJOR BUSHNELL.

Maj. Douglas R. Bushnell, son of Francis W. and Louisa Bushnell, was born in Norwich, Conn., June 17, 1824, where the first years of his life were spent, and where he received a thorough education and adopted the profession of civil engineer, in which capacity he was connected with the railroads in the vicinity of his native place.

In 1845, he removed to New Hampshire, and still following his profession, was employed on many of the railroads in that and the adjoining State of Vermont.

At Highgate, Vt., on the 16th of September, 1849, he was married to Miss Emily J. Edson, an intelligent and accomplished lady, in whose refined taste and congenial society he found the counterpart of his own cultivated mind; and he participated in unusual domestic happiness until duty called him to offer even this precious boon upon the altar of his country.

In the fall of 1850, falling in with the tide of emigration which was then wending its way toward the fertile prairies of the Great West, he came to Illinois, and located at Rockford, to which place he removed his family the year following. After a three years' residence there, he in the meantime being connected with the Galena and Chicago Union Railroad, he located his family in Sterling. While here, he was prominently connected, as engineer, with the Dixon Air Line Railroad, and as chief engineer, superintended the construction of one of the main roads in the northern part of Iowa, running westward, and also the Sycamore branch of the Galena and Chicago Union Railroad. When the Sterling and Rock Island road was projected, he was called to the position of chief engineer, and most successfully he performed his duties.

In the spring of 1861, when the first call was made for troops to maintain our integrity as a nation, and to repel the treasonable assaults of Southern disunionists upon our glorious inheritance of unity and liberty, Major Bushnell was among the first to respond. Prompted by a sense of duty to his country, and impelled by the true spirit of patriotism, he added his name to the muster-roll of Honor, and went forth to battle for the Right —to lend the aid of a true heart, an intelligent mind, and a strong arm, in the defence of his country's institutions.

At Sterling, scores of resolute men, among whom were the most intelligent, wealthy and influential of her citizens, left their counters, their workshops, their offices, and their farms, to volunteer for the defence of the dear old flag, and immediately commenced drilling for the service.

They expected no light work, and raised no questions of bounty or pay. They only knew their country was in danger, and their bosoms burned to avenge her wrongs. Such were the heroes of the 13th Illinois Infantry, and such were the men of Co. B. To be chosen leader of these brave sons of Sterling, was an honor not to be lightly esteemed, and in electing D. R. Bushnell for their Captain, they manifested their appreciation of his ability, experience, and many virtues. The company was presented with a beautiful flag by the citizens, with appropriate ceremonies; and with an affectionate adieu to his three lovely children, and a tender "farewell" to the brave woman, who bid him "God speed" in this glorious cause, Capt. Bushnell hastened to join the regiment in camp at Dixon.

The early volunteers having been accustomed to civil liberty, were not prepared to endure the restraints of military duty, and to some, Capt. Bushnell's strict and thorough discipline seemed severe; but in a short time, they learned to prize him all the more for this qualification.

From Dixon, the regiment was ordered to Rolla, Mo., and there, during the summer of 1861, Col. Wyman was in command, and Capt. Bushnell, acting Major. At the request of Gen. Totten, who was personally acquainted with his abilities as an engineer, he was put in charge of the construction of a fort at that place, which was completed under his supervision, and afterwards pronounced one of the strongest and most complete of its size in the United States. It was proposed to name it after its scientific constructor, but Capt. Bushnell, with his characteristic modesty, declined the honor and gave the preference to his superior officer, and it is now called "Fort Wyman."

In March, 1862, the regiment joined Gen. Curtis' army at Pea Ridge, and in all their toilsome marches through southern Missouri and Arkansas, Capt. Bushnell was acting Major, and by his sagacity and uniform sympathy with the wearied but uncomplaining soldiers, won the confidence and affection of officers and men. After the arrival at Helena on the 14th of July, he was frequently put in command of expeditions into the surrounding country. In one of these, he was sent to the St. Francis River, with a detachment of the 13th Illinois and 14th Iowa, and from the plantations of Generals Pillow and Brown, he brought away a large quantity of corn and quite a number of cattle. In Gen. Hovey's expedition to the Coldwater and Tallahatchie Rivers, Capt. B. had command of 200 of the 13th; and, after a successful raid in the enemy's country, and destroying the railroad at Oakland Station, they returned to Helena, where they remained until the 22d of December. The regiment was then put under the command of Gen. Sherman, in Gen. Blair's brigade, and ordered immediately to Vicksburg. After arrival there, the "Old 13th" was placed in the advance, and was the first Illinois regiment to assault the enemy's works. In all the engagements at Vicksburg previous to December 29th, Capt. Bushnell led his own brave company of Sterling boys; but upon the fall of Col. Wyman, he was promoted to Major of the regiment.

On the 29th occurred the memorable charge upon the rebel riflepits at the foot of Walnut Hills, at Chickasaw Bayou, in which the 13th lost 30 killed and over 100 wounded. Major Bushnell highly distinguished himself for coolness and courage, by advancing within a few rods of the enemy's works, under a fire that swept the ground on which he stood.

On the 10th and 11th of January, 1863, we find him displaying the same heroic devotion at the assault and taking of Arkansas Post. After this, his engineering abilities were again called into requisition during the seventy-five days the regiment was at Young's Point, digging canals, building levees, and erecting fortifications to operate against Vicksburg.

In Gen. Steele's raid upon Deer Creek in April, in the march upon Grand Gulf and Jackson in May, and in the terrific assaults upon Vicksburg in June and July, Major Bushnell was ever at his post—shrinking from no toil, privation or danger to which the regiment was exposed. In Gen. Sherman's operations against Johnston, after the fall of Vicksburg, Major Bushnell acted Lieut. Col. until they returned to their summer quarters, August 13th, 1863.

Thus, from a modest, retiring citizen, he had changed to an undaunted, war-begrimed hero. His fine form had lost none of its gentlemanly bearing; but the realities of cruel war had stamped upon his face a sternness which was unnatural, but which befitted the soldier. The iron had entered his soul, and his dark, piercing eye had too often looked upon death, to droop beneath the gaze of any man, or quail before any form of danger; yet, in the recesses of his heart, there was the same affectionate tenderness, which had so endeared him to his family and friends. He could still weep over the sufferings and trials of his companions, and a simple flower would awaken all the fond recollections of a far-off, peaceful home.

He had risen high in the estimation of his superior officers, and had he been as ambitious for office as he was to be useful, he might have arrived at greater distinction, but would have been less a hero. His only desire was to discharge faithfully his duty to his country, and then return to the bosom of his family; and now, as he drew near his last battle, and the images of his absent loved ones rise before him, his affectionate letters to them breathe more earnestly this longing desire. In one of these he says:

I pray God, at the end of my service, I may be restored to my beloved family in safety, but *more especially I pray, that the cause in which I have staked my life and my honor may succeed.*

Never since the night at Gethsemane was that prayer, "Not my will, but Thine, be done," more fervently uttered.

He had passed safely through the storm of shot and shell in the fierce contests of Lookout Mountain and Missionary Ridge, on the 24th and 25th of November, and was now hopeful that he should live to see the end—to see the rebellion crushed, and to see his country again united and happy; but the God of Battles had ordered it otherwise.

On the morning of the 27th, the 13th Illinois Infantry held the extreme right before Ringgold, and was ordered by General Osterhaus to advance rapidly over an open field, which was covered with shells, canister and bullets, like hail, to a few houses in front, from which they might drive off the artillery-men of the enemy. This they accomplished in magnificent style, and gained the position, which they held, in spite of the murderous fire from the gorge in front and the hillside on the right.

Gen. Osterhaus, in his report of this battle, says:

The 13th Illinois remained, undauntedly keeping up a vehement fire. These struggles, during which so many deeds of bravery were exhibited, lasted from 9 a.m. to 1 p.m., our infantry fighting against the combined forces of the enemy.

The artillery coming up, the rebels were soon driven from the gorge, and the victory won. But the glad shouts of triumph which rent the air, fell unheeded upon the ear of the gallant Major Bushnell. He had given his life this day as a sacrifice for his country's honor, and a more patriotic or pure heart was never laid upon her altar. While assisting some of his men to place a rail in front of them for their protection, a musket ball came crashing through, and, striking him in the left temple, passed into the brain and killed him instantly.

Lieut. Col. Partridge communicated the sad intelligence to Mrs. Bushnell, in the following letter:

CHATTANOOGA, TENN., Nov. 30th, 1863.

MY DEAR MADAM: The painful duty has devolved upon me, as the commanding officer of the 13th Regt. Ill. Vols., of sending to you the last remains of your precious husband. The sad news has already been broken to you, I am informed, by sympathizing friends. The 13th, officers and men, sympathize heartily with his bereaved family. He died in defence of the cherished institutions of his country. He died in his place, as a brave and gallant soldier should; and although, when you think of the desolate condition to which you and yours are reduced by his untimely fate, the thought may give you no present comfort, believe me, that when you relate to your children, in after years, the fate of their lamented parent, the fact that he was stricken in his place on the field of battle, struggling with the old 13th to put down this accursed rebellion, will be full of comforting circumstances.

I remain yours to command,   FRED'K W. PARTRIDGE.

Lieut. Joseph Patterson, of Co. B, 13th Illinois, in a letter to his father, whose residence is near that of the late Major Bushnell, says:

We mourn exceedingly the death of our gallant Major, and sympathize deeply with his bereaved family. * * * I feel deeply for Mrs. Bushnell and her little, fatherless children. It will tend to alleviate her distress to know that her husband fell, fighting in defence of his bleeding country. The Major was a courteous gentleman—a true patriot, and, as an officer, *unequalled in the regiment.*

The body was embalmed and sent home in charge of Sergt. Harvey, accompanied by a brother of the deceased, the Rev. F. H. Bushnell, of Louisville, Ky. At Chicago it was met by a deputation of the citizens of Sterling, by whom it was escorted to that city, where, on its arrival, it was taken in charge by the Masonic fraternity.

At the funeral, the Rev. Mr. Wilkinson, of Chicago, delivered an eloquent address, from which the following is an extract:

We are met together here to pay the last sad honors to the remains of our lamented friend and fellow-townsman—the noble gentleman, the brave soldier, the gallant officer—Major Douglas R. Bushnell: to mingle our tears with those of his bereaved family, and to give the best sympathies of our hearts as an offering of love to them, and a tribute of honor to the departed. It were sad enough to do this under any circumstances. Had he been gathered to his fathers in a good old age, like a shock of corn fully ripe, having done his work, and written his history in the records of your material prosperity and social progress, even then we must have laid him to rest with weeping hearts and eyes. But not thus has his end come. In the prime of life, in the midst of his usefulness, the full strength of his manhood fitting him for greater efforts, and the maturer development of his mental powers marking him for more successful achievements—he is gone; another victim of this accursed rebellion, another sacrifice to the bloody demon of secession, another jewel added to the countless price that loyalty is paying for the suppression of Southern treason —that patriotism is offering for the preservation of our beloved country. On the field of battle, where the shot fell fastest, and the iron storm raged the sorest, there, at the post of duty, our brother met the summons of the destroying angel, and laid down his sword forever. We mourn his loss. We sorrow for the afflictions of his bereaved friends. We bow in humble submission to the Providence that has permitted this afflictive dispensation.

While thus "weeping with those who weep," it is my privilege to pay my feeble tribute to his memory.

As a citizen, he is known to you all as upright, honorable, courteous and

8

true. No taint of crime dims his bright escutcheon—no breath of calumny dare sully his fair fame.   All knew him to respect, admire, and love.

As a soldier, it is the unanimous testimony of fellow officers and of his men, that he was ever faithful in duty, ever firm, yet gentle, in discipline, true in his friendships, and unfaltering in his courage.   Death found him, where he might have found him at any moment of his career as a soldier—*at his post.*

From the church the body was taken to the cemetery, accompanied by the martial band and the Masonic lodges of Sterling and Dixon, and followed by a large concourse of sympathizing citizens. Houses of business were closed, and flags, draped in mourning, waved solemnly as the procession moved along. At the grave, the impressive burial service of the Masons was read, and the mourned dead was lowered to his last earthly home, enshrouded in the stars and stripes, beneath whose folds he received the summons which called him to another world.

> " Aye, leave the stripes and stars
> Above him, with the precious cap and sash,
> The mute mementoes of the battle's crash,
>   And of a hero's scars.
>
> A hero heart is still.
> And eyes are sealed, and loving lips are mute
> Which bore on earth the spirit's golden fruit.
>   But peace ! it was God's will."

CORPORAL ORMSBY.

Corp. JESSE HARRISON ORMSBY, son of John Ormsby, enlisted at Chicago, on the 30th of July, 1861, in Co. I, 42d Regiment Illinois Volunteers.   He went from there to Benton Barracks, St. Louis, Mo., and from thence to Jefferson City ; thence to Springfield, and other places in that State—sometimes guarding wagon trains, and almost the whole of the time on the move, until they got to Tipton, where he was taken with the measles.   He was doing well, but on removing him from his tent to the hospital, he suffered a relapse, and died very suddenly on the 18th of December, 1861, in the twenty-third year of his age.

CAPTAIN SHEPLEY.

Capt. CHARLES H. SHEPLEY, eldest son of James C. and Mary S. Shepley, was born in Tunbridge, Vermont, on the 10th of February, 1841. When he was but seven years old, his parents removed from Tunbridge to Bradford, and from thence, in 1854, to Chicago.

At an early age, the subject of this sketch evinced a lively interest in military affairs, and in numerous instances gave his friends reason to suppose that whenever a fitting opportunity offered itself, he would exchange the avocations of a citizen for the honors, duties and dangers of a soldier's life.

In 1856, young Shepley joined Col. Scott's National Guard Cadets—afterwards better known as the Zouave Cadets—and continued an active member until that organization was disbanded, being one of the company on their famous tour to the principal eastern cities, in the summer of 1856, when their splendid drill exercises excited the enthusiastic admiration of countless thousands.

When, in the spring of 1861, the rebellion culminated in the bombardment and capture of Fort Sumter—by a traitorous faction who had taken up arms against a government which had never wronged them—then the heart of young Shepley became fired with a holy ambition to give his services, and if need be his life, to his dearly loved country. Having obtained the consent of his parents to enlist, he at once accepted an offer to become the 2d Lieutenant of Co. K, in what afterwards became the 19th Regiment Illinois Volunteers. On the 21st of April—only one week after the fall of Sumter—Lieutenant Shepley bade adieu to his parents and friends at home, and went with his company to Cairo, where he remained about one month, when they were ordered to Springfield. From thence they came to Chicago, and acted as escort on the occasion of the funeral of the late Hon. Stephen A. Douglas. In a few days after this event, Co. K and several other companies were organized into a regiment, and designated as the 19th Illinois —Colonel John B. Turchin, commanding.

Soon after its organization, the 19th was sent into Missouri. It was not long after leaving Chicago before the subject of this sketch was promoted to the 1st Lieutenancy of his company. Early in the fall, the regiment, in accordance with an order from headquarters, started for Washington, but on the way, a sad railroad casualty occurred in crossing a bridge over the Wabash river, which quenched the life of many a gallant soldier, and brought sorrow to many a desolated family circle. Immediately after this catastrophe, the regiment went to Cincinnati, and from thence was sent into Kentucky. On the 26th of October, while at Elizabethtown, in that State, Lieut. Shepley was chosen Captain of Co. I—a position for which his excellent personal qualities, combined with his superior skill in military science, rendered him eminently qualified; for, though not yet twenty-one years of age, Capt. Shepley, by his indefatigable industry in the improvement of all his opportunities, had acquired a practical knowledge of military tactics superior to that which most officers of riper age are apt to possess after years of active service.

On the 10th of February, 1862, while the regiment was quartered at Bowling Green, Ky., Capt. Shepley was made the recipient of an elegant sword, sash and belt, from the members of his company, as a token of their high esteem for their gallant commander and noble-hearted brother in arms. This splendid gift was accompanied with a brief presentation speech by Private McDowell, to which Capt. Shepley happily and feelingly responded.

While the 19th Regiment was stationed at Murfreesboro, Tenn., Capt. Shepley met with an accident which resulted in his death two days afterwards. On the 21st of March, while quietly engaged in loading his pistol, the weapon suddenly discharged itself, the ball passing into and nearly through his body, producing a fatal wound. He lingered till early on the morning of the 23d, when, despite all the surgical skill and kindly attentions put forth in his behalf, Capt. Shepley was compelled to yield up his young life while bright hopes and well-merited honors were clustering around him. He had often expressed to his fellow soldiers a desire that if he must lose his life in the war, it might be his privilege to die on the battle-field, rather than in camp or on picket duty. But that wish was not to be gratified; and yet those best acquainted with him know that he died none the less a hero than if his life had been taken by the hand of the enemy amid the carnage of battle.

His loss was deeply felt by his company and regiment, for none knew him who did not respect him for his noble, manly virtues, and more than ordinary talents, while those who were his intimate friends, loved him as a brother. Generous, truthful, ambitious to acquire honorable distinction in his chosen profession of a soldier, but even more ambitious to serve his country in her time of peril; with a high order of talent, combined with a firm, high-toned sense of moral rectitude, which made him scorn to do a wrong act, whether in the army or the walks of civil life,—Capt. Shepley was a model whose example young men might follow with safety to themselves and benefit to society.

Immediately after his demise, the remains of Capt. Shepley were placed in a handsome metallic coffin, generously procured by the regiment, and transmitted to Chicago for interment. On Tuesday, April 3d, the funeral obsequies took place. The remains of the young and gifted officer were followed from the residence of his parents to Trinity Church, by a large procession of citizens, preceded by a numerous and an imposing military escort. At the church, the services—conducted by the Rev. Dr. Pratt—were of the most solemn character, and nearly every one of that vast assemblage, whether citizen or soldier, wept as those weep who mourn the death of a beloved friend. The services concluded, all that was mortal of this estimable young officer was borne away to a quiet resting-place in Rosehill Cemetery, which is now overshadowed by a monumental column.

Thus early in life, and early in the war, perished Captain Charles H. Shepley, who, at the hour of his death, was aged but twenty-one years, one month and thirteen days.

LIEUTENANT COLONEL WEBB.

Among the patriotic and brave men who have fallen victims to this unholy rebellion, none have met a more untimely fate than Lieut. Col. LYSANDER R. WEBB, of the 77th Illinois Infantry. Beloved by an unusually large circle of friends, a fine speaker, a ready and vigorous writer, had he lived, bright honors awaited him. We bewail the sacrifice.

Col. Webb was born at Pittsfield, Mass., December 30, 1833, and being early left an orphan, went to reside with his guardian, Hon. William Shepard of Chester. When of suitable age he entered Yale College, but his protector dying a year or two after, he quitted the college before graduation and became an assistant editor on the Springfield (Mass.) *Republican*. In 1857, he came to Illinois, where he was connected editorially with the Waukegan *Gazette*, and, in the following year, assumed a similar position on the Peoria *Daily Transcript*. In 1859, he commenced the study of the law; in 1860, was admitted to the bar, and continued in the practice of his profession until the summer of 1862. At that time, in response to the call for 300,000 volunteers, he raised a company, which, on the organization of the 77th Regiment, became attached to it as Co. E, and its Captain promoted to the Lieut. Coloneley. Soon after, the regiment was ordered to Cincinnati, and from there joined in Gen. Buell's unsuccessful pursuit of Bragg. From that time until the fall of 1863 they were constantly on the move. From December 27th until January 1st, 1863, they took part in Gen. Sherman's attack on Vicksburg; January 11th, they were at Arkansas Post, where they lost fifty men in killed and wounded; May 1st, at Port Gibson; a few days after, at Champion Hills and Black River Bridge; at Gen. Grant's long siege and final capture of Vicksburg; and in July, at the siege of Jackson, Miss.

During the winter of 1863–4, Col. Webb was detailed for the

important post of Commandant of the Convalescent Camp of the 13th Army Corps, located at New Orleans. This responsible and arduous duty he conducted with great credit to himself and to the entire satisfaction of his superior officers, who only consented to relieve him that he might take charge of his regiment after repeated requests on his part. In March, he joined the 77th at Berwick Bay, and, after leading them in the long march up Red River, appeared at their head for the last time at the disastrous battle of Sabine Cross Roads, on the 8th of April, 1864. While gallantly cheering on his men, he was shot by a bullet, which pierced his head. Deprived of their leader, the noble 77th suffered fearfully, and of the 400 men who went into the struggle, but 153 remained to tell the tale.

Col. Webb was a staunch and earnest Republican, and boldly stood by his principles when to do so was a sure road to unpopularity. He was heart and soul with the administration in every effort to maintain the union and put down the rebellion, and was a powerful advocate of all those measures.

In 1858, he married Virginia, eldest daughter of Charles Ballance, Esq., of Peoria, who is left to mourn the loss of her brave and gallant husband, but not alone—the memory of such men lingers in the hearts of a grateful country, and his life will be measured by deeds, not years.

The following extracts have been made from the many letters written by Col. Webb to his friends. He vividly portrays the events passing under his review; and the last one he was permitted to write, displays a feeling which entitles him to honor and his memory to unfading recollection.

ON BOARD STEAMER "ARGYLE,"
NEAR VICKSBURG, MISS., Dec. 25, 1862.

I have just read the private circular from President Lincoln, who says the *Mississippi must be opened.* The rebels, to the number of 120,000, are concentrated at Vicksburg, strongly fortified, and a great battle must undoubtedly occur. To-morrow we sail up the Yazoo River to a rebel fort, sixty miles up, take it, unite with Grant, and march on Vicksburg. There are tears in my eyes as I write this letter, and reflect that it may be the last you will receive from me. Believe me, however, in view of the good I hope to do for our wretched country, there are no regrets in view of danger.

(After Sherman's attack on Vicksburg.)

MILLIKEN'S BEND, Jan. 2, 1863.

Since my last letter to you important events have been going on in this command. Sunday morning last, our division landed twelve miles from the mouth of Yazoo River, and immediately disembarked. The other three divisions of the army had disembarked before us. The 1st brigade started, and we followed, over a muddy road, leading through a densely-wooded bottom in the direction of Vicksburg. After marching about four miles we heard the action commencing on our extreme left, and it soon became general along the whole line of the last three divisions. Our division halted for about a quarter of an hour, when an order came for our regiment to advance and drive in the enemy's skirmishers on the right. As we filed past the other regiments, the only words spoken were: "What regiment?" "77th Illinois," our boys would answer proudly, conscious that the advance given us was a mark of honor. * * * * Some eleven or twelve rebels were killed in this skirmish—not one of our men either killed or wounded, though two or three had holes shot in their clothes. I attribute our good fortune to the superiority of our arms. Towards night, word came for us to contract our line and fall back. We did so, and not daring to make fires, lay upon our arms all night. I could hear the town clock in Vicksburg strike the passing hours, and the cars rattle all night long. * * * * Wednesday and Thursday were quiet days along the whole line. It was evident our force was insufficient to take the place, and neither Banks nor Grant could be heard from. Meantime, the rebels were hurrying in reinforcements, and studying mischief of some sort. Our brigade built a long line of rude but strong fortifications, and determined to "die in the last ditch." Thursday night, however, about midnight, the whole army commenced a noiseless retreat to the boats. We have fallen back to Milliken's Bend, and thus far, the movement is an acknowledged failure. What will be done next remains to be seen. McClernand, it is said, supersedes Sherman in the command. If so, he will either take Vicksburg or lose half of his forces in the attempt. The place is strongly fortified, and must be got, if at all, by a large force and by desperate fighting.

FIELD OF BATTLE, POST OF ARKANSAS, Jan. 13, 1863.

I have escaped unhurt. We have had a fine battle, and have won a most gratifying victory. 7000 prisoners, 8000 stand of excellent arms, and 20 cannon, are its fruits, besides an immense quantity of ammunition, commissary and quartermaster stores. The fight opened Sunday noon, and lasted four or five hours. Such a thunder of cannon and roll of artillery have seldom been heard in any battle. Fort Hindman, the captured stronghold, is a small but exceedingly strong fort, surrounded by rifle-pits, abattis, and other means of defence. Our regiment has won, by its gallantry, distinguished honors. When the white flag was raised by the rebels, our flag-bearer being wounded, Major

Hotchkiss seized the regimental flag and charged through the ditch, while I followed him. I assisted him up the ramparts, and climbed up after him. I do not think I ever shouted so loud in my life as when we seized the staff and waved the flag of the 77th over those rebel fortifications. The whole regiment was speedily inside the fort, and as a mark of honor, Gen. Morgan placed us in command of the fort and in charge of the prisoners.

Again, at Milliken's Bend, April 9, 1863, he writes:

To-day, our division was reviewed by Gen. Grant. There are no marching orders as yet, though large movements are in progress. You will soon hear of a ditch dug five miles below our camp, not yet made public, and not known to the enemy. The Lake Providence ditch, Yazoo Pass expedition, etc., are, in my opinion, only so many blinds to mislead the rebels. I shall be much disappointed if we are not soon in the rear and on the flanks of Vicksburg, with the enemy comparatively cooped up and at our mercy. Do not be discouraged about our success, or apparent want of success, rather. *We shall have Vicksburg.*

NATCHITOCHES, April 5, 1864.

It is not probable now that I shall have any opportunity of seeing you until the war is over, for it is not my present intention, health permitting, to leave the army for the North again until I can leave it for good. Were it consistent with my duty, I should resign my commission this fall, upon the expiration of two years of service. It would be pleasant to be relieved of the toil, the hardships and dangers of my present life, and return once more to the comforts and joys of home and friends; but I honestly would feel ashamed to do so.

Many things in the management of the war disgust me—as they must disgust everybody—but my heart swells and my blood boils when I think of the terrible ruin which the Vandal hordes of treason are still attempting to accomplish. The complete overthrow of this Rebellion, mighty as it is, *must* be accomplished at any and every sacrifice. There must be no idle repining over this "cruel war." We must work, and sacrifice, and suffer, looking to *victories* alone, at any cost of precious human blood, as the paths to honor, peace and happiness.

No, I *cannot* resign. I must remain here at the post of honor, and danger, and duty—here with those comrades in arms, endeared to me by common impulses of enthusiastic patriotism, common trials in our country's cause, and common dangers in the fierce hour of battle. Do not smile at these, perhaps, too rhapsodic words. Remember that I *feel* what I say.

LIEUTENANT COLONEL CHANDLER.

The subject of this sketch, Lieut. Col. GEORGE W. CHANDLER, one of the bravest, most efficient and humane of the many accomplished officers Illinois has sent to the field to aid in crushing out the great "Southern Rebellion," was born in the parish of St. Armand East, Missisquoi county, Canada East, August 27th, 1832.

His grandfather, Daniel Chandler, was from Hartford, Connecticut, and had the honor of being a soldier in the Revolutionary War. In 1800, he removed to Canada, where the father of our hero, Horace M. Chandler, was soon afterwards born.

The mother of Col. Chandler was born in Windsor, Vermont —a lady in every way worthy of her noble son, whose loss she now so sadly mourns.

Col. Chandler received a good common school education in his native parish, and completed his studies at the academical institution in Bakersfield, Vt. In his boyhood days, and while he lived in Canada, he was highly respected and much loved by all who knew him.

In the spring of 1851 he went to Montreal, where he was employed as an accountant in the exchange office of George W. Warner, where he remained three years. He still continued in this vocation in a large manufacturing house until September, 1855, when, like thousands of others, thinking to better his condition, he removed to Chicago, Illinois.

Soon after his arrival in Chicago, he became connected with the banking house of George Smith in the capacity of bookkeeper, and shortly after took the initiatory steps towards becoming a naturalized citizen of the United States. He continued with Mr. Smith until the year 1859, when he was tendered the appointment of head bookkeeper in the City Comptroller's office, which he accepted, and filled with much satisfaction to the officials and the public, and with credit to himself.

LIEUTENANT COLONEL CHANDLER.

He possessed rare qualifications as an accountant, and retained his position until the advent of the opposing party into power, when he was displaced for political reasons only.

He was a firm and consistent Republican in politics, but not a violent partisan. Immediately after leaving the Comptroller's office, in the summer of 1862, the President having called for 300,000 volunteers, he determined to devote his whole energies to his adopted country, and soon obtained authority from the Governor of the State to raise a company of three year's troops for one of the three Chicago regiments then being raised under the auspices of that patriotic and liberal body of merchants, the "Chicago Board of Trade." In this undertaking he was ably assisted by a private named George A. Sheridan, who subsequently became a Captain in the "2d Board of Trade" (88th) Regiment Illinois Infantry. Together, and subject to the charge of Mr. Chandler, they raised two companies, and upon their organization, Mr. C. was unanimously elected Captain of the first company, which became the "banner company" of the regiment, under the name of the "Kimbark Guards," and the second company chose for their captain, A. C. McClurg, naming it the "Crosby Guards,"—the former in honor of George M. Kimbark, and the latter in honor of U. H. Crosby, both prominent citizens of Chicago, who rendered Col. Chandler and his lieutenants much valuable service in organizing the two companies.

Upon the organization of the regiment, Frank T. Sherman was appointed Colonel, A. S. Chadbourne, Lieutenant Colonel, and Capt. Chandler being the *unanimous* choice for the position of Major, he was duly commissioned as such, November 8th, and ranking from September 4th, 1862.

Previous to the departure of the 88th from Chicago, Major Chandler's many personal friends presented him with a complete uniform and outfit, including sword, revolvers, etc., as a slight testimonial of their appreciation of his virtues as a citizen and a friend, and an earnest of the success they hoped him to achieve.

After having remained a few days in camp at Cottage Grove, near Chicago, the 88th took their departure for the field—leav-

ing early in September, 1862, and reaching Perryville, Ky., in
time to take an active part in that spirited and bloody battle,
entering the fight and maintaining their ground with a determination which would have done credit to a band of veterans.

The 88th participated in Gen. Buell's campaign in Kentucky,
and in every engagement of importance fought by the Army of
the Cumberland, under Generals Buell, Rosecrans and Sherman,
—in all of which Major Chandler was conspicuous and gained
for himself distinguished honors. After the battles of Murfreesboro and Stones River, Major Chandler was appointed by
Gen. Rosecrans to command the "Brigade of Honor," which
he decided to form, to be composed of men selected from the
different regiments engaged in those battles, who had made
themselves most conspicuous for deeds of bravery and gallantry,
in honor of their services, and as an incentive to his army's
future acts of courage and daring. In consequence, however,
of the depleted ranks of the various regiments, it was not
deemed advisable to carry out the formation of the "Brigade
of Honor," although the *Roll of Honor* was completed, by
designating the names of the brave men who would compose
the brigade, whenever it might be thought proper to have it
organized.

The appointment of Major Chandler to the command of such
a band of heroes, was indeed the highest compliment the General commanding could have bestowed upon him, and an evidence of his exalted opinion of him as an efficient and skillful
officer. How well Maj. Chandler merited this enviable appointment, his many brave and gallant acts, and his universally
acknowledged competency as a commander, have since attested
in every battle fought by the Army of the Cumberland up to
the assault of Kenesaw Mountain, where he sealed his devotion
to his country with his life's blood.

After his appointment to the command of the "Brigade of
Honor," the line officers of his regiment presented him with a
very fine and valuable sword as a token of their esteem and
appreciation of his soldierly qualities—a gift highly prized by
him, and most meritoriously bestowed.

At the battle of Stones River, an incident occurred, which

vividly illustrates the cool and undaunted courage of our hero when in action and under fire.

During the engagement, the 88th being on the skirmish line, a battery was posted on an eminence in their rear for their support, firing over them with solid shot and shell, and Major Chandler having occasion to ride out in front of the skirmish line to give some necessary order, a misdirected shot from the battery in the rear struck his horse in the side, passing entirely through him, cutting the Major's overcoat, pants and saddle in its passage, and killing the horse instantly. The horse sank to the ground, and Maj. Chandler, although partially stunned from the shock received, with the utmost coolness, raised himself to his feet, and turning to his men, and swinging his sword above his head, exclaimed—"Give it to them, boys, I am not dead yet!" He had hardly spoken, however, when a minie ball passed through the fleshy part of his ear, making a slight wound, to which he paid no regard until the battle was over.

Maj. Chandler was a man remarkably free from all profanity and dissipation, never having been known to taste of spirituous liquors or use a profane word while in the army or previously; cool and courageous in the face of danger; an unusually humane commander; a strict though impartial disciplinarian, and possessing rare qualities for a brave and efficient officer.

At the battles of Chattanooga and Lookout Mountain, Major Chandler took a distinguished part, and at the battle of Chickamauga conducted himself with a heroism unsurpassed. During this entire engagement he persistently refused to dismount from his horse, (being the only officer in his brigade who remained mounted,) and in answer to the earnest and tearful pleadings of his comrades, he replied—"My place is on horseback; and, as I am satisfied I can be of most service here, I shall remain."

Thanks to his heroism, by remaining mounted, he was enabled from his elevated position to discover a flanking movement of the enemy just in time to save his own brigade from capture.

Subsequent to the battle of Stones River, Col. F. T. Sherman having been placed in command of a brigade, and Col. Chadbourne being absent from the field most of the time, on account

of illness and on detached service, Major Chandler had almost
continued command of the regiment up to the battle of Chickamauga, when Lieut. Col. Chadbourne again assumed command,
but afterwards resigned. Owing to this vacancy, Maj. Chandler
was promoted and commissioned Lieutenant Colonel, October
31st, taking rank from October 14th, 1863.

At the storming of Mission Ridge, Col. Chandler particularly
distinguished himself, and his gallant regiment had the proud
honor of being the first to plant their colors upon the enemy's
works, the Col. himself being one of the first within the rebel fort.

Annexed is an extract from a letter to a personal friend, written at midnight, after the storming and taking of Mission Ridge:

DEAR FRIEND:

I am cheating myself out of the sleep I ought to have, to do some writing,
and will steal time to say a word.

We have this day accomplished that which the nation ought to feel proud
of, and grateful to us for doing. I do not write this in any boasting spirit,
but I feel that the blow has been struck that will cause the tottering to its
very foundation of the so-called "Southern Confederacy." God grant that it
may be so.

You will have read ere this reaches you, in the city papers, the telegrams
of good news, and also the details of the storming of "Mission Ridge," a
position considered by the enemy as impregnable to any assault.

It was _glorious_ to see the "old flag"—the stars and stripes—that proud
emblem of Liberty and Freedom, cross the upper line of the rebel rifle-pits
and wave triumphantly on the top of the "Bald hills of Mission Ridge." It
was all the more glorious to me to know that the 88th Regiment Illinois
Volunteer Infantry was the first to carry her colors across that line of works,
and wave them defiantly to the retreating enemy.

We are off in the morning, God knows where, _I_ don't, but feel certain that
it is to strike again for the death of the bogus Confederacy; hence go willingly.
We are reduced terribly in officers and men, but still in good heart, and must
work while the iron is hot. Lieut. Charles T. Boal has telegraphed you the
casualties, which you have no doubt received, and from which you will per-
ceive I escaped unhurt. I little expected when near the top of the ridge to
escape with my life, but had I been killed, I should have died as I would wish,
were I to be killed in battle, on the field of duty, fighting for the best Government God ever gave to man.

In a subsequent letter, referring to a set of resolutions adopted
by the "peace-on-any-terms" party in the Illinois Legislature,
in which they denounced the Government and took sides with

an arch-traitor, (whose name shall be unhonored here,) lauding him as a "pure and noble patriot," he says:

It seems strange, *very* strange to me, that men, who claim to be honest men, can oppose the efforts of their own Government in maintaining its laws, and thereby itself. Political corruption is at the bottom of it, and he who in times like these clings to any party except the Union-saving party, does not deserve the title of an American citizen or a man. You and I desire peace, and who does *not? We* also desire the war to continue yet longer. This may seem a little paradoxical, and I will explain. We desire the war to continue, because it is the *only* road to honorable peace, and without more fighting the end of that road cannot be reached. Those who favor the withdrawal of the "Federal Armies" from the field, that peace may be had, are "liars, and the truth is not in them." They know well enough that such action would not bring peace and save the Union, for their brother traitors of the South have told them so. They know well enough that the only solution to the problem is bitter, cruel war, for their brother traitors of the South have told them so. *You* feel embittered towards those men, but what think you are *our* feelings; we who, as it were, have taken our lives in our hands to go forth in battle array to meet those traitors who are manly enough to take arms and stand or fall by their principles? We loathe and detest them. When listening to the booming cannon, to the sharp crack of the rifle, and the zip–zip–zip of the minie bullet which carries death in its flight—what think you then are our feelings towards those traitors of the North who oppose sending more men into the field? We forget them, and think of the more manly ones of the same species who are fighting us in the field. I have a kind of admiration for the men composing the rebel army, compared with their brother traitors in the North, and always feel like treating them with respect; but if I should go North, and one of those most contemptible of the human species—a Copperhead—should open his batteries on me, he had better say his prayers for fear he would not have time afterwards. I say we forget them here when in presence of their more manly brethren of the South, but we none of us will forget them after this rebellion is crushed, as it surely will be, and we return to our homes.

God grant that light may soon enter the hearts of these men, and bring them to a realizing sense of their duty to their country in this hour of our nation's trial.

I tell you, sir, to know that while we are freely giving our lives to sustain our Government, these Northern traitors are using every available means to crush us and our Government, is humiliating indeed, and a sad reproach to the honor of the North. I could weep over their mistaken course, but tears would have no effect upon him who has murder in his heart.

I tell you, my kind friend, that every word spoken by these fiends, and every act in opposition to our Government, at this time, is a minie bullet sent into our ranks, the results from which, in killed and wounded, no one can tell. But while we soldiers in the field so deeply mourn the acts of these Northern traitors, we call upon you and all loyal men to falter not at all. Go on in your noble efforts to crush out the monster. Strike whenever and wherever you find the iron hot; for, while we are combating the enemy here, we want to feel that our friends, the unconditional war and Union men and loyalists, are doing their part at home. Let the soldiers but feel thus, and they will do their part nobly and well.*

From the capture of Mission Ridge to the storming of Kenesaw Mountain, Ga., Col. Chandler's regiment was continually in front, and day after day were on the skirmish line, doing noble execution, and always fully sustaining the excellent reputation both he and they had so honorably gained, and received from their Commanding General his thanks for their efficiency and conduct during the terrible campaign.

When it was decided to storm the enemy's works at Kenesaw Mountain, it was understood that the 4th corps, Gen. Howard commanding, was to be held in reserve, having been continually in duty on the skirmish line for many days, but when the time came for the charge to be made, this corps was sent to the front, an evidence of the confidence reposed in their superiority and gallantry. In this charge Col. Chandler lost his life, being shot through the body while leading his veterans against the rebel works. The following letter shows forth the particulars of his death:

In the Field, near Marietta, Ga.,
June 28th, 1864.

Geo. M. Kimbark, Esq., Chicago, Ill.:

Dear Sir,—I am pained to write you of the death of Lieut. Col. George W. Chandler, who was killed yesterday in a charge upon the enemy's works at this point, by a musket shot through the body. Death followed the wound almost instantly. It is unnecessary for me to express to you the sorrow which his loss occasions me, for you know my high estimation of his character, (shared by all who knew him here and at home,) and the warm friendship which has existed between us. The service has, in him, indeed, lost a capable, efficient officer, his regiment a brave and gallant leader, and his brother officers a comrade with whom they have been proud to do battle, and to whose efficiency and continued, faithful performance of duty, much of the reputation of the 88th is due. It is strange and mysterious that one should have escaped so many perils and dangers to fall at last in the closing struggle of the war, but I know that, on his part, the sacrifice of his life for the cause of the nation was willingly and cheerfully made: his patriotism was untainted, unselfish and rare.

---

* These are, indeed, the words of a pure and patriotic heart, and like as a voice from the grave, should scorch the class at whom they are cast.

He died as he would have wished—on the field—without pain or suffering, saying only—"Give me some water and let me die." * * *

All that I can offer in aid of his friends will be gladly done. We are still in the midst of the campaign, when to end, no one knows. The work before us is yet hard, but will be accomplished. Very truly yours,

GEORGE W. SMITH,
Major Commanding 88th Illinois Volunteer Infantry.

A letter from Col. F. T. Sherman, chief of Gen. Howard's staff—dated "near Marietta, Ga., June 27," giving an account of the repulse at Kenesaw Mountain—says:

Lieutenant Colonel George W. Chandler, of the 88th, was almost instantly killed at the head of his regiment—one more has been added to the list of the noble and pure of our land who have laid down their lives in defending the right. May he rest in peace.

On the afternoon of July 4th, 1864, a despatch from Captain H. H. Cushing at Nashville announced to his unsuspecting friends the sad and serious intelligence that "Colonel Chandler's remains were on the way to Chicago by express," being the first announcement of his death. Immediate steps were taken for arrangements to pay due respect to the remains, and on the following morning, "on 'change," at the Board of Trade rooms, Col. John L. Hancock, President of the Association, introduced to the audience George M. Kimbark, who announced the mournful information he had received in fitting terms, and offered the following preamble and resolutions, which were unanimously adopted:

WHEREAS, Providence in its wisdom has stricken down upon the field of battle the late noble, efficient and gallant Lieutenant Colonel George W. Chandler, commanding the 88th Regiment (2d Board of Trade) Illinois Infantry, and thereby bereft us of a friend with a heart awake to all the kind offices of a noble and christian spirit, and the nation of one of her most earnest and ardent supporters; therefore, be it

Resolved, That we do humbly bow ourselves before Almighty God in sincere mourning for one we loved, and for one in whom the nation has lost a pure and noble patriot, a gallant and fearless defender. Brave in battle, earnest in the cause for which he has so gallantly laid down his life, beloved by all who knew him, we honor his memory, and deeply mourn his irreparable loss.

"None knew him but to love him,
Nor named him but to praise."

To his aged parents, sister and brothers, although in a foreign land, we offer

10

our heartfelt sympathy in this the hour of their affliction, and tender them as our boon of consolation the proud name their noble son and brother has left behind him, both in civil and military life——a record resplendent with deeds of kindness, heroism, and pure and noble manliness, with the assurance that, while we deeply mourn his loss, we shall ever cherish in our hearts fond remembrance of his many virtues.

Resolved, That these resolutions be published in each of the daily papers of the city, and that copies be sent to his relatives and friends, and that the officers and members of this Board, in a body, follow Colonel Chandler's remains to the cars which are to bear them to his friends and final resting place.

Resolved, That the President of this Board appoint a committee of five to meet other committees at the Tremont House this evening, at 7½ o'clock, to make arrangements for paying a suitable tribute to the remains of the honored dead.

In accordance with the above resolutions, a Committee of Arrangements was appointed, consisting of Messrs. Kimbark, Tucker, Munn, Wicker and Rumsey. The President of the Board, Colonel Hancock, was subsequently added.

A meeting was held at the Tremont House in the evening, at which were present the Committee of the Board of Trade, and many of the friends of the deceased. Mr. Kimbark was appointed Chairman, Lieut. George Chandler, Secretary, and Col. Hancock was requested to obtain a military escort.

A committee of three was appointed by the Chairman to draft resolutions. This committee consisted of C. A. Gregory, Edson Keith and John Tyrell. These gentlemen retired, and soon returned with the following resolutions, which were unanimously adopted:

WHEREAS, It has pleased God to remove from our midst George W. Chandler, Lieutenant Colonel of the 88th Regiment of Illinois Volunteers, killed while gallantly leading his command against the rebels at the battle of Kenesaw Mountain; and

WHEREAS, We desire to express our appreciation of his worth as a man and a soldier; therefore,

Resolved, That we, in our intercourse with Colonel Chandler in civil life, have ever found him to be a gentleman in every respect, and an upright and honorable man. His associates in the service also were forced by his admirable conduct upon every occasion, whether in the camp, upon the march, or on the field of battle, to acknowledge him pre-eminent for cool courage, soldierly ability, and regard for the welfare of his comrades, and conspicuous for daring gallantry.

Resolved, That our army has lost, by the death of Lieut. Col. Chandler, a good soldier, and our country a brave defender.

Resolved, That we condole with the relatives and friends of Col. Chandler, in the loss which they have sustained by his death.

Resolved, That we sympathize deeply with the officers and men of the 88th Illinois Volunteers, in their loss of a beloved comrade in arms, and a faithful friend.

Resolved, That a copy of these resolutions be sent to the parents of Col. Chandler, and also a copy to Col. F. T. Sherman, with a request that they be read to his regiment, and also that they be published in the Chicago daily papers.

The old members of the 88th were appointed a committee for the reception of the remains.

The body of Col. Chandler reached Chicago on the 6th July, in care of Capt. H. H. Cushing, Q. M. 4th Army Corps, Department of the Cumberland, inclosed in a handsome metallic burial case. On the morning following, the remains were taken to Bryan Hall and laid in state, appropriately and beautifully decorated with many handsome wreaths of flowers and four American flags, (one of which he had fought under at the battles of Perryville and Stones River,) gracefully grouped at his head, with the sword, with which he had carved his bright name on many a hard-fought field, laid across the coffin over his manly breast. The sword was thus inscribed:

Presented to Major George W. Chandler, after the battle of Stones River, by the line officers of his regiment, on the occasion of his being appointed by Major General Rosecrans to command his "Brigade of Honor," in consideration of his gallant services in the field.

At 12 o'clock noon, the hall was opened to the public. All the afternoon a saddened throng of citizens, in whose grateful hearts the story of his gallant deeds seemed freshly written, passed in with softened tread and faces clouded with the general grief, to look upon the coffin which held the corpse of the departed, and the true sword with which he had carved for himself so honorable a name.

At half-past 3 o'clock, detachments of the 8th and 15th Veteran Reserve Corps, under command of Maj. Skinner, together with the pall-bearers, citizens and military, the guard of honor, composed of the members of " Co. D.," members of the City Government, Board of Trade, Mercantile Association, Young Men's Association, Young Men's Christian Association, and citizens, marched to the hall, headed by the excellent band of the Veteran Reserve Corps.

The large concourse which had assembled completely filled the hall, except the open space in the centre where the seats had been removed, and which had been kept clear by the police. In this open space was placed the coffin and its decorations, the stand of regimental colors gracefully drooping its folds over his head.

At 4 o'clock, the relations of the deceased, with the pall-bearers, military escort, and guard of honor, took their positions around the coffin, when a dead-march was executed by the band. The Rev. Rob't L. Collier, of the Wabash Avenue M. E. Church, then read appropriately selected portions of the scriptures; after which he addressed the assembly in a few remarks suggested by the occasion. He said:

No draping more glorious can hang around any man's coffin, than that you have hung around these remains. The white in these flags is the true symbol of national purity; the red, the symbol of the bloody struggle through which it was established, and is now being redeemed; the stars, the crown which is now awaiting in heaven its gallant defenders.

The name of the departed is only one in the long list of those who have gone from among us to do nobly and die bravely. Col. Chandler was a young man, and the noble elements of his character might have long thrown their lustre upon his life, and upon the lives of his companions and friends, but that another and higher power called him forth in the hour of public peril to die for his country. I knew *Mr.* Chandler well; he was a pure and generous man. I have heard of *Col.* Chandler that he was a humane and brave commander.

We shall never see him here again. But we have the memories of his pure life and unselfish nature, of his gallantry, and of his death. These will never forsake us, but will journey on with us until we meet him. We find him an altar on which to consecrate a higher patriotism and a holier devotion to his country, to our country, and to God.

Prayer was then offered, and the benediction pronounced; after which, the remains were removed, and the procession formed in the following order:

Chief Marshal, Col. Joseph H. Tucker.
Veteran Reserve Corps Band.
Military Escort, composed of detachments from the 8th and 15th Regiments
Veteran Reserve Corps.

MILITARY PALL-BEARERS.			CITIZEN PALL-BEARERS.
Lieutenant Chas. T. Boal,			R. Sherman,
Lieutenant S. Titsworth,			Edson Keith,
Lieutenant F. C. Goodwin,	Ex-Officers of the 88th.	HEARSE.	Leroy Swamsteadt,
Lieutenant Geo. Chandler,			Samuel J. Glover,
Lieutenant H. C. McDonald,			U. H. Crosby,
Lieutenant G. F. Bigelow,			L. Sherman,
"Co. D." Guard of Honor in citizens' dress.			"Co. D." Guard of Honor in citizens' dress.

Assistant Marshall, Col. J. M. W. Jones.
Officers in the Army and Navy.
Mayor and City Officers.
Board of Trade.

Assistant Marshal, George M Kimbark, Esq.
Executive Board and Members of Young Men's Association.
Mercantile Association.
Officers and Members of Young Men's Christian Association.
Citizens generally.

On the arrival of the remains at his former home in Canada, a very large concourse of his friends, acquaintances and citizens assembled to pay the last, sad tribute of regard to him who they so dearly loved and respected.

A funeral discourse was delivered by Col. Chandler's former pastor, the Rev. Mr. Lindsay, aged 84 years, the resolutions adopted and sketch of the ceremonies at Chicago read from the pulpit, to the great gratification of his relatives and friends; after which, all that remained of that once brave soldier and noble man was followed by sad hearts to his final resting-place, where an appropriate monument will be erected to his honored memory. "Peace be with him." It is sweet to die, so nobly, so manly and pure, a death all might envy.

Dying, he has left behind a proud and honorable record worth having lived for. Such names and such heroes will gleam brightly on the pages of our nation's history, not dimmed because they are many, but brilliant and prominent each in the resplendency of their glorious deeds, as the galaxy trails its band of brightness athwart the heavens, to be readily resolved by the observer into single stars.

COLONEL MILLER.

Col. SILAS MILLER was born in Tompkins county, in the State of New York, on the 15th of April, 1839. His father moved to Aurora, Kane county, Illinois, in August, 1842, and died when Silas was five years old, leaving a wife and six children in rather destitute circumstances. Mrs. Miller continued keeping house, and maintained her children together until Silas (the youngest of the family) was ten years old, at which period they all began to earn their own support, when Mrs. Miller suspended housekeeping.

Silas commenced his education under the direction of A. P. Farnsworth, in the school-house standing on the ground now occupied as the Public Park, and upon the identical spot where his funeral sermon was preached. He possessed a decidedly independent disposition from his infancy, and at a very early age manifested a very great liking for books and study. He was a very apt scholar, and while in school, was always two or three classes ahead of the other children of his age. His favorite study was mathematics.

When he was but ten years of age he started in business for himself. His first efforts were upon the farm of M. N. Norris; consideration to be received—what he wanted to eat and wear. This arrangement kept him alive and in clothing, but did not leave him much ahead except in years and muscle. He followed farming only a short time, and even that under several different landlords. The last agricultural employer soon returned him to his friends with the advice, that he "could never make a farmer out of Silas, as *he had altogether too many books in his head!*" After being convinced of his shortcomings and unsuitableness as a farmer, Silas, unsubdued, determined to change his tactics and try another occupation. It was an absolute necessity. He was here and must live, and that principally by the sweat of his own brow. The next and only thing that presented itself was the printing business. He concluded to accept—yes, he would even become a printer's devil, and live upon his own resources and earnings, rather than depend on the assistance of others. In the spring of 1853 he entered the office of the *Aurora Beacon* as an apprentice.

From the day that the long-legged, white-headed boy Silas entered the printing-office he became a changed being; a new ambition took possession of him, and he seemed to live a different life. He had found his affinity among the types and papers, which opened up to him a fresh field for study and thought, all strange and new, but in accordance with his hopes and manly aspirations. He labored there faithfully for nearly two years, discharging his duties in a satisfactory manner, when he struck higher, and obtained a situation in the news-room of the Chicago *Evening Journal*, where he remained for almost two years. During this time he never entered the theatre or visited any other place of amusement, but labored faithfully night and day, always economizing and saving his money, with which he was to defray the expenses of his intended studies. He has related to the writer that during all his then residence in Chicago, he did not go three blocks from his boarding-house, except as he went to and from his work at the *Journal* office. At this time his acquirements in the ordinary branches of study were excellent, he having spent *all* his leisure hours for two years in preparing for his future studies. He learned and labored regularly from sixteen to eighteen hours every day of the time he worked in the *Journal* office. After leaving, he again returned to Aurora, and recommenced work in the *Beacon* office. After a short while, he entered Clark Seminary as a student, attended several terms in that institution, at the same time working in the *Beacon* office all the spare intervals he could find, to enable him to defray his expenses at school.

From Clark Seminary Silas went to the State of New York, and spent two years at Fort Edward Seminary. During the last year of his membership of this academy, he was the acknowledged leader of the school in oratory and literary composition. When he returned from Fort Edward, he entered the office of Charles Wheaton as a law student. He spent the winter of 1860 in teaching school near Bristol, Kendall county.

From his school he returned to Wheaton's office, and resumed his law studies, in which pursuit he was engaged on the rebellion breaking out, when he exchanged his books for the sword, in defense of his government and its laws.

In April, 1861, soon after Fort Sumter was fired upon, he enlisted as a private in Co. C of the old 7th Regiment. On the organization of the company he was elected 2d Lieutenant, and before the regiment left Springfield, he was promoted to the 1st Lieutenancy, serving in that capacity three months, the term of his enlistment. His regiment was among the first that arrived at Cairo, and notwithstanding the incompleteness of their outfit, and the consequent deprivations and hardships they endured, the young Lieutenant returned to Aurora unsatisfied. The object for which he enlisted was not obtained; the rebellion was not crushed. Armed traitors were still in the land threatening the life of his government. This he would not submit to. He had sworn to keep his sword unsheathed until either himself or the rebellion died.

True to his pledge, he was among the first to advise and urge the formation of the 36th Regiment Illinois Volunteers, and as soon as his three months term of enlistment expired, he returned to Aurora, re-enlisted, and incited others to do the same, until Co. B was filled. Upon their organization, he was unanimously elected Captain. He left Camp Hammond, Aurora, along with his regiment, on the 24th of September, 1861, and went with it to Rolla, Mo.

After the regiment was organized, he sought and procured all the various published works on military tactics, and applied himself diligently in learning the principles and rudiments of war and military science. In this, as in everything else, he was *thoroughly* thorough. The bugle calls and various drills, especially the skirmish, were his daily lessons and constant themes. So diligently did he apply himself, and so thoroughly did he accomplish his self-imposed task, that he soon was the recognized drill-master of the regiment. Although the youngest Captain, he was the umpire to whom was referred all regimental disputes and disagreements as to drills and military science.

He was not satisfied to simply possess this information himself. He worked hard and urged strongly to have it promulgated to the regiment. At first he appointed certain hours every day, when he demanded the attendance of the lieutenants and non-commissioned officers of his company, and instructed them in the bugle calls and skirmish drill. So persistent was he in this custom and exercise, that the balance of the command considered his bugle and its squeaking cry a nuisance. They did not understand nor appreciate its importance. He did, and therefore persevered.

His studious habits and officerlike conduct soon attracted the attention of his superiors, and when any feat of special consequence was to be performed, Capt. Miller, with his lively and vigorous Co. B, were quite sure to be selected. During the early Missouri and Arkansas campaign, he did good and important service. At Pea Ridge, when Price and his Missouri rebels were first met by Curtis and Sigel, Capt. Miller and skirmish tactics were brought into immediate requisition. The enemy was met, secreted; skirmishers were needed to hunt them up. Capt. Miller, with Co. B, and his heretofore unwelcome bugle sounds, now became an object of regard and admiration. His shrill bugle calls now became forcible music. They meant business. Now we could discern their use, which he had comprehended months before. He and his company were called for by Gen. Sigel, and immediately sent forward as the first skirmishers of that army and campaign. And most gallantly did they respond and efficiently accomplish their task.

From that day Capt. Miller's reputation as a thoroughly drilled skirmish officer was a fixed fact. From that day up to the time he was wounded, in all the various battles in which the 36th participated, he was certain to be assigned the *responsible post in charge of the skirmish line*. It was his pleasure and duty to face the first rebel bullets and exchange the first leaden compliments with the enemy in a majority of the battles of the Southwest.

When the regiment was sent to Mississippi and stationed at Rienzi, the extreme outpost of our army, it became necessary to advance a force beyond the main body as a picket. Again Capt. Miller was selected and placed in command, and, as on all other occasions, he performed his duties well. Here it was that he first formed the acquaintance of his much esteemed friend, Maj. Gen. Phil. Sheridan. That intimacy grew into a mutual, life-long friendship. From that time until Gen. Sheridan left the Army of the Cumberland, Captain (then Major, then Colonel) Miller was one of his most intimate friends and constant supporters. While stationed at Rienzi, Col. Greusel was placed in charge of a brigade, and Capt. Miller in command of the regiment. From Rienzi, Miss., to Cincinnati, O., and thence to Louisville, Ky., thence through the Buell Kentucky campaign and the battle of Perryville, the regiment was commanded by Capt. Miller. Never did any officer do better, or give more general satisfaction than he did in this terrible fight. His command, who had always admired him, now loved him.

In September, 1862, he was commissioned Major of the regiment, and continued in command during its sojourn at Edgefield, Mill Creek, and on the march from the latter place to Murfreesboro, Tenn., and during the first days' fights of that memorable struggle. On the morning of the 31st day of December, 1862, he was wounded and captured by the rebels. Though maimed, crippled and bleeding, he was marched to the rear, and thence transported to Atlanta, where he was placed in prison, in company with many of his brother officers. From Atlanta he was conveyed to Richmond, and located in the notorious Libby Prison for safe keeping. He was held as a prisoner of war for over four months, and then exchanged. On getting his freedom, he paid a hurried visit to his home in Aurora, spent his twenty days' leave of absence, and then left for the front to join his regiment in fighting the enemies of our government.

During his incarceration at Richmond, both the Colonel and Lieutenant Colonel resigned, and in March, 1863, he was commissioned Colonel of the regiment, although he was but twenty-three years of age, and quite beardless.

For instance, to illustrate his youthful look and appearance, the following incident is *apropos:* While at home on the above-mentioned furlough, he was in Chicago looking at some military goods, in company with several other officers of his regiment, and he inquired to see some shoulder straps. The clerk, a wise-looking individual, said: "Which do you desire, first or second Lieutenant?" His comrades considered it a rare joke, and frequently told it on the Colonel.

He took part in all the various encounters and skirmishes in Rosecrans' advance from Murfreesboro to Chattanooga, and fought on the field of Chickamauga, where the 36th suffered severely. Again, he and his regiment were engaged at Mission Ridge, where he commanded a brigade, and won new laurels both for his bravery and military sagacity.

After the battle of Mission Ridge, he went with his command into East Tennessee, and there endured one of the most severe campaigns that has been made during the war.

Notwithstanding all these things, in January, 1864, he and his handful of remaining heroes re-enlisted for another three years as veterans. They received a furlough of thirty days, and came home to enjoy it. But there was too much matter of fact—too much business about the Colonel to enjoy furloughs or other inactivity. True to his government and his nature, he hurried his regiment back to the field of duty as soon as the time of leisure expired. His command was returned to East Tennessee, and marched from thence back to Chattanooga, and then started with Gen. Sherman on his eventful campaign to Atlanta.

He participated in all the engagements between Chattanooga and Kenesaw Mountain, where he received the fatal wound. In most of them he had his old place—*the skirmish line*.

From his brother officers in the 36th we learn that he had a positive presentiment that he should be hit in this campaign. Before the battle of Resaca he conversed with the Lieut. Col., and told him that he felt that he should be hit, but nevertheless he could and would go into the fight and do his duty. Escaping from that battle unhurt, he, notwithstanding, did his duty faithfully, and exposed himself unreservedly and fearlessly.

Again, before the battle of Dallas, he repeated his apprehensions of his fate, and instructed the officers of his regiment that if he fell, he desired them, if possible, to secure his body and send it to his friends in Aurora for interment. He said that he did not wish to remain alone down in that rebel country, but added that, in no event did he want them to abate their efforts against the enemy on his account. He said, "FIRST WHIP THE ENEMY, THEN LOOK AFTER ME!" They tried to persuade him that his fears were unfounded; said that he had passed through so many engagements unhurt, that they could not think he would meet such a fate now. He coolly replied— "Boys, this thing isn't played out yet!" True enough, it was not.

He who had fought his way from a private to the coloneley of his regiment, was a doomed man, and he, brave soldier, felt it. Still he would not falter. He kept his perilous place, *the skirmish line*, until the last moment, on Monday morning, the 27th of June, when he fell, seriously wounded, with drawn sabre in hand, gallantly leading his men in the charge on Kenesaw Mountain. He was immediately carried to the rear, where his wound was examined and dressed by the surgeon in charge, and found to be through the right shoulder and shoulder-blade, shattering the latter badly. While upon the operating table, undergoing a severe surgical operation, he inquired how the contest was going, and how many wounded men had been brought in. Chaplain Haigh replied, "Fifteen, and all from the 36th Regiment." He exclaimed, "My God! they will murder all those dear boys," and then wept like a child.

Although seriously and mortally wounded himself, yet his thoughts and anxieties were concerning the results of the fight and the welfare of his men. Brave, unselfish Silas! What a loss to the service, and especially to his regiment, to have him fall in the midst of the impending struggle.

He was sent from the front to Chattanooga, and from there to the officers' hospital in Nashville. The weather was extremely hot, the distance so great, and the accommodations so poor, that he suffered severely in being transported from the front to Nashville. He knew and appreciated the extremity of the situation and the necessities of the case, and therefore bore all the incurred torture with his usual soldierlike fortitude.

Arrived at Nashville, he immediately telegraphed to his

brother, and for Dr. Young, an old acquaintance, and formerly Surgeon of the 36th Regiment. Harvey Miller and the doctor left immediately, and when they arrived at Nashville, they found him indeed severely wounded. The doctor and his friends remained with him constantly from that time until he died, on Wednesday morning, July 27th, just one month from the day he was wounded.

The weather during the entire month was excessively hot, and unfavorable for wounded men. Gangrene soon made its appearance in its worst and most persistent form, requiring severe surgical operations, and the severest remedies known to the medical profession. All these means were most faithfully applied and persevered in, but all to no purpose. Empyema finally supervened, and the courageous soldier who had braved almost everything, now surrendered up his life without a murmur or a struggle. When he was told by his physician that he could not possibly recover, he considered a moment and then said, "Doctor, I do not like to hear it." This was all the regret he uttered.

He was a true soldier to the last. His soul was in the cause. During his four weeks' suffering, his whole anxiety was concerning the army and its achievements. When awake or asleep, while sane or delirious, he talked about the army, his regiment and its boys. Several hours before he died he became somewhat unconscious, and talked incoherently. He was back to his old place on the skirmish line, urging on the boys and reporting to Gen. Howard. His last words were: "*Keep down, and keep your eyes peeled!*" In a word, *he died on the skirmish line.*

The announcement that Col. Silas Miller was dead, and his remains were then on their way to Aurora for interment, went with a sad and heavy pressure to the heart of every person in that city, he was so universally beloved. Thousands of the citizens waited on the Friday evening for the arrival of the train, and received in mute sorrow all that remained of him whom they had but a few short months before bidden adieu with cheers and vivas, and in whom in never-betrayed confidence they placed the welfare of brother, husband, son and father.

The body was taken to the residence of James G. Barr, Esq., and lay there, visited by hundreds who desired one glance at the inanimate clay, until the funeral ceremonies on the Sunday afternoon.

The Colonel having been made a Freemason in 1861, that ancient fraternity took in charge the ceremonies of the occasion, inviting to join them such military men as might be able and inclined. At three o'clock, "Jerusalem Temple" Lodge, with invited brethren from Aurora Lodge, Oswego, Batavia and Geneva, numbering 300, all clad in appropriate mourning, left Jerusalem Temple rooms, and escorted by a company of military under Captain Pritchard, and an honorary corps of old officers—all marshaled by William H. Hawkins—took up their solemn line of march to Mr. Barr's residence, whence the hearse and mourners were escorted to the Park. Here at least 4000 people were gathered, to pay their final tribute to the brave. The funeral services were led in a beautiful hymn by the Congregational choir, followed with prayer by Rev. Mr. Bugbee, an oration by Rev. Dr. Forrester, and prayer by Rev. Mr. Brown from Oswego. From the park the funeral train passed to the cemetery, marching to the grave notes of "Pleyel's Hymn." On arriving there, the interesting services of the Masonic order were read. Each brother cast upon the coffin lid his sprig of evergreen, emblematic of eternal life; the military salute was fired, and all that was mortal of our beloved friend and brother, the noble man, the devoted and patriotic soldier, was consigned to the earth "from whence it came."

CAPTAIN CHANDLER.

Capt. KNOWLTON H. CHANDLER, son of Marcus and Martha Chandler, was born on the 30th of August, 1830, in Connecticut. He and his parents emigrated to Illinois in the year 1834.

From early childhood he was remarkable for his amiable disposition, and by his noble and upright conduct won the love and esteem of all who knew him. He atten'ed school until he arrived at the age of seventeen, when he entered his father's store at Chandlersville as clerk, and remained there two years.

In the spring of 1853, he started for California by way of the plains, and arrived there on the 24th of August. For some time he worked in the mines, but this business getting distasteful to him, he became proprietor of the City Hotel in St. Louis, California, and continued so until he left the country. After an absence of five years he returned home and engaged in the lumber business in Bath, Mason county, but spent most of his time in Chandlersville, in a drug store of which he was a partner. While thus engaged at this latter place, he was elected Police Magistrate, which office he held until he entered the army.

Although devotedly attached to his home and friends, when the first call was made for troops he offered his services to his country, raised a company and tendered them, but the quota being filled, they were rejected. For this company the ladies of Chandlersville made a beautiful flag, and when it was presented, Capt. Chandler responded, saying, that whenever he should go, that beautiful emblem of Liberty should bear him fellowship. At the battle in which he lost his life, that flag was torn to shreds.

When the second call for troops was made, he was offered the 1st Lieutenancy of a company got up by the people of Virginia and Chandlersville, which position he accepted. This company went into the service as Co. F of the 19th Regiment Illinois Volunteers.

Capt. Chandler followed the fortunes of the glorious 19th Illinois through all the hardships and disasters met by that gallant regiment. Capt. Allard, who commanded Company F, having resigned his post, Lieut. Chandler was promoted to the Captaincy on the 1st of December, 1861.

His was a noble, generous and impulsive nature—a man who would live or die, sink or swim with the stars and stripes. At the battle near Murfreesboro, when the left of the Federal army was about to be turned by the impetuosity of the rebels, and Gen. Rosecrans asked "who would save the left?" Col. Scott replied—"the 19th Illinois!" and while that regiment of heroes advanced to meet the shock, the gallant Chandler led his company through a storm of leaden hail until he fell dead, shot through the brain, on the 2d of January, 1863. Though his military career was brief, his name will be revered and honored as one of the heroes that fell in saving the Army of the Cumberland from disaster and defeat.

So falls the brave; so does stern war mark its victims. His sisters' warm affection—the love of his men, who regarded him as a brother—could not turn aside the fatal bullet. The endearing memories that cling around his name, and the hope of meeting him in the grand army above, where all are victors,— are all we have of our departed friend. When this bloody war is over, when the country is purged of treason, and when the marble shaft—commemorative of noble deeds and a country saved—ascends high towards heaven, the name of Chandler will be there.

ADJUTANT HALL.

Adjt. HENRY WARE HALL, son of the Rev. Nathaniel Hall, was born in Dorchester, Massachusetts, on the 21st of March, 1839. He was a pleasant child, not precocious, but fair to look upon; docile, affectionate, quick-witted, and sweet-tempered; easily managed at home, and always a favorite with his mates. His boyhood was a boyhood of health and gladness. He was a joy to himself, and a joy to those who watched over him as their first-born.

When he was nine years of age, he became a pupil of one of the public schools, and afterwards entered the High School, leaving it to his own credit and that of his accomplished teacher, fully prepared, for admission into Harvard College, in 1856, as a member of what is known as the class of 1860.

Henry remained two years at Cambridge, and then—that he might have a better chance, which he readily accepted and grandly used—entered Antioch College, Yellow Springs, Ohio, in charge of his father's friend, Hon. Horace Mann. He finished his course in that institution, with honor, in the summer of 1860, and passed the following autumn and winter in Dorchester, reading, and making up his mind what profession to adopt. He finally decided to be a lawyer, and to reside at the West. He was a student in Chicago when the war broke out; and, after fitting himself in a drill-club, early joined the 51st Regiment Illinois Volunteers as Lieutenant of Co. B. He was soon made Captain; subsequently resigning that rank, in the belief that he could thereby be more useful, to take the position of Adjutant, which he held to the time of his death.

The regiment served in the expedition down the Mississippi, at Island No. 10, and at Corinth. It afterwards joined the forces under Rosecrans, fought at Stones River, and took part in the campaign to Chattanooga. In the battle of Chickamauga, early in the autumn of 1863, Adjt. Hall was severely

11

wounded. He was taken prisoner whilst in the field-hospital, and paroled. On hearing that his son lay wounded, Mr. Hall, after a tedious, anxious, and hazardous journey, found him less dangerously hurt than he had been led to fear, and brought him home a convalescent, to be soon made strong and whole again by breathing his native air. He remained until December, when he left to return to St. Louis, to be ready for duty as soon as he should be exchanged.

He had the pleasure of seeing his regiment at Chicago whilst enjoying the furlough it had obtained by re-enlisting; but he could not go back with it. Not until the campaign in Georgia, under Sherman, was he released from his parole, and allowed to go to the front. He made all haste to go; hurrying along what to him was the path of duty; well knowing, from his past experience, that it might be, as it proved to be, hurrying to meet death. He had hardly been a month at his post, when, on the 27th of June, 1864, the 51st Illinois led an assaulting column, on Kenesaw Mountain. Adjutant Hall was in front, cheering on the men, when he fell at about eleven o'clock in the forenoon. The attack was unsuccessful, and our forces were driven back. Some of the soldiers of the 51st were wounded in daring but fruitless attempts to reach his body. It was recovered the next day under a flag of truce, and buried in a retired spot within our lines; the grave carefully fenced and marked by his surviving comrades. It was found ten steps from the breastworks, struck by nearly a dozen bullets. His death must have been instantaneous. The enemy spoke of his daring gallantry, and met the application for his remains and sword with courtesy and kindness.

His distinguished gallantry as a soldier, combined with many noble qualities both of head and heart, made him greatly beloved by all his comrades; and when he fell so gloriously on Kenesaw, leading his men to the cannon's mouth, a spontaneous tribute of affection and respect was offered by many brother officers in view of what they deemed a mutual loss.

Col. (now Gen.) Bradley writes of him:

His loss comes nearer to me and hurts me more than any that has ever fallen on us. He was, in many respects, the foremost man among us, and in capacity and cultivation, had few equals. He was a natural leader, and his courage was equal to any man's. He was the most gallant man I ever saw, and a splendid fellow in all respects.

Capt. Waterman writes:

On the 28th of June, a truce having been arranged, Col. Bradley and myself went out and recovered his body. He probably died instantly, as he was pierced by at least ten balls. The rebel Col. Rice spoke of him as one of the bravest of men, who had attracted and received the admiration of his soldiers, for the manner in which he led the regiment. He was the first from our circle from Chicago to go, and while we live, the memory of him will live with us.

Capt. Wiseman writes:

Col. Rice and other rebel officers who were there at the time, said he was one of the bravest and most gallant men they had ever seen, and seemed to regret the necessity of firing on so brave a foe; "but," said the Colonel, "it was dangerous to let him come further." (They had reserved their fire until the attacking column was within a few rods of their entrenchments.)

Surgeon Magee, in concluding a letter, says:

In conclusion, I wish to say, that in the death of Adjt. Hall, our regiment has sustained a loss which cannot be repaired. As an officer, he was always prompt and efficient, whether in the office or field. He held the universal confidence, respect, and esteem, not only of his own regiment, but of all his associates.

Major Rust writes:

The intellectual capacity and culture of Adjt. Hall were recognized by all his associates; but it was his noble manliness, and unselfish friendship, that endeared him to me. * * His was a cool courage, born of a sense of duty, giving him, in the seething cauldron of battle, the complete control of all his faculties.

COLONEL HARMON.

Col. Oscar F. Harmon was born in Wheatland, Monroe county, New York, on the 31st of May, 1827; his birthplace one of the "choice places of earth." His father, Ira Harmon, and his grandfather, Dea. Rawson Harmon, are well known by the people of that county as among the early settlers of that justly celebrated town.

His boyhood and early manhood were spent on the farm and in school; and though he did not receive a college course, he yet had a fine education. The hardy labor of the farm caused him to be "well grown," and of a manly form, and, standing six feet four inches, gave him the air and appearance of one of "nature's noblemen," which he truly was. He had a generous and noble heart, always open to friends and friendship.

He was the second of a family of six brothers; and he was the first of the family (including his parents) to fall—the first to pass over that "bourne from whence no traveler returns."

He united with the Baptist Church of his native place, at an early age, and ever after remained a consistent member.

After the completion of his academic course, his first year and a half were spent in the (then) popular law school of Prof. John W. Fowler, at Ballston Spa, N. Y., and subsequently he passed another year and a half in the office of Smith & Griffin, at Rochester, N. Y.

In the month of March, 1853, he removed to Danville, Illinois, where he entered upon the practice of his profession, and subsequently with Hon. Oliver L. Davis. He pursued his professional career with distinguished success until the summer of 1862. Few men in the profession of law have deserved and enjoyed in an equal degree the public confidence. Respectable, but not greatly excelling in forensic ability, he stood unrivalled in his remarkable accuracy as a pleader and in the reliability and soundness of his counsel and opinions, and in those qualities which entitled him to a character, often supposed to be too rare in the profession, of an honest lawyer. He possessed a singular power, evidently unconscious, but not less real, of winning the hearts of all around him. Acquaintance with him soon begat esteem, and esteem quickly ripened into affection.

Soon after his establishment at Danville, he was married to Mrs. Elizabeth C. Hill, a most estimable lady. His amiability and affection in his family diffused happiness throughout the entire household, insomuch that the sojourner of a few weeks would depart expressing the regret that the pleasantest interview of his life was passed.

He served one session in the Legislature of his adopted State in the winter of 1859, as a member of the Lower House. He then continued in the practice of his profession at Danville, in connection with Hon. Oliver L. Davis, until the spring of 1861, when his partner being elected Judge of his circuit, he continued alone till he entered the service.

At the opening of the war he was among the leaders of the first military organization in his town. His position from first to last, was for the preservation of the Union at any cost. During the first year of the war, important business responsibilities made it impossible for him to enter active service, but the struggle in his mind in the midst of duties apparently conflicting, was constant and painful.

At length, in August, 1862, the desire to serve his country in her army could no longer be repressed, and sacrificing a lucrative business, the society of an affectionate family, and all the congenial pursuits of life, he went forth to share the fortunes of war. He was elected to the command of the 125th Regiment Illinois Volunteers, which position he held with increasing popularity until his death. Kind and affable in all his relations as an officer, he was nevertheless prompt, faithful and laborious in the discharge of duty, successfully striving to bring his regiment to the highest standard of military efficiency.

His regiment first went to Cincinnati, thence to Louisville, and from there, by forced marches, to Perryville, where it participated in the short but severe contest at that place. They were afterwards stationed at Nashville for nearly a year, where the 125th became a model regiment. They were then moved to Chattanooga, where the regiment remained till after the battle of Missionary Ridge, in which it took only a slight part. It then went to Knoxville, under Brig. Gen. J. C. Davis, for the relief of Burnside, when everything was endured, by forced marches, and exposure, and lying on the ground without tents, that men are capable of enduring. On the opening of the spring campaign in 1864, the regiment, now as heretofore in the division of Gen. J. C. Davis, and in the brigade of Col. Dan. McCook, started south under Sherman. It went through all the lesser battles previous to the desperate charge upon Kenesaw Mountain, with small losses; and Col. Harmon having never received a scratch, his friends had fondly and flatteringly come to believe that God would protect him and bring him safely through. None, then, but those who have experienced the same, can tell with what crushing weight the tidings of his fall and death came to his family and a large circle of friends.

On the 27th of June, 1864, in the terrible assault upon the rebel position at Kenesaw Mountain, his regiment was assigned to the most difficult point. The brigade commander, General McCook, mortally wounded, was carried to the rear, and his command devolved upon Col. Harmon, the next in rank. But within the space of a few minutes, as he was cheering on his gallant boys, with sword drawn and uplifted above his head, and in front of his regiment, a ball struck him in the breast, and he fell, exclaiming, "I am shot dead," and in a few minutes expired.

He leaves a wife, who was most sincerely and strongly attached to him, and four young children—the eldest nine years and the youngest fifteen months; thus sundering the strongest ties that ever bound man to earth.

He wrote to his wife on the evening before, and again in the morning at daylight, before the assault, that he dreamed on the night before that she and his mother came to see him, and that they "bid him good bye," and that the parting was enough to make "angels weep;" yet, he adds, (and a presentiment of his approaching death must have then weighed heavily upon him,) "if I fall, I shall fall at my post."

He is gone. He sleeps with the heroes of all time. And

though many, perhaps, as great and good as he have died as bravely in their country's sacred cause, yet it is the spontaneous sentiment of all who knew Col. Harmon, that no more noble offering than he has yet been sacrificed as the price of a nation's redemption.

LIEUTENANT YORK.

Lieut. JOHN YORK was born on the 8th of November, 1816, in the district that now composes Morgan county, then in the Territory of Illinois. His father, William York, was one of the early settlers of that section, and in politics always adhered to the old Democratic faith—always for his country, no matter who were its enemies. He fought in the war of 1812, and in the Black Hawk war of 1832.

Lieut. York lived and worked with his father on the farm until 1847, when he was married to Miss Precious Lake on the 16th of October. When the county was formed from the territory of Morgan, he was left 'a resident of Cass, in the Indian Creek Precinct. He resided during life in the neighborhood of his birthplace, except for the term of eighteen months that he spent in the State of Louisiana. For a number of years he was an earnest, active party man of the Democratic creed, and for two or three terms was elected Precinct Justice of the Peace.

In the fall of 1861, as early as he could leave his crops and his family in a situation to allow his absence, he took a position as private in the army. On September 7th, he joined the 32d

Regiment Illinois Volunteers, at Springfield. The regiment not being then filled up, he was sent back to the vicinity of his home on recruiting service, and by his energy raised thirty men in Cass and Morgan counties. With these he was attached to Co. H, Capt. Duncan commanding, and elected 2d Lieutenant.

During the winter of 1861–2, he endured hard service, but was in no prominent engagement until the battle of Shiloh, on the 6th and 7th of April, 1862. At that fight his company was in the heat of the contest at an early hour on Sunday morning, the 6th, at which time they got partially scattered, and Lieut. York taken prisoner, his side arms being taken from him. He was held until night, when he escaped and joined his command the next morning. On the 7th, he was again much exposed to the enemy's fire, and in the course of the day was struck with three balls: one going through his shoulder and collar bone, one through his arm, and one spent ball struck him in the side, breaking one of his ribs. After keeping the field for some time in this wounded condition, he became exhausted by the loss of blood, and was sent to the rear. A few days afterwards he was placed aboard of a steamboat, and sent home, where he arrived on the 17th of April. His wounds becoming very painful, fever set in, which progressed beyond the control of his physician, and he gradually sank until he expired on the 9th of May, 1862.

Lieut. York was a patriot, and an active and efficient officer. He loved his country, and fought and died in its service, leaving a widow and five children to mourn his loss and revere his memory.

COLONEL GREATHOUSE.

AT the commencement of this unhappy Rebellion, among the many brave men who, inspired by an American's love of country, shouldered the musket in behalf of our common birthright — constitutional government — must be remembered the subject of this sketch, not then arrived at the years of manhood.

Col. LUCIEN GREATHOUSE was born in Carlinville, Illinois, in June, 1842, where his father, a lawyer by profession, had emigrated a few years previously from Shelby county, Kentucky. In 1844, his father returned to Kentucky, where he now resides. At the age of twelve years, Lucien came back to Illinois, where he had brothers and sisters, part of the time attending the college at Lebanon, Ill.; and when away, still assiduously pursuing studies in which he took, for so young a lad, wonderful delight. For many months it was his practice, after attending to various duties through the day, to sit far into the night, wringing from his Greek and Latin grammars that solid foundation from which, in conjunction with other studies, he might arise the educated man.

At fifteen, he entered the University of Bloomington, Indiana, and graduated at sixteen years of age, with all the honors, and, as the president said, at an earlier age than any former graduate of that institution. Returning to Illinois, young Greathouse studied law, and was admitted to the bar, making, by his kind and genial disposition, hosts of friends wherever he was known. About this time the Rebellion was inaugurated, and a company of volunteers being raised in Fayette county, Lucien enlisted as a private in the ranks, determined, as he said, to do his share in defence of law and order.

His three months' service in the 8th Illinois Regiment, under Col. Oglesby, though not called into active service, was a fine school to instruct him in military tactics, as well as to inspire him with that ardor in the cause which, in his after campaigns, so distinguished him.   At the close of this term of a hundred days, he went to Hardin county, and with the assistance of a brother—John C. Greathouse—raised a full company for three years or the war, and was elected Captain, forming the initial company of the 48th Illinois Regiment, at Camp Butler.

At Fort Donelson, he was first baptized in battle, where the regiment and his company lost many in killed and wounded. Afterward, at Shiloh, his gallantry was conspicuous as he stood at the front, and when the rebels were making a charge directly upon the brigade to which he was attached, his shout of "stand firm" will not be forgotten by those of his company who survive the war.   Soon after he was commissioned Major, his regiment was stationed for several months at Bethel, Tenn., and again at Germantown, doing guard duty.   His regiment, then attached to the 16th Army Corps, was ordered to Vicksburg. After the fall of this Gibraltar of the Mississippi, our hero, then Lieut. Col., but in command of the regiment—their Col. (Sanford) commanding the brigade—writes:

After celebrating the July fourth of our fathers in the rebel stronghold, seeing the gridiron flags hauled down and draped, taking a drink in token that we were glad it was over and the shells done coming, we took up our line of march in the dust and heat of dog July.   Our army corps, then the 16th— and the 9th Army Corps, Burnside's Rappahannockers, moved to attack Gen. J. E. Johnston, with his so-called army of forty thousand, across the Big Black.   Arrived at Black River, twenty miles in rear of Vicksburg, the 48th acted as advance pioneers in the face of the enemy, who changed base as soon as we crossed over.   We followed them, attacking frequently that Confederate rear you've heard so often mentioned; having frequent skirmishes with it until they reached Jackson inside their works.   We sat down under their fire until July 16th, when we made a general charge on the left—the Rappahannockers and we upon their forts and rifle-pits.   Our regiment marched against their siege guns and field pieces, firing shot and shell, grape and canister, on clear open level ground for half a mile at double-quick, until within two hundred yards of their works, when, being the entire and only advance at that point, we (or the men) lay down on our faces and held the position half an hour, waiting for the "Yankee" column to advance "which it didn't," and after receiving two successive orders, I moved the regiment to the rear by the right flank, to a tolerably protected position, until we were relieved at 3 o'clock P. M.   We lost our Major (Stevenson) in the charge, and several other brave and useful officers, and many men.   The Rebs, evacuated that night and saved us many lives, and some little glory, for I should have taken the regiment over those works at sunrise if they had been there, just as I did when we leaped over and discovered they were gone. As the sun rose above the hills, the regimental banner of the 48th Illinois waved over the State House, causing a shout to be raised on the left, that went down to the right like the rush of a flame over the prairies.

In speaking of the march from Vicksburg to Jackson, he said it was one of the saddest of sights to see the men marching under the intense heat of a July sun, with their tongues parched and protruding from their mouths for the lack of water, and, as they grew weaker, dropping from the ranks to die, or fall into the hands of the enemy. The advance upon Jackson was the first contest of importance after young Greathouse took command, and to mark the appreciation they earned, Gen. Smith issued the following complimentary order:

HEADQUARTERS 1st DIV. 16TH A. C.

LIEUT. COL. LUCIEN GREATHOUSE:

Sir,—I desire to thank you and the gallant officers and men of your command, for your good conduct in all the fighting we have had to do in our advance upon Jackson. Please make known to your noble regiment the high estimate which is placed upon such heroism as it has exhibited. May you all be spared in the future even as miraculously as you have been in the past.

WM. G. SMITH,

Brigadier General Commanding 1st Div.

Subsequent to the fall of Vicksburg and second capture of Jackson, the 48th formed a part of the 15th Army Corps, and Col. Greathouse now hoped his regiment might obtain some rest. But no. Chattanooga was in danger, Knoxville threatened, and who but Gen. Logan's invincibles must take boat to Memphis, march by land three hundred miles, fight the battle of Chickamauga, and again take up the weary tramp to raise the siege of Knoxville—a march of one hundred and seventy-five miles and back, without shoes, the men in many instances tying rags, torn from their clothes or blankets, round their feet to protect them from the sharp frozen ground, and subsisting on the country.

About this period the time of three years men was expiring, though many regiments re-enlisted in a body. The men of the 48th were called together, and their young commander, Greathouse, (the Col. having resigned sometime previous,) addressed them in a spirit-stirring speech, promising that, if they re-enlisted, he would share their fortunes in every campaign; pointing out that however grandly they had fought and suffered in the cause of their country, they could make their record still more glorious and be hailed as a nation's deliverers by striking a few more blows at their rapidly-failing enemy. In answer to this appeal, his regiment, reduced to a little over four hundred men, re-enlisted and went home on furlough to rest and fill up their depleted ranks.

At Centralia, the 48th Illinois Regiment was feted by the citizens and Governor of the State, and young Greathouse made the recipient of a splendid sword by his officers as a testimonial of his worth, and soon after, as Colonel of his regiment, recruited to near eight hundred strong, departed to join Gen. Sherman in his wonderful march to Atlanta.

As an evidence of his devotion to the cause and labor for the welfare and efficiency of his regiment, Col. Greathouse did not pay even a passing visit to either of two sisters while home in Illinois, although he well knew they almost idolized him, but wrote that the imperative duties of his command occupied all his time, and that he "must go on and fight until the last rebel was either armless or soulless."

Gen. Sherman's memorable march on Atlanta is now matter of history. The 48th, always in the van, over mountain, river and plain, had its full share of hardships and loss in that continued skirmish and battle for three hundred miles: not without honor, for high encomiums were passed by General Logan and others on the chivalrous commander of the 48th Illinois and the obedient and brave daring of the officers and men of that regiment. At Kenesaw Mountain, Col. Greathouse was struck on the head by a piece of a shell, which stunned him for several hours, but not to create unnecessary alarm, he characterized as "a slight hurt."

Ever mindful of the welfare of his men, and quick to appreciate merit in his officers, he was beloved by all his regiment; while his good judgment in military affairs, his soldierly deportment and integrity, made his worth duly known and commented on in the General's marquee.

He was in politics a Democrat—but a Democrat of the Jacksonian school, like Sherman, Grant, Logan, and others, who reiterate the oath by their deeds that "the Union must and shall be preserved." And here let us chronicle, as the words of our hero, the most withering sarcasm or expression of merited scorn ever hurled at the disciples of a Northern projector of what is termed the Chicago platform. Said he: "The time will soon come when the history of that class of Northern men will be engraven on copper plates, bound in nigger skin, and on the lowest shelves of hell, form the Devil's library to all eternity." Once on being accused of Abolitionism—"No," said he, "as the son of a slaveholder, my education and prejudices are all the other way, but I am fighting for the perpetuity of a republican form of government."

Said he, in a letter to his father, for whom, if for any one, he would have moderated his opinions :

My destiny is identical with the success of the cause I maintain, the triumph of the arms I support, whether that success is achieved under an *abolition* or *conservative* administration—that is in this country. If we fail, and I admit *no such possibility*, then I will not plume my wings like a whipped cock within sound of the crowing of a victorious adversary, nor live an humbled existence where I can hear the chidings of those friends whose counsels I forsook to follow the promptings of my own judgment. I would rather freeze with the Esquimaux, or starve and die of sheer filth, in the dens where the Hottentots wallow. In short, if we fight the old ship through, and come out keel downward, with the old flag flying gloriously at the mast, as well as ever, in spite of the beaten villains that dared to insult it—I'm all right, and will not curse the fate that ordered my being. If we fail—I'll go down with the glorious riddled old hulk, with the torn flag, with sword or bayonet in my hand—and if I can't shout, then I'll sink with a *groan* of defiance, and a moderate invocation of left-hand blessings, on the first knave that spoke his country's ruin, in the utterance of the word secession!

In the action of the 21st of July, before Atlanta, second in severity only to those of the 22d and 28th following, our boy Colonel was ordered to charge with his regiment the enemy's works, while some new disposition was being made of other troops. Across an open field he led his men to within a hundred yards of the rebel guns, losing thirty-five men, and keeping the enemy employed until he was ordered to retire. Such

chivalrous daring, witnessed by the brigade and division commanders, elicited the highest compliments,—one saying of him,
that "where other men were brilliant, Col. Greathouse blazed."

On the 22d of July, 1864, when the reckless bravery of the
rebels was met by the spartan valor of the boys in blue, far in
the advance, with five companies of his regiment following his
lead, Col. Greathouse had mounted a line of breastworks,
cheering on his men, when a rebel sharpshooter laid him low.

Alas! for our gallant brother. At the very time when life
is most promising—he was but twenty-two—at the very gates
of a rebel city in the heart of a rebel State, he laid down his
young life for his country amid the din of that thunder which
he too truly said was "God's answer to the wish of man's heart
and the pleading voice of his hope."

When their Colonel fell, the men of the 48th, by command
of F. H. Farrell, Captain of the Colonel's former company,
and a firm friend in all his campaigns, bore his body back,
often pausing to repulse repeated charges of the enemy, until
within their lines, they "laid him down with his martial
cloak around him." Some three weeks afterwards, his brother,
T. Greathouse, procured the body and took it to Vandalia, Ill.,
where the remains lay in state for twenty-four hours, and then,
in a grove of oak, were buried with military honors.

COLONEL MULLIGAN.

Col. JAMES A. MULLIGAN was born in the city of Utica, New York, in the year 1830. After the death of his father, which occurred when young Mulligan was but a child, his mother removed to Chicago, where she subsequently married Mr. Michael Lantry, who also died in the early part of 1864. James, at an early age, gave promise of a vigorous mind and noble principles. He was educated at the University of St. Mary's of the Lake, and in college, both with professors and with pupils, stood highest among the high. He was a member of the Roman Catholic Church, and proud of his identity with its faith, being a regular communicant from his boyhood up to the time of his death.

In 1852, '53 and '54, he read law at the office of Arnold, Larned & Lay. He was a close student, but the law was not his only study. The whole field of literature was to him as an open garden of flowers and fruit. After leaving college, and before entering on the study of the law, he accompanied Mr. Stephens on one of his expeditions in Central America, and he often delighted his friends with his eloquent description of the scenes he had witnessed, the perils he had passed through, and the adventures he had encountered. In 1854, he edited, for a short time, a religious weekly paper, published in Chicago, called *The Tablet;* but, in 1856, he commenced the practice of the law.

He always had a taste for military life, and even while a law student, he volunteered as a private in the Shields Guard, a fine company of men, whose physical appearance was made the more striking because of the enormous shakos that formed part of their uniform. In this company he was soon promoted to a Lieutenancy, and afterwards became its Captain.

In 1857–8, he desired to see life at the Capitol, and through the kindness of Senator Fitch, he was appointed by President Buchanan to a clerkship in the Interior Department. He spent one winter in Washington. During the time he held office under Buchanan, he was an outspoken, fearless advocate of Douglas, and feeling the position embarrassing to those who had obtained his appointment, he resigned his situation and returned to Chicago. Before going to Washington, and after his return, he was in a law partnership with Henry S. Fitch, who, during the last part of Buchanan's term, was the United States' Attorney for the district. During all this period, he was a constant contributor to the newspaper press.

In October, 1858, he was married by the Rt. Rev. Bishop Duggan, to Miss M. Nugent, an accomplished lady of Chicago.

When the war broke out, he was Captain of the Shields Guard, and proposed to organize a regiment of Irishmen, which was accomplished; but others were elected to its command, he being given but a subordinate position. The supply of volunteers was so great, that the State authorities could not accept it. Mulligan, however, was not to be repressed in that way. He obtained from the dying Douglas a letter to Secretary Cameron, who at once gave him authority to raise a regiment. In a few weeks he succeeded in enlisting as fine a regiment as ever left Chicago; he was made Colonel, and was at once sent to Missouri. The regiment left Chicago on the 15th of July, 1861, 1064 strong, for Quincy; and from there started down the Mississippi to St. Louis. Remaining there a day, they left for Jefferson City, with orders to cut their way through to the threatened town of Lexington. He had with him about three thousand men and five pieces of artillery. Price, with his 15,000, soon surrounded Lexington, demanding its surrender. Such fortifications as limited time permitted, were made, but had the fortifications been half as strong as was the will of the commander to defend the town, Price would never have succeeded. For nine days the heroic Colonel maintained the unequal contest, and it was not until he had neither ammunition, water, nor food, that the demand for surrender was complied with. The officers and men were paroled, and allowed to return; Mulligan, however, refused a parole, and being joined by his wife and babe, was carried off as a prisoner by Price, who treated him with the most marked kindness and respect. Early in November, he was exchanged for Gen. Frost.

On the 8th of November, the Common Council held a special session, and appointed a committee to act with a committee of citizens to receive him on his return to Chicago. A train of cars, containing over six hundred persons, left the city on the afternoon of November 8, 1861, and proceeded to Joliet. That town was in a blaze of light to welcome the gallant fellow. As he stepped upon the platform, he was greeted by the Rev. Dr. Butler, the chaplain of the regiment, with a kiss upon the cheek, which affectionate demonstration was received by the multitude with the most deafening cheers and applause. Judge Van Buren then addressed him a welcome on the part of the committees representing the authorities and citizens of Chicago. To this address he responded, saying, among other things:

Actuated by a love of this, my country, I entered the fight now waging in this Union, with as gallant a band of men as ever contended against enemies. All I ask is that I may be enabled, with as little delay as possible, to lead them back again, and show the foes of the Union that there are men in the North who will fight to their death in defence of the Constitution and the laws.

These words were prophetic—he did fight to his death in support of his country, its flag. its Constitution and its laws.

On his arrival in Chicago, his reception was truly magnificent. He was escorted to the Tremont House by a military and civic procession numbering many thousands. He was there formally greeted by B. F. Ayer, Esq. Col. Mulligan responded most feelingly, and in conclusion said:

I am now and forever for the Union, in life and to the death. In bidding you good night, I do so with the hope that when I again meet you, I will be at the head of my old regiment, with my face towards Missouri, and my sword striking the rebellion.

The regiment, which had been in Camp Douglas, was recruiting and guarding the rebel prisoners, but early in the spring of 1862, was ordered to Western Virginia.

After his return from Missouri, Col. Mulligan visited Washington, and while there, President Lincoln tendered him in person the commission of a Brigadier General. Mulligan asked if he could take that rank and his regiment continue in whatever command he might have. The President replied that as a

12

Brigadier he must be separated from the Irish regiment, and take such command as would be assigned to him. Col. Mulligan thereupon, after thanking the President, declined the promotion.

His career in Virginia was a succession of dangerous enterprise; though only a Colonel, he was charged with the responsibilities and the command of a Major General. Gen. Kelly, the department commander, placed great reliance on Mulligan and his men, as they never failed in doing their duty. On Sunday, the 24th of July, 1864, at the battle of Winchester, Col. Mulligan, in command of a division, was sitting erect in his saddle, and with hat off, was inspiring to deeds of valor those brave troops who loved him so dearly, and who recognized in him the attributes which constitute the heroic soldier, when a minie ball passed through his thigh and he fell from his horse. His staff gathered around him, and, assisted by the brave men of his command, endeavored to bring him off the field. It was almost certain death to every man who approached him, and yet the gallant men of the Irish Brigade, with their colors planted close to his body, rallied around him, determined, if possible, to bear their leader off the field; but the enemy, perceiving the intention, concentrated their whole fire on them for a moment. Lt. Nugent, Col. Mulligan's brother-in-law, and an officer on his staff, was wounded in the leg, and at the same moment his horse was killed. Turning to the Color Sergt. of the 23d Illinois, he took the colors from him and desired him to assist in carrying the Colonel off the field. Limping along, he had not proceeded many steps before he received a second wound and fell, exclaiming, "Colonel, I am shot." Mulligan then addressed the men around him, and told them to save the flag and themselves, as it was useless to try to rescue him. "Boys, don't lose the colors of the Irish Brigade," was the last brave-hearted remark he uttered to his comrades. He was found some hours after by the rebels, and lingering for two days, his life-work bravely ended.

During all his campaigns, his young and devoted wife accompanied him. She followed his march, and when he stopped, she and the little ones joined him. When danger threatened, or a fight took place, she merely retired to a place of safety, that she might be near, and in case of casualty, that she might hasten to his side. When he was besieged at Lexington, she was in the vicinity, and when he was carried off a prisoner, she followed him into captivity, and stayed with him during those long months, sharing his prison fare and life. Upon the appearance of rebels in Western Virginia, Mulligan and his men marched out to meet them; she remained, watching and praying for his safe return. The news of the fight, the retreat, and of her husband's wounds and capture, reached her in her place of refuge. Prompted by a wife's devotion, and with all the hope and anxiety of a mother, she, without a moment's delay, sought the enemy's lines, and by a woman's tears, won permission for Col. Mulligan's wife to enter. She hastened on, but, alas! too late. The eyes that so often looked on her with love had been closed by stranger hands, in the enemy's camp. The father of her children was dead. Nor did that blow fall alone. By the side of her brave and gallant husband fell also her heroic and noble brother—both at the same time, upon the same field. Noble, daring, fearless soldiers, they gave to their country their own lives, and the happiness of their loved ones forever.

Col. Mulligan was an accomplished gentleman. Well educated, he was gifted with a mind capable of making that education of practical use to himself and to his country. He was an able writer—clear, bold, concise, yet thorough; his literary productions are remarkable for their energy, fearlessness and eloquence. As an orator, he had few superiors. Of a commanding presence, excellent voice, and unbroken flow of language, he never failed to win the attention and deserve the admiration of his listeners. In all the names who will go down to posterity, as the names of those who fell in this infamous rebellion, there will be no name of a nobler man, braver soldier, or generous friend, than that of Col. Mulligan.

The announcement of his fall cast a gloom over the whole community, and his last utterance of devotion to the stars and stripes found a response in the hearts of the people, who resolved that they would honor his remains and sympathize with his bereaved wife and children. Accordingly, meetings of the citizens were held, and committees appointed to carry out a concerted plan of arrangements. His coffined body was brought to Chicago, and laid in state in Bryan Hall, where a constant stream of admirers passed in and out for a whole day. On the next morning, the remains were placed in a festooned funeral car, and the cortege moved to St. Mary's Church, where Dr. McMullen delivered an affecting discourse, of which the following is the closing extract:

Oh, my country, that you had more such heroes! Oh, that protestations to you were not mere verbiage in the mouths of many! Oh that you could find more Christian men, whose patriotism is the spontaneous growth of virtuous hearts, with roots fixed deeply in eternal truth! Then might thy beauteous plains be spread out to-day covered with the abundance of smiling peace, rather than be made the graveyard of thy children. Thy rivers seek the interminable ocean, which girds thee round, white with a commerce bearing blessings to the needy of other lands, rather than crimsoned with fratricidal gore. You want heroes whose devotion to you cannot be purchased by the dross of earth—whom deadly envy and foul ambition cannot tempt to rise against their common mother! You want them, but, alas, you find too few! But you shall have them yet, children of the church of Christ, whom she shall have nurtured at her breast, strengthened with that nourishment which the blood of her most holy spouse imparts. They shall be the heroes whom you seek; they shall be your devoted children in truth—heroes in war, and heroes in peace—like him who to-day lies sacrificed for thee.

Then all that remains to us of the bravest and truest, we consign to a sacred resting-place, a hallowed shrine, a Christian hero's grave. We will lay them where the wild flowers bloom, fit emblems of the purity of that spirit which enlivened them. We will lay them where the free winds play, the purest dew-drops fall, and where the first glances of the king of day, after having touched the bosom of Lake Michigan, shall rest, and throw around them a little garb of glory, a faint resemblance of that in which the soul is blessed with God.

After the services were over, a procession, consisting of civic and military bodies, marched with solemn music to the cars for Rosehill Cemetery, where all that was mortal of the Irish-American hero was consigned to the peaceful tomb.

The following lines, signed H. E. H., appeared shortly after the death of the gallant Mulligan:

> Harp of Erin, pour thy wailing
> Sadly o'er the battle plain:
> He who loved thy songs of freedom,
> Sleepeth now among the slain.

'Mid the shock and cry of onset,
  Whizzing shot and bursting shell,
Leading on his gallant legion,
  Bravely there our hero fell.

Ne'er from mortal lips came utterance
  Of a sentence more sublime—
"Lay me down and save the flag, boys!"
  It shall live through coming time.

Let the sea-green flag enfold him,
  And the banner of the stars
Spread its constellation o'er him,
  While he sleeps from toil and scars.

Let the voice of woe be silenced—
  Strike a war note wild and shrill;
Let it ring like calls to battle,
  Over every vale and hill.

As it rolls across old ocean,
  From each sea-washed beach and crag,
Sound that cry, so full of grandeur—
  "Lay me down and save the flag!"

CORPORAL KIDSTON.

Corp. JOHN KIDSTON, son of William and Ann Kidston, was born at Port Glasgow, on the Clyde, Scotland, in the year 1839. He came to this country in 1855, where, with an excellent education, he hoped to raise himself socially far above the scale that he might have had the opportunity of doing in the land which he had left. Not without friends, however, did he arrive here, and he found it a more pleasant task in encountering the difficulties and trials of a stranger, to have the benefit of their experience and advice.

Brought up in the vicinity of hoary-peaked mountains which overlook the distant ocean, and where freedom sits enthroned, he inherited the sentiments of antipathy to slavery which his forefathers possessed from generations now passed away.   Believing, also, that liberty and bondage were incompatible together in one nation, and opposed to Christianity and the teachings of his youth,—in his manhood he looked with abhorrence upon those wicked ones who plunged his adopted country into war, and resolved to give his aid in restoring peace—a lasting tranquillity—by conquering his country's enemies.

With this resolve, he enlisted at Aurora, Kane county, on the 12th of August, 1862, as a private in Co. E, 124th Regiment Illinois Volunteers—Col. Thos. J. Sloan, commanding—who left Camp Butler on the 6th of October, for the field, 866 strong.   During their dreary and trying march to the Tallahatchie, in the attempt to reach Vicksburg by land, he was appointed Corporal on account of his good behaviour.   He was engaged in a number of battles previous to Champion Hills, on the Black River, Miss.—fought on the 16th of May, 1863—where he was struck, while charging on a rebel battery, on the upper part of the right breast by a minie ball.   After lingering in the hospital for three days, he died of his wound. Corp. Kidston had particularly distinguished himself, and was soon to be promoted for his bravery in action.

When writing to his uncle, Alexander Kidston, of Chicago, sometime before he was engaged in the series of battles he had come through, he said "he was prepared for whatever the Lord was pleased to send."

His betrothed reached Chicago from Scotland only to find her lover—a corpse—killed, doing his duty bravely as a defender of his chosen country, and he now sleeps near the sound of the Father of Waters rushing on to the sea—surging a requiem for the noble dead whose blood hath made it free.

LIEUTENANT CAPRON.

LIEUTENANT CAPRON.

Lieut. HORACE CAPRON, JR., was born in Prince George's county, Maryland, on the 27th October, 1839, and removed to Illinois with his father in 1854. His constitution was good—his figure symmetrical and well proportioned. Accustomed to exercise in the open air, having been early taught to ride on horseback, he was by nature and education well fitted for the duties of a cavalry officer.

His fondness for history, and particularly of wars, was early shown. He delighted in reading Froissart's Chronicles and historians of ancient wars, and often referred to those renowned warriors (whose deeds stand there recorded) with much enthusiasm, as though anxious for an opportunity to witness, if not to be an active participant in, similar scenes.

The opening of this deplorable war found him in the vigor of manhood, with all his predelictions and temperament ripe for the coming struggle. His grandfather served under General Washington in the war for our independence, and his love of country was instilled into the youthful mind of his grandson by tales of the battles fought and sieges of that eventful period. At the first tocsin sounding to arms from the walls of Sumter, he responded to its call.

The first service in the cause of his country was as a private in the 8th Illinois Cavalry—Colonel Farnsworth—a regiment which has carved out its own fame upon the battle-fields on the Rappahannock, the Chickahominy, and at Antietam. With this regiment he fought through all its campaigns in 1862. The manner in which he performed his part let the records of the regiment show. At an early day he was appointed Sergeant, and after many hard fought battles, and numerous hand to hand encounters, he was promoted Brevet 2d Lieutenant for bravery on the field.

At the formation of his father's regiment in the autumn of 1862, he was mustered out of the 8th and commissioned as 1st

Lieutenant, Co. A, 14th Illinois Cavalry, which company he was commanding when he received his death wound at Tuckaseeget, North Carolina. In a few days more he would have received further promotion, his Captain having resigned.

Lieut. Capron entered the army almost a boy, he being only twenty-four years of age at the time of his death; but his record is one of the brightest in the annals of the war. He was energetic, persevering and daring, proving himself to be every inch a hero. Whilst in the 8th Illinois Cavalry, he was the favorite of the entire command, not only because of his gentlemanly bearing, but also in consequence of the marvelous bravery he displayed. His commanding officers recount with enthusiasm his heroic deeds, and to use the expression of one of them who was an eyewitness to his performances, " he knew no fear;" and upon the battle-field he seemed to have the heart of a lion and strength of a giant. But perhaps the best illustration of this point is the fact that when the officers of the 8th Illinois Cavalry met to select six of the bravest men in the regiment to receive the " Gold Medal of Honor," the name of Horace Capron, Jr., was unanimously placed at the head of the list, and was thus acknowledged by one of the first regiments in the service to be the bravest of the brave. On the medal was engraved,

TO SERGEANT HORACE CAPRON, JR.,

FOR GALLANT CONDUCT AT CHICKAHOMINY AND ASHLAND.

June, 1862.

The career of this young officer after he joined the 14th Illinois Cavalry as Lieutenant fully sustained his former reputation, and has proved him as brave an officer as ever drew a sword. Patient, enduring, and untiring; cool, and unruffled in the hour of danger, he was never absent from his post up to the time when he fell at Tuckaseeget.

From his bright record we glean a few instances of his courage in the crises of battle. Hours have been passed in the bivouac and around the camp fires at night by his brave companions and followers in recounting them, and, as many of these examples occurred during the rapid marches in which the

14th Illinois Cavalry has been constantly engaged, they have not been given to the public.

On the 18th September, 1863, the 14th Regiment Illinois Cavalry was marching in front of the 2d Brigade, 2d Division, with the 8th Tennessee Cavalry as advance guard. On approaching the ford of the Holstein River at Kingsport, Tenn., the advance guard was suddenly checked and thrown back in the utmost confusion upon the main column by a withering fire from a heavy concealed force of the rebels. The Colonel commanding the brigade at once ordered Col. Capron to move with his regiment by the right, crossing the river lower down, and if possible to get in the rear of the enemy, which was accomplished with as little delay as the nature of the stream would allow. At this point an advance guard of two companies, commanded by Lieut. Capron, was thrown forward to feel the enemy and ascertain his position, followed closely by the residue of the regiment. On reaching the road leading from Rodgersville to the ford, it became necessary to pass a deep stream through a covered bridge, the advance moving up on the gallop, (expecting that the enemy's attention would be engaged in front by the remaining forces of the brigade.) On entering the covered bridge, they were met by a volley from the rebels, who had been suffered to withdraw quietly from the ford and take up a new position under cover, to meet the movement of this regiment. The result was for a moment stunning, but only for a moment, for this gallant young officer, perceiving at a glance the position of things, and feeling that any hesitation would be fatal, gave the order to charge, and heading the column, sabre in hand, fell upon the enemy with such impetuosity, that they were completely thrown into confusion. When the head of the column came through the bridge, the scene was perfectly astounding; the enemy were completely ridden down and rolled into the dust, in a hand to hand encounter. They were routed and followed up for ten miles, capturing their wagon train, camp equipage, hospital wagon, with two sets of fine surgical instruments, and nearly all their arms; the road for the whole distance being completely strewn with arms and equipments, a number killed, and 40 taken prisoners, the balance escaping by taking to the bush.   The enemy proved to be the 1st Tennessee Rebel Cavalry—Col. Carter.

No action has occurred showing more fully the importance of coolness and resolution in the moment of greatest danger, and the boldness and dash necessary to carry it through successfully.

In the fights at Blountville, Zollicoffer, and Bristol, he performed an active part in September; and on the 11th October, in the fight at Richtown, where the 14th at first, and then the whole brigade, attacked the rebel General Williams' Division, routing and driving them to Virginia—Lt. Capron was among the foremost.   They again met the enemy on the 15th at Blountville, when four companies were held in readiness to make a charge to break the rebel lines and drive them from their stronghold.   The bugle sounded, and, led by Lt. Capron, they charged into the 2000 rebels posted behind fences, houses, logs and trees.   Here the Lieut. showed his superior coolness and judgment amid showers of bullets, as but few have witnessed. He posted his men to do their deadly work as if on parade drill, when but a moment of thought could pass before the work itself *must* be done.   The least falter would have been death to them all; as, in this case, they were not supported by other troops.   The enemy were routed by one-tenth of their number and put to flight.

In the fight at Bean Station, on the 16th of December, which continued for four days, when Longstreet's whole force attacked our cavalry corps, Lt. Capron was again prominent.   It seemed as though everything was being lost by the powerful force thrown against them.   No infantry coming to their relief, the enemy pressed with all the power of superior strength: yet, amid the din of battle, our men stood boldly up to their work, resisting the foe, and contesting every inch of ground, although overpowered by numbers.   Here, in such a place, Lt. Capron coolly gave orders and sent reports.   When our right was driven back, and the 14th exposed to a flanking fire, and had, in addition to this, to fight their way around the spur of a mountain, hand to hand with the enemy with their revolvers, many were falling dead or wounded, among whom was a young lieutenant —Lieut. Capron seized him, and, while directing his men to "hold the enemy," carried him off the field, thus saving him from the hands of the rebels, and probably from death. Such coolness and duty performed have not been surpassed.

On the 30th of January, 1864, they received orders to move from Tuckalucha Cave *via* Cedar Cave, over Great Smoky Mountain and up the Little Tennessee River into North Carolina, and attack and destroy a camp of Indians and rebels under Col. Thomas, the old Indian agent. They moved forward, marching day and night, over mountains and deep gorges, and over a country destitute of forage or subsistence, arriving on the 2d of February—Lieut. Capron, as usual, in the advance. Three miles out, he captured a rebel scout of five men, and within one mile of the camp captured their picket of seven men, thus making the way clear for surprise. After moving within sight of the camp, with four companies they charged forward, completely surprising them, yet they made for the hills and bushes, forming and some of them fighting desperately. The Indians, numbering about 200, fought bravely, but, to their infamy, most of the white men ran. After the first struggle was over, Lt. Capron, with two companies, was sent to capture some Indians who had escaped on the left and rear. He moved upon them, and finding the rebels in position—a line of about thirty men—he ordered a charge, which was successful in taking or killing all of them. While leading this charge, and while three rods in advance of his men, the rebels fired a full volley upon him, and he fell, mortally wounded, no more to wield his gleaming sabre in the cause he loved so well. Thus, while his parents have lost a kind and affectionate son, and his friends a noble companion, the regiment has lost an accomplished, brave and efficient officer—endeared to them by the trying scenes through which they had passed, and by the ties that try and prove men—and the country has lost a true patriot, one who always felt and said nothing was too great to give that this government might be preserved. No *if* or *and* had a place in his patriotism. Bold, energetic, free, outspoken, ever ready for duty, his motto was—

"Down with the rebels, let them be whom they may."

He has died the death of a soldier. He has fallen in the prime of life, on duty, inspired by his love and devotion to the cause of freedom. He has fallen on the field, with his armor buckled, battling for the great principle which nations revere. His duty has been faithfully performed; and the consolation remains to his surviving comrades, as well as his bereaved friends, that he died in defence of a cause thus heroically expressed:

> " Then up with our flag where'er it may call,
>   And freemen shall rally around :
> A nation of heroes that moment shall fall,
>   When its stars shall be trailed to the ground."

The following is an extract of a letter from Lieut. Col. D. J. Hynes, of the 17th Illinois Cavalry, but formerly Captain of Co. G, 8th Illinois Cavalry, to Lieut. Capron's father:

In common with the whole of his old comrades-in-arms, of the 8th Illinois Cavalry, the sad intelligence of our noble friend's death fell like a pall upon our hearts, and pervaded, probably, with a sadder gloom those whose good fortune entitled them to call him friend—and amongst the latter, myself. Having known him as a schoolmate, and later, embarked in the same glorious cause in a company, being about his age, and from other ties which are unnecessary to mention, it is but natural that we became attached friends, and also that I should not allow his death to pass without some remembrance.

He was an ardent, thorough devotee of liberty, in its broadest and holiest meaning, and consequently his whole soul was possessed with the good work in which he was engaged, and for which he laid down his life. His own bright sabre never flashed with such lustre, as did his bright, flashing eyes, when, with all the chivalric bearing of his young manhood, he was fearlessly riding in the van of a desperate charge. His quick decision, clear judgment, comprehensive grasp of the situation and coolness, had already distinguished him in the regiment, and his friends confidently predicted for him a brilliant career, and have watched with admiration the star of his glory in its ascendancy.

I could relate an hundred incidents of his remarkable gallantry in action, but to his father, who has seen him in service, it would be superfluous, and consequently, I will content myself with one remembrance which now forcibly presents itself to my mind. The enemy, after being driven from Middletown, Md., (in the first Maryland campaign,) sent their wagon train, under a heavy guard, by the road leading to the left over the Potomac at Berlin, while their main body retreated, skirmishing with us, in the direction of the afterwards bloody field of Antietam. A detachment from the 1st Cavalry Brigade, under our friend, the late noble Major Medill, was sent in pursuit of the train. Your son's company was among those who composed the advanced guard, and upon coming up with the rebels, charged with the impetuosity which always characterized the 8th Illinois, and owing to the superior numbers with which they had to contend, were compelled to retire in some disorder. Horace was amongst the most conspicuous in rallying the men of his company, and leading back a few whom he had gathered together, to inspire the others with confidence, never spared the spur until he had struck the advancing rebels, and the most of his few heroic companions had been wounded and captured. Treating with contempt the loud cries to surrender which greeted him, he turned his horse and rode for his company, who were just recovered and advancing again. Horace noticing their hesitancy in firing upon the enemy lest they might hit him, and having only an eye for the chastisement of the foe, cried out, "Shoot! Shoot! It don't matter if you do kill me; shoot, and you'll kill enough of them to make up for it!" and had not fairly reached his friends before he, in turn, turned upon his pursuers, and with sabre alone, made some of them bite the dust. When it was all happily ended, the men and officers, with one accord, greeted him with hearty cheers and warm congratulations. When asked why he did not rather surrender than run the risk of almost certain death, he replied that "Once having turned his horse's head toward his friends he knew his body at least would be carried in, and further, it would not sound well at home, that I had surrendered without being mortally wounded." * *

Appropriate resolutions of respect and admiration of his bravery on the battle-field, and also of sympathy with his relatives in their bereavement, were passed by the commissioned officers of the regiment and by the non-commissioned officers and privates of Co. A, which were forwarded to their commander, Col. Capron.

His body was brought home to Peoria, under charge of Lieut. Rowecliffe, for interment. The Masonic fraternity and the military paid the last, mournful rites to their departed companion, whose deeds entitle him to rank as one of the bravest heroes of the war.

LIEUTENANT APTHORP.

Lieut. GEORGE HENRY APTHORP was born near Quincy, Illinois, on the 9th of August, 1841. He was the third son of the Rev. W. P. Apthorp; the first and second being also in the army —one under Gen. Grant, and the other at Hilton Head and Florida. At the time of his mother's death in 1853, when the family was much scattered, he was put on a farm near Denmark, Iowa, for a year, and then went into the preparatory department of Iowa College, at Davenport, where he remained a few years. After this, he went east to Massachusetts, and spent some time at Mr. Hunt's Seminary at N. Bridgewater, and afterwards at the High School at Andover. From thence he retraced his steps westward, and went into Wheaton College, Du Page county, Ill., nearly supporting himself while there. Residing in this county when the war broke out, he was impelled, by his love of country, to enlist. He entered the three months service by joining a battery of light artillery, when he was sent to Cairo. Here he was taken sick with bilious fever, and barely escaping with his life, returned to Wheaton when he became able to travel.

On the next call for volunteers, George enlisted in the 105th Illinois Infantry, and was elected Corporal. This regiment was sent to Kentucky. They did not see much active service at first, but were employed in guarding railroads, often in unhealthy situations, so that his company lost many of its men through malaria. After about a year's service, he applied for and obtained a commission as 2d Lieut. in Co. E of the 14th U. S. C. I., when he was ordered to Chattanooga, which was shortly after that place came into the possession of the Federal forces, and where the 14th remained for some time in garrison. He was promoted to a 1st Lieutenancy in the same regiment, but in another company, three months before his year expired. In these offices (or after becoming an officer) he was employed in various expeditions against different rebel commanders. At one time they had Morgan within their reach, and early in the morning were ordered to enter the camp in silence to surprise them while asleep, but the plan miscarried, and the noted rebel with his command escaped.

The last expedition but one in which Lieut. Apthorp was engaged was as a part of Gen. Rousseau's force to operate against Wheeler and Forrest. They met various parties of rebels, and had some sharp engagements, the enemy always retreating. He was also in the battles at Alatoona and Dalton.

On their return to Chattanooga, they were in a few days ordered into Alabama. During that short respite, he wrote to his father his last letter, detailing some of the narrow escapes he had, and how good his health was through all hardships, night marches, out in rains without even a blanket for shelter, and living without rations sometimes; and in spite of these vicissitudes, he continued the same. It was but five days after that, on the 29th of October, 1864, in a battle near Decatur, Ala., he was slain, together with another Lieutenant of the same company, in a charge on a detachment of Hood's army.

His body was immediately taken to Chattanooga, and by the kindness of Capt. Vallette, of the same regiment, embalmed, placed in a metallic coffin, and sent to Davenport, Iowa, where a discourse was preached by Rev. W. Windsor, of the Congregational Church, and the day following the remains were taken by his father to Port Byron, Ill. Some friends gathered at the grave, and after an appropriate prayer by the pastor, his body was lowered to its last resting place to await the Resurrection. He lies by the side of his mother, and near a former schoolmate of like age, who was killed in the battle of Murfreesboro.

Lieut. Apthorp bore a high character while in the army as a brave soldier and a gallant officer, and won the affection of his comrades by his affability and kindness. His motives in joining the army were not from mere love of adventure or excitement, but from a sense of duty. A friend writes:

After enlisting in the 105th, he was at our house until he went into camp. My wife said to him, "Why *did* you enlist?" "If all refuse to enlist," said he, "that can go as well as I, very few would go. The country needs an army, and it is my duty to go." Thus he said and thus he acted, although he well understood the evils and the hardships of an army life; all of which were far from being congenial to his quiet and unobtrusive disposition.

Capt. Vallette, in writing to Lieut. Apthorp's father of his character as a man and a soldier, says:

I believe George to have been a true Christian, and let me sympathize with you in your bereavement. His loss will be deeply felt in the circles of his friends and comrades-in-arms. Let the thought that he died in the just cause of his country assuage the grief that must be yours; and you may have the knowledge that Lieut. Apthorp always acquitted himself nobly both as an officer and soldier.

Capt. Meteer, of Co. K, also writes:

CHATTANOOGA, NOV. 15, 1864.

REV. W. P. APTHORP:

Dear Sir.—I return to you a letter written to my 1st Lieutenant, your son. Of course, you have heard of his death from wounds received in the charge made by our regiment on half of Hood's army, Oct. 29th, at Decatur, Ala. It was a very heavy blow upon me and the regiment. He had been with me about three months, and I never was associated with a better soldier, a purer patriot, or a more companionable man. He was very quiet, and somewhat difficult to become acquainted with, but he had a strong hold on the affections of those who knew him. My men almost worshipped him; and when some one cried, "Lieut. Apthorp is killed," my whole company seemed ready to die rather than leave his body, and amid a shower of balls and the crash of shells, one sergeant and five men brought him off the field, though in a terribly mangled state, having received several shots while he was borne in their arms.

My house seems broken up. Everything about my tent reminds me of Apthorp. Every little contrivance for convenience and neatness speaks of him. I am passing through the saddest period of my life.

There is, however, one thing which comforts me, and I know it does you— *he lived a Christian and died a Christian.*

I remain, yours truly,

J. H. METEER,
Capt. Co. K, 14th U. S. C. I.

Such is a brief history of one of the many generous spirits who have given their lives for their country in her hour of need.

LIEUTENANT COLONEL BROSS,

LIEUTENANT COLONEL BROSS.

Lieut. Col. JOHN A. BROSS, fifth son of Deacon Moses Bross, (now of Morris, Ill.,) was born at Milford, Pike county, Pennsylvania, February 21st, 1826. Having completed a thorough academical course at Chester Academy, Orange county, N. Y., then taught by his brother, William, now Lieut. Governor of Illinois, he commenced the study of law at Goshen, N. Y., and, removing to Chicago in 1848, concluded his studies in the office of Hon. Grant Goodrich. For sometime he served, with credit to himself, as Assistant United States Marshal; after which, he devoted himself to the profession of law, particularly the Admiralty practice, at once entering upon and holding an honorable position at the Bar. Ever acting with strict integrity, he won the entire confidence of all with whom he was connected.

When our flag was dishonored, his impulse was to rush to the rescue, and he was only deterred, because men with fewer ties binding them to their homes, were offered in greater numbers than the Government would accept. Having counted the cost, and fully determined that *duty* led him to the field, if needed, he responded when in 1862 there appeared some difficulty in raising men. He recruited a company, and was made senior Captain of the 88th Illinois Volunteers.

A month after leaving home found him in the battle of Perryville, Ky., where his conduct gave him rank as one whose cool bravery could be relied on in every emergency. This reputation he afterward sustained at Stone River and Chickamauga; at the latter place particularly distinguishing himself.

Early believing that the Government should use all the resources within its reach, and that black men would fight as well as white, he responded to Governor Yates' call to raise a colored regiment in Illinois, and entered upon his duties with energy. Owing to tardy action by the Government, great

13

numbers of colored men had already gone to regiments formed elsewhere. Having six full companies, they were formed into the 29th U. S. C. Infantry. He was commissioned Lieutenant Colonel, and in April, 1863, assigned to Gen. Burnside's 9th Corps. The corps having gone to the Army of the Potomac, he was ordered to Camp Casey, near Washington, and placed in command of a brigade, with which he moved to the front on the 1st of June, and until July 30th was with the troops in the trenches before Petersburg.

The regiment had so rapidly attained skill and proficiency as conclusively to show that black troops readily become equal to white, if placed under efficient officers. When it was known that the colored division was to make a charge, the 29th was selected to lead it. This honor they accepted, and nobly performed its attendant desperate duties. The mine was exploded early on Saturday morning, and it is believed, had the assault followed immediately, the works would have been easily secured. But there was a fatal delay. Then Gen. Ledlie's division advanced, but failed to proceed beyond the crater formed by the explosion. After this it was impossible to accomplish anything, as the rebels had brought troops from miles around to oppose any further advance. The colored division were, however, ordered to charge, and heroically rushed forward. On passing the mine, they were exposed to a merciless fire in front, as well as an enfilading fire right and left. They fell in great numbers, but the 29th, with the Colonel at their head, led the way without faltering. One after another, the color-bearers were shot down, but still brave hands upheld the flag. After five had thus fallen, Col. Bross, seizing the colors in his own hand, bore them to the top of the works and planted them on the parapet, the farthest point reached by our troops. But heroism was of no avail. Most of the officers were either killed or wounded; the enemy's numbers were overwhelming, and the order was given to retire. While seeking to extricate his men, the fatal ball entered the left side of his head, and he sank without a groan; and, as one who witnessed it said, "all that a Christian patriot can achieve by dying for his country, he gloriously won."

Col. Bross was married on the 5th of June, 1856, to Miss Belle A. Mason, daughter of Hon. Nelson Mason, of Sterling, Ill., whom he leaves with a little son of four years ever to mourn the loss of one peculiarly fitted to render home happy.

In person, Col. Bross was of commanding appearance; about six feet in height; slender, but firm and erect. His features regular and finely moulded, and his whole countenance indicative of strongly marked character. His native refinement and genial, unassuming manners, rapidly made him friends; while his unselfishness, almost feminine gentleness and regard for the feelings of others, sincerely attached them.

As a Christian, he was exemplary, earnest and faithful; not making religion obtrusive, but ever showing that he was actuated by high and noble principles.

As an officer, though strict in discipline, his uniform, courteous, kind behavior, secured to him the love and respect of all fellow commanders and the devotion of his men. Interesting himself in their moral and religious behalf, they felt in him they had a friend, and repaid his efforts with an almost idolatrous affection.

In early manhood, leaving parents and home, wife and child, position, and all that man holds dear, he gave his life for the country he so ardently loved;

> " And though the warrior's sun has set,
> Its light shall linger round us yet,
> Bright, radiant, blest."

SERGEANT CRAWFORD.

Sergt. E. A. CRAWFORD was born on the 30th of June, 1829, in Beaver county, Pa.   In 1856, he removed to Warren county, Ill., with his family.   In August, 1861, he enlisted in the 36th Regiment Illinois Volunteer Infantry, when he was immediately appointed 3d Sergeant, which office he filled with great satisfaction to his superiors and fellow-soldiers.   When any particular guarding was to be done, he was the Sergeant appointed, and was respected by all.

He was with the regiment during their long encampment at Rolla, and started with them when they left to chase Price, but was detailed before they got to Springfield, Mo., to guard the equipments that had to be left behind when they thought they were going into an engagement with that rebel.   This duty he had to perform very much against his inclination, as he wished to be in front; but his officers decided that he should remain. He was the only sergeant that had a family, and they thought he would not there be exposed to so much danger.   It was not long, however, till he was appointed to ride express, and carry the mail.   This was a very dangerous business, several carriers having been shot at; but he got through without much trouble. Part of the time he had to attend to forwarding express horses from Rolla to Springfield, and was always kept busy, if he was not marching.

He was at Lebanon, Mo., when the battle of Pea Ridge was fought.   He then expressed a regret that he was not with the regiment, but said he must be content to serve his country in whatever way he was commanded.   About the 1st of May he and seven others commenced marching after the regiment, but they did not overtake them until the 22d, at Cape Girardeau.   He was with them at Rienzi, Miss.; through their travels and marches, both by cars and on foot, to Cincinnati, Covington, Lexington, and Louisville, and was in the battle of Perryville, where his comrades were shot by his side, but he escaped unhurt.   He was with the regiment in that long and dusty march through Tennessee, where they suffered so much for water. About the middle of December, 1862, he was sent to the hospital at Nashville, Tenn., with camp sore-eyes—was there at the time of the battle of Murfreesboro; and hearing that his brother-in-law, J. B. Edgar, was wounded, he started for the front, but his eyes getting worse, he was sent back to the hospital, and there, on the 29th of January, he took erysipelas fever, which ended his days on the 9th of February, 1863.

He was a good soldier, and, we trust, a good Christian. His mother died when he was in the fifth year of his age; but he had the guidance and admonition of a very pious father. In 1852, he joined the Associate Church at Darlington, Pa. In this connection he remained until he removed to the West, when he united with the Reformed Presbyterian Church of Monmouth, Ill., and remained in it till the time of his enlisting in August, 1861. He was a kind and affectionate husband and father; but, when the war broke out, he said he could not stay at home when his country needed his services. He said he thought it the duty of Christians to fight for their country and their honor. He said he could not enjoy peace if he did not help to fight for it. His farewell words to his wife, on bidding her adieu, were—"Mary, hear whatever you may of me, you will not hear of me being a coward." In all his letters, during his eighteen months' service, he complained not, except at the time his infant son died, in July, 1862. He wished to get home, but was denied, and the only endearing alternative he had was the comforting and consoling epistles he wrote to his wife and four remaining children.

In his last illness, when asked what were his prospects for eternity, (by his kind brother-in-law, Dr. J. Wylie, who attended and nursed him in his own room in the hospital at Nashville,) he said, for the sake of his family, he would like to live a little longer, but was resigned to God's will, and gave great satisfaction concerning his hopes of salvation. He warned all not to put off a preparation for death until a dying hour. He said it was impossible for him, in his weak and nervous condition, to concentrate his ideas on any subject.

He became irrational for some days at the last; but the night before he died, he suddenly regained his lucidity for a few moments, and chanted the 100th Psalm nearly through, saying he had often sung that psalm and tune at church—(being clerk both at Darlington and at Monmouth.) He then, in a most fervent prayer, commended his spirit to God who gave it, and his family to the care and protection of his covenant-keeping Creator.

He died in the thirty-fourth year of his age, at Hospital No. 5, Nashville, and was buried in the cemetery there—far from home and friends, but where many loved and martyred heroes lie side by side, sleeping the sleep of the brave.

PRIVATE EDGAR.

Private JOHN BOYD EDGAR, only son of William and Elizabeth Edgar, was born in Brighton township, Beaver county, Penn., on the 3d of September, 1839. Early in life he was deprived of the love and counsel of a pious mother—a loss he deeply felt. Having a desire to see more of the country than that which bounded his father's farm, he left home on the 20th October, 1860, to visit a sister residing in Illinois. Being highly pleased with the country, he determined to make the West his future home, but the breaking out of the rebellion soon caused him to change his mind. Having been in declining health for several years, he debated with himself about the propriety of enlisting; but an ardent love of country prevailed, and he could not stand idly by and see that flag he loved to look upon dishonored. In Warren co., Ill., on the 1st of August, 1861, he joined Co. C, 36th Regiment Illinois Volunteers.

He was with the regiment in all its encampments and marches after Gen. Price through Missouri and Arkansas, and though frequently staring starvation in the face, he complained not. He was in the battle of Pea Ridge, under the "fighting Dutchman," Gen. Sigel, of whom he always spoke in terms of the highest commendation. In this battle he escaped unhurt, but through fatigue and lack of food, he was unable to go on picket for a few days, though he stood guard when he had to be assisted to rise and walk with a cane,—the only excuse from duty during his actual service. In writing home about this time, when they were almost without anything to eat, some shoeless and scarce of money, he said: "I do not mind it at all. I am willing to endure far more to aid in putting down this cruel war; and if peace was once more established on a firm basis, they might place me on the highest peak of the Rocky Mountains, without a penny in my pocket, and I would be content."

He assisted to place the stars and stripes on the Ozard Mountains. Soon after the battle, his regiment was sent to Corinth, where they arrived just in time to see the rebels leave. They marched 240 miles in nine days, over hills and valleys, through woods and streams, knowing not where they were going, or what was expected of them. Of the scenes connected with that march he never could think without experiencing a feeling of horror. They were sent from Corinth to Cincinnati, to repel Bragg's invasion; thence to Louisville. He was in the battle of Perryville. His clothes did not escape so well as he, for they bore the mark of rebel bullets.

His next battle was that of Stone River, Tenn. On Wednesday morning, Dec. 31st, 1862, the division beside Sheridan's (the one he was in) gave way, leaving that General's force to bear the whole charge of the opposing column. The 36th charged across a field on the enemy. They were ordered thrice by their officers to retreat, but they did not understand, and kept on, dealing death all around, until compelled by overpowering numbers to fall back, which they did reluctantly, and only when they knew resistance was madness.* In retreating, he received a fatal shot. His blanket had shifted, impeding his progress, and, halting a moment to arrange it, he became the victim of a

* He afterwards heard from a rebel, who was engaged in the fight, that they charged on five full regiments.

sharpshooter. He said his feelings were indescribable when he saw the rebels charge past him on his comrades. He gave up all for lost; but soon the scene changed, and back came the rebels pell mell, our men in close pursuit. On seeing the old flag, he made an effort to greet it with a cheer, but was unable. He was shot in the right side, the ball passing through the bowels, and striking his cartridge box, prevented it from coming out.

He was taken to a house where a number of wounded were lying, but, unfortunately, they all fell into the hands of the enemy. He was so severely injured that he could not be taken to Richmond with those who were captured, and the rebels attempted to parole him, although he did think he never would rise again from his pallet. He would not take the oath, but they took his hand and wrote his name, which act he did not consider binding upon him to observe. While lying in this house, our officers were not aware that it was used for hospital purposes, and accordingly gave orders to demolish it by shelling, as the rebels were using it as a retreat for their sharpshooters. The pitiful wounded were soon covered with pieces of falling timber and plaster, which caused the yellow flag to be hoisted, and prevented what otherwise would have been a heart-rending scene. Five days he was in the enemy's hands, during which he suffered extremely from want of attention. He was then taken to Nashville Hospital No. 2, where he remained for over six months, when he became able to walk a little through the room on crutches.

He longed to see his old home once more. He thought that he could travel if he had some one to assist him in getting through. With this purpose, his brother-in-law went for him, and after some delay in getting his papers made out, he at length got his discharge on the 9th of August, 1863, and on the 19th he recrossed his father's threshold. He was so rejoiced at being again amongst familiar friends, that he exerted himself too much, and unfavorable symptoms soon made their appearance. In nine days after his arrival, his wound opened afresh, which prostrated him, and he was unable to sit up, while he suffered extremely. The best medical skill and counsel the country could afford availed nothing. His case was a singular one, as attested by the hundreds who visited him in his last illness. His sufferings were borne with Christian resignation and patience; but nature could not always endure, and on the morning of the 20th of August, 1864, just twelve hours more than a year after arrival at home, his spirit gently passed away to the bright regions of peace, where war is unknown.

During his long, painful confinement, which continued nearly twenty months, he manifested the deepest interest in the progress of the war, frequently expressing a wish to recover that he might re-enter the service. Knowing this to be impossible, he desired to live to see the end of the rebellion, and the stars and stripes waving throughout the whole country; but this also was denied him. He was a member of the Reformed Presbyterian Church at Monmouth, Ill., and died in the full hope of a Christian's faith—a brave soldier of the Republic.

LIEUTENANT JOHNSTON.

Lieut. ROBERT A. JOHNSTON was born in the city of Philadelphia. When he was quite young, his father removed to Northwestern Ohio, where he still resides. Robert left home at an early age, and came farther west to better his fortunes. He married and settled in Logan county, Illinois. At the breaking out of the Rebellion, he enlisted in Co. B of the 2d Illinois Cavalry Volunteers, under Capt. (now Major) Larrison. He was with his company in the actions at Fort Donelson, at the capture of that formidable fortress, and also Shiloh. His company was afterwards stationed at Columbus, Ky., and engaged in scouting West Kentucky and Tennessee. By his success, he was appointed Sergeant, and while stationed at Union City, Tenn., became a terror to guerrillas and their less noted companions, the smugglers.

He was appointed Lieutenant of the 4th U. S. Col'd Heavy Artillery, in August, 1863, and was ordered with Lieut. Moss,

of the same regiment, to Union City, on recruiting service.
Here he greatly distinguished himself by his daring. On one
occasion, in the month of August, 1863, he, with Lt. Moss and
James Clark, (who was killed in the massacre at Fort Pillow,)
went twenty-five miles southwest of Union City, and brought in
forty-four colored recruits at a time when it was considered
unsafe for less than a hundred men.

Lieut. Johnston was ordered to Paducah and Fort Pillow
successively on the same duty, and left the latter place a week
before its capture by Forrest. He then remained on duty with
the regiment until ordered to Pine Bluff. In view of his meritorious services, Lt. Johnston received promotion as 1st Lieut.
on the 1st of July, 1864, and was assigned to Co. I of his
regiment. While at Pine Bluff he encountered and killed a
guerrilla captain, singlehanded, without injury to himself.

Many incidents are recited of Lieut. Johnston, which show
his skill and bravery, but none more so than the following,
which relates to the crowning act of his life, when he fell,
pierced by the bullets of the enemy.

A part of his regiment were out on a recruiting expedition,
when they were unexpectedly attacked by some of Forrest's
roving banditti, outnumbering them more than two to one;
but, at the command of Lieut. Johnston, his brave colored boys
rushed into line as undaunted and as immovable as the granite
mountains of New Hampshire. The enemy came on, expecting
to annihilate them completely. Three times they charged the
heroic band, and three times they were repulsed with heavy
loss, when they retired from the field, utterly routed and defeated, leaving their dead and wounded in our hands.

Here Lieut. Johnston fell; but, like the true soldier, he fell
with his "face to the foe," and died in the triumphs of victory.
The loss in the death of this gallant officer was great, but the
success complete.

He was buried with military honors beside the place where
he fell—Pine Bluff, Tenn., near Fort Donelson. Many tears
will be dropped upon the grave of this "martyred hero," and
the name of Lieutenant Johnston will live in the annals of his
country long after *we* shall have passed away.

COLONEL MUDD.

COLONEL MUDD.

Col. John J. Mudd, the subject of this sketch, was the second son of Stanislaus and Eliza Mudd, and was born in St. Charles county, Missouri, on the 9th of January, 1820, his parents having emigrated from Kentucky the year previous.

In 1832, his father died of that terrible scourge, the Asiatic cholera, at Louisiana, Mo., leaving a wife and six children. A few months subsequent to his death, the family moved to Pike county, Ill., and settled near the town of Pittsfield, where our young hero lived until he arrived at the age of manhood.

About the year 1844, he united with the Christian Church, of which he lived a consistent and exemplary member until his death; ever showing, by his habits and general deportment, his love for the great truths and doctrines of the Bible. For the last twenty years of his life, he was particularly interested in the religious culture and moral training of the young, never failing to interest himself in Sabbath schools, whenever an opportunity was offered.

The year following the discovery of gold in California, he made an overland trip to that land, returning by sea; and the year following that, made a second trip. On those long and weary journeys, which were so trying to the principles of men, bringing out man's worst nature in all its sad deformity, he faithfully and patiently carried out the principles of virtue and benevolence, prompted by the generous impulses of a noble and sympathizing heart. Many sick, discouraged and unfortunate travellers to the land of gold, were assisted and comforted in their extremity, and brought by him safely to the end of their journey, who, but for his kindly aid, would never have reached their destination. He gave of his supplies until they were exhausted, and was compelled to replenish at exorbitant prices.

Shortly after his return from his last trip, he was married to Miss Celestia R. Dunham, on the 4th of November, 1852. In the spring of 1854, he removed to St. Louis, Missouri, and engaged in mercantile pursuits in the firm of Mudd & Hughes. He soon took a prominent position among the merchants of that city, as a man possessing business talents of the highest order. His strict integrity in extensive commercial operations—fine, social qualities, and untiring devotion to the welfare of his friends, endeared him to all who came within the sphere of his influence. He remained in St. Louis until 1859. In the autumn of that year, he removed to Chicago, and entered into business in that city, with his accustomed zeal and fidelity— doing a prosperous and lucrative trade. He here, as elsewhere, soon won the love and confidence of a large circle of admiring friends.

Upon the breaking out of the great Rebellion, from purely, patriotic motives, and an undying love for Republican principles and institutions—leaving home, family and friends, all of which he fondly loved—he offered his services to his country.

In October, 1861, he was commissioned 1st Major of the 2d Illinois Cavalry. The regiment went immediately into active service, being ordered to Paducah, Kentucky. In the service, as elsewhere, he soon proved himself capable and trustworthy. His devotion to the interests and welfare of the soldiers under his command, and the courtesy and uniform kindness in his deportment to and intercourse with his brother officers, won for him the love and regard of all.

He, with his regiment, took an active part in all the operations of the siege of Fort Donelson. After the surrender of the Fort, Major Mudd, learning that a man with important papers was effecting his escape, pursued him beyond our lines, when he met a citizen who begged for his promise of security, which was readily given. While they were riding toward the town of Dover, two other citizens joined them, who also asked for and received his pledge of protection. While conversing on the exciting events of the day, the first one, who (the Major after- wards learned) was a notoriously desperate character, fell in the rear, drew his revolver and fired at the Major, inflicting a severe and dangerous wound near the spine. The Major put spurs to his horse, and the cowardly traitor fired again, without effect, then wheeled his horse and fled.

On his way to our lines, and while suffering acutely from his wound and loss of blood, the Major captured a rebel Lieutenant, and compelled him to ride into camp in advance, having just realized the true import of "southern chivalry" and honor. In the confusion and rejoicing consequent upon taking the rebel works, and the amount of labor the surgeons had to perform in the field, he had considerable difficulty in finding one to examine and dress his wound. The ball could never be extracted. The wound healed slowly, and he never fully recovered from its effects, carrying the rebel lead with him to his grave. He was at home a short time on leave of absence; and when he was again ready to take the field, he was ordered on detached service as Aid on Gen. McClernand's staff; the duties of which office he faithfully discharged, until that officer was relieved of the command of the 19th Army Corps, during the siege of Vicksburg.

He was at the siege of Corinth, Miss., and shortly after its evacuation, was sent by Gen. McClernand to Washington City on business. Before his return, Lieut. Col. Hogg, of the 2d Illinois Cavalry, was killed in the battle of Britton's Lane, Tenn. Immediately on his return, he received the Lieutenant Colonel's commission of the regiment. In the following winter, he was engaged in the military operations at and near Holly Springs, Miss.; and in the battle of that place, not only refused to surrender, but with a part of his regiment, cut his way through the rebel forces and escaped, his daring and gallantry making him the hero of that affair.

In the winter of 1863, Col. Noble, of the 2d Illinois Cavalry, was mustered out of the service, and Lieut. Col. Mudd was promoted to the colonelcy of the regiment. In the following spring, the regiment was ordered to Milliken's Bend; and on the way they landed at Greenville, Miss., had a battle with the rebels, and completely dispersed them. The regiment then re-embarked and proceeded to its destination.

In all the battles and operations of Gen. Grant's campaign, from Grand Gulf to Vicksburg, he was actively engaged; and at the battle of Black River Bridge, particularly distinguished himself by his prudence and heroism.

During the siege of Vicksburg, he was in command, super-intending the obstructing of the roads and approaches to the city, so as to protect Gen. Grant's rear from any attack that General Joe Johnston might make to relieve Pemberton's beleaguered army, which duty he faithfully and judiciously performed.

A few days before the surrender of the rebel army and the city of Vicksburg, while reconnoitering in the Black River swamp, he was fired on by a concealed foe, at short range, one shot taking effect in his face, just below the left eye, the ball lodging near the ear: the other struck just above the collar-bone, and passed nearly out on the shoulder, and was afterwards taken out. From these wounds, he bled profusely; and, but for the timely assistance of his aids, must have been taken prisoner, they supporting him on his horse until he arrived at a place of security at the house of a widowed lady, who did all in her power to render him comfortable, when a surgeon came with an ambulance, and conveyed him to safer quarters. He again returned home, and soon recovered from these wounds. During his absence, his command was ordered to New Orleans, where he quickly joined it. The regiment accompanied Gen. Banks in his Texan campaign, and he was engaged in its operations, battles, and many skirmishes, acting as Brigadier General.

During the winter, his health becoming much impaired by the hardships and exposure he had undergone, he obtained leave of absence, to return home and recuperate. On arriving at New Orleans, he received orders to recruit his regiment. He immediately went to Springfield, Illinois, and opened a recruiting office. In the meantime, a large majority of the regiment re-enlisted as veterans, and came home on furlough. In a few weeks, the ranks of the regiment were filled, and it was ready again to take the field. They arrived in St. Louis, Missouri, on their way south, when, on the 30th of March, the Veteran Reception Committee of that city gave the heroic Colonel and his gallant soldiers an enthusiastic reception and a sumptuous dinner. They took ship on the 3d of April for New Orleans, and immediately on their arrival, were ordered to Baton Rouge, where Col. Mudd received an order from Gen.

Banks to report, without delay, to Gen. McClernand at Alexandria, La., as chief of staff.

On the first day of May, 1864, he embarked on board the steamer City Belle, and on the 3d, left the mouth of Red River for Alexandria. At 3 P. M. of that day, when at Dunne's Bayou, five miles above Snaggy Point, the guerrillas opened a masked battery upon the steamer, consisting of two pieces of artillery, at first, firing solid shot. The second shot killed the pilot, and broke the wheel; the fifth entered one of the boilers, causing it to explode. The boat soon became so disabled that it was unmanageable. Col. Speigle, of the 120th Ohio Infantry, was the senior officer in command. In a few minutes after the attack was commenced, he was killed. Col. Mudd then took charge, and ordered the engineer to run the boat ashore, but his efforts proved fruitless. All this time, a perfect storm of leaden hail rained upon the ill-fated steamer; the rebels, after the fifth shot, firing grape and canister at short range, every discharge doing fearful execution. In this terrible extremity, the gallant Colonel put a life preserver around Mr. Daniel Bates, who swam ashore, carrying a line, intending to land the boat, and make a dash at the guerrillas, who were inferior in numbers to the troops on the steamer. At this critical juncture, a shot struck the Colonel in the forehead, when he fell and instantly expired. The vessel was surrendered. The guerrillas robbed the living and the dead, took the body of the Colonel ashore and buried it, marking the spot, and then burned the steamboat. Of the 600 soldiers on board, about 160 escaped; the remainder were either killed or captured. Mr. Daniel Bates and the Colonel's orderly escaped, and arrived safe at Alexandria. In a few days after, they returned and exhumed the body, placed it in a wooden box, and took it to New Orleans, where they procured a metallic coffin, and accompanied it to Pittsfield, Ill. A funeral sermon was delivered, and the body followed to its home in the city of the dead, by a sadly, bereaved family, and hundreds of sorrowing friends.

Thus fell, at the post of duty, another victim at the shrine of rebellion. Let his own words, in a letter to his wife, on the eve of an engagement, prove his sincerity and devotion:

"I go forth to battle—if I fall, the blood of another martyr will enrich the soil, to nourish the tree of Liberty."

In his death, our country has lost a pure patriot—the army, a gallant and skillful officer—society, one of its brightest ornaments—his wife and little daughter, all there is in a loving husband and fond father—and an aged mother, a supporting staff in her declining years.

The writer was acquainted with the Colonel for twenty-seven years; most of that time, intimately so. Knew him in all the relations of life—as a son, dutiful and affectionate—as a husband and father, devoted and loving—as a Christian, consistent and zealous—as a friend, ardent, kind and obliging—as a man, noble, pure and honorable—and as a soldier, gallant and patriotic, possessing a devotion to liberty and his country, that prompted him to willingly offer his bleeding body upon the altar of the Republic's glory and honor.

DOCTOR COATSWORTH.

DOCTOR COATSWORTH.

Dr. GEORGE COATSWORTH was born on the 3d of February, 1832. His parents, who were Scotch and English, migrated from England to Canada, and settled in Romney, fronting Lake Erie. Here they purchased a farm, where, in due course of time, George, who was the youngest in a family of three sisters and five brothers, was born. His father was much respected, and held many important offices throughout the country. George, a handsome, promising lad, who attracted much attention, was sent early to the district school, in which he soon outstripped his young companions. Mathematics were his special *forte;* but he was an adept also in all departments, and had made considerable proficiency in other branches while he was yet of tender years.

At the age of twelve, he was placed under the care of an Episcopal clergyman, for instruction in the languages, preparatory to his choice of a profession; but his parents soon discovered that the very light of the household had gone out with him, and he was recalled, after an absence of one year.

He was subsequently sent to Caradoc Academy, a school of high standing in London, C.W. Here he remained some years, and left the college with honors. He was sent next to the Medical University at Buffalo, N. Y., where he applied himself closely to study for three consecutive years, spending most of his intermediate vacations in the hospitals of New York city, and graduating with the highest commendations of the Professors, both for his medical and anatomical knowledge.

On returning home, his next step was to seek a field for practice, near a medical college if possible, that he might thus enlarge his experience and learning. To this, however, there were many obstacles. His friends refused to part with him; and, having expectations from his father's estate, he yielded to their entreaties, and settled in the town of Kingsville, a charming, little place, on the banks of the Erie. Here he met with

good success, and soon commanded an extensive practice. His
large, social nature, which was ever the charm of his character,
drew around him an extensive circle of admiring friends; and
at the age of twenty-three, he was a man far beyond his years
in social as well as professional influence.

About this time he met with, and afterwards married, Miss
S. S. Flood, a lady of liberal education and fine, natural ability.
To a bright, genial, and sunny nature like his, a happy union,
such as this proved to be, was all that seemed necessary to complete and crown his manhood. He had his struggles, like the
rest of us, and also his triumphs; but he was so fortunately
tempered, that he was not discouraged by the former, nor un-
duly elated by the latter.

On the 27th of May, 1856, he was commissioned as Surgeon
in the 4th Battalion of Essex (Canadian) Artillery, an office the
duties of which he discharged with his usual zeal and conscien-
tiousness. This was his first introduction to military life—the
presage of that brief but honorable career in which he subsequently distinguished himself, and finally closed his humane
labors. It soon became evident, even at this early period, that
he was not destined to be tied down to a small country town.
His reputation had traveled considerably beyond the "parish
boundaries," and intimations were not wanting that he must
seek his fortunes in a wider sphere, and enlarge the province
of his usefulness. He also felt that Kingsville was not his final
resting place, although he was content to work on, and bide his
time. His friends were most anxious that he should remain
amongst them, and his unhappy father—in imbecile affection
for his favorite son, whom he could not bear from his sight—
thought to coerce his residence by cutting him off with a shilling,
a piece of injustice which he was actually allowed to perpetrate,
we fear, without overmuch remonstrance. On the death of the
old gentleman, to whom George had always been a loving and
dutiful son, he felt free to make a home in the place of his choice.
The community in which he practised had become greatly attached to their young physician, and were almost ready to claim
him as personal property; but, regardless of the many inducements which were held out to him to remain with them, he closed

his business; and amid the tears of many, and the deep regrets of all, he bade adieu to the scenes of his nativity, exchanging the grasp of old-timed and well-tried friendship for the cold recognition of a strange and populous city.

On the 28th of March, 1857, Dr. Coatsworth, with his young wife, took up his abode in Chicago, Ill. Letters of introduction had been tendered him from his old tutors in Buffalo to some of the leading physicians in the "Garden City," which were accepted, and from which we quote as evidence of the high esteem in which he was held by those most competent to form a judgment of his professional abilities and character.

Prof. Hamilton says:

My esteemed young friend, Dr. Coatsworth, a late graduate of our college, is worthy of any attention you may bestow upon him.

Prof. White:

He is one of our finest graduates, and a young man of rare talents. The attention you may please to show him for my sake, I have no doubt you will be happy to continue for his own.

Professors Flint, Dalton and others gave similar testimony, and the medical fraternity of the city took him cordially by the hand. He became at once, a member of the Cook County Medical Association, and soon after entered into partnership with Dr. Wardner, under the firm-name of "Coatsworth & Wardner." (The latter gentleman now a Brigade Surgeon in the army.) After more than a year's successful practice, the firm was dissolved, owing chiefly to a strong desire which had possessed Dr. Coatsworth of becoming acquainted with the laws of his adopted country. He may have imagined also that the kind of talents which he possessed might be turned to a more remunerative account by the study and practice of law—especially as a pleader at the bar—than by following the profession of medicine. Various motives no doubt operated upon him, and entered into the decision to which he finally came. He was young, and not without a manly ambition to make the best of his abilities. He had good reasoning and analytical powers, a fine voice, and a commanding presence—faculties and qualities of essential regard to forensic success. The Law, at all events, was an untried field to him, and much as he loved his profession, there might have been still more weighty inducements than any now named to tempt him to try his fortunes in that new region of intellectual enterprise. It is certain, however, that he did not act from mere caprice in thus abandoning the old for the new profession; and thus much is necessary to be said, by way of justifying him from any charges of that nature.

He was presented with the following resolutions upon his leaving the Cook County Medical Association:

To Dr. GEORGE COATSWORTH, OF CHICAGO:

Dear Sir,—At our last meeting, it was communicated to us that you had ceased to be an active member of the medical profession, and had become identified with the Bar of this city. And although very loth to lose you from our number, yet to express to some extent the warm friendship we bear you, and the high appreciation we entertain for your acquirements as a physician, the following resolution was offered, and unanimously passed:

WHEREAS, Dr. George Coatsworth, a member of this society, has withdrawn from professional intercourse with us, and entered upon the practice of law,—therefore, *Resolved*, That he retires with our profound respect for his many attainments, and our best wishes for his success in the new sphere which he has chosen.

Similar good wishes came in from all quarters where his friends were, and that is, from every quarter, for he was a man without an open enemy! He forthwith began the study of law with zeal and earnestness. Never did student work harder. He had an insatiable thirst for knowledge, and the day seemed too short for the gratification of his intellectual appetite. Often has he been left at night with a book in his hand and a lamp by his bedside, and found next morning still hard at work, accumulating material on which to build a future reputation. The money crisis, which had been tightening its coils for so long a time around the Empire City of the West, had this winter reached its climax; and many men were driven to abandon professional life, by the sheer force of circumstances. Not so this brave student! "*Nil desperandum*" was his chosen motto; and "who help themselves, God will help," were his frequent words of self-encouragement. He was never downcast, or disheartened. A great, indomitable courage lay at the bottom of his nature, and he was always equal to his necessities: studying a new profession, paying his debts, and supporting a family, when most men at that time found it hard to perform any one of these duties.

After the necessary preparatory study, he was admitted to the Bar of the State, and practiced at the Chicago Bar in partnership with Lester L. (now Aldermen) Bond. As a lawyer, he gave great promise. Judge Manierre said of him:

Young Dr. Coatsworth is destined to become one of the leading spirits of the West. He possesses undoubted talent—a superior education—breadth of mind, and depth of soul, which, combined with an agreeable address, great energy and force of character, must make him successful—and that largely.

This law dream, however, soon ended. His "first love," who had never ceased to follow him in his truantings from her, soon began to beckon him with the privileged fervor which belongs to that estate, and he could no longer resist her blandishments. He had gained—if not all he strove and hoped for—priceless wealth of knowledge in his legal studies, which, to him, was sufficient and all remunerative.

There is no doubt that he would have been a successful pleader if he had continued at the Bar. But the invitations of friends; the pressure it might be of still more weighty matters —(for we speak entirely without authority upon this subject)— as well as his early love for the medical profession, induced him to return to it, and give up his life as a sacrifice to its duties. An unseen hand—visible only to the eye of faith—there was in this guidance of the wanderer back to the profession wherein lay the true sources of his power. He also had a mission to perform, of which, happily for himself, he was unconscious to the last. Hence, he never presumed upon it, as so many do, who fallaciously imagine that such is their case, but he labored on with heart and soul, and the full, broad, deep strength of a right healthy man until his course was run.

During the intervals of business, when he was not engaged in curing the bodies of his fellow-men, he was earnestly devoting himself to a proper understanding and application of those intellectual remedies which the moral reformers of his time were propounding for the cure of the social estate. He was an active, member of the "Good Templars," and belonged to the Chicago

Lodge. He was an eloquent speaker, a good lecturer, and a ready writer; and his friends were frequently charmed with the productions of his pen, as he travelled from place to place.

We now come to a new era in his brief and chequered life. When the war clouds of 1861 burst upon us, he was among the first to give up the comforts of home, and rally to the national standard. Here was a wide field opened to his active benevolence and enterprise—and here, he could best discharge his duties as a patriot. Going to Springfield for examination, he was one of the few who, at that time, took a first-class certificate, and was at once commissioned as Surgeon of the 22d Regiment Illinois Infantry.

On returning to Chicago, his friends, always ready to strengthen his hands and sustain his high purposes, presented him with a handsome sword and belt, accompanying the gift with the following welcome and cheering words:

DR. GEORGE COATSWORTH,—Allow us to make you this slight present as a token of our esteem for your character and talents. Called from civil life, as you are, by the exigencies of our common country, we, for our part, know of no better way of expressing our regard for you than by confiding to your hands this sword—an emblem of the power which defends our common homes, etc., etc.

The Doctor's regiment was first sent to Bird's Point, where the surrounding marshes and miasma caused such extreme debility in the army, that many physicians were entirely unfitted for duty. Dr. Coatsworth, however, was of so strong and vigorous a constitution, that he was not in the least affected by the poisonous emanations of the locality. He undertook and accomplished the work of three sufficient men, struggling bravely through it, under a torrid sun and surfeiting atmosphere. In vain his brother officers admonished him to "beware!"—telling him that his turn would come next if he did not husband his resources—always ending with the kind reminder, "We cannot do without you;"—duty was the only mandate which he obeyed. Such services as he rendered could not be hidden. They had a public as well as a private recognition, which nerved him, if possible, to still greater activity. The Chicago *Journal*, speaking of that time and circumstance, says:

The hospitals over which Dr. Coatsworth has charge, are models in their neatness and general management.

The Medical Board of Inspectors reported the same hospitals as the finest and best attended of any on the Point. His supervision was over all his work, and his attention to his patients incessant.

But the strongest man can be bowed down, and so he found it. A slow typhoid fever now seized upon his manly frame, and for a while, there was a life and death struggle between them, the fever being at last thrown and conquered, and the Doctor once more on duty. He was soon destined to see a more active service than ever he had yet witnessed and endured. The engagements of Farmington and Belmont introduced him at once to the shambles of the battle-field, where he became acquainted at first hand with the most fearful and bloody mutilations to which his practiced art had hitherto been applied. He was so successful here in his treatment even of the worst cases, that he was soon afterwards—19th February, 1862—assigned Post Surgeon at Paducah, Ky. Here he had ample scope for the exercise both of skill and kindness. All the severely wounded from the battles of Fort Donelson and Pittsburg Landing were placed under his immediate care. His skill in surgery was acknowledged by the Medical Director and others of the profession, to be unexcelled by any practitioner in the U.S. service. Here he won not only professional laurels, but the hearts of all who knew him. And indeed, no man ever more truly or worthily deserved gratitude from those under his charge than he. Night seldom brought repose to his weary frame and faculties. After contending all day with disease and the arch-enemy, Death; after putting forth against them all the armories of his power and knowledge—all the energies of his indomitable will, and the magnetisms of his intellect, he would pass the night also at the bedside of the dying, comforting and cheering them in their last moments, until the trembling spirit left its frail tenement to find its way across the troubled waters of the ever-present and mysterious Jordan.

His endurance was immense. He has been known to stand by the surgical table in the hospital and operate continuously

for three successive days and nights, with but one hour's rest
in twenty-four ! This was killing work, it is true, but the
men also were dying—would have died but for his kindly-cruel
knife. The Chicago *Journal* speaks of him and his exertions
at this time in a most friendly manner:

> The central hospital at Paducah is under the very able management of Dr.
> Coatsworth, who is a man of great executive ability and medical skill. It is
> but fair to state, that the wounded upon whom he has operated have all,
> more or less, recovered—the army rule being, for the most part, that one
> operation is equal to one death! Most of the Doctor's patients are getting
> along finely, and are rapidly recovering. A better man could not have been
> chosen for the place which he so faithfully and so admirably occupies.

The New Albany *Ledger*, of about the same date, said:

> Dr. George Coatsworth, who was transferred from his regiment on account
> of his medical skill, and is now in charge of Paducah Hospital, is a man of
> more than ordinary talent, and is admirably fitted, in every respect, for the
> responsible place which he now holds. A more suitable person could not
> have been chosen from the whole division.

And such, indeed, was the universal testimony.

After four months of laborious service at this station, he was
recalled to his regiment, and went through the exhausting toils
of a mid-summer campaign in the interior of Alabama. Soon
after the evacuation of Corinth, he resigned, for the sole purpose of recuperating his health, which had been much shattered
by his long labors and marches. He returned once more to
his home in Chicago, where his numerous acquaintances gave
him a warm and hearty welcome.

Through the persuasion of many of his old friends, and a
conviction that he had not yet paid his full debt to his adopted
country, he was induced to enter the service once more, and, on
the 4th of September, 1862, was commissioned as Surgeon of
the 88th (2d Board of Trade) Regiment Illinois Infantry—Col.
F. T. Sherman commanding. The Chicago *Tribune* notices his
appointment in the following terms:

> Col. Stokes has appointed our fellow-citizen, George Coatsworth, M. D.,
> Surgeon of the 2d Board of Trade Regiment of U. S. Volunteers. In this
> appointment Col. Stokes has not only given new evidences of his fitness for
> his position, but has gratified the wishes of a large portion of our community.

Dr. Coatsworth has been in the service for fifteen months in the position of Surgeon of the 22d Regiment Illinois Volunteers. At Belmont, he was regimental surgeon, and after the battles of Fort Donelson and Shiloh, he was detached from his regiment and placed in charge of the general hospital at Paducah, Ky., when the most severely wounded of those bloody battles were put in his care. After remaining there three months, he rejoined his regiment, and was at Monterey, Farmington, Corinth and Boonville, Ala. During all of this time, he was constantly engaged in the duties of his profession, and there are few surgeons connected with our army who have done as much service to the country as Dr. C.

We congratulate the officers and soldiers of the regiment upon this judicious selection of their chief medical officer.

Entering upon his duties with renewed health and ripened professional experience, the old intellectual fire and generosity of nature, which had marked his previous career, were soon again apparent, and he became the idol of his regiment. In the battle of Perryville, where he was under a long and heavy fire, he displayed much coolness and courage; and his efforts were untiring to relieve all who suffered in the conflict. Officers and men were all one to him on the great levelling platform of the battle-field—and he made no distinction between them. In a letter to a friend, he says:

To heal and sustain an officer in the hour of need, is commendable—but how much greater is the humanity that cheers and prepares for battle the poor friendless private, who offers up his life upon the altar of his country, and committing his soul to God, marches at another's will and bidding, to the cannon's mouth for his destiny!

Dr. Coatsworth was everywhere complimented upon the neatness, order and cleanliness of his hospitals; and at Perryville, Gen. Sill, commander of division, said that he had the best regulated hospital he had seen in the service, and he recommended it as a model to others.

After hunting guerrilla bands four months, and passing through one of the most toilsome marches that has been made during this wicked rebellion, the regiment was at length sent to Nashville, Tenn., where they reasonably expected a short respite from a sod pillow and uncooked rations. Alas for their hopes! The bloody battle of Stone River commenced immediately, and raged for days with all the fury, as the soldiers expressed it, of a "Hell broke loose!" As the men were swept from the ranks like grass before the scythe, Dr. Coatsworth was in their midst, binding up the broken wounds and cheering the spirits of the mangled soldiers, who looked to him as their only salvation. Heart-rending was the sight to witness those fine manly fellows, who, but a moment before, were in the full glory of manhood, the blood-rush of battle on their cheeks, unconquerable courage in their hearts, and each hand mailed for victory, thus suddenly, at the blast of a trumpet, cut down by an invisible enemy, helpless, torn asunder by unspeakable agonies, crying in their blood for help, and crying, alas! too often in vain! Dr. Coatsworth saw thousands of such sights as this, and he was always ready to help the poor sufferers to the best of his ability.

At the battle of Stone River, there was for days scarcely a cessation in the roar and thunder of the warfare. Now near, now distant, it rose, ebbing and flowing, heaving and surging, like a vast sea of fire and flame; the cries of the trodden and wounded drowned in the madness and clamor of the conflicting hosts and the rolling of the mighty drums. The Doctor was on the very edge of the battle, his ears appalled every now and then by hideous death yells, and his heart smitten by beseeching eyes appealing to him not in vain, so long as his strength lasted. For forty-eight hours did this monstrous phlegethon of human strife and passion rage and boil in the depths of the Stone River valley; whilst Dr. Coatsworth, all that time without food or rest, continued his almost superhuman labors, fascinated by them, drawn from the relief of one poor soul, only to put his merciful hands upon some other equally as necessitous and importunate—and so on, as it seemed to him, in an endless succession of shattered and mutilated bodies. Still he never stopped nor faltered. Like one fulfilling some dreadful destiny, with no hope nor rest in the background of the future, so he worked until his strong frame gave way, and he sank, utterly exhausted, into that pitiless grave from which he had rescued so many others during this tremendous battle.

Long will the tragedy of his death remain in the minds of those who witnessed the sacrifice! It is to us one of the grandest, most touching and divine pictures which the war has contributed to humanity and to art.

The greatest agony of his dying moments seemed to be that his idolized wife could not be near him to minister to his wants; she who, to quote his oft-repeated language, "had been to him the stimulus to all high and noble ambition; the benefactor, and guiding star of his life."

Thus died on the 9th of January, 1863, one of the noblest heroes of this cruel rebellion.

The following resolutions, expressive, to some extent, of the feelings of his regiment on his decease, were sent to his bereft family:

The officers of the 88th Regiment Illinois Volunteers, deeply feeling the loss of their Surgeon, Dr. Geo. Coatsworth, who died of pneumonia, at Murfreesboro, Tenn., January 9th, 1863, were called together by Col. Sherman, when a committee, consisting of Lieut. Col. Chadbourne, Capt. Sheridan, Capt. McClurg, and Lieut. Bigelow, was selected to draft resolutions expressive of their feelings. Lieut. Col. Chadbourne, on presenting the resolutions, remarked, that he did not feel that the occasion was an ordinary one; that he was opposed to the usual way of calling meetings and passing the customary resolutions. He believed that every one present felt the loss of a true friend in the death of Dr. Coatsworth. The resolutions passed were as follows:

WHEREAS, Providence has seen fit to remove from us our Surgeon, George Coatsworth, by death—*Resolved*, That we, the officers of this regiment, tender to his family our heartfelt sympathy in this their sudden bereavement. We bear willing tribute to his many excellencies of character and his greatness of head and heart. To us his death is an irreparable loss, and to the profession of which he was so able a member. In our friend we recognize a man of more than ordinary ability and attainments. Our respect and love for him increased as a continued daily association with him developed those traits of character which a less intimate acquaintance would fail to discover. We feel that not only has the regiment, by his death, lost a true friend and skilful surgeon, but the profession one of its clearest thinkers, most devoted students and accomplished operators. But, though the loss is hard to bear, we find relief in the fact, that he died in the noblest way a man can die—at his post, in the laborious and faithful performance of his duty.

F. T. SHERMAN, *Chairman.*

J. SEYMOUR BALLARD, *Secretary.*

Among the most touching reflections upon his death, is the following letter, forwarded from the camp of the brave 88th to his bereaved wife:

HEADQUARTERS 88TH REGIMENT ILLINOIS VOLUNTEERS, CAMP BRADLEY, NEAR MURFREESBORO, TENN., Jan. 11th, 1863.

MRS. DR. COATSWORTH,—Allow us to present to you a copy of resolutions passed at a meeting of the officers of this regiment, expressing our respect and love for your deceased husband, and our deep regret at a loss which we must mourn in common with. We feel a delicacy in intruding upon the sacredness of your grief; but, as we take pleasure in being the keepers of his later reputation, we feel ourselves privileged to approach you with our heartfelt testimony. And let us assure you, that these resolutions are couched in no idle words merely, but rather that we deeply feel every word in them, and much more than we expressed. Dr. Coatsworth had been with us for some months, but we had just begun truly to know him. Every day as it passed showed us more and more the keenness of his intellect, the kindness of his heart, the genial nature of his disposition, and the strength of his character. The future opened up before him in all the brightness of its possibilities, and he had long resolved upon a life of earnest labor and its attendant rewards and honors. But this was not to be. The clouds seemed only rolled away for a moment, that his sun might set in its natural brilliancy. At the opening of the battle of Murfreesboro, he entered on his labors with that earnest zeal which always characterized his devotion to his profession. Night and day he labored unceasingly. Rest he forsook, and scarcely paused for necessary food. For forty-eight hours he thus labored, forgetful of himself, and only anxious to relieve the sufferings of others, until even his mighty strength gave way, and he sank into that grave from which he had rescued so many. It was for others to die on the field of battle by the bullets of the enemy; he died no less gloriously at the post of duty.

Again, let us offer you our most sincere and heartfelt sympathy. As you mourn the most devoted of husbands, so we mourn an endeared friend, and, through his mastery of his profession, an invaluable protector.

We invoke for you, in your bereavement, the guidance and protection of that Providence who doeth all things well.

We remain, Madam, very sincerely and respectfully,

F. T. SHERMAN, Col. 88th Ill. Inft.
A. S. CHADBOURNE, Lieut. Col.
G. W. CHANDLER, Major.
A. C. RANKIN, Surgeon.
J. C. THOMAS, Chaplain.
And all other officers of the regiment.

On hearing of her husband's illness, his devoted wife set out with all possible speed to reach him. The road was infested with guerrilla bands; rail tracts were being torn up, boats burned, and women injured; but her love was strong, her courage great; and alone in the night, she undertook the hazardous journey, resolved that no obstacle should keep her from her husband's side. But alas! before she reached him, stranger hands had closed his eyes, and angel spirits had borne him hence. The sun of her day had set in early morn.

The remains were forwarded from Murfreesboro to his home in Chicago, where, owing to interruptions caused by bushrangers, they were not received until two weeks after his decease. His many friends in the city awaited them with every demonstration of respect and sorrow. The profession of Chicago took notice of his death in the following words:

At a meeting of physicians, who were called together for the purpose of drafting resolutions expressive of their regret, Prof. N. S. Davis said, that "it gave him pleasure to state, that Dr. George Coatsworth was a very highly esteemed member of the Chicago Medical Society, and while living, enjoyed the confidence and esteem not only of its members, but of the profession generally; that in scientific and professional attainments, as well as high social qualities, he had but few equals in the profession of our city." The following resolutions were then adopted:

WHEREAS, George Coatsworth, M. D., formerly a member of this society, died while in the noble discharge of his duty as a surgeon in the volunteer army of Tennessee; therefore, *Resolved*, That in the death of Dr. Coatsworth, this society has lost one of its most valuable members, and the army one of its most skillful and efficient medical officers. *Resolved*, That we sincerely sympathize with the family and friends of the deceased in their deep affliction. *Resolved*, That a copy of the foregoing preamble and resolutions be furnished to the city papers and to the widow of the deceased.

Dr. Allen, of the army, wrote:

It was with deep feelings of sorrow he heard of the death of his esteemed brother Coatsworth. He was a man of rare professional acquirements, and brilliant scientific attainments. Gifted with a massive brain, he had stored it industriously and with care. He was a cheerful companion, a faithful friend—a man who could chain the attention of his friends for hours with sallies of wit and eloquence—a man of broad and generous views, and known as one of the best surgeons in the whole army.

Mr. Simmons, Medical Director, said—

There was nothing mediocre about Dr. Coatsworth. His executive ability was much above par; and that, during the many years of his connection with the U. S. Army, he had met with no mind superior to that of his young friend.

Dr. T. R. Austin, Surgeon in charge of Post Paducah, Ky., wrote of him:

It was my good fortune to become acquainted with the late Surgeon, Geo. Coatsworth, while in Paducah, he having been appointed to the command of the Central Hospital of that place. Dr. Coatsworth labored in that position with the most unremitting ardor. Exceedingly skillful in his profession, an expert and scientific operator, he won the love and admiration of all his associates, and endeared himself to those who came under his care, by his kind attention to their necessities. Thoroughly versed in scientific lore, he was also a laborious student, and a close observer of all that would tend to advance surgical knowledge. He was also practically conversant with his duties, and discharged them nobly. And although we cannot understand why one so eminent in his profession, so highly gifted in intellectual attainments, and whose mind was so richly stored with professional and literary knowledge, should so early be removed from our midst; yet He, who is his own interpreter, will soon make it plain. I feel deeply that I have lost a dear friend and brother, with whom I had often taken counsel, and whom I had hoped to meet frequently again upon earth. While we grieve for his loss, let us remember all that was good, ennobling and great in his character; how many sorrows he soothed, how many tears he wiped away, and how many sufferers he relieved. Professionally, Dr. Coatsworth had but few equals; socially, no superiors. He had faults, (and who has none?) for he was mortal; but they were few, and he had MANY virtues.

Through the entreaty of a brother, and a regard for an aged and doting mother, the remains were taken to the maternal home for interment, it not being known until after his burial, that, in the event of his death, Dr. Coatsworth wished to be placed in Rosehill Cemetery, near his city home, where a fitting monument will be erected to his memory.

Funeral services were held over his remains in Chicago, previous to their removal East. On this occasion, Rev. Dr. Swazey, who officiated, said:

Our esteemed friend, whose great loss we deplore, has finished his course, and all that is left of his once manly form lies before us, "sunk in that little measure." His bereaved wife is sorely grieved; her heart is rent asunder! but she and we also are comforted not only with the thought that God, the merciful Father, who noteth even the falling of a sparrow, has brought this grief upon us, but that our beloved friend died in the service of his country. He literally laid down his life for others. There is nothing that makes life so noble, so grand! His name will bear this lasting honor, that, while many are living ingloriously at ease, he gave his life for the bruised, the wounded, and for all who love our country! Much of the spirit of our Saviour is manifested in this man's death, and great will surely be the reward.

After proper services, the remains were conducted to the cars, and in charge of his brother, taken East, where a large funeral took place.

And thus crowned with the glory of a ripe humanity—all his duties nobly done—has passed away forever from the earth one of our best and bravest citizen patriots. He is numbered with the vast army of martyrs, who, from all the ranks and conditions of men, have gone forth at the summons of their country, to rescue the Republic from the hands of rebels and barbarians. Of a comparative lowly estate, like a million of others, he has risen by the grandeurs of his character, to a high moral position, and his name and memory are embalmed in the immortal record of his time.

> "Only the actions of the just,
> Smell sweet, and blossom in the dust!"

GENERAL RANSOM.

Brigadier General THOMAS EDWIN GREENFIELD RANSOM was born at Norwich, Windsor county, Vermont, on the 29th day of November, 1834. His father, Col. Truman B. Ransom, was born in Woodstock, Windsor county, Vt., in 1803, and was for some time President of the Norwich University in that State. In this school the military element was made prominent. The students were regularly trained in the manual of arms, and obtained great proficiency. They made a tour, as far as Boston, in the summer of 1846, and attracted much attention. They were called Norwich Cadets. Thomas was then about thirteen years of age. The military element of the school must have made a deep impression upon the susceptible nature of young Ransom.

On the breaking out of the Mexican war, his father promptly placed himself at the head of the 9th New England Regiment of U. S. Volunteers, and went to the field. All New England, howsoever divided the people may have been as to the justice of the war, awards him honor, as a gallant leader, worthy even of a better place. After participating in several battles, and in every instance displaying distinguished ability, he fell at the storming of Chepultepec, September 13, 1847, which made a deep impression upon the public mind when the sad announcement of his death appeared. The qualities of the son were, in a conspicuous degree, those of the father. Col. Ransom had more of the military officer in his demeanor than the General, had more sternness of manner, but in all true traits which render a man dear to those who know him best, they were much alike. The mother of the General is still living, and is represented as a lady of high endowments and culture.

Gen. Ransom removed to Peru, Lasalle co., Illinois, in the spring of 1851, and in the fall of 1855, with his uncle, G. W. Gilson, became interested in the land agency firm of A. J.

Galloway & Co., at Chicago; and, at the same time, did business in the firm name of Bell & Ransom.

At the announcement, in April, 1861, that Fort Sumter had been fired upon and the national flag dishonored, young Ransom sprang to the defence of the Union. Between Saturday night and Wednesday morning, he raised a company for the 11th Illinois Infantry; at 5 o'clock of the latter day, had the men in Springfield, and before he slept, he and his company were accepted into the service. Upon the organization of the regiment a few days after, he was elected Major. In June following, he was promoted to Lieutenant Colonel. He was commissioned Colonel a few days before the battle of Shiloh, to date from July 16, 1862, the day of the surrender of Fort Donelson, *vice* W. H. L. Wallace, promoted to a Brigadier Generalship.

At Shiloh, he led the regiment through the thickest of that bloody fight, and though wounded in the head early in the engagement, remained with his command throughout the day. He assisted Gen. McClernand in rallying an Ohio regiment that was falling back on his right, and forced them to move forward with his own troops upon a rebel battery. In the official report of this battle, Gen. McClernand spoke of Col. Ransom, at a critical moment, "performing prodigies of valor, though reeling in his saddle, and streaming with blood from a serious wound."

In the spring of 1863, he was elevated to the rank of Brigadier General, to date from Nov. 29, (his birthday,) 1862, for distinguished services at Shiloh, and at the siege of Corinth. In the memorable siege of Vicksburg, he commanded a brigade, and won fresh laurels, as he had in every other branch of the military service with which he had been united. The fortifications which he built during that siege still remain, and bear his honored name.

Gen. Ransom was connected with the famous Red River Expedition. His coolness and daring at the unhappy battle of Sabine Cross Roads, saved that branch of the army which he commanded from complete and overwhelming disaster.

Gen. Ransom was four times wounded: At Charleston, Mo., Aug. 19, 1861; at Fort Donelson, Feb. 15, 1862; at Shiloh, April 6, 1862; and at Sabine Cross Roads, Louisiana, April 8, 1864.

15

The wound received at Sabine Cross Roads was severe, and brought him to Chicago, where he received the congratulations of a grateful public. He needed rest. He had been in active service continually, in Missouri, Kentucky, Tennessee, Mississippi, Georgia, Alabama, Louisiana and Texas; but on the 27th of July, even before his limb was quite restored, feeling that the exigencies of the cause in Northern Georgia demanded his services, he returned to the front, where he best liked to be. Through the remainder of the summer he was in good health, and took an active part in the duties of that momentous campaign. He was in the battle of Jonesboro, his command forming a part of the left wing, and was one of the rejoicing host that entered the city of Atlanta soon after it was abandoned by the opposing army.

Ready for new victories, as yet not seriously harmed by lead or steel, he, to whom death had so often looked but not yet called away, was now to receive the summons which sooner or later comes to us all.

The early part of October found him sick. His disease assumed the form of dysentery. As it was needful for his command to proceed to Rome, he started with it, and though the disease was constantly weakening him, he insisted on going forward with the troops. Sometimes he rode at the head of the column in an ambulance, taking the saddle only as the advance guard became engaged with the enemy. Generals Sherman and Howard, and their respective medical directors, suggested to him the propriety of allowing himself to be reported sick, and thus relieve himself of duty; but his decision was unalterable; "*I will stay with my command until I leave in my coffin,*" was his final answer to all such suggestions. On the 26th of October, still moving forward, there was a decided change in him for the worse. His death was hourly expected, but his vigorous constitution and strong will carried him through that sudden relapse, so that on the morning of the 27th he took his place in the ambulance, and bore the fatigue of the day remarkably well. The next day he was worse again—too ill to ride any longer, and so his comrades placed him upon a litter, and with a regiment for an escort, they bore their beloved General forward.

Light were their feet, but heavy were the hearts of his brave men that day. The next morning they resumed their march, but at 11 o'clock the column was halted. The young leader could go no further. His precious life was fast ebbing away. The Surgeon informed him that he could not survive but a few hours. The announcement did not alarm him in the least. Looking up, with a cheerful expression, the brave warrior said: "*I am not afraid to die; I have met death too often to be afraid of it now.*" His mind was clear and vigorous. Calling his Aid-de-Camp to him, he delivered to his care several messages of love for relatives and friends, gave directions as to private business, and waited cheerfully, with triumphing Christian trust, for the rapidly approaching hour. At forty-five minutes past 2 P. M., Oct. 29th, when near Rome, Ga., his spirit took its flight to the God who gave it, uttering, to the latest moment, words of love and happiness. He was twenty-nine years and eleven months old. Few lives, though numbering threescore years and ten, have exhibited more maturity of character, or rendered larger service to mankind. Among his last words was this remarkable sentence: "*I have tried to do my duty, and have no fears for myself after death.*"

As soon as the sad event was known in Chicago, a meeting of the General's friends and admirers was convened at the Tremont House, when a dispatch from Chattanooga was read by Norman Williams, Esq., intimating that the remains were on the way to this city. Thereupon, appropriate committees were appointed to make the necessary arrangements for a public funeral to the young martyr hero, on the 6th November, 1864.

The body lay in state at Bryan Hall, and for four hours the tide of life flowed steadily and solemnly by the catafalco. The hall was draped in mourning; floral wreaths and immortelles strewed the coffin; the General's good sword lay across his breast, and the flag, under which he fought and died, was flung over the narrow house.

The funeral service at the hall, consisting simply of the impressive ritual of the Episcopal Church, was pronounced by the Rev. R. H. Clarkson, D. D.; upon the conclusion of which, he delivered a short address, paying a glowing tribute to the memory of the General. During these exercises, the various divisions of the funeral procession were forming in the places assigned them. Masons, with their emblems draped in mourning, and sable banners fluttering in the breeze, were wheeling slowly into line; squads of soldiery were fileing through the street, to the strains of the "Dead March;" the firemen took up their position; and at 2 o'clock, the funeral pageant commenced its march. Solemn and slow tolled the city bell—minute guns were fired—flags throughout the city were displayed at half-mast—and November's leaden sky and sighing wind added befitting gloom to the scene, as if nature itself were touched with human sympathy. On the procession arriving at the old cemetery, a detachment of the Veteran Reserve Corps fired a salute over the body, and with Masonic rites the remains were deposited in a vault, to await a fitting receptacle at Rosehill.

The following is an extract from an obituary sermon, delivered by Rev. W. H. Ryder, D. D., Pastor of St. Paul's Universalist Church of Chicago, at the request of a number of the friends of the lamented General, taking, for his text, 1 Sam. ii. 30—"Them that honor me I will honor:"

As I see the patriot hero borne along the rough highway, mile after mile, upon the shoulders of his comrades, asking for no greater privilege than the opportunity of continuing to serve his country, yet realizing, as he must have done, that he was rapidly nearing the shore of that undiscovered sea that rolls round all the earth; as I hear, in imagination, his cheerful words, look into his sunny face, and listen to his testimony to the value of the Christian religion, interpreted in the light of the divine goodness; as I think of what he was, so young, so promising, and yet so crowned with the confidence of his countrymen, and so esteemed by all who knew him—it has seemed to me that the death was not only befitting the life, but rounds his brief but brilliant career into an example that must exert a salutary influence upon thousands now living, and is worthy of being placed high in the list of those names which the historians of this war for the defense of the National Union, will preserve for the admiration of future generations.

We shall not attempt an elaborate analysis of the character of the deceased. Certain of his prominent traits, those most conspicuous and instructive, are all that we shall attempt to indicate.

1. General Ransom was retiring and unostentatious. There was no strut about him. He was simple in his manners. Quiet, unobtrusive. In a

company of gentlemen he would not have been selected as a military man, according to the people's estimate. His power was always in reserve for occasions—and the greater the occasion, the deeper the peril, the more capable did he show himself to be. Ambitious—meaning thereby desire of power or eminence—he was not. His ambition was to honor his country—the service—to quit himself as a man should, acting in such a presence and such an hour. Whether General Ransom would have risen to the rank of a *great* leader—*i. e.*, whether he would have gained a still higher grade, and filled it with the same distinguished success which graced all the positions he occupied, is now a question which can never be decisively answered, and which, perhaps, it is not worth while to tarry long and consider. One thing is quite certain: had he been the chief in command of the Red River Expedition, that blundering campaign, if undertaken at all, would have had a very different issue. And it is a pretty safe rule, that he who does best when most is demanded, is capable of doing more than he has ever yet done.

2. General Ransom was a kind, pleasant, sympathetic man. He had a sunny face, a clear, cheerful eye. He attached people to him; they loved him, for he was good; they honored him, for he was brave. There are those here who knew the kindness of his heart, and who loved him with all the reverence of grateful affection. A dutiful son, an appreciative relative, a faithful friend, a patriot hero, he deserves well of his countrymen, and will long be honored in the sanctuaries of a thousand hearts.

3. General Ransom's patriotism and high moral tone proceeded from conviction—were the outgrowth of inward stability. The springs of his action were deep. Hence he was true in danger, and uniformly prepared for the duty when it came. Hence, also, he did not degenerate into the temptations which beset the service, or lose that strength which comes from Christian integrity. These traits would have served him in any calling. And had he lived to the allotted age of man, it is more than probable he would have held fast to the principles which distinguished his youth, and ended his career in a life of the largest usefulness.

MAJOR BOWEN.

Major RODNEY S. BOWEN, severely wounded at the battle of Franklin, Tenn., 29th November, 1864, died at officers' hospital, Nashville, 3d December following, aged 31 years.

Major Bowen was born in Herkimer county, N. Y., and the only surviving child of Dr. A. W. and Mrs. Mary C. Bowen, who removed with him to the present site of Joliet, Illinois, in 1834. Constitutionally feeble, he was almost wholly deprived of attendance at school; yet, with his mother's aid, and an aptitude for learning, he acquired intelligence and a fair education. In his youth he was noted for manliness and a retiring disposition.

In 1859, he removed to Wilmington, Ill., and was, for a few years, engaged in business; but his health failing, he sought the labors of out-door life. In 1855, he married Frances, daughter of the late Dr. Todd, of Rockville, Ill., and, at the breaking out of the rebellion, was living comfortably on his farm at Wilmington. With restored health, he felt it a duty he owed his country to assist her in this her hour of need. Brought up with the care and tenderness of an only child, he was by public opinion exempt from the first call for 300,000 volunteers, as being unequal to the hardships and privations of a camp life, yet his patriotism overrode all minor objections. He said he "should feel ashamed to sleep in a comfortable bed at home while so many thousands were lying on the ground deprived of the comforts of life for his protection."

Leaving family and business in the midsummer of 1862, he obtained permission from Gov. Yates to raise a company, was chosen its commander, and in about thirty days was mustered into the 100th Regiment Illinois Volunteers as its senior Captain. With the earnestness which characterized all his actions he entered upon his new duties, determined to serve his country faithfully and well. In this he persevered to the end.   In

August, 1862, the regiment was ordered to Louisville, Ky., under the lamented Col. Bartleson, to avert the threatened raid of Gen. Bragg, of the Confederate army, and followed that rebel over half of the State of Kentucky, compelling him to retreat to Middle Tennessee. In this, one of the hardest campaigns of the war, when nearly one-half of the new recruits succumbed to the severe marching and oppressive heat of September, Capt. Bowen was ever at the post of duty, and earned the love and respect of his men for his humanity and kindness.

At Bardstown, Ky., Gen. Hascall rode up in front of the 100th Regiment, and, addressing them, said: "You are about to meet the enemy, and if you *run*, I have a regiment (pointing to the 26th Ohio) placed in your rear to shoot you down." Capt. Bowen, heading the skirmish line, ordered the advance, in expectation of a fight within a short distance. The men, biting their lips with wounded pride, sprang forward at the command, nor did they stop for fences, thickets or swamps, until the rebel cavalry retreated out of sight: but, though respecting Gen. Hascall for his bravery, they did not soon forget his imputation upon their untried courage.

At Lavergne, the 100th Regiment was highly complimented. Its position was, as usual, on the left, and companies A and B were in the skirmish line: their charge through the town swept everything before it, and the regiment received the commendation of the General in command. It was again in the thickest of the fight at the battle of Stone River, losing several officers and about forty men killed and wounded.

Capt. Bowen continued in command of his company during the fighting from Murfreesboro to Chattanooga; was at the taking of the latter place, and in the terrible fight at Chickamauga, where Colonel Bartleson was taken prisoner. At the storming of Mission Ridge, he was acting Major and severely wounded, but, being helped upon a horse, he did not leave the field until the victory was complete.

Joining his regiment again at Loudon, East Tennessee, he was in all the battles from Chattanooga to the crossing of the Chattahooche river, near Atlanta, where he was disabled by severe inflammation of his eyes and ordered to Lookout Mountain Hospital. "His coolness in battle, and his calmness under fire," says his commanding officer, "were heroically displayed in the battles of Resaca, Rockyface, Newhope Church, and Kenesaw Mountain."

On all occasions he did his duty as a soldier, but the devastation of war, and particularly the wanton destruction to private property, were repugnant to his instincts. In a letter to his mother, in October, 1864, from Chattanooga, he says:

The yard in which we are encamped, shows signs of having once been filled with choice shrubbery. There is a magnificent vine of the Eglantine species still showing signs of life over the front door of the mansion—our dining table stands upon what was once a bed of flowers—a peach tree, that was capable of bearing bushels of fruit, serves us for a hitching post—a few honeysuckles still remain to mark the paths—and our cook hangs his wiping cloth upon a shrub of some choice kind unknown to me; and, although the owner is said to be rebellious, I could not have been the first to trample upon such a place. The remembrance of several such spots that you have spent time, taste and labor upon, and that I have occasionally assisted in forming, will always prevent me from laying ruthless hands upon what are among the pleasant things of life. The soldier first takes the fence to cook his coffee, only one or two pickets or boards—the next soldier, another; and before you are aware, there is no protection left. Then some careless teamster comes crushing along with his six mules and heavy government wagon, and the iron enters the soul of the chivalry. They have sown the wind, and are now reaping the whirlwind. They have sown the dragon's teeth, and the armed men that spring up are now tearing out their vitals.

At Atlanta, Capt. Bowen received his Major's commission, and continued with his regiment until he received his mortal wound while in charge of the rear guard at the battle of Franklin, Tenn.

Naturally of a retiring and religious turn of mind, he had long been a firm and consistent member and one of the wardens of the Episcopal Church of Wilmington.

A thorough conviction that his country needed his services, was his only motive for enlisting in her cause, and the final crushing out of the rebellion the end at which he aimed. In the language of one of his fellow officers, "he lived a Christian and a gentleman, and died a soldier and a hero."

COLONEL BRYANT,

COLONEL BRYANT.

Col. JULIAN E. BRYANT was born at Princeton, Ill., November 9, 1836. He was the second son of Arthur Bryant, who emigrated from Massachusetts to Illinois in 1830, and was one of the earliest settlers in Bureau county.

He had no other facilities for acquiring an education than those afforded by the schools in that locality. From early boyhood he showed an unusual taste and talent for drawing; and while at school took lessons in drawing and painting, which he practised in leisure hours under circumstances not the most favorable. At the age of twenty-one, he determined to qualify himself for the profession of an artist; and in the fall of 1857 went to New York, where he remained until the next summer, studying and sketching from nature in the vicinity. After pursuing his studies for about a year at Princeton, he went in 1859 to Bloomington, and was for sometime connected with the Normal School of Illinois as instructor of drawing. He afterwards took apartments in the city, and painted several large landscapes for the Natural History Society, which now adorn its rooms. He also executed many other pieces, which are scattered over the country. Some of his paintings are quite fine, and gave assurance of future eminence in their author as an artist.

In the summer of 1861, Col. Bryant, together with Major Elliott of Princeton, raised Co. E of the 33d Regiment Illinois Volunteers, and was elected 2d Lieutenant of that company. In June, 1862, he was promoted to the 1st Lieutenancy. His first year of service was spent in Missouri and Arkansas. In the march of Gen. Curtis' army through Arkansas to Helena on the Mississippi river, he was engaged in the battle of Bayou Cache, where Col. C. E. Hovey, with less than 300 men, routed a troop of 3000 Texan cavalry and Arkansian conscripts—a battle of no great importance, but deserving of notice for the

disparity of numbers in the forces engaged.   Our troops buried
117 dead rebels on the field.

In the fall of 1862 he was detailed on the staff of Gen. C. E.
Hovey, and while holding that position was present at the unsuccessful attack of Sherman upon Vicksburg, and soon after,
at the storming and capture of Arkansas Post.

Early in 1863 he was appointed Major of the 1st Regiment
Mississippi Infantry, which afterwards took the name of the
51st U. S. Infantry, (colored,) and entered actively upon the
business of enlisting, organizing and disciplining the blacks for
soldiers.   He was engaged in the bloody fight of Milliken's
Bend, and was conspicuous for his gallantry and energy in
rallying and leading on the troops after they had been driven
to the brink of the river.   As an illustration of the desperate
character of this battle, it may be stated that many of the blacks,
although wounded, still continued to fight.   One, particularly
noticed by Col. Bryant, had been shot through the jaw.   When
our troops were forced to the water's edge, he washed away the
blood, and with his jaw shattered and hanging loose resumed his
place in the ranks and fought like a tiger.

In the fall of 1863 he was promoted to the rank of Lieutenant Colonel.   For nearly a year he was stationed at Goodrich's
Landing and Lake Providence, making occasional expeditions
into the country around, and engaged in frequent conflicts with
rebel troops and guerrillas.

In September, 1864, he was commissioned as Colonel of the
46th Regiment U. S. Infantry, (colored,) its former commander
having resigned.   This regiment was composed of excellent
material, but badly disciplined, and considered notoriously the
"hardest" regiment in the department.   By his energy and
skill he soon brought it into a state of discipline and efficiency,
which received the unqualified approbation of his superior officers.   While in command of the 46th, he was successively
stationed at Vicksburg, Memphis and New Orleans.   In the
beginning of May, 1865, he was ordered to Brazos Santiago,
Texas, to relieve a regiment that had been sometime stationed
there.   On the 14th of May, three days after his arrival, he
was drowned while bathing in the Gulf of Mexico.

Gifted with fine talents and imagination—enterprising, industrious and persevering—cultivated and refined in mind and manners,—Col. Bryant was distinguished as a young man of great promise among the many who went from Northern Illinois to the war.   In all the relations of life his principles and conduct were pure and upright; and it is no slight consolation to his bereaved friends to know, that amid the trials and temptations of a military life, he retained all his purity and force of character.   He raised himself from the rank of 2d Lieutenant to that of Colonel solely by his own merit, without assistance from the influence of any one.   Among the officers of the 33d Illinois he was accounted one of the bravest and best.   Cool, prompt and resolute, his presence of mind never forsook him in time of danger.   Although engaged in many desperate conflicts and often narrowly escaping, he was never seriously wounded. He possessed a hardy and enduring constitution, which enabled him to withstand, with almost entire impunity, the fatigue and exposure of long marches and the miasm of Mississippi swamps. After passing unharmed through almost four years of hardship and danger, he was struck down when the prospect of safe return to the loved ones at home seemed near and flattering. About three months before his death he tendered his resignation, but it was not accepted.

Col. Bryant was greatly beloved both by his soldiers and brother officers.   One of the latter, writing from Mobile, speaks thus of him :

Never before, it seems to me, did so young an officer gain the love and respect of army associates in the degree that was felt for him.   Not only his superiors and equals in rank, but also his subordinate officers—all spoke of him at all times with the highest praise; all deplore his loss as that of a warm personal friend.

Another writes :

Truly he was one of earth's noblemen.

"None knew him but to love him,
Or named him but to praise."

He was a good and dutiful son, a tender and affectionate brother, a kind and sympathizing friend, a true Christian, and a brave and loyal soldier.

The following resolutions show the estimation in which Col. Bryant was held in the regiment which he commanded. Resolutions of similar character were passed by the officers of the 51st Colored Regiment, with which he was formerly connected.

At a meeting of the officers of the 46th U. S. Colored Infantry, held in their camp at Brazos Santiago, Texas, May 15th, 1865, Lieut. Col. Will Lyon was called to the chair, and Asst. Surgeon James H. Bennett chosen Secretary. A committee, consisting of Captain M. M. Kingsbury, Adjutant B. F. Hudson and 2d Lieut. Thomas V. Smith, were appointed to draft a series of resolutions. The following preamble and resolutions were adopted:

WHEREAS, It hath pleased Almighty God to call from our midst our esteemed and beloved commander, Col. Julian E. Bryant; therefore,

Resolved, That Col. J. E. Bryant, by his strict impartiality, his promptness and decision as an officer, and his valor in the field, won our highest respect and esteem, and by his brilliant qualities as a scholar, and the many traits that distinguished him as a gentleman, our warmest friendship and love.

Resolved, That in view of his untimely fate—cut off in the very flower of his manhood—snatched from the field of glory in which his talents had already marked him pre-eminent—taken in an instant from the position of responsibility which he occupied in respect to the regiment,—we do deeply feel his loss, and realize that the energies of the entire regiment are paralyzed by the removal of its chief.

Resolved, That he, having, by his affability and gentlemanliness, gained our warmest friendship and love, we do most sincerely mourn his departure from among us, as the loss of a dear friend and cherished companion.

Resolved, That the Government has in him lost a brave, efficient officer and a true and unflinching patriot, whose great aim was his country's glory, and whose life was freely placed at her disposal.

Resolved, That we extend to his bereaved family our deepest sympathy in the hour of their affliction, and that we transmit to them a copy of these resolutions.

W. LYON, President.

JAMES H. BENNETT, Secretary.

LIEUTENANT STEWART.

Lieut. ALEXANDER STEWART, third son of Alexander and Margaret Stewart, was born in Glasgow, Scotland, on the 17th day of December, 1831. His father enjoyed civic honors, and being the most extensive thread manufacturer in Bridgeton, near Glasgow, he was thus enabled to afford his offspring the opportunities of a good education, which Alexander acquired in early boyhood. Subsequently, he was apprenticed to a silk mercer in London, where he remained four years, when he took a dislike to the business, and forsook it for a more congenial employment. He next entered the mercantile house of Messrs. J. & W. Campbell, of Glasgow—a firm whose business connections permeated the whole civilized world.

Lieut. Stewart immigrated to this country in 1852, and for some time resided in the city of New York. While there, he married Miss Sarah Ann Clark, and soon after, moved to the city of Chicago, where he commenced business with his brother, John, as a wholesale grocer.

The St. Andrew's Society of Illinois claimed him as an honored officer, during the years 1859–60, and his zeal in discharging the onerous duties of his position reflected his estimation of the benefits of association in relieving the distressed belonging to the land of his nativity.

When the first gun of the rebellion startled the nation, Lieut. Stewart manifested a desire to raise his arm in defence of the Government, but owing to the limited number of troops that were called for or accepted by the authorities, he, like thousands of others who were ready to lay down their lives for their country, failed to find a place in the army.

Early in December, 1862, an opportunity was offered him, which he gladly accepted, and he threw up his business for the purpose of raising volunteers for the 12th Illinois Cavalry—a regiment then recruiting at Camp Douglas. He devoted his entire time and available means to the work, and was highly successful.   The nucleus of the regiment was only formed when it was ordered to Camp Butler, near Springfield, to complete its organization; whereupon, the commanding officer—Colonel Arno Voss—recommended Lieut. Stewart for the position of Battalion Adjutant, to which place he was duly commissioned and mustered.

The regiment was ordered to Virginia in June, 1862, where it participated in the battles of Darkesville, Harper's Ferry, Falling Waters, Aldie, Middlebury, Dumfries, and twenty other contests of greater or less importance, including Gettysburg,— in nearly all of which Adjt. Stewart was engaged, and bore himself with credit.

Not the least important event in the history of his regiment was the part it performed in the great cavalry expedition towards Richmond, known as the "Stoneman Raid," in April, 1863.   The 12th was detached from the cavalry corps for a special work for which it was known to be eminently fitted, and sent by the shortest route to the neighborhood of Richmond to cut Lee's communications in that direction, while the main body of the corps moved to the rear of the Confederate army, south of Chancellorsville.

The regiment on this raid was under the command of Lieut. Col. Hasbrouck Davis, who, in the absence of the regimental Quartermaster, called Lieut. Stewart to perform the duties of that officer.   Col. Davis knew well the nature of the arduous and difficult work before him, which was to approach the rebel capital as near as circumstances would permit; to sever all railway connections, burn all important bridges, and capture or destroy all Confederate public property; and having accomplished which, he was to report with his command to the nearest Federal post or camp.   The expedition was a success. The command met the enemy several times, but nowhere was it driven from its purpose.   Several million dollars worth of public property was captured or destroyed; all railroad connections were cut and bridges burned; besides, many prisoners were secured, and much valuable information in regard to the enemy was gained.   In all this work, Lieut. Stewart did efficient and needful service, and displayed a thorough knowledge of all things appertaining to the Quartermaster's department. .

The 12th Cavalry was the first to return to Illinois to reorganize as a veteran regiment. It was thus favored in view of its glorious record in the field, as well as on account of its depleted ranks.

Soon after the return of the regiment to Chicago, and during its reorganization, Lieut. Stewart was detached, at the request of the mustering and disbursing officer of the post, to take charge of the Quartermaster's department of the recruiting rendezvous of Northern Illinois, and when the regiment again went to the field, he was still retained.

In this new position an immense amount of labor devolved upon him, mentally as well as physically. It was no mere honorary or nominal position, surrounded by a retinue of assistants, for he conducted the whole duties unaided save by one clerk, whom he paid from his own salary. While thus employed, the effects of his long exposure and hardship in the field became manifest in the rapid decline of his health; but he labored on, apparently forgetful of his own interests, until he was conquered by disease. He died, after a brief confinement to his bed, on the 9th of April, 1864, leaving a wife, a little son, and a multitude of friends, to mourn their irreparable loss.

His remains lie in Rosehill Cemetery, where he was buried with military honors and the imposing rites of the Masonic fraternity, of which he was an active and esteemed member.

> Hands fraternal took him home
> To where the weary masons lie.

CAPTAIN RUTISHAUSER.

Capt. KARL A. RUTISHAUSER was born in the canton of Thurgau, Switzerland, on the 16th of February, 1840. He received his education in the canton school at Frauenfeld, where he applied himself to the study of medicine. After emigrating to this country, he entered the Humboldt Institute at St. Louis, where he graduated and obtained his diploma as Doctor of Medicine. While in that institution, the rebellion broke out, and he entered the ranks first formed at St. Louis. Having enjoyed the benefits of a military education, which all students in Switzerland possess, he was soon promoted to a Lieutenancy in Shuttner's Regiment, and acted as Adjutant during the three months' service; after which, he was appointed as Surgeon at Rolla, Mo., under orders of Gen. Sigel.

His anxiety to fight the traitors, and to protect the Government of the United States—impelled naturally by an inborn love of freedom and hatred of slavery inherited by the natives of the land of Tell—induced him to enlist again as a private, on the 17th of September, 1861, in a company formed at Somonauk, Ill., and on the 25th of December, he was mustered in for three years at Camp Douglas, Chicago, as Captain of Co. E of the 58th Regiment Illinois Volunteer Infantry, in which his father, Isaac Rutishauser, was then appointed Lieutenant Colonel.

The 58th left camp on the 11th of February, 1862, before it had been thoroughly organized, and without the necessary drill, for Cairo, when it was ordered to Fort Donelson, and on the 14th of February, the regiment was on the battle-ground at the fort. Capt. Rutishauser, with his command, was immediately detailed for skirmish duty, which was said to be, in consideration of lack of drill, very well performed. On the 15th, the regiment was ordered to mount the so-called bloody hill, when it was received with a heavy fire of batteries in ambush.

By his courageous example, he encouraged his men and materially aided his father in saving the regiment from destruction.

On the 6th of April, 1862, when the army was surprised at Pittsburg Landing, he was successful in providing his company with better firearms, which he distributed to them while in line of battle and in action. He fought valiantly throughout the whole day, until half-past 5 o'clock, when the enemy gained advantages on the right and left wings of the line of battle, and the 58th was then surrounded and taken prisoners. In this onset, Captain Rutishauser was wounded by a ball entering the skull, which brought him to the ground. His knowledge of the medical art persuaded him of his hopeless condition; but he nevertheless kept up a strong and manly disposition, so that, when visited by his father, who was also wounded, he said: "Father, console yourself; you have yet children at home who love you, and I die willingly. I die with honor." After which, he tore the straps from his shoulders, and with his cap, pierced through by the fatal lead, handed them over to his father, with the wish that they might be preserved and taken home to his friends. The interview was short, and ended in Lieut. Col. Rutishauser being marched to the rear; afterwards suffering during long, weary months in Southern prisons without any knowledge of the condition of his lamented son.

After reinforcements had reached Pittsburg Landing, on the 7th April, the enemy was driven back. Capt. Rutishauser was then taken from the field and carried on board a steamer for St. Louis, where he was cared for by his former teacher and friend, Dr. Hammer, Director of the Humboldt Institute. The tedious delay of ten days in reaching St. Louis had a very depressing effect on his condition, and with untold agony he yielded up his young life as a sacrifice on the altar of duty and patriotism, on the 18th of May, 1862. His remains were, with appropriate ceremony, interred in the St. Louis cemetery of the Holy Ghost.

SERGEANT HUDSON.

Sergt. Oscar M. Hudson, the only child of James and Maria Hudson, was born in Marlow, Cheshire co., N. H., in the year 1848. His parents emigrated to Illinois in 1851.

When the rebellion broke out, and a call made for 75,000 men, he enlisted in the 20th Regiment Illinois Volunteers—Col. C. C. Marsh commanding, which was quartered at Joliet. When the regiment was mustered in for three years, he was discharged on account of ill health. He remained at home, however, but a short time before he went forth a second time, in December, 1861, and enlisted in the 1st Battalion of the "Yates Sharpshooters," when he was appointed Sergeant. He was at the battle of New Madrid, under Gen. Pope, and at Corinth, Miss. While there, encamped in a swamp, he contracted a disease which carried him to his grave, on the 30th August, 1862.

Oscar was a youth of fine talents and personal worth—a brave soldier boy, beloved by all his comrades.

CORPORAL HEGANS.

Corp. Nelson Hegans, son of Michael and Susan Hegans, was born in Johnson co., Ind., in 1839. He moved, with his mother, from there to Jersey co., Ill., in 1851; and when the war broke out, like thousands of our heroes, the call for volunteers found him at the plow. Feeling it was his duty to give all the aid he could in suppressing the rebellion, he enlisted at Carrollton, Greene co., in Co. C, 61st Regiment Illinois Volunteers—Col. Fry. He was soon elected Corporal, and his Captain appointed him Color Guard. One month after the regiment was organized, they left for Tennessee, and were engaged at the battle of Pittsburg Landing, where Corp. Hegans was wounded. He was taken from the field and sent to the hospital at Savanna, where he expired on the 12th of April, 1862.

CAPTAIN LESTER.

CAPTAIN LESTER.

Capt. THOMAS T. LESTER, son of William and Jane Lester, was born on the 13th of July, 1839, in the town of Howden, Yorkshire, England, a city somewhat famous for its horse-market. Thomas, with his parents, left their native shores of Old England on the 27th of September, 1853, to try their fortunes in the West, and in due time arrived in Chicago, when he engaged with Thos. George & Co. to learn the business of brassfounding. He proved a competent workman, being guided and thoroughly instructed by his foreman, Alex. Barnet, in all the intricacies of the trade. After remaining four years, during which his health was slightly impaired, he concluded on changing his employment for something more congenial. He then became a dry goods clerk in the store of W. R. Wood & Co., and continued there until he responded with his services to his adopted country's call for defenders.

Upon the first indications that the South had determinedly resolved to destroy the Union, and that the Constitution of the United States was seriously in danger of being made a reproach and a byword among the nations, with no less enthusiasm than the sternest patriot whose grandsire had fought in the revolutionary war, he buckled on his armor to go forth in their defense. Before the boom of the first gun was heard, he seemed to have had a premonition that the great issue could only be settled by the arbitrament of the sword, and with this idea, he connected himself with one of the independent companies of the city—the Anderson Rifles—to qualify himself should the emergency arise. When the call came, he was one of the number selected by the Union Defence Committee, for his soldierly qualities and gentlemanly bearing, to officer a regiment being raised under their auspices, and known as the Chicago Legion; better recognized now, however, both to friend and foe, as the 51st Illinois Veteran Volunteers. The position assigned to him was 2d Lieutenant of

Co. E, but upon an election of officers in the company, he was unanimously chosen 1st Lieutenant.

The regiment left Camp Douglas for active service on the 14th of February, 1862, and arrived at Cairo, when they were assigned to Gen. Paine's Division. On the 10th March, they joined Gen. Pope's Army at New Madrid, Mo. The arrival of the division settled the fate of that rebel stronghold; for, after throwing up works and mounting guns within seven hundred yards of the fort, and opening upon the astonished foe with such an effective fire, they had only to move in the following morning and occupy the formidable fortress which the enemy had abandoned during the night in a terrible rain storm. Indeed, so hastily was the movement made, that candles were left burning; champagne, half drunk, at one of their tables, and the corpse of one of their officers in a coffin unburied.

The 51st, 10th, 16th and 22d Regiments Illinois Volunteers, under command of Gen. Paine, were the first to cross the Mississippi to the Tennessee shore, and march on Tiptonville, to head off the rebels who were trying to escape from Island No. 10, and succeeded in capturing six thousand of them under Gen. McCall, besides all the heavy artillery and ordnance stores collected there to oppose our passage. This movement has been justly characterized by Gen. Halleck as one of the most brilliant achievements of the war. On the 10th April, the regiment returned to New Madrid, and on the 14th moved with the remainder of Gen. Pope's Army down the river to Fort Pillow, which was bombarded for several days; but before any definite results were attained, they were ordered to join Gen. Halleck before Corinth, and arrived at Pittsburg Landing on the 21st, forming part of the grand advance under that General. From the 23d of April until the 29th of May, they were day and night upon the skirmish line, or supporting it.

At the battle of Farmington, on the 9th of May, the whole brigade, consisting of the 51st, 22d, 27th and 42d Regiments, narrowly escaped capture: only the cool courage of officers and men, under the generalship of John M. Palmer, saved them. They were attacked by three rebel divisions, and for three hours successfully maintained their position. Lieut. Lester, commanding the color company upon this occasion, nobly won the esteem of his superior officers and the implicit confidence of his men by his coolness and presence of mind.

After the evacuation of Corinth, on the 30th of May, the regiment was foremost in the pursuit of the fleeing rebels, going as far as Boonville; then they returned and went into camp at Big Springs, Miss.

Lieut. Lester, being recommended, received orders upon the 9th of July to return to Illinois on recruiting service. On the 21st the regiment moved to Northern Alabama, and occupied the Memphis and Charleston Railroad, from Courtland to De-catur. Upon Gen. Bragg's advance into Tennessee and Ken-tucky, the division, now commanded by Gen. Palmer, were compelled to retreat in the direction of Nashville, where they arrived on the 11th September, to find themselves with Gen. Negley's Division isolated and cut off from communications with the north.

As soon as connections were again opened by Gen. Rose-crans, Lieut. Lester joined his command with a reinforcement of sixty recruits for the regiment, more in number than the combined results of all other detailed officers from the brigade. The brigade was now transferred to Gen. Sheridan's Division, when, shortly after, the memorable battle of Stone River was fought. The great loss in officers again placed Lieut. Lester in command of his company.

The regiment remained here until sufficient rations were got up and such works erected as to make the necessity of another evacuation of the State out of the question; and, on the 24th of June, again the army of the Cumberland moved out to meet the enemy. The result was the brilliant campaign in which Gen. Rosecrans forced Gen. Bragg successively from all of his strategic and fortified positions—Shelbyville, Tullahoma and Bridgeport, across the Tennessee River—thus freeing the State of Tennessee of all rebels in arms. Then the army rested until the 2d of September, when Georgia was first made to feel the terrible results of rebellion. Through the battle of Chickamau-ga, that fearful carnage of life; through the battle of Mission Ridge, fighting in the clouds, Lieut. Lester passes unscathed, winning new laurels for deeds of daring, and survives the untold hardships of that march to the relief of Burnside in East Tennessee, a campaign the most severe that an army has witnessed during the rebellion—made by men without shoes, tents or blankets in midwinter.

Lieut. Lester, in consideration of well-earned services, received his commission, on the 6th of October, 1863, as Captain of Co. K, and was second in command of the 51st. He re-enlisted with his regiment for three years more, or during the war—until the success of the cause which induced him to sacrifice the social comforts and the society of loved ones at home was complete.

While in Chicago on furlough, Capt. Lester, with a number of other officers, entertained Gen. Sheridan in the Sherman House, who was on his way to command the Army of the Shenandoah. He afterwards expressed a high opinion of that brave General, and said that wherever he lifted the sword he would give telling blows. How true his judgment has been proved.

The regiment returned from their veteran leave of absence in time to advance with Gen. Sherman in the great campaign which terminated in the capture of Atlanta; but among the first of that series of bloody scenes at Resaca, on the 14th of May, in the front of battle Capt. Lester fell, pierced through the head by a rebel bullet—here ending a life of much promise —one of the noblest sacrifices received upon our country's altar.

Before the engagement, Capt. Lester, in conversation with a brother officer, Lieut. Hills, told him that the night before he had a presentiment of a soldier's fate. He then gave him his brother's address in Chicago, with other requests as to his effects, and took his place in the regiment before the fatal ball sped on its course. We append an extract of Lieut. Hill's letter, showing the movements of the regiment at the battle of Resaca and the manner of our hero's death:

The enemy had evacuated Dalton, and we were pressing their rear very closely, seven miles from that place. We found them strongly intrenched in front of Resaca. Before the battle commenced on the morning of the 14th, our brigade halted to receive the news of Grant's victory over Lee in Virginia.

Of course, all of us felt happy, but none more so than your brother. He seemed to be in ecstasies. In less than three hours he was dead. I will give you the particulars. The 23d Corps had made a charge on the rebel works, and drove them from their first line. We were ordered in to relieve them. Marched across an open field, (under a heavy shower of shell and canister,) where many of the regiment were wounded. We gained the woods, and were ordered to relieve some regiments on the right, who were being hard pressed and had no ammunition. To the right we went. The regiment was formed in a hollow, and opened a hot fire on the enemy, who had fallen back to their second line of works. We had remained there about two hours, when I was called upon by Lieut. Grey, of our regiment, who silently pointed to the body of my brave Captain. I looked at him, and at first could hardly realize that he who had been so merry a few hours previous was dead. I went to the body; that was no time for regrets. It pained me to see him dead, so young, and full of ambition and hope.   *   *   *   *   *

We, as a company, had only been acquainted with him as a *man* for the short space of nine days; but during that time, he was loved and respected both as an officer and a gentleman. As for myself, he was all that I could desire for a social companion.

The following letter to Capt. Lester's brother, from his superior officer, indicates a warm and feeling heart :

HEADQUARTERS 51st ILLINOIS INFANTRY,
KENESAW MOUNTAIN, GA., June 25th, 1864.

DEAR SIR,—I have had it on my mind to write you ever since the death of your brother on the 14th of May. Constant work in the field has left me no opportunity to do so until now.

You will not doubt that Capt. Lester's brother officers esteemed his generous and manly qualities at their full worth, nor that they mourn his sudden and early death. You have the sympathy of all his companions, and I wish, as the commanding officer of the regiment, to express to Capt. Lester's family and friends their sorrow and sympathy.

Your brother earned our esteem by his gallant conduct on various fields, and he died in the front of battle while heading and directing his men. He had few superiors as an officer, and as a companion he was genial and kind.

We shall cherish his memory as one of the most gallant of our number.

With much esteem, yours, etc.,
L. P. BRADLEY,
Col. 51st Illinois.

His loss was deeply felt and mourned by all who knew him, for his life in the army had been one of work. Never absent from his command except when ordered—*never in the hospital*—his comrades saw no dangers but what he cheerfully shared.

Joined to a pleasing exterior, he possessed in a remarkable degree the power of interesting and pleasing all with whom he was thrown in contact. Straightforward and manly in all his dealings—honorable as a soldier knows honor—generous and unselfish to a fault; with ideas of friendship that made no sacrifice too great for those he loved—always prompt in the discharge of his duty,—he was, in every sense, the beau ideal of a soldier, and has left behind him from a soldier's grave a character that we all might emulate, that we all should envy.

PRIVATES.

CHARLES H. CONNER.

Private CONNER was born in Maine, Cook county, Illinois, on the 18th of August, 1840. Previous to the breaking out of the rebellion, he was engaged in farming. When the news came flashing over the wires of the terrible disaster to our army at Bull Run, he, with thousands of other brave men, rushed to the country's rescue. He joined Co. F, 39th Illinois Volunteers (Yates Phalanx) during the latter part of August, 1861, and served his first three years with the "Army of the Potomac," after which he re-enlisted as a veteran.

In writing home in regard to the course he had taken, he said:

I have made up my mind that my country needs me, and I shall fight till the flag again floats over every inch of American soil.

He bore an active part in the engagements before Petersburg, during August, 1864, and was taken prisoner on the 16th, in a corn-field, by three rebels, the only capture from the 39th on that occasion. He with others were first sent to Belle Island, and immediately put on short allowance. Afterwards they were removed to Saulsbury, N. C. Here their sufferings were terrible, and equalled only by those of the Andersonville prisoners. Food, consisting of corn and cobs ground together, which was the allowance for one day, was consumed at one meal. They possessed scarcely clothing enough to cover their nakedness, and even this was alive with vermin. Still hardly a complaint escaped them, until the mail carrier announced the arrival of letters for the prisoners. Those who possessed enough to pay the postage were indeed happy, while others, who were unable to pay, saw those messages of love torn in strips and scattered to the wind.

It was then that strong men, who had never flinched on the battle-field, sobbed like children, while others muttered their curses. The day of retribution or relief to them seemed afar off.

He was exchanged early in March, 1865, after an imprisonment of seven months; but he was so reduced by exposure and starvation, that he died, March 15th, 1865, in the hospital at Annapolis, Maryland.

Instead of the glad tidings of returning home, his friends heard of his sudden decease. An only brother went to Annapolis, where he got his body embalmed, and brought it under his mother's roof, when, after solemn funeral services, his remains were laid to rest beneath the waving willow in the family burying ground.

———

Some of the more fortunate of the prisoners, on being exchanged and landed in Maryland, set to work and embodied their tale of suffering in verse, a copy of which is appended. It is entitled "The Song of Union Prisoners from Dixie's Sunny Land."

AIR—"Twenty Years Ago."

Dear friends and fellow-soldiers brave, come listen to our song
About the rebel prisons and our sojourn there so long;
Yet our wretched state and hardships great no one can understand,
But those who have endured this fate in Dixie's sunny land.

When captured by the chivalry (?) they stripped us to the skin,
But failed to give us back again the value of a pin,
Except some lousy rags of gray, discarded by their band;
And thus commenced our prison life in Dixie's sunny land.

With a host of guards surrounding us, each with a loaded gun,
We were stationed in an open plain, exposed to rain and sun;
No tent or tree to shelter us, we lay upon the sand—
Thus side by side great numbers died in Dixie's sunny land.

This was the daily "bill of fare" in that secesh saloon—
No sugar, tea or coffee there, at morning, night or noon;
But "a pint of meal, ground cob and all," was serv'd to ev'ry man,
And for want of fire we ate it raw in Dixie's sunny land.

We were by these poor rations soon reduced to skin and bone,
A lingering starvation—worse than death! you can but own.
There hundreds lay, both night and day, by far too weak to stand,
Till death relieved their sufferings in Dixie's sunny land.

We poor survivors oft were tried by many a threat and bribe,
To desert our glorious "Union cause," and join the rebel tribe;

Though fain were we to leave the place, we let them understand
"We'd rather die than disgrace our flag!" in Dixie's sunny land.

Thus dreary days and nights roll'd by—yes, weeks and months untold,
Until that happy time arrived when we were all paroled;
We landed at Annapolis, a wretched looking band,
But glad to be alive and free from Dixie's sunny land.

With many—as with Charles H. Conner—their living freedom was to die.

NOAH MITCHEL.

Lieut. Luff, of the 12th Illinois Cavalry, writes:

HEADQRS. 1ST CAV. DIV. ARMY OF THE POTOMAC, }
CAMP NEAR CATLETT'S STATION, VA., 6th Sept., 1863. }

NOAH MITCHEL was the first who fell of the brave men whom I have the honor to command. On the 7th day of September, 1862, the company, under Capt. Grosvenor, charged upon 280 of Ashby's Cavalry at the village of Darksville, Va. Mitchel was foremost in the charge, and made a dashing and daring attempt to capture the rebel colors. When he had nearly accomplished his object, and his hand was near the prize, he received his mortal wound—a rifle bullet through the body. I visited him the next day. He was pale, and the mark of death was on his brow. I spoke of his gallant conduct, and expressed my sorrow at his doom. He replied that "he had done only his duty, and met his fate without murmuring." As he had lived a brave soldier, he suffered as a true patriot. He was removed to Harper's Ferry, where he died on the 13th, and was buried during the memorable bombardment before the surrender of that place by Col. Miles.

ABRAM WEAVER.

Private WEAVER, the subject of this sketch, was born in Sodus, Wayne county, N. Y., on the 30th October, 1839. He was the third son of Henry and Helena Weaver, and lived with his parents in Sodus until 1856, when the family moved to Loda, Iroquois co., Illinois. Here he principally followed the plow up to the time of his enlistment.

At the first call for men to suppress the rebellion, he was anxious to offer his aid, but yielding to the solicitations of his aged parents, he remained with them until the call for "six hundred thousand more," when they finally yielded to his importunities, and, with his younger brother, he enlisted in the 88th (2d Board of Trade) Regiment Illinois Volunteers, on the 1st of August, 1862. He passed safely through the battle of Perryville; endured nobly and without a murmur the fatigue of forced marches, and was ready to sacrifice comfort, health and even his life (so full of promise) upon the altar of the country he loved so well. At last, we find him with his regiment at Murfreesboro, where, on the 30th of December, 1862, he was the first of his company to fall, being shot through the heart by the unerring aim of a rebel sharpshooter.

There are none among the many thousands who enlisted in the volunteer service that did so with purer or more patriotic motives than Abram Weaver. He went forth with the blessing of pious parents and the best wishes of all with whom he associated. He performed faithfully all the duties of a soldier, and at last fell at his post with his armor on. The soft Southern winds blow over his lonely grave, and fond hearts are left to deplore their loss.

STEPHEN C. KENNEY.

Private KENNEY was born in the town of Livermore, Oxford county, Maine, on the 16th September, 1831; enlisted in the 100th Regiment Illinois Volunteers, Co. E, Capt. Bartlett, on the 25th September, 1862. He served under Gen. Buell, in the Kentucky campaign; was present at the battle of Stone River, and while standing guard over a pile of knapsacks, he was seized with pleurisy and inflammation of the lungs. His comrades placed him under an open tent, where he lay in great distress until the conflict was over. He was then taken to Nashville, where he died on the 7th of January, 1863, and was buried in the Soldiers' Cemetery at that place.

JONATHAN D. BLANCHARD.

Private BLANCHARD was born in Rutland, Rutland county, Vermont, in the year 1840, and with his parents emigrated to Illinois in 1844, where he lived until the second year of the rebellion, when he enlisted in the 100th Regiment Illinois Volunteers (Col. Bartleson) on the 8th of August, 1862. The regiment left Joliet on the 2d of September for Louisville, Ky., where, under Gen. Buell, the duty of marching bore hard upon some of the untried prairie boys of the West, but they endured unflinchingly. About the 1st of December, they moved to Nashville, Tenn., where he was seized with a painful sickness, during which he was never heard to complain, but lay on his pallet of straw, and lingered on until the 7th of February, 1863, when he bade adieu to all earthly strife.

FERDINAND F. FOWLER.

Private F. F. FOWLER, eldest son of Henry B. and Esther D. Fowler, was born on the 5th September, 1841, in the town of Naperville, DuPage county, Illinois.

Reared amid the peaceful tranquillity of a country home, his feet trained beneath its hallowed influence to walk in virtue's ways, he had but just entered upon the threshold of a promising manhood when the cry of "TO ARMS" broke upon the startled ear of the North. Inheriting a frail constitution, and never strong of limb or robust of body, yet, from the first outbreak of the rebellion, he burned with patriotic ardor to go forth in defence of his country and his country's laws. Restrained from this for a time by the advice of physicians and the counsel of friends, nevertheless he watched with nervous anxiety the progress of the war. At length the trumpet call for "six hundred thousand more" rang out in clarion tones over the land, which told to every patriot heart of liberty's necessity. Then, forgetful of self, and impelled by a love of country which could no longer brook restraint, he enlisted on the 20th of August, 1862, in Co. D, 105th Regiment Illinois Volunteer Infantry, and eagerly marched to the rescue. Thenceforth he sustained the fatigue and encountered the hardships incident to an active campaign until prolonged ill-health compelled him to leave the ranks and accept the tendered position of Captain's Clerk. Here winning the respect of both officers and men by his cheerful assiduity, he ably and faithfully discharged the duties of the post up to 1st February, 1863, when he was entirely prostrated by pneumonia. From this attack he partially recovered, but alas! only to find himself hopelessly wrestling with that dread foe, the phthisis. It being painfully evident to all that he was beyond the reach of human skill, the Regimental Surgeon procured him an honorable discharge from the service. Summoning all his remaining strength to the effort, and animated with the hope of again meeting the loved ones at home, on the 12th of March he left the hospital in Gallatin, Tenn., with tottering limbs and emaciated form, and on the 14th arrived at the residence of his father in Warrensville, where he lingered with labored breath until the 19th March, 1863, when he departed for that better country "where the wicked cease from troubling and the weary are at rest."

DANIEL H. FOWLER.

Private D. H. FOWLER, younger and only brother of the subject of the foregoing sketch, was born on the 11th April, 1844, in the town of Naperville, DuPage county, Illinois.

Young in years, but mature in thought and action, he was a noble specimen of that energetic, high-toned manhood which nowhere on earth finds a more congenial soil or takes a readier root than in the breasts of the intelligent, self-reliant youth of the "Garden State." Hence, when in the autumn of 1862, the defeat of our arms seemed most imminent, actuated solely by patriotism—the noblest passion which can animate a man in the character of a citizen—he cheerfully resigned home, its ease and pleasures, for the toil, privation and danger of the tented field. Enlisting, August 5th, 1862, in Co. B, 105th Regiment Illinois Volunteer Infantry, he manfully marched to meet the embattled host of treason then flushed with victory and exultant with success. But while thus heroic in spirit, and willing to do and to dare for the right, his body soon proved unequal to the self-imposed task. Gradually sinking under, yet resolutely enduring the terrible vicissitudes inseparably connected with a soldier's life, at length, worn by exposure and enervated by disease, he was reluctantly forced to enter the hospital at Gallatin, Tenn., where he soon after died, March 21st, 1863, just forty-one hours after the decease of his brother.

www.ingramcontent.com/pod-product-compliance
Lightning Source LLC
Chambersburg PA
CBHW021034030726
47496CB00006B/1531